Annie Edwards

Philip Earnscliffe

Or, the morals of May Fair. A novel

Annie Edwards

Philip Earnscliffe
Or, the morals of May Fair. A novel

ISBN/EAN: 9783337241001

Printed in Europe, USA, Canada, Australia, Japan

Cover: Foto ©Andreas Hilbeck / pixelio.de

More available books at **www.hansebooks.com**

PHILIP EARNSCLIFFE;

OR,

THE MORALS OF MAY FAIR.

CHAPTER I.

It was a cold, gusty evening. Although the middle of May, the wind, as it swept up from the sea, howled round the Tête Noire rocks with more of the fierce melancholy of December than of that "sweet sighing" which should belong to the month of flowers; and the rain beat in torrents against the grey old walls and narrow casements of the Manoir de Kersaint, as it loomed grimly through the gathering mists and dying twilight. The Manoir was situated in one of the wildest parts of Western Brittany, and was a gloomy looking building at all times—even with the summer sun shining on its many-paned windows, scutcheoned doorways, and high-pointed slate roofs; but doubly so, when, as was the case during six months of the year, the storms of the Breton coast beat around it, with groans, and shrieks, and tremulous wailings, which, to the superstitious peasantry of the district, might well seem like voices from the ghosts of shipwrecked mariners—many of whom every winter found a watery grave among the shoals and rocks of that cruel shore.

The Manoir stood about a league from the nearest town, and with no hamlet or cottage in its immediate neighborhood. It was close to the sea—which, indeed, in stormy weather often dashed its foam against the windows on that side which faced the bay—while between the house and the shore lay a garden, only exposed to the south, and sheltered even in winter from the rude north and north-western blasts. This garden was old-fashioned, stiff, and quaint; with a terrace overhanging the beach at the farther end, flights of broken steps, an ancient sun-dial, and the remains of a fountain—all records of the palmy days of the château, and the stiff taste of a by-gone age—but pleasant in summer, when bright flowers, tended by no unloving hands, decked its borders, and ripe peaches and grapes hung upon the warm southern wall. On this evening, however, the garden looked desolate in the fast falling shadows, and the early flowers lay crushed and soiled under the heavy rain. The court gates communicating with the road on the other side of the house were firmly closed for the night: the watch-dog lay silently sleeping in his kennel; and only through one of the lower windows the uncertain flickering of a wood fire gave token of life, and the presence of human beings in this dreary habitation.

But, however cheerless the scene without, within that room was light and warmth, and a little group, so happy in themselves, as scarcely even to bestow a thought upon the drifting torrents of rain upon the windows, or the wind that screamed and eddied in the immense old chimney. The room was itself a vast one, with a lofty painted ceiling, and floor of many-colored woods, arranged in arabesque patterns. The faded furniture was of the style belonging to the reign of Louis Quinze, and conveyed an instant idea of former courtly days, and more ample means than were possessed by the present inhabitants of the Manoir. On the walls hung a goodly array of portraits—blooming, powdered, and wreathed with flowers; doubtless, some of them representing the fair chatelaines of Kersaint, who had once reclined on those very high-backed chairs of cramoisi damask which now stood grimly ranged under their lifeless effigies. The enormous chimney-piece was of white marble, sculptured over with innumerable bands of roses, and figures of love and graces; whose projecting heads occasionally caught a rosy glow from the capricious flickerings of the well-piled wood fire. Before this fire was a little group of three persons, and their appearance seemed to harmonise strangely with the old-world room they inhabited, although, at the same time, they gave it a warm and household aspect. It was, indeed, an "interior," upon which an artist's eye might long have rested with delight, half lit up as it was by the ever-changing light from the hearth.

At intervals, pale, fitful gleams bathed the figures, and the whole room, then, quickly dying away into the red glow of the embers, left the large *salle* alternately black and sombre, or quivering for a few seconds in a soft half-shadow. Anon this wandering light would fall upon some projecting gilding of the picture-frames, covered with medallions and crowns of carved wood, then on the massive furniture, plated in brass and ebony, or the delicately-cut cornices of the wainscoting; and then, as one brand fell extinguished and a new flame broke from a different side of the fire, objects visible before returned again into obscurity, and other bright points stood out from the darkness. Thus the eye could gradually trace every detail of the picture. First the painted ceiling, bedecked with azure and stars; then the heavy console, supported upon four huge silver tritons, now darkened and tarnished with age; lastly, the fringed hangings of crimson damask, at the extreme end of the room, which, covered with wavy reflections, seemed to advance and recede mysteriously in the undulating rays of the fire.

In a large arm-chair, drawn towards the centre of the fire-place, sat an elderly man of grave and noble exterior. He might, perhaps, have been about fifty; but study and an expression of habitual melancholy, joined to delicate health, made him look some years older than he really was. His high, pale brow was perfectly bare at the temples, in which the blue veins were painfully visible, and around the eyes was that hollow rim which bespeaks the slow, sure progress of life's decay. His tall figure was somewhat bent, and his white, thin hands hung with an attitude of weakness upon the arm of the chair. A rough deer-hound was at his feet; he was old and grey, but still bore traces of the strength and beauty of his youth. His wiry coat of a deep brindle hue, his black eyes, long, sharp muzzle and dark ears, still soft and silky, all bespoke his high race and pure blood. He had rested his head upon the invalid's knee, and now stood gazing up in his face with a tender, melancholy expression, as though he could read, in his brute love, the signs of suffering so plainly written there; but when his master occasionally passed his hand over his shaggy neck, the creature's eyes softened and dilated with pleasure, and his long tail swept from side to side upon the hearth. At length, he gave a little bark of impatience, as the object of so much love still kept his face averted, while he looked down at a young figure on his other side, and only extended an unthinking caress to the hound.

"Jealous, as usual, old Bell!" said a childish voice. "Father, if you even look at me too long, that creature barks." And the speaker, leaving a low stool by the hearth, came and seated herself by her father's feet, and held up her little fist in the old hound's face.

She was a young girl of scarcely sixteen, and a countenance of more perfect, and almost infantine sweetness, it would be difficult to conceive. It was just one of those faces so rarely met with, except in some picture by one of the old masters. Her hair, of a rich chestnut brown, hung in a flood of light upon her neck, and, forming a waving halo round her head, added to its pure Madonna-like character. She was very fair, with all the first blush of childhood upon her cheeks, and her small white hand shone like a lily upon Bell's grizzly coat. Her eyes—of so deep a blue that in this light they seemed black—were fringed with the longest eyelashes; and clearly-defined, dark eyebrows gave a character to the otherwise soft countenance. In person she was tall; and, though so young, there was already promise of the richest lines of contour in the graceful shoulders, and full and exquisitely-proportioned bust. As it had never entered into her head, or that of her father, that she was approaching the age of womanhood, she was still dressed like a mere child, in a little muslin frock, without any ornament of lace or ruffle, and so short in the skirts as to allow a full view of her tiny feet in their well-worn house slippers. *She* had no melancholy expression, like poor Bell, as she looked up into her father's face; but continued laughing, and chattering, and playing with the dog, occasionally resting her head against her father's knee, or stroking the thin hand which hung listlessly at his side.

Another figure sat somewhat apart from the two principal ones; but still near enough to enjoy the warmth from the fire, and mix with perfect freedom in the conversation. This was Manon, Marguerite's former nurse, and now their only attendant, who, with a respectful familiarity still to be found amongst servants in the remote part of France, always took her place near the evening hearth, gazing ever and anon at her master, then at his child; but with the eternal stocking forming under her busy fingers, and which appeared to require neither light nor thought to aid its progress. Manon was a woman of about five-and-forty, perhaps older, for hers was one of those faces which never look young, yet on which, after a certain time, years and years pass away and leave no further trace. She had the hard Celtic features peculiar to Brittany, and wore the usual costume of the peasants—the white linen headdress, short dark petticoat, enormous apron, and bright handkerchief pinned across her bosom, over which hung a large silver crucifix.

The conversation was carried on in good French, which Manon understood well, although Breton was her native tongue. Marguerite spoke with the perfectly pure accent of a born French child; but her father, although possessing a thorough knowledge of the language, still bore traces, in the pronunciation, of being an Englishman.

"How delightful to think that summer is come!" said the girl, pausing in her play with Bello. "Do you know, father, the hawthorns are in full blossom on the warm side of the orchard, and the young linnets are hatched, and Bruno thinks I shall have some roses in a fortnight? What a pleasant summer we shall have, darling old father!—you will get so strong in the sunny, open air; and, till you are well enough to walk, Manon and I will take you down in the garden-chair to the shore, and you can sit quietly and enjoy the fresh sea breeze, while Bello and I run about on the sands, and keep watch over you."

She looked so hopeful and happy, that her father had no courage to tell her he saw small prospect of any summer weather making him strong again. His lips never could approach that cruel subject when talking to his child; although he had several times confided his forebodings about his state to the old servant.

"Well, Marguerite. I hope this is not your idea of summer," he answered, smiling; "listen to the wind and rain as they drift against the window. Where will your early flowers be to-morrow?

"Only beaten down for a day, father; by Sunday they will be fresher than ever, and I shall make Manon the first bouquet she has had this spring to take to mass with her."

For Manon was, of course, a rigid Catholic, and, on fête days and Sundays, thought nothing of the long, rough miles she had to walk to the nearest town to church. The rain or snow—indeed, nothing but the illness of her master—had ever kept her at home; and, in fine weather, Marguerite frequently accompanied her. Mr. St. John had reared her in his own simple faith, but utterly apart from all sectarian prejudice; and it gave the poor child such pleasure to go to the old cathedral with Manon, and see the pictures, the rich vestments of the priests, the acolytes swinging the incense, while the sun poured through the stained window over the altar; above all, to listen to the solemn peals of the organ, and the sonorous chanting of the priests, that her father was glad for her to have this one enjoyment; and, in time, the cathedral became to her childish fancy all imaginable beauty, grandeur, and sweet music combined. She had a passionate love for music herself, and Mr. St. John also thought it good for her to have the opportunity of gratifying it, and of hearing any other harmony than that of her own voice—although, to him, that was worth more than all the music on earth.

"And if Sunday is fine," Marguerite continued, "I may go with Manon, petit papa?—that is, if you are very well, and quite sure you will not want me——"

"And if we have no more rain between this and then," chimed in Manon. "The roads are not in a state for your little feet, mamie dame! When I went to church last Sunday, I had often to wade through the mire and bog well nigh up to my knees. Luckily, I had wrapped my white stockings round my prayer-book, and put them in my pocket, before I set out."

"Oh, Manon, how I wish I had seen you!" cried Marguerite; "you must have looked so droll, with your large ancles all covered in mud. Never mind, Bello, you shall come too, and carry me through these wonderful torrents on your back," and she shook her long, bright curls over the hound's eyes to wake him. He made a start, but, on seeing how matters stood, only gave his usual impatient bark, and, turning his head resolutely towards the fire, went off again to sleep. Mr. St. John closed his eyes, wearied, as he generally grew towards evening; and there was no sound for some minutes but the occasional click of Manon's knitting-needles, or the little hissing voices from the wood fire, and the eternal pattering of the rain. Marguerite was just meditating going in search of her kitten to rouse up Bello and make them all less silent, when the old clock in the hall struck nine.

"Supper-time already!" she cried, jumping up. "How late we are to-night! Come, Manon, let us get lights at once, and make the omelette."

Manon carefully folded her work, having first removed the disengaged pins from their place in her black hair, and struck them with much precision through the stocking; then she placed it all in the ample pocket of her apron, and followed Marguerite to the door. They felt their way through winding passages and down many treacherous descents, until they reached the kitchen, where Manon, after considerable groping, struck a light, and they began their evening labors.

The kitchen was a low, dark, vaulted room, so large that it seemed to extend under the whole ground floor of the house; and the one candle and few expiring embers on the hearth, instead of lighting its obscurity, appeared only to render it more intense. There were strange old closets and projections, behind which a dozen men might lie concealed, in this kitchen; and a ghostly owl took delight in flapping his wings against the casements of an evening; so, altogether, Manon was not fond of frequenting it alone after twilight, and generally persuaded mademoiselle to accompany her—for Marguerite was not afraid of ghosts or owls, and she also liked to assist with her own hands in preparing her father's supper.

Manon on her knees, quickly succeeded in fanning the wood embers into a blaze; the savory omelette was soon upon the fire; the roasted potatoes among the ashes declared to be done to perfection; and then Marguerite filled the kettle, and got ready the little tea-service. Mr. St. John retained his old English liking for tea at night; and it was his daughter's pleasure to arrange it for him herself, and to take care that it was strong and well made. Her father's cup of good tea was the one extravagance of their household. She looked like a little fairy, contrasted with Manon's solid form, while she flitted about, searching for the different objects she required, among the uncouth shadows of the place; and her white, slender hands, and that nameless air of high birth which was visible in each of her movements, seemed strangely at variance with the place and her occupation. She went on chatting merrily to Manon in her sweet, full voice, while the old servant, although perfectly familiar, invariably answered in a tone of respect which, even to strangers, would have expressed the difference of condition, and her own sense of it.

"This has been a long day, Manon," said Marguerite, suddenly.

"My days are never long, mademoiselle; and to-day I have been looking over the last year's preserves to see what we must make this summer. Will you believe it, ma mie, two jars of my best green-gage were empty? and I never knew the mice to touch them before."

"The mice, you silly old Manon! more likely Bruno!"

Manon almost dropped the pan containing her omelette, and her eyes flashed fire. "Bruno!" she exclaimed. "If I thought that lout—that idiot—that cochon de paysan —had touched one of my master's green-gages, I would——Bruno, indeed!"

"There," cried Marguerite, "I have made you happy for the night in giving you Bruno's sins to think over. Do you know, Manon I wish sometimes that Bruno, or you, or some one, would do something really wrong? I am so tired of nothing happening."

"Nothing happening!" echoed Manon. "Why, Gilbert, the pedlar, was here yesterday with all the news from Quimper; and Friday eight days M. le Curé met us in the road; and, in three weeks we shall have the fair at N—— Mon Dieu, it seems to me that a great deal happens!"

"Does it?" answered Marguerite, dreamily; "well, I suppose so. But sometimes, lately, I have wished for something more—I cannot exactly tell what. What can I want Manon?"

If Manon knew, she did not choose to speak; but, inspecting the omelette closely, she declared it to be done à ravir; and then, remarking that the carafe was empty, went off to fill it with fresh water, while Marguerite, who had to arrange the tray, forgot all about her own question.

And now the repast was ready, and carried in by Manon, Marguerite preceding her with a light. The snowy cloth was laid, the invalid's chair wheeled round to the table, and Manon had taken her place behind her master, when an event suddenly occurred—for certainly the first time, at such an hour, within a dozen years—which made them all start with astonishment: the great bell of the court-yard rang. Mr. St. John looked uneasy, as an invalid always does at any unexpected interruption of his usual existence. Manon exclaimed, "Mon Dieu!" and crossed herself; Bello, awakened this time in good earnest, gave a long, unearthly, howl, which was echoed by the fierce barkings of the watch-dog without; while Marguerite clapped her hands with delight at "anything happening." Manon was the first to speak.

"Oh, master, they must be robbers—there can be no doubt of it; no visitor ever comes to Kersaint, and the country people know me better than to dare ring at the great bell at this hour: we shall all be murdered. Ah, bon Dieu, and all the saints, help us!"

Marguerite laughed aloud, and Mr. St. John answered—"No, good Manon; if robbers were to attack a house like this, which is not likely, they would not enter by the garden, and not warn us quite so loudly of their intentions. It is, more probably, some wayfarer overtaken by the storm, and seeking a night's shelter."

"Then come, Manon," cried Marguerite, seizing a light with one hand, and the servant's sleeve with the other; "let us open the door at once, and admit this poor traveller to our fire. Father, tell her to come with me!"—for Manon visibly hesitated, and drew back.

"Nay, Marguerite," he answered, "though I have small fear of robbers, yet, at this unusual hour, it would certainly be well to hold some parley through the little lattice, before opening the gates. I will go myself, and ascertain the character of our visitors, and do you remain here until my return;" and he rose feebly from his seat. But to the last proposal his daughter and Manon made so instant and decided a resistance, that Mr. St. John soon obliged to give them their own way. He must remain quietly by the fireside, while they proceeded to the lattice; and if, after scrutinizing the strangers, they were not satisfied with their appearance, Marguerite would return and tell him the result; and Bello, meanwhile, should go as their protector. So they left the room; but Manon first placed the omelette and potatoes on a stand before the fire. No excitement made her forget her master's comfort; and, although she had just declared that they would all be robbed and murdered, she seemed to think it well to keep the supper hot until the completion of the tragedy.

The little window mentioned by Mr. St. John had formerly belonged to the concierge, or, in more ancient times still, to the manoir-warden, and was scarcely more than a loop-hole through the solid masonry on the outer side of the court facing the road; so that, in daylight, it commanded a good view of any person standing before the gates. Having lighted a lantern, Manon undid the manifold bolts of the house-door, her healthy, red face being, by this time, several shades paler than usual, and accompanied by Bello, they both ran through the rain, across the courtyard, and gained the shelter of the great outer gates. There, a winding stone staircase led them up into the small chamber, or, more properly speaking, look-out—for there was scarcely enough room in it for more than one person at a time—in which the loophole window was placed. After some difficulty, Manon undid the rusty fastenings of the casement, and, with considerable trepidation of manner, looked out first. But such a torrent of rain and sleet beat into her face as nearly blinded her, and she quickly drew back her head, exclaiming angrily—*Milles tonnerres!*" which, under the circumstances, was not inappropriate. Marguerite, with a stifled laugh, next attempted, but with almost similar success. They had entirely forgotten that, while the light from their own lantern rendered their movements perfectly clear to any person without, they were themselves unable to see an inch after the profound darkness of the night.

"What shall we do?" whispered Marguerite, upon whose courage the gloom and uncertainty were beginning to tell a little; "had we better go down and speak through the door, or——"

"Return to the house at once, and not look at them at all," added Manon, quickly, as another vigorous peal of the bell close beside them made them both start again.

"No, no, Manon, it may be some poor travellers seeking for shelter, as my father said. Let us first fasten up the chain, so that they cannot enter, and then open the gate an inch or two, and speak to them."

Manon unwillingly complied; and after much delay, caused by the trembling of her great strong hands, the gate was opened. She was, by this time, so gasping and frightened, that she could not get out a word; so Marguerite advanced her own face to the small space which was left open, to be speaker; while Manon held the light, exactly where it was in no service in seeing the strangers, but fell full upon the girl's figure, and long streaming hair; and old Bello snarled and showed every tooth in his head, as he stood, waiting to seize upon anybody's legs who might enter.

"Who are you?" said Marguerite, rather faintly, in French, of course; "and do you wish to come in?"

Whether it was this question, or the sight of the enraged old hound, and Manon's terrified face, or all combined, which produced the effect, is unknown; but a suppressed laugh was the first reply. Marguerite's courage returned at the sound.

"Turn the lantern this way, so that we can see them," she whispered, looking round. Manon did so, and the light streamed—not upon a band of robbers—but upon the face of one young and handsome man, who, perfectly drenched with rain, stood outside in the road.

"*Eh, mon Dieu!*" exclaimed Marguerite, reassured in a moment, "if I had only known it was you. Wait one moment, please," and, aided by Manon, she hastily withdrew the chain, having first silenced Bello with an admonition to be friendly, which he appeared rather imperfectly to understand, as he still continued showing his teeth, and uttering a low, dissatisfied growl. The stranger entered, his cap in his hand, and the water literally streaming from his clothes and hair, and began an apology for disturbing them, in tolerable French, but which Marguerite knew in a moment to be that of a foreigner.

"I am so glad you have found our house," she replied, in English; "my father will be delighted to see you, and he is an Englishman. You are very welcome to Kersaint."

The young stranger looked well pleased with his reception; and, when he had assisted in replacing the chain, they all crossed the court together. But, after entering the house, and just as Manon had re-fastened the bolts, while Marguerite was waiting impatiently to conduct the visitor to Mr. St. John, Bello overturned the lantern, which had been placed on the floor, and they were suddenly left in utter darkness.

"Never mind," cried Marguerite, laughing, "I know the house quite as well at night as in the day. Give me your hand, please, and I will take you to my father."

The stranger resigned his hand, nothing loth, to her little warm touch; and she led him on through endless windings and passages, occasionally saying, "Now down one step—now up two steps," until he began to think he was in some enchanted house without an end. At length, they reached the door of the *salle*; there Marguerite whispered, "Just wait one moment here, while I go in; for my father is not strong, and I must prepare him to see you;" and, entering the room, she closed the door, with the simplicity of a child, exactly in his face; while Manon made many apologies, and vainly groped about for a light.

"It was a traveler, and I have let him in, father. He is quite young, very handsome, and an Englishman—and, oh, so wet!" cried Marguerite; while the stranger, just outside the door, naturally heard every word.

"An Englishman!" echoed her father, rising from his seat, and an expression of pleasure crossing his face. "An Englishman at Kersaint!—this is, indeed, strange—after more than fifteen years, to meet one of my countrymen again! Well, he shall receive all the welcome we have to offer; but where have you left him, child?—not still shivering in the cold, I hope?"

"Oh, no, father!" returned Marguerite, triumphant at her own management. "He is quite close—only just outside the door;" and she returned to open it. Mr. St. John advanced to meet the stranger, with the easy courtesy of a man who had been long used to good society. He shook his hand, and made many excuses for their suspicious mode of giving him welcome, adding—"But as I have lived in this lonely spot for sixteen years and you are my first evening visitor,

you will understand that we are somewhat
cautious of opening our doors after nightfall."

The Englishman said that he ought to
apologise himself for disturbing the household at such an unseasonable hour. He was
traveling through Brittany alone, and on foot,
and, having lost his way, had been overtaken
by the storm, and was almost blinded with
the beating rain, when he suddenly found
himself under the walls of the chateau, and
rang the bell, in hopes of finding it inhabited.
"Although," he added, "with little expectation of meeting so kindly a reception;"
and he glanced at Marguerite.

"But now," returned Mr. St. John, "before you partake of refreshment, which you
must so greatly need, or even approach the
fire, you must at once change your dripping
garments. Manon, take this gentleman to
my room, and help him to find whatever he
requires among my wardrobe."

The stranger, however, pointing to a small
waterproof knapsack slung across his shoulders, said he was, fortunately, provided with a
dry suit of clothes, and, in five minutes,
would be ready to join them at the supper-
table; and he then accompanied Manon, up-
stairs. It was not long before he re-appear-
ed. In the meantime, Manon had added
some dainties from her store-room to their
repast, and Marguerite prepared some fresh
tea; while her tongue ran on in a perfect
maze of delightful bewilderment at the adventure.

"My own countryman—the first I ever
saw but you, father—and so handsome, and
such a soft voice! I never saw anything like
it all before. Oh! we must ask him to stay
a long time at Kersaint—it will be such a
new life for us to have a visitor; and—and—
I shall have no time to go with you to church
on Sunday, Manon."

<hr/>

CHAPTER II.

THE entrance of the stranger cut short
Marguerite's words; and the little party
soon sat down to their evening meal. Bello, although partly reassured, kept very close
to his master, and occasionally eyed the new
comer from under his shaggy brows with no
friendly expression, as though aggrieved at
this interruption of their accustomed life;
but upon the human members of the lonely
household the guests quickly produced a most
favorable impression. Mr. St. John's pale
face grew almost animated while listening to
his lively account of his Breton adventures;
Marguerite's open delight expressed itself
both in looks and words; and Manon, who
could not understand the conversation, leisurely surveyed his handsome face and fine
linen, and mentally decided that he was a

worthy guest to sit at *their* table. It was
certainly a face upon which nobility—if not
of birth, that of soul—was legibly written.

The Englishman was pale, and though
young—apparently about four or five-and-
twenty—had already that care-worn look
which can arise only from some deep sorrow,
or a too early knowledge of life and its passions. His forehead was high and fair; his
features regular, and nobly cast; and his
eyes, somewhat deeply set, had a mingled
expression of grave intellect and youthful
softness, which gave a peculiar charm to his
face. He was rather above the middle height,
but slightly made; and Manon thought she
had never seen such small fair hands before.
Marguerite's gaze was quite as free as the
old servant's; but what she noticed most
was the kindly expression of the stranger
when he addressed herself, and the unusually musical tones of his voice. And, as Marguerite's world had hitherto been limited to
her father, the cure, Manon, and the Breton
peasants, it is not surprising that her admiration for their new guest bordered upon the
enthusiastic.

"I hope you like our Bretagne," she said,
when a pause emboldened her to speak.

"What I have seen of it and its people
as yet," he answered, "has interested me
greatly; especially in this wild, sea-side district, where I hope to linger away half the
summer" (her face grew so bright). "But
you say *our* Bretagne—have you then given
up your claim to be Saxon, as the people
here call us?"

"Ah!" answered her father, "poor little
Marguerite forgets sometimes that she is
English. She was born in this old house,
where her whole childhood has since been
passed; and has never known anything but
the rocks and forests of Brittany. You are
the first Englishman, excepting myself, that
she has ever seen; and, but that I make it a
point for her to read with me in her own
language every day, she would long ago
have been French in that as in everything
else. Even as it is, I suppose, she speaks
like a foreigner; for Manon is much with us
in our primitive life, and we never converse
before her in a language she cannot understand; and our good friend the cure, who
occasionally spends the winter evenings with
us, has been Marguerite's French teacher
from her infancy."

"I certainly thought your daughter was
French," replied the stranger; "though
speaking English unusually well."

"Ah! I want practice," replied Marguerite, rather indignantly; "for, father, you
know you read all day, except when you are
teaching me, and then in the evening we
must talk French for Manon. Now that
monsieur is come, however," she added, "I
shall have some one to talk to;" and she
glanced at the young Englishman, who could
not forbear smiling at her childish expres-

sions, and utter absence of what is usually called manner. He resumed his conversation with Mr. St. John, but in a few minutes Marguerite rose, and going to her father's side put her arm round his neck, and whispered something. He smiled and shook his head; but she insisted, and then looking towards his guest, Mr. St. John said—"Although my little daughter has been brought up among wilds and deserts all her life, she has still the natural curiosity of her sex at heart; and cannot rest until she has heard the name of our visitor."

"Oh! petit papa," interrupted Marguerite; "when you know I wished you to ask for yourself, and not for me!" and she blushed crimson; but still fixed her eyes intently upon the young Englishman, as though the subject were one of all-engrossing interest.

For a moment the young man looked somewhat confused, and the slightest shade of color rose in his own face at the question; but quickly recovering his composure he replied, "I am only too happy to satisfy mademoiselle's wish. My name is Philip Earnscliffe." And his tone seemed to imply that in hearing that answer, his new friend would at once be acquainted with h s history. But Mr. St. John simply bowed with the air of one who hears a perfectly unknown name, and Marguerite communicated the discovery to Manon in French, adding in a whisper, "that she thought Philip Earnscliffe the most beautiful name in the whole world;" while the stranger himself was evidently relieved at the unconscious manner of his host on hearing his name.

"And now, Marguerite, as your own curiosity is satisfied, perhaps you will tell Mr. Earnscliffe how we out-of-the-world people call ourselves," said her father.

"Pray do so," added the stranger. "I may now confess that, for the last hour, I also have wished to ask that question."

They had left the supper-table, and were all seated round the fire; Marguerite in her old place at her father's feet, with her arm over Bello, who was gladly forgetting his injuries under the influence of warmth and sleep; and Mr. Earnscliffe placed where his eyes could rest fully upon the little group. Marguerite looked up at him, when her father spoke, with that full, confiding gaze, never seen save on the face of a child, and replied gravely—"My father's name is Percy, and mine is Marguerite Lilla St. John. Marguerite, after my little sister, who died before I was born, and Lilla," she added, very softly, "after my own dear mother. I never saw her, monsieur; she left us alone," touching her father's hand, "when I was born."

Her father's face clouded at these recollections; and he soon grew so pale and silent, that Manon, who was hovering about the background, came forward, and reminded him that it was long past his usual hour for rest; then, turning respectfully to Earnscliffe, she said—"My master is not very strong at present, sir; and mademoiselle and I are obliged to keep watch over his health."

The guest having entreated that Mr. St. John would not remain longer, out of ceremony towards him, he rose; and then the Englishman first fully saw how thin and weak he was. He extended his hand to Earnscliffe, and said, kindly, he should hope on the morrow to rise stronger, and be better able to entertain him, adding—"At all events, my little one will be only too delighted to show you all the walks and wonders of the neighborhood; and I hope you will spend as long a time at Kersaint as you can find anything to interest you."

Earnscliffe heartily accepted this invitation, and, after bidding him "good night," his host withdrew—first kissing his daughter, and saying, in a low voice, "But you, my child, can stay up longer and entertain our guest."

"And not help you, father?"

"No, not to-night, darling." And he took Manon's arm, and walked to the door.

Marguerite had a confused idea that politeness required her to remain by the visitor's side; but when she saw her father, for the first time since his last serious illness, going up to his room without her attendance, the tears rushed into her eyes, and she turned round to Earnscliffe—"Oh! I must go with him, sir, if you please. I will not be long—but, indeed, I cannot see him walking so feebly, and not help as well as Manon!"

Earnscliffe begged her to do so; and, running lightly to her father's side, she supported him with her own firm young arm; while the poor invalid smiled gratefully at his child's warm love, which nothing could for a moment turn aside.

The stranger was left alone, and stood gazing at the door through which Mr. St. John and his daughter had disappeared; and a gloomy expression crossed his face, as he recalled the scene he had just witnessed. "This dying man," he thought, "living in the midst of a dreary solitude, and with pain and suffering written upon his features, possesses the priceless treasure of human love, which I, with youth and health, have never found in the world. He is happy in all the first affection of that girl's young heart. And what a lovely being she is!" he continued, to himself. "With the unconscious grace of a perfect woman, and the artlessness of a child. How she looked at me, and smiled, and then turned away her little head, blushing, only to look again a moment afterwards!" He thought for some minutes, then said, half aloud—"It will be better for her, and for me, too, perhaps, that I should leave them to-morrow morning;" and he turned round, and walked up and down before the fire.

But, as still he continued alone, his late companions seemed gradually to lose their recent tangible forms, and to fade into a mere creation of his own brain. The lonely spot in which he had suddenly met two such beings as Mr. St. John and his daughter—the manner of their introduction—the chateau with its old-world furniture—the dim outline of the gigantic hound who lay outstretched upon the hearth, and the weird voices of the storm, which still beat against the windows—all combined to give to the evening's adventure something dreamy and unlife-like; and Marguerite seemed to him more like some Breton fairy, than a real blooming inhabitant of that gloomy house. "She is a mere child, too," he went on at length—"a lovely little meadow-daisy—but no more! What can she be to me, but a pretty, wild idea for the heroine of my next book? Why, her whole innocent life precludes any other thoughts, even if my own position did not. I will stay and make this fresh nature my study, and leave them in a few days. I have had enough of love"—he smiled bitterly—"without adding another failure to my experience; and if I do create any feeling in this girl's heart, it will be only the awakening of a first fancy, no deeper than that of a child for a new toy. All her love is given to her father; and if it were not so, she would run small danger from me."

The door opened, and the little meadow-daisy entering herself, interrupted his meditations upon her. She approached him, her face radiant with a grave happiness.

"You have done my father good already!" she cried. Although he is tired, he is so cheerful, and glad to have heard an English voice. Manon says—and she understands well about his health—that it will do him more good than taking all the medicines in the world to have a new companion. I know so little, you see," she added, humbly, that I am not enough for him."

Earnscliffe thought how charming it was when a woman knew so little; but he checked a rising compliment, and only inquired if her father had been long ill.

"Oh! do not call him ill," she answered, with a look of sudden terror. "Surely you do not think that my father is ill?"

Her voice faltered; and, to the beseeching expression of her eyes, Earnscliffe could only answer, gently, "that he meant Mr. St. John appeared delicate and to require care."

"Yes! he is not very strong at present; but then, you know, we have had a long, cold winter, and he has not had much opportunity yet of recovering from his illness in the autumn, when he had a lingering, low fever. Now that the summer has come, he can be out all day in the garden, and gain his strength. Should you not think he will be quite well in two or three months?"

Earnscliffe tried to join in her hopes, although his own conviction was that Mr. St. John had not long to live; but her terrified look at the mere idea of her father being seriously ill, made him turn from the subject, and he began inquiring how she spent her own time in summer. This was a theme on which Marguerite could be eloquent. She told him of all the wild haunts on the seashore—of the distant caves among the St. Hernot rocks—of the one small, sunny bay so hard to reach, even at low water, but where you were sure to find the most beautiful shells and sea-weed—of the high cliff, from whence there was the widest view—of the ruined chapel—the heath—the fir-forests—the meadows, now full of primrose and hepatica—the hawthorn lane, with the linnet's nest—and, lastly, of their own orchard and garden; ending it all with—"But, if to-morrow is only fine, I will take you to see our walks, and then you will believe what a happy place this is in summer."

He listened with evident interest, and encouraged her to proceed with her descriptions. It was something strangely new to him to listen to such conversation as hers; and he found a singular pleasure in gazing down upon her animated features, and hearing all her childish accounts of her life. Marguerite soon forgot that she had only known him two hours; and when Manon at length entered, she found the guest still standing by the fire, with Marguerite close to his side, speaking very earnestly, and looking up in his face.

"Monsieur's room is ready," said Manon; "and, after his cold drenching, he should endeavor to get a good night's rest—it is past eleven o'clock."

"Past eleven!" echoed Marguerite, who had never been up so late before. "Why, how quickly the time has gone! I thought it was only ten minutes since my father left us."

It was impossible for the stranger not to feel somewhat pleased at this naïf acknowledgment, from such a mouth; and as he looked on her glowing face, he thought he had never, among all the beauties of London, seen any one to compare with the little meadow-daisy, Marguerite. She held out her hand with the most perfect frankness, wishing him "Good night;" and Earnscliffe followed Manon up the oak staircase, and along the winding passages of the first floor, to the room prepared for him—a quaint, old chamber, all hung with faded blue arras, and where he could hear the loud beating of the waves close under the windows: but a cheerful wood fire blazed on the hearth, and made him seem welcome.

"Good night, and sound sleep to Monsieur," said Manon, as she handed him light, and took a last look round the room, to see that all was in comfortable order for the stranger. Then she closed the door, and descended to her young mistress. Marguerite was still standing in the same place, with Bello sound asleep at her feet, wishing the morrow were come, and wondering why the whole world had suddenly grown so bright.

"Is it not delightful, Manon?" she exclaimed, as her nurse re-entered.

"What, ma mie?"

"Why, having a visitor, of course—and *such* a visitor! Oh! Manon, how unlike any one here, with his gentle manner and low voice! And he spoke so beautifully to my father—and yet did not mind listening to my childish talk. Did you ever see any one so handsome?"

"This young man is good looking," replied the other, in a tone which sounded very cold to Marguerite, "and his shirt front is of the finest batiste I ever saw; but he has a look at times which is much too grave for such a young face. I don't believe his life has been as happy as ours, ma mie!"

And Manon was right.

CHAPTER III.

PHILIP EARNSCLIFFE had lived and suffered more than the generality of men at six-and-twenty. His parents both died during his early childhood, and circumstances had thrown him, when a mere boy, upon the treacherous sea of London society. Gifted to no common extent—handsome, warm-hearted, generous, and, above all, the heir to an immense fortune, Earnscliffe had not wanted friends. Few, indeed, could look on his fair, noble face, or hear the tones of his singularly sweet voice, without becoming interested in him; but, unfortunately, his lot lay among a class of persons, of all, the least likely to conceive really disinterested attachments, or to assist in the formation of a character, which natural softness and absence of all self-reliance made only too ductile.

Philip's mother was a woman of high family—which family she was considered to have irrevocably disgraced, by eloping with her brother's tutor at the very time her mother was planning her marriage with a hoary-headed foreign prince. Mr. Earnscliffe was a gentleman by birth as in feeling, and was also a scholar of no mean attainments; but he was poor, and without connection or influence in the church; and all the happy married life of Philip's parents was spent in an obscure and very small living in the north of England. For the outraged family of

Earnscliffe's wife would not bestow any of their church patronage upon the man who had disgraced them; and, indeed, held no communication whatever with their daughter from the hour of her marriage. Philip was the only offspring of the union, and all the fond love of these two gentle hearts was centered in their lovely, promising child.

But when the boy was about four years old, Mr. Earnscliffe's health, at no time robust, began visibly to decline. The strong, vigorous air of the north had never suited him, although he had not felt himself justified in giving up his small living for this cause; and not until it was too late, did his agonised wife read in his face, and in the evasive answers of the country physician, that the fiat had gone forth—and they were to part. But, from the first, something told her she would not long survive her husband. She had been his so exclusively, from the moment her own family cast her off, and in their lonely life they had seen so little of any but each other, that her very existence seemed bound up in that of Earnscliffe, as every will and thought of her heart were dependent upon his. Had it not been for the child, perhaps neither of them would have greatly grieved to leave the world, where they had met with so much neglect. But their child—their unprotected, unprovided-for child—to leave him, was indeed the bitterness of death; and all the thoughts of both turned unceasingly upon him, and the stranger hands into which their unstained jewel was to be committed.

Mr. Earnscliffe had one brother, many years older than himself, and a man of enormous property, amassed solely by his own endeavors, in India. Their father was a man of small fortune, and not able to give both his sons a college education; so the elder, and stronger one, had to make his way for himself; while the delicate, gentle Herbert was destined for the church from his infancy. A mere lad, with a few pounds in his pocket, Miles Earnscliffe started, and worked his way out in a merchant vessel. On his arrival in India, he got one of the most menial offices in a large mercantile firm; one of the partners having picked the boy up for his shrewd face, but without recommendation. A dogged, untiring perseverance and thorough integrity, united, certainly, to some degree of good fortune, raised him step by step, from errand-boy to clerk—clerk to manager—manager to partner—until, at length, Miles Earnscliffe was one of the wealthiest merchants in Calcutta; and thirty years after he had left his country a friendless, penniless youth, he returned to it with boundless wealth, and as many friends as he had rupees. He had never held much communication with his brother, and was ignorant of his marriage, or its results. Shortly after his return, however, he received a letter, in which Herbert, after warmly congratulating him on his brilliant fortunes, gave him a sketch of his own life—of his marriage, and present condition—concluding with a hope that, for the future, the brothers would see more of each other than their divided state had hitherto permitted. But with the suspicion which long years of lonely labor, and distrust of every one but himself, had engendered, Miles Earnscliffe thought that the gentle, affectionate letter contained some covert request for money; and as he read, every feature in his face worked with rage. Of poverty—as poverty—he had, like all self-made men, the most utter contempt; but when to this was added education, refinement, and the profession of a gentleman, he could scarcely keep his hatred within bounds. He crunched the letter up, flung it into the fire, and paced up and down his lordly room, muttering aloud—" So, my fine gentleman brother, whose white hands were not made for work—with your college education, and brainful of Greek and Hebrew—you have married a noble, titled beggar, whose family despise and scorn you; and I —the low, vulgar, hard working tradesman-brother, am to help you and your grand lady-wife to live! Never, by —— !" And, leaving his untasted breakfast, he sat down, and wrote Herbert a coarse, unfeeling letter; which the latter read once, destroyed, and never even mentioned to his wife.

And thus ended the brothers' intercourse. But when death was upon him, and Earnscliffe looked in his little Philip's face, pride died in his heart. He forgot the past insult, and only remembered his isolated position, and that his brother might be the child's powerful friend and protector for life. Accordingly, after deep deliberation, he made a new will, appointing Miles sole guardian of his son, and leaving the small property he had to bequeath to his care. This done, he consigned the future to the hands of Providence; rightly judging that his brother's iron heart might more readily soften to the child as an orphan than during his parents' lifetime. In three months from this time Philip's father and mother were dead. Miles read the announcement of his brother's death in the paper; and, a few weeks afterwards, that of his wife, and something human smote at his heart as he thought of the child; but pride forbade him making any inquiries about " pauper relations."

It was now late in the autumn; and, one cold, stormy night, Miles sat alone in his splendid dining-room, over his wine. He was abstemious from long habit, and never took more than two or three glasses; so now he sat, with his empty glass at his side, watching the bright logs crackle and blaze upon the hearth, and listening to the mournful soughing of the wind, as it beat fitfully upon the windows. It sounded to him like the voices of the poor trying in vain to enter the rich man's dwelling, and the unusual thought made him turn restlessly in his easy chair.

" Will the evening papers never come? " he exclaimed, after again waiting long and silently. " It is cursed lonely to-night." And the weary Crœsus rang the bell impatiently.

At that moment, a knock—a little fluttering knock—came at the dining-room door. " Come in !" thundered Miles. " What the devil are the idiots at now? scratching like rats, instead of bringing me my paper? "

The door opened slowly, and only after repeated turnings of the handle, and in came —to old Miles's amazement, and almost horror—a child—a very small, young child, dressed in the deepest black, and with long fair hair falling all round its face and neck.

" What the—— !" he began, hastily, starting to his feet; but the words died unfinished on his lips—as still, slowly, but without the slightest trace of fear or shyness, the child continued to approach him. When he was quite near, he looked up in Miles's face, and touching his hand with his own little cold finger, said—" Are you my uncle? If you are, I have brought you a letter from my papa;" and he pulled a sealed envelope from under his dress, and held it up to him.

Earnscliffe was a cold, hard, suspicious, worldly man; but he was human—and in every human breast lurks the tie of blood, and pity for a fatherless child. And as Philip, in all the confidence of childhood, stood looking up in his uncle's face, his lips parted, and the golden curls falling back from his open brow, he recalled so strongly, in his infantine beauty, the image of his own father—whom Miles had last seen, long years before, a bright-eyed boy, hanging round his neck, and weeping before he went to India—that his usually hard feelings were softened in the sudden remembrance of his youth; and, seizing his nephew in his arms, he kissed him with more tenderness than he had shown to anything for years. Philip wound his little arms round his neck, and stroked his cheek. His parents had prepared him to love him, and with the ready warmth of his nature, he already clung to the uncle, who was to supply their place to him. Supply their place—poor child !

On his mother's death, their nearest neighbors, a farmer and his wife, had taken Philip to their house, as they had already promised Earnscliffe, and comforted him, in their homely fashion, during his first passionate sorrow; but three weeks had now elapsed, and already his pale cheeks were more blooming, and he began again to laugh merrily over his play. In childhood, three weeks is an eternity of grief. The good farmer had himself journeyed with Philip to Miles Earnscliffe's door, and there left him, as his father requested, merely asking the servants to allow the boy, unannounced, to enter his uncle's presence. At first there was considerable demur amo ng these grand gentlemen as to the propriety of this proceeding; but Phillip settled the matter for himself by walking through them all with the air of a young prince, and knocking at the first door that took his fancy, which chanced to be that of the dining-room; and thus, as we have seen, introduced himself to his uncle's notice. Philip still nestled in his new protector's arms, when the door noiselessly opened, and the stately butler entered, contrition and apology duly impressed upon his fat features.

"Indeed, sir, it was quite against my knowledge, sir——" he was beginning, when he suddenly stopped. The sight of Miles Earnscliffe—of *his* master—with a child in his arms, so astonished the worthy man, that he was—to use his own words when describing the scene afterwards—"took all of a heap," and the unfinished sentence gurgled and choked in his throat.

Miles set the boy hastily on the ground, enraged that one of his own servants should have witnessed his emotion, and, red with passion, demanded what he meant.

"I did not know, sir," replied the gasping butler, "that you might like to be interrupted, sir—I thought——"

"And who requires you to think, sir?" was the reply. "My nephew can go where he pleases in my house, and enter my dining-room when and as often as he likes without the interference of my servants. Send Mrs. Scott at once," he added, as the butler, very crest-fallen, left the room; and he was again alone with the new-comer, who hoped his uncle would never look so angry at him as he did at the big man with the white head and black breeches.

Mrs. Scott, a thin, starched, unpleasant-looking, middle-aged female, was much aggrieved at hearing of the unexpected addition to the household. On the strength of many extraordinary accounts of wealthy nabobs espousing their own housekeepers, she had been always pleased at the isolation in which her master lived, and was disposed to look with no favorable eye upon any new claimant of his attentions. However, she put on her sweetest smiles as she proceeded to the dining-room, and entered, with the blandest of curtsies to Miles, and what she meant for an encouraging, motherly look at Philip, who immediately grasped his uncle's hand the tighter.

"Mrs. Scott, my nephew having arrived some days earlier than I expected, you have as yet received no orders for his reception. You will now see a room prepared for him for to-night, and to-morrow have nurseries and attendants got ready for him at once."

The housekeeper, with venom at her heart, smiled most sweetly at this announcement; and when Earnscliffe added—"And now take him with you for whatever refreshments he requires," held out her hand with great kindness to Philip: but the child turned away from her, and looked imploringly at Miles.

"Oh, let me stay with you this once, uncle; I like to stay with you, and I don't love her," pointing to Mrs. Scott. "I will be so quiet here." Miles chuckled at this speech and at the housekeeper's visible discomfiture; and dismissing her, now fairly boiling over with indignation, prepared himself to spend the evening alone, in company with his brother's child. He sat down in his arm-chair, and Philip, drawing a little stool to his feet, seated himself also.

"This is how I used to do at home with my papa," said the boy; "and he gave me my dessert on a plate."

"Oh—oh!" said Miles, "I see through it all now" and he filled a plate with peaches and grapes, and handed it to him; "it was for the sake of the dessert you wished to stay with me." Philip jumped up, his face all in a glow of indignation. He had never even been accused of untruth before.

"You may keep your fruit," he said, pushing the plate as far as he could upon the table; "I won't eat it. I wanted to stop with *you*, and never thought of your dessert till you gave it me"—and his eyes flashed again. Miles was more pleased at this display of spirit than even with his former caresses; and, drawing him to his knee, said he did not doubt his truth, and only meant to joke him.

"Oh," returned Philip, brightening up, "if you were only in joke, of course, that is different, and I don't care a bit; but you said it so like earnest"—and all his anger vanished. So again he sat down, the plate in his lap, and began his fruit. How fair he looked, with the red firelight dancing on his long, waving hair, and white neck and arms, which shone like marble upon his sable dress, dividing the fruit with his rosy fingers, and every minute looking up and smiling archly at Miles.

"You have very good fruit, I think, here; we had only apples and plums at home, though they were very sweet, too. I never saw fruit like this before."

"I should think not," said his uncle, complacently. "You will see a great deal in my house that you never saw before."

"Shall I?" returned Philip, with much animation. "Oh, tell me what!" and, having finished his dainties, he came and stood close to his uncle's side. "Can you tell stories?" he whispered—as Miles remained silent—looking inquiringly up into his face.

"Well," he replied, "I suppose I could if I tried."

"Then, please let me sit on your lap, and tell them to me till my bed-time;" and, without further invitation, he seated himself on his uncle's knee, folded his hands, composed himself comfortably to listen, and then said, "Begin." And old Miles began, awkwardly enough—as might be expected of a man who had never talked to children in his life—and in a very low voice, as though he were half ashamed of himself. But Philip saw no defects or hesitation; and, when he came to stories of parrots and monkeys, clapped his little hands with delight, and cried out, "Tell it again—tell it again!"

So Miles told it again; and went on improving until Philip was fairly in ecstacies, and thought he had never seen such a funny man as his uncle. Miles Earnscliffe a funny man! And thus passed the evening. At length the child's head drooped, and his eyes grew heavy with fatigue, and his uncle said he must go off to bed.

"Yes, directly," said Philip. Then he lingered and looked rather shy—"but I want to say something first. When my mamma was alive, I used to say my prayers to her. Oh, uncle, let me say them to you this one night, because I am all alone here, and I don't like to say them to Mrs. Scott."

Miles assented with a husky voice; and the child knelt down, and, folding his dimpled hands on his uncle's knees, said his evening prayers, concluding with "God bless papa and mamma"—poor little fellow!—as though they still needed the weak, imperfect prayer of their child.

And now he is gone; and Miles sits long by the red fire-light, with new thoughts in his heart, and a softer expression on his hard face, and his dead brother's open letter in his hand.

CHAPTER IV.

PHILIP was thus installed in his uncle's house; and, in one of those sudden revulsions of the heart, to which the hardest of human beings are subject, Miles Earnscliffe had soon conceived an almost passionate love for the child. After living all his life distrustful and alone, a natural source of affection was at length opened for his hitherto barren feelings, and they seemed more intense from the very fact of having been so long pent up in his own bosom. Philip was soon paramount in the house. Mrs. Scott the boy seemed to look upon as a natural enemy; and, after a six weeks' war, Mrs. Scott was dismissed. He had a cheerful young relation of his old friend the farmer for his own attendant, birds and pets for his amusements, a Shetland pony to ride—in short, a flood of sunshine seemed to have broken upon the house, which used to be so "dull and dignified."

Miles was more happy in the change than he would acknowledge to himself. To hear Philip's little voice, as he played about the room during breakfast—to have him prattling at his knees, in the long winter evenings—to look in his fair face, and feel, "he, of my

own blood, and not a stranger, shall inherit my wealth"—all this gave him a living interest in his life, and in his riches, which he had never felt before. As the boy grew older, he was formally announced by Miles to be his heir; and it is needless to say what numbers of friends awaited young Philip in the world. Although his uncle himself hated society, his pride was gratified by all the attentions showered upon his heir; and he would chuckle to himself as he thought "how much love would Phil's grand relations have shown him, if he had not been adopted by his vulgar old uncle?"

For gentle reader, the family of Philip's mother—with that beautiful constancy to a rich relation, so frequently to be observed in the world—although they had cast off a daughter of their house for marrying a poor man, were exceedingly anxious to court the poor man's rich brother. Miles had himself abandoned Herbert in his poverty; but he felt the greatest disgust at their meanness, and insulted his lordly relations on more than one occasion when he chanced to meet them in the world. After his adoption of Philip, however, and as the latter grew up, he began to relent towards them, for the child's sake; for he wished his nephew to have an introduction to the very society he had himself always affected to despise. The first amiable advances on the part of the eccentric Mr. Earnscliffe—very rich men are only eccentric never rude—were met cordially; his former rebuffs were forgotten with true Christian charity; and Philip found a score of affectionate grand-parents, uncles, aunts, and cousins all ready to love him. As Herbert Earnscliffe's son, they would, probably, have considered him a common-place, uninteresting boy; but, as Miles Earnscliffe's nephew, every one discovered that he had inherited his father's wit, and his mother's beauty. It happened that all these praises were, as regarded Philip, true. He grew up exceedingly handsome; with more, perhaps, of that beauty which awakens interest from the intellect shining through the outward form—than of the mere physical perfection which attracts the common mass of people. And yet Philip's features, of themselves, were all good and finely chiselled. The Grecian nose, and full, poet mouth, might have borne the most critical scrutiny; although it was in his brow, and deep, spiritual eyes, that lay the rare charm of his face.

He went to Harrow, and did not shine there; some of his masters pronouncing him merely idle, others a dunce. But when Miles, in stern displeasure, questioned the boy upon these evil reports, Philip's only reply was—"Uncle, I have as much ability as any of my masters, though I cannot learn as they teach. Take me from school, and let me study at home, and I will be a greater man than any of them." Miles would do nothing of the kind, so Philip remained at

Harrow the usual number of years, and left it with the proportionate amount of ignorance and Greek, which can't be acquired at an English public school. But his mind had not lain idle all this time. His education had been—not in the wretched daily routine of immoral classics—but in his life. In his school friendships, and dislikes; in all the varieties of human life—although only that of boys—which he had learnt to analyse; in his own transition from childhood into youth; in the long summer walks among the Harrow hills; in his solitary evening dreams under the starlight, his poet's mind had gradually dawned. And at the end of five years he left school, no scholar, but a genius.

"What are you at, Phil?" his uncle would exclaim testily, when he was continually filling endless sheets of writing-paper, and absenting himself from all his old amusements; and Phil had not the moral courage to say "he was writing a book;" knowing well that Miles was no lover of authors, and would, probably, not be pleased at the prospect of having one in his own nephew; so he evaded the question, and kept his papers out of sight, but, in his own study, returned with redoubled ardor to his occupation, made all the sweeter from having to be pursued by stealth. As his work grew, and he felt within him the wonderful power of creative genius strengthening, day by day, his love for his art increased tenfold. It was with Philip no wish for fame, no feverish desire to be heard of, but the mere delight of creating, which impelled him to write; and with extraordinary rapidity the book proceeded. Full of faults it was, both of diction and composition; but with frequent touches of pure pathos, vigorous conception, and a shrewd and caustic wit, which bespoke the early dawnings of no common mind. At length, he finished it. One summer midnight, he wrote the last line; and then, for the first time, he felt that he had succeeded. Although no eye but his own had ever read a word of his writings, something within him said that his was not like the generality of books, and that he was to be one of the few who rise apart from the common leaven of humanity. He extinguished his little lamp, and, throwing open his window, walked out upon the balcony.

The summer night, with its thousand voluptuous odors—the soft, warm air—the deep sky above—and the stars, those mysterious types of immortality, which seem, in every deep emotion, to have kindly sympathy with the heart of man—all harmonised with his own happy feelings. Nature seemed bidding him welcome among the poet band, who alone interpret her rightly, and are her apostles to the weary children of the world. He remained long, building a hundred bright dreams for the future—those first visions of fame than which the hopes of love are not sweeter—and when he at length retired to rest, he slept not; for now other and more practical thoughts arose upon his mind.

How should his first work appear before the world?—should he publish anonymously, and unknown to his uncle, trusting merely to his own merit for success? At first, he liked the idea, but then his heart revolted against even a temporary concealment from Miles; he thought of the old man's disappointment at his Harrow failures, and felt he should confide his secret to him, and let him participate with him in his hopes and triumph. Then, again, he thought of his uncle's sarcastic remarks about authors of fiction—"trashy rubbish," as he called novels; and so the hours passed, in a conflict of opposing plans, until daybreak, when he rose to read and re-touch portions of his work. When he came down to breakfast, next morning, his heavy eyes bore ample testimony to the way in which he had passed the night. He had decided to broach the subject at once: and his manner was constrained, as he seated himself and began his breakfast, without knowing what he was about.

Miles eyed him sharply; he had watched Philip much of late. His abstraction, his late hours, his pale cheek, had not escaped his notice; and a suspicion had arisen, the bare thought of which filled him with horror—the boy must have fallen in love. Of course, he looked forward, some day, to his marrying a woman with rank or money; but of love, or youthful romance, he had almost a greater horror than of poverty, and he was resolved to cure all such nonsense in its beginning. He had never known a similar weakness himself, and classed it with measles, and other childish disorders, that must be gone through. He only wished his nephew had had the good grace to keep clear of the contagion.

"What ails you, Phil?—with your ghostly white face—helping yourself three times to sugar, and crumbling your bread all over the table-cloth—do you hear me, sir?"

"Yes, sir," said Philip, looking very guilty; "I—the fact is—I—"

"Oh, yes, it is all coming!" groaned Miles, internally; then he added aloud, with sarcastic politeness—"Pray take your time, nephew; I am in no hurry."

"I fear you will not be pleased, uncle. I should have told you sooner, but——"

"But what, sir?" interrupted Mr. Earnscliffe, angrily. "I know the meaning of your hesitation, and your blushes, and your modesty. Tell me the woman's name, you love-sick young idiot, at once, and have done with it."

"The woman's name!" said Philip, looking up in amazement, and with his face exceedingly red. "It has nothing to do with any woman in the world. I have written a book, sir," bringing out the last words with an effort.

Miles heaved a colossal sigh of relief; he drank an entire cup of tea—buttered some toast—looked Philip full in the face—and then went into a hearty fit of laughter. "So you have written a book? oh!"

"Yes, sir. I am glad to see you so amused." Philip had already too much of the author in him, not to feel offended at the way his important announcement was received.

"A book—ho! ho!—don't be angry; and what are you going to do with it?"

"Publish it," he returned, shortly,

"Well, I suppose, at your age, you must do something ridiculous; and it is so infinitely better than the other thing, that I feel actually relieved. But a book—well—what is it all about?"

"Perhaps you would like to hear some of it?" replied Philip—he could not long be angry with his uncle—"I should be glad to read you some of my scenes."

"Is it in verse? No. Well, that is a comfort. A novel, I suppose? I thought so. I am an excellent judge of that valuable class of works, and shall be happy to give you my criticism. We will publish it, by all means (without our name, if you please); and I daresay our first success will be such, as to make us leave book-writing alone for the future."

And in this cheerful strain Miles finished his breakfast. He loved Philip deeply, but it was not in his power to refrain from saying spiteful things, even to him; and looking upon him with all his good looks and noble qualities, as no genius—there was really, to him, something quite ludicrous in this new idea of authorship.

"I shall be in the library at eleven, punctually, for the reading, Phil," he said, as they parted. "Bring the shortest chapters"

Philip went sadly to his own room. He was very young; and his uncle's sarcastic manner had fallen like a pall upon all his bright hopes.

"Yes," he thought, "I daresay he is right. I have no real genius; and the world will think so, too." He took his manuscript in his hand, and turned the leaves over with a feeling of disgust. "And all this, that only last night I thought was to live for ever, is, perhaps, worthless nonsense." And he began, bitterly, to read a passage aloud. But, even as he did so, the feeling under which that very passage was written—a description of genius slowly conquering difficulties, and rising above this world to another —returned to him, and his own words became his comforters. "I *have* genius!" he exclaimed, aloud, "I know—I feel it. My uncle has not heard any of my writings yet; and, even when he has, and if he judges ill of it, it shall not alter me. I must succeed." He laid down the manuscript; and walking up and down the room, waited impatiently for the appointed hour, when he descended—his work under his arm—to the library. His uncle was already there.

"Heaven help me!" he exclaimed, half to himself, but, of course, meaning Philip to hear; "I expected one, or, at most, two, quires of foolscap, and, behold! as much paper as goes to a family Bible." Then he added, aloud—"Well, how much are we to get through at one sitting?"

"As much, or as little, as you like," replied Philip, laughing; "I will read you a scene here and there; and when you are tired you can tell me."

"Don't fear. I shall not forget that," was the answer, as Philip seated himself at the table.

Who does not remember the nervous, choking sensation in the throat, when one was about to read one's first composition to a relation? No after ordeal among editors and publishers can ever come up to it. He arranged his papers—turned, and re-turned them, to find an effective part—and then glanced at Miles. He was comfortably seated in his easy chair, by the open window— his hands folded over his ample waistcoat, and his eyes fixed upon the ceiling, with an expression of mock resignation, very trying to a young author. His feet were outstretched in an attitude of excessive ease; and over his head he had thrown a large silk handkerchief—his usual prelude to falling asleep.

"Are you ready, uncle?"

"Quite, Philip—the day is hot—and if I *should* go to sleep, you must wake me, and not be offended!"

And, at length, after clearing his throat twice, the boy began. Miles expected a great deal of nonsense about love and sentiment; but Philip knew his taste too well to choose such scenes, even had there been much about love in his work, which there was not. He selected a portion of the book where the workings of an erring, but originally noble nature, were developed; and there was a vigor and truthfulness in the way this character was brought out, of which Miles, who had seen so much of life, was fully able to judge; for, although he knew nothing of books, he was well versed in the darker parts of human nature. The description was one of a youth, who, by slow and gradual stages, becomes a gambler; for years plays, as men term it, with honor; and, at length, in a moment of uncontrollable temptation, makes another downward transition, and is a felon. Then he analysed, at some length, the passion which had led the youth on into crime, and painted minutely its terrible pleasures and irresistible fascinations. A passage or two may be quoted, as giving some idea of the general style.

"The love of gambling," he read, "is more intense than was ever the love for woman; more intoxicating, more fervid, and actually, in its deeds of self-abnegation, more heroic. With the mere vile end of gold for the reward, what blind and boundless sacrifice, what changeless courage, what unfailing ardor is evinced in the pursuit! The true gambler conquers or falls, with the coldness of a stoic; passing, in an hour, from the highest to the lowest grades of society, without a change of features. Still, hanging over the green cloth, where the demon of play enchains him, he experiences in one night every vicissitude of our life. First king, then slave, he leaps over, in one bound, the enormous space that separates these two men in the scale of human existence. What will he be when he leaves this fevered den, a prince or a beggared outcast? weighed down with countless gold, or despoiled of the last poor gem which glitters on his hand? He knows not—he scarcely cares. For, after all, it is *not* the lust of gold which chains him to his consuming life. It is the loathing of repose, and love of the fierce excitement caused by these eternal gains and losses. Gold becomes his life—his mistress—his one desire—his avenging fiend—his god; and yet it is not gold for its own sake that he covets. This ceaseless combat for a shadow, no sooner caught than it again eludes his grasp, and which he loses almost with pleasure, that he may re-commence the struggle, is to him, at length, as the very breath of his nostrils. In time he has no other life but this life; every softer feeling of his nature is sacrificed to the infernal fever that consumes him. Love, self-esteem, friendship—even the blandishments of mere sensual pleasure—what are they to him, whose delight it is to have his own heart throb with agony, his blood boil, his brain reel madly; who throws his life, his fortune, his honor away at one throw of the dice, or risks them, piece by piece, in a slower and more exquisite torture? What are the excitements of our life to him? puerile and childish.

" The ocean could as soon sink into eternal calm, the eagle be happy without wings, as he return to the peaceful monotony of common existence. Oh! what patriots would have lived for their country alone—what lovers have sacrificed their life and honor for their mistress, if the same fire had ever burnt in their breasts which lights up the hollow eye of the gambler!"

Philip went on reading several pages; at length he stopped, and stole a glance at his uncle. He was not asleep; his eyes were fixed intently upon the boy's face, his head bent forward in a listening attitude, and the handkerchief lying unheeded upon the floor.

" Are you tired, uncle?"

" No."

" Shall I go on?"

" No. Philip, answer me one thing, and truly; how did you learn all you have just read to me? where did you get your experi-

ence of a gambler's life and feelings? From what you have read—or—but, no, it is impossible that you could have seen such things at your age."

"Uncle," returned Philip, quietly, " I cannot tell you how I learn anything that I write; as you say, it cannot be from my own experience, and I have read so few novels that I do not think I have borrowed much from them. I suppose, in this case, it must partly be from what I have read and heard, but much more from imagining what *must* be the state of a man's mind under one powerful and all-engrossing passion. Further than this, I cannot explain how or why I have written."

Miles looked into the frank young face, and believed him. He was shrewd, and not without ability, of a certain kind, himself; and, though Philip's was of a higher and very different order, he was able to recognize the youth's dawning talent at once. But he paid him few compliments.

" I do not deny, Philip, that I am altogether surprised at what I have heard of your writing. You shall begin this evening, and read the whole work to me through. Afterwards, I suppose you will publish it. Well, I never thought you would end in being an author."

The readings were long, often extending until after midnight—for old Miles grew more interested in the plot than he acknowledged —and, when it was finished, he was as anxious as Philip about the publication; adding, at last—" and, I believe, after all, it may be as well to publish it under your own name."

In a few weeks the book was in the press.

Philip had small difficulty to contend with at the commencement of his literary career. Had he been an ordinary youth of eighteen, struggling on without friends or fortune, his talents would have undoubtedly remained the same, but his success might have been different—I mean the success of his first work, not his ultimate fame as an author—and therein lies a great distinction. The rugged path to be toiled up in early youth—the neglect at first—the harsh criticism—the slowly-dawning fame, are the very circumstances which have braced up and fostered many a youthful genius; while, on the other hand, there is scarcely a more perilous test of real worth, than for a first work to be brought out under all the accidental advantages of a name and fortune, excellent publishers, and friendly critics. But the result at the time is unquestionably far pleasanter.

At eighteen, Philip found himself a successful author—a lion in London society; with as great a share of adulation, and as many pretty women ready to be in love with him, as might have turned many an older head. He was naturally no coxcomb, and became as little one as was perhaps possible; but no handsome young author, courted as he was, could remain long free from the per-

2

nicious effects of such a life; one of the greatest evils of which was, that his mind, instead of the quiet and repose necessary after the feverish haste in which his first book was written, was kept in a constant whirl of excitement, when it should have been acquiring new and healthy vigor for its next labors. At the end of another year, however, he again published. The success of the work was great—perhaps, greater than had been the former one—but it was a false success this time—that of society. In the world the book was indiscriminately praised, its faults, which were many, were unnoticed, and the really true and beautiful parts overlooked. Only a few grave critics were more sparing in their praises than before; and hinted that if the third work of the young author were again as intrinsically poorer, as was this one, compared to the first, his literary career would be over. Philip felt the truth of these remarks deeply, and resolved to profit by them, and withdrew himself awhile from the noisy world of London, ere he again attempted to compose.

Miles gladly seconded his intention; for all Philip's success and engagements had naturally deprived his uncle of much of his society, and they were both looking forward, with pleasure, to spending some quiet months at a place of Mr. Earnscliffe's, far away in the north of England, when a new train of events arose, which altered their plans, and colored the whole of Philip's after life.

When he again wrote, it was to be under very different circumstances.

CHAPTER V.

PHILIP EARNSCLIFFE was already looked upon as one of the best *partis* in London. Joined to all his own attractions, he was the acknowledged heir of one of the richest men in England; and many a wily mother and innocent daughter had combined their united snares around him. But Philip, although he had had a dozen admirations, had never fallen in love. Perhaps he had as yet had no time to do so; or, more likely, he had been thinking too much of himself to bestow undivided attention upon any other object. However this might be, he only laughed, when his uncle used to ask him, at breakfast, "What silly face he had become enamoured of the evening before?"—and always said he should have no time to think of marrying, for the next ten years, at least. He little knew how near his fate was upon him.

One of the houses at which he was the most intimate was that of Lord St. Leger, his maternal uncle. The noble lord was himself as disagreeable a person as you will often meet with, and possessed scarcely an idea beyond his own dignity and the dicebox, while of principle he was most singularly and entirely void. His wife was not a whit inferior to himself in coldness of heart —or, rather, in the complete absence of what common people term natural affection. She had, however, a fair, kindly face—a plausible manner—a soft voice, and was generally spoken of as a very charming woman indeed. Few claims to popularity go deeper.

They had only one child, a daughter; and Lady Clare St. Leger inherited many of the qualities of both her parents—although these were, of course, somewhat glossed over by her youth and personal attractions. She was several years older than Philip, and had already attained the age of five-and-twenty —an age at which most girls, in her position, would have been some years married. But, although she had had several offers, and one lover, none of her suitors had been considered eligible, either by herself or her parents. Time wore on, however, and every year Lord St. Leger became more anxious for his daughter to marry a wealthy man. Beneath his cold, white, unmeaning face, lurked the fire of many an evil passion; and the gambling-table had long been making fearful inroads upon a fortune already crippled with youthful extravagance.

Lady St. Leger was equally desirous that Clara should make a distinguished marriage; but she had always looked less to mere money than to high birth and position, until one day, when her husband abruptly acquainted her with the darkening state of his own affairs; adding, coarsely, "and it would be well, madam, for you to make a last effort to marry your daughter, or I reckon she will have little chance soon of finding a husband at all. Unless something very unforeseen occurs, you may look forward, in the course of the present year, to being the wife of a beggar." Lady St. Leger pondered deeply over this fearful intelligence—the most fearful that can be conceived to a heartless woman of the world. The prospect of poverty was, to her, the prospect of disgrace, loss of position, influence in society—all that constituted her life. Without domestic affections, resources in herself, or religion, she looked upon a beggared future as far worse than death itself; and, with a desperate determination, she resolved to marry Clara at once. She felt that upon that alone hung their last chance. But to whom? She turned over in her mind all the men who had ever shown her daughter any attention, and even those who had not; and as, one by one, the most eligible rose before her, she felt that Clara, at five-and-twenty, had small prospect of succeeding where she had failed at eighteen: she was getting somewhat thin, of late, and had not too many partners at balls during the present season. Suddenly a new thought flashed across Lady St. Leger; she half smiled, and deliberated long—but the deliberation seemed, at last, favorable, and her thin lips parted disdainfully, as she muttered aloud, "Well, I suppose it must be so; I must marry my daughter to young Earnscliffe."

Later in the day she sought for Clara, and found her alone in the drawing-room. She was neither working nor reading, but sitting in the twilight, with her eyes fixed upon the fire, and her hands lying listlessly in her lap. She was paler even than usual, and her long light hair, thrown back from her face, revealed lines which had already lost the rounded contour of early youth. Lady St. Leger looked at her for a few seconds, and then, approaching noiselessly, laid her hand on her shoulder.

"Clara!"

"Yes, mother."

She never turned her head.

"What are you thinking of, child, sitting alone in the dark?"

"I was thinking of Harry, mother."

"Of Harry!" returned the other, with cold contempt. "Well, I should not have expected that my daughter would think of Harry Douglas again, after the lapse of eight years. A poor penniless young sailor, who presumed to talk to you of marriage."

"Aye, is it not ridiculous?" she replied, with a bitter laugh. "For I refused him—at your bidding, certainly, but also through my own pride. And for eight years—you remember rightly, mother— I have planned, and plotted, and acted, in the hope of becoming the wife of a dozen other men, and have not succeeded. And now—a worn and wearied woman—I can yet think of him and of my girlhood, and shed tears for both, as I have done to-day. But I do not feel that I shall shed many more." She clasped her hands upon her knees, bowed her head upon them, and was silent.

"Clara," resumed her mother, after a pause, "listen to me. You have been a dutiful daughter, hitherto "—she moved impatiently—"and have never opposed my wishes. Now, the very existence of your father and myself may depend upon you. Our affairs, it matters not how or why, are in the most desperate condition, and to your marriage alone can we look for help. If you were to marry a man of property, we might yet————"

"Well!" said Clara, suddenly looking up, "I understand you. Who is it to be? what happy man am I this time to try to win for my husband?"

Her mother even was rather taken aback at her hard, cold manner, but she soon recovered her composure; and turning her face a little aside, answered quietly, "Your cousin Philip."

"Philip Earnscliffe?"—"Yes."

"Mother, are you dreaming? Why should I marry that boy? Surely you do not care

for his handsome face or his genius?" she added, with a sneer.

"Clara, Philip's uncle is the wealthiest commoner in England. His nephew is, certainly, only his presumptive heir; still, every chance is in his favor. Old Earnscliffe would probably make handsome settlements; and, at all events, it is the best *parti* you have any chance of making, and he will be easily won."

"He is not likely, with his poet's fancies, to fall in love with me."

"At twenty, a vain youth will fall in love with any woman who shows a preference for him. Leave everything to me, my darling; only act as I wish you, and in a few weeks you will be Miles Earnscliffe's niece."

"And *his* wife. Well, as you will—his or another's; it is all the same. Only one thing, mother—get it over as quickly as you can, and let me have as little to do with it as possible. And once more she sunk into her old listless attitude. Her mother pressed a kiss upon her forehead, and then, quite delighted at Clara's acquiescence, fluttered gaily out of the room.

Thus was Philip's marriage projected.

Lady St. Leger was naturally a clever woman. Long experience in the world had given her an extensive knowledge of the foibles of human nature, and she had an inborn talent for scheming and manœuvering. It would not be interesting to the reader to follow her minutely in the way she plotted for Philip. The crowning scene of her endeavors it will be enough to relate.

One day, about a week after the interview with her daughter, Philip was to dine with them alone. He frequently did so, partly on the score of relationship, partly because he rather liked his cousin's society. In spite of her pale face and moodiness, there was something about her which interested him, although she was certainly the last woman in the world with whom he could have fallen in love. In her calm, sensible conversation he found a pleasant contrast to the blooming, exuberantly happy and excessively amiable young ladies he generally met with in the world. Clara rather liked him, too, in her own cold way; and looking upon her cousin in as one she would, at least, never be called upon to win, her manner with him had always been friendly and natural.

Philip found Lady St Leger alone in the drawing-room. She received him affectionately, and made many inquiries for his uncle; but, after these first customary greetings were over, he perceived that she was silent and abstracted. Her face was averted from him, and occasionally she sighed, as if unconscious of his presence.

"You are not well, I fear," he said, kindly; "or something has occurred to depress you."

She raised a little mass of deep lace to

her eyes—that action being considered a symbol of feminine agitation—and was silent. Philip became interested, and pressed her for a reply.

"Ah, Philip!" she cried, seizing his hand—her own was still white and soft as a girl's; "none but a mother can know how I suffer. I feel that it is imprudent, but I cannot conceal it, even from you; the sad truth has broken upon me so suddenly. After watching the infancy of an only child, seeing her grow up to womanhood, and never once in her life having breathed a reproving word to her; now, in the brightness of her youth, to know that she is pining, altering day by day. Oh, Philip! my heart will break under it!" and the lace was again in requisition.

"Is Clara—is my cousin ill?" he inquired, anxiously.

"Yes, she is ill, and with a worse malady than any bodily ailment. Philip, for some months I have perceived that she was restless and unsettled; she has cared less for society, her gay cheerfulness has decreased" (Philip never remembered her being very cheerful)—"her cheeks have grown pale; and yet, when I have questioned her upon her health, she has always replied, 'she was well—quite well—quite happy.' But a mother is not so easily deceived. I have watched more closely every indication of her feelings, and, at length, only two days ago, an accident discovered to me my poor darling's secret. Clara oh, how can I tell you! you of all others!" (her voice sank until it was scarcely audible) "my child is the victim of a deep—and too much, I fear, unreturned—attachment."

"Good heavens! how little I should have supposed it possible. Believe me, dear Lady St. Ledger, I fully sympathise with you in your anxiety; but what man can be insensible to the preference of so gentle a being as Clara?"

Philip had not the slightest idea which way his afflicted relative was drifting. He only felt real concern at Lady St. Leger's communication, not unmixed with astonishment that she had selected him for a confidant on such a very delicate subject as her daughter's unrequited love; while the lady's inward reflection was, "Stupid creature! I shall have to tell him in so many words."

"I cannot tell you more; perhaps I have already said too much. I believe it would kill my poor child if she thought I had revealed her secret—and to you; for, once, when I remarked upon her altered looks, and said I must ask you to cheer her with some of your right poetic thoughts, she exclaimed, 'Not him, mother!—not one word to my cousin, or I shall die!' and her very lips turned ashy pale. Oh, Philip! it was then that I first suspected the cruel truth. But hush! here she comes!"—and at that moment the door slowly opened, and Clara entered. She was dressed in white, with only a bouquet of natural moss-roses in her bosom, and looked younger and fresher than usual—with her long, pale hair falling in a cloud upon her transparently fair neck, and a somewhat heightened color in her face. When she saw her mother and Philip alone together, the color deepened to a crimson blush, and she averted her head as they shook hands.

The last words of Lady St. Leger had caused an extremely painful sensation to Philip; and Clara's evident embarrassment at seeing him only confirmed his half-formed fear, that he was the object of her attachment. Although she was not a girl he could love, she was gentle, and certainly pretty; and he had always felt a kind of pity for her companionless life. Nothing could have given him more sincere pain than the idea which had been forced upon his mind; and he allowed Lady St. Leger to talk on without reply, while he became as silent and embarrassed as his cousin. Lord St. Leger, however, soon entered, and dinner was announced, Lady St. Leger whispering to him as he handed her to the dining-room, "Not a word—not a look—as you value my poor darling's happiness."

The meal passed off slowly. Lord St. Leger was out of temper, as usual, and spoke little. Clara was perfectly silent; and although Lady St. Leger and Philip exerted themselves to talk, their conversation was evidently constrained. Soon after the ladies had left the table, his uncle begged Philip to excuse him, saying he had an engagement which obliged his attendance; so Earnscliffe was compelled to join his aunt and cousin in the drawing-room. But he had a gloomy feeling—a sort of presentiment of evil—upon his spirits, and he would much sooner have left the house. He found Clara alone. She was seated by a small table, at the further end of the room, apparently intent upon the book she was reading. As he approached, his heart fluttered slightly at seeing it was one of his own works. He was too young to be insensible to the attachment of any woman; and his cousin had never appeared to him so interesting before.

"I wish you had a better book to study, Clara," he said with rather a forced smile.

She turned and looked at him—that fixed, steady look which, had he lived longer, he might have known no woman could bestow upon the man she loved—and again a deep, painful blush overspread her face, coloring even her neck and arms. How should he know that it was a blush of burning shame? There was but one way to interpret her confusion after the half-confession of her mother; and it was an interpretation too flattering to his vanity to be doubted. She loved him! Poor Philip felt himself getting rather confused, too, and seated himself quite close to her, without knowing exactly what he was about.

Clara bent over her book again, and sighed—no acted sigh. Whatever her emotion at that moment, it was real, although it arose not from love to her cousin. She felt that her mother had spoken; and all the lingering pride of her girlhood was warring against the worldly obedience to which she had been trained. When she looked in Philip's bright, young face, too, she felt more than her usual disgust at the part she was acting. This time she was not trying to win a mere man of the world, but to deceive a frank and truthful nature. She remembered him as the one friend she had ever possessed since her childhood; and, even now, the thought of speaking openly to him, and saving them both, struggled in her bosom.

"You are ill, dear Clara—your color changes every minute!" He took her hand, and was shocked at the clammy, death-like touch.

"Not ill, Philip. I am ill in mind only. Cousin" (her cheeks were again on fire), "I fear my mother has spoken to you—my mother——"

But her proud lip could not speak those humiliating words, and quivered with agitation as she vainly tried to continue.

Unhappily for himself, poor Philip was too generous to allow her to do so. He reflected not that on a few words of his the aftercoloring of his whole life might depend; and that, in saving her a passing humiliation, he was about to sacrifice himself for ever, without one warmer feeling than pity in his heart. He only saw a broken-hearted girl trying, with pale, trembling lips, to exonerate herself in his eyes for having given him her love unasked, and all the noblest feelings of his nature were awakened. Throwing his arms around her, he whispered, before she could speak another word, "Oh, Clara, confide all your sorrow to me—for I love you!"

She had not then the principle to withdraw, though she shuddered in his embrace; and the recollection of the warm love she had once known for Harry Douglas came like a mockery to her, even at that moment, when, with a selfish, unbeating heart, she was about to give herself for life to another. Her cold lips were pressed unresistingly to Philip's, and he poured forth passionate words which, in the excitement of the moment, he actually himself believed were genuine.

When Lady St. Leger entered the room, after a reasonably long time had elapsed, her delighted eyes beheld them standing together near the fire, Clara's face deeply flushed, and her eyes cast down, and her companion speaking in low but animated tones, with her hand clasped in his.

It was late that evening when Philip found himself on his way home, excessively bewildered at all that had passed, and the accepted suitor of Lord St. Leger's daughter.

CHAPTER VI.

It would be difficult to describe Mr. Earnscliffe's feelings on hearing of Philip's sudden engagement to his cousin. Of course, he flew into a great passion at first, and refused point-blank to give his consent, saying "the boy had been decoyed, inveigled, taken in." But this he would have considered it a sort of duty to do, whatever project of marriage had been formed by his nephew without his own advice. On cooling down, and reflecting more calmly, however, the leading weakness of the old man's nature was immensely flattered at the idea of the St. Legers—the proudest people amongst the whole English nobility—catching eagerly at *his* heir. It had always been his secret hope that Philip would one day marry into a noble family, and thus unite in his posterity his own hardly-earned wealth with aristocratic blood. As he thought over it he became gradually more reconciled to his nephew marrying so young, and at length grew really friendly to the match, although he made himself thoroughly disagreeable to everybody, long after he had, in his own mind, determined to consent. Lady St. Leger's expectations, however, of handsome settlements, on the part of old Miles, were grievously disappointed. A few days after he had given his tardy consent to the engagement, Philip hinted delicately that it was probable his future father-in-law would be desirous of an interview, on business, with him.

"Then, let him come here, Phil! I am quite ready to tell him my intentions towards you: and I hope his daughter's prospects are one-tenth part as good as your own—though I much doubt it."

Philip thought it would be well for his uncle to wait upon Lord St. Leger—Miles did not.

"Not a bit of it—it is all their doing! They want to marry into my family, not I into theirs. You know," he added, maliciously, "the proposal was not made in my drawing-room, after dinner. Don't distress yourself, Phil; your noble father-in-law will find out his way to me, when money is to be talked of, without our assistance."

And he was right. Two days afterwards, the proudest gentleman in England was standing nervously in old Miles's study for half an hour, waiting to see him, while Miles finished his luncheon.

"Don't fret yourself, Phil," he remarked, as he leisurely rose from the table; "my lord has had patience, I have no doubt."

When he entered the study, Lord St. Leger advanced warmly to meet him. "My dear sir——"

"How are you? Pray sit down, and we will at once begin the business you have come upon."

"Your health, my dear Mr. Earnscliffe?"

" Is excellent, my lord. I am as clear in my head as I was fifty years ago, when I started life the lowest clerk in a merchant's office. You are aware that I am a self-made man, Lord St. Leger. Without birth, connection, or any advantages but my own brain and perseverance, I became what I am. Pray seat yourself, and we will enter into accounts at once. As you are the young lady's father, and I am only Philip's uncle, you will, perhaps, first have the goodness to state the settlements you propose making upon your daughter, and I will then tell you my own intentions towards my nephew.

Lord St. Leger's face had grown several shades more sallow than even its usual cadaverous hue, during Miles Earnscliffe's little speech. The old merchant, with spiteful pleasure, had purposely recalled his own humble origin, and made his noble companion feel, to the full, the true position in which they stood to each other. It was with an immense effort that he swallowed his proud indignation, and brought out a few common-place remarks—very courteous ones, but not at all in answer to Miles's question.

" But the figure, my lord ? " he said, sharply, drawing an immense sheet of blue paper before him, and placing his pen in the extreme left hand corner, as though the whole page would be required to note down Lord St. Leger's magnificent intentious. " I am a plain man, as you know ; and, though I have greatly objected to the whole thing—thinking Phil, with his unsettled position and love of society, far too young, *and* unsteady, my lord, to marry—yet, as everybody else seems bent upon it, and the poor boy feels his honor engaged—may I trouble you to pass the ink ?—thank you—feels his honor engaged—why, I have given my consent. And the only thing now is for you and me to decide upon the settlements, and let them marry ; and, considering my objections to the engagement from the first, I think I am now acting generously in meeting you half way about the money."

Lord St. Leger bowed and smiled. He was bland and courteous, made vague promises, and commented largely upon the other's well-known riches and generosity ; but it was all of no avail. Nothing led Miles for one moment, from their actual business ; and, after his lordship's most flattering speeches and graceful perorations, he invariably returned to the original question—" Then what amount will you settle upon your daughter ? "

" At length, after as many wily turns and fine sounding phrases, " signifying nothing," as would have done credit to a Vienna note, Lord St. Leger was beaten. Brought to the actual point—but still with an attempt at dignity—the answer came out. " In the present state of the country—the difficulty of getting rents—and some slight embarrassments of his own, which would, he trusted,

soon be over, he could give his daughter—nothing."

" Very well, my lord," said Miles, with one of his pleasantest smiles, and carefully replacing his unsullied paper in a portfolio ; " t en I believe our conversation is at an end. I had proposed to settle the same sum as yourself upon your daughter ; I will do so now, and it rests with you that the amount is so small. With regard to my nephew, I have long since made my will, and at my death he will inherit all my property. His marriage—should the projected union still be carried out—will not alter my intentions towards him, poor fellow ! and during my life-time, I shall allow him what I consider sufficient—not more. It is well that he should also depend upon his own exertions."

Lord St. Leger rose, his face livid with rage at his utter failure, but his presence of mind still not forsaking him. At that moment of supreme disappointment, he felt that it were better to marry his daughter to Philip, although without settlements, than not to marry her at all ; and, taking Earnscliffe's hand, he expressed with dignified composure his regret that he was not able to act as he himself wished on the solemn occasion of his only child's marriage, thanking him at the same time for his generous intention of making settlements equivalent to his own upon Clara. And so, with still a calm exterior, but in his bosom a very hell of hatred towards his future connections, he left the room.

" I knew how it would be," muttered Miles, after he was gone. " They are selling their nobility for my money—and poor Philip is just to be thrown in, as the least important part of the bargain. Hang the fellow ! with his white, deceitful face, and glib words. He was as difficult to be brought to speak as an attorney. And his promises, and his grand words, and his inquiries about my health—my health ! ho, ho ! when he would like to see me drop down dead on the wedding-day ! However, I will say one thing for him—he behaved like a gentleman."

It is not necessary to speak much of Philip's courtship. Having got into the entanglement, he tried hard to make himself believe that he had done so wisely, and of his own free will. He consequently endeavored to be in love ; and then, finding the task somewhat tedious, only wished the whole thing were over. He was young and hopeful, and life for him held out so wide a field of ambition, he saw before him such long years of success in the world, that his marriage did not appear an all-important event. He had never felt anything of love beyond mere boyish fancies, or that vague yearning for ideal beauty, which is part of a poet's temperament ; and any idea of domestic happiness had never crossed his mind. He was fond of society, where he shone supreme—those refined circles of the great London world, to which he had universal *entrée*; but he also delighted —and who does not at twenty?—in another society, far more brilliant and less restrained, that of artists and actors—those delightful *petits soupers*, after the opera, where all was mirth and laughter, and of which he had not yet learned to weary; the rehearsals, the pretty faces that smiled upon him; in short, all the mimic but exciting life of the greenroom. It would have taken a passionate love, a most sweet and winning wife to convert Philip Earnscliffe, at twenty, into a domestic husband. And he married Lady Clara St. Leger. The preliminaries of the marriage were speedily got over. There was no reluctance of the bride, no tearful wishes for delay on the part of the bride's mother; and the bridegroom, if not ardent about his marriage appeared extremely anxious for the termination of his courtship. Mr. Earnscliffe, after all, made the young couple a handsome allowance, and they took a furnished house in Park Lane for the coming season.

By tacit consent neither of them spoke of any tour after their marriage. Their honeymoon was to be passed at the estate in Yorkshire, whither Miles and Philip had talked of going previous to his engagement, and afterwards they were immediately to return to London. Philip seemed suddenly to have given up all his intentions of solitude and improvement, and to think more of society than ever; and Clara remained passive whatever was planned for the future.

The wedding-day came, and they were married. Lord and Lady St. Leger showed the proper amount of feeling at the touching event, although the bride was cold and tearless. There was a profusion of silver and orange flowers, school-children with baskets of lady-looking green leaves, and pretty bridesmaids, and meaningless young men, and pompous old relations. Speeches were made and healths drank; and the bride's mother kissed the bridegroom, who appeared uneasy and nervous, as though he were just beginning to realise the meaning of what he had been about. Old Miles, in a blue coat and gilt buttons of antique workmanship, looked exceedingly out of his place, and made sarcastic remarks to everybody. And so the happy morning went off; and the bridal pair departed, and the guests after them; and the father and mother were left alone, to think over their daughter's marriage. Miles drove back to his house about ten miles from town—the house in which he had first received little Philip—and the remainder of the day hung heavily upon him. He walked about his gardens with less interest than usual, and at six he sat down to his lonely dinner. It was, of course, a thing of frequent occurrence for him to dine alone, but then he always knew that Philip was enjoying himself in the world, and thought of all the good stories he would tell him at breakfast next morning; for Philip knew the pleasure this gave his uncle, and never failed in being punctual at the morning meal. Now it was different; his life was again to be lonely, and for ever. Philip might come as his guest—but that was all; he was married, and every other tie would be broken.

After dinner he sat long by the fire; and, as he watched the red logs sparkle, his memory recalled that winter evening when the little, bright-haired child first appeared at his lonely hearth. He traced all his young life since then; his childhood, which had made the silent house so joyous with his shouts, and laughter, and thousand affectionate, winning ways; his holidays, made happy at Christmas with his skating and sledging, and noisy in-door games; even happier at Midsummer, when Miles took him to the seaside, and used to sit on the beach, watching the boy swimming, delighted, over the smooth summer sea. Then he thought of the unexpected outbreak of Philip's genius —his success in the world—his own gratified pride in his nephew's distinction; and he felt he had never known how much he loved him till now.

"And I let him marry that idiot's palefaced daughter!" he exclaimed bitterly, aloud, "for her rank and birth, as though *they* would make his home happy, when I might have prevented the whole thing by one word of disinheriting him. Married, and not yet one-and-twenty; my poor boy!"

He remained long looking vacantly at the fire; and, at length, tears gathered slowly in the old man's eyes. They were the only ones shed on Philip's wedding-day.

CHAPTER VII.

ALONE in the country, in the depth of winter, Philip found his honeymoon amply long enough to awaken him to a true sense of the error he had committed. He soon saw that he had allowed himself to be drawn into marriage with a woman to whom he was indifferent; while, before he had been married many days, doubts had already dawned upon his mind as to the real motive of Clara in becoming his wife. When he was relieved from the necessity of constantly acting love himself, he had time to observe her more closely; and he was forced to admit that her cheeks were just as pale, her spirits as dull, now that she was his wife, as they had been six weeks before, when her mother represented her as pining under a hopeless attachment.

Was it possible, he asked himself, that she had acted with duplicity, and married him without love, only because he was his uncle's heir? The thought filled him with ineffable disgust. He was far too proud to recriminate or demand an explanation, so he remained silent; but, in these first days of married life —so rarely ruffled by suspicion—a feeling of estrangement had already risen in Philip's heart towards his wife. Besides this, *he* was in the very brightness of life and youth; and there was something excessively irksome to him in Clara's cold, silent companionship. For what had appeared gentleness in a cousin was very insipid in a wife. She could neither warm into admiration at his conversation—which, to all others, had so rare a charm—nor share in his enthusiastic visions for the future. A monosyllable, a quickly-fading smile, was her usual reply; and the bridegroom soon longed impatiently for the termination of those endless thirty days, which, according to the laws of English society, it is necessary for newly-married persons to spend in banishment.

"Are you fond of the country, Clara?" he asked, the night before their journey homewards, as the long winter evening passed slowly by.

He had been reading—she gazing in the fire (it was a peculiarity of Lady Clara's that she never worked); and a sufficiently long time had elapsed without either of them speaking a word.

"I, when I was quite young"—how the expression jarred upon Philip's ear—"I greatly preferred the country; I think, then, I should have liked to remain for ever among the Highlands of Scotland, which I happened to visit when I was about seventeen"—her face grew soft, for a moment, at the recollection—"but after that I returned to London, I was presented, and since, I have, of course, been so continually in society, that I have never had time to think of a country life; for, even in the country, at Christmas, one has as much gaiety as in town."

"And now?"

"Now? Oh, of course, you prefer being in London, do you not?"

"But for yourself?"

"For myself, I am indifferent." And the conversation closed.

She *was* indifferent to almost everything now. With her marriage had ended even her old friendship for Philip; she knew well that he did not love her, and she could not forget the unworthy manner in which he had been won. It was a perpetual wound to her pride, and she cared not that her manner betrayed the coldness of her feelings; indeed, she preferred her husband should no longer believe her more attached to him than she was in reality. It was a relief to both when they returned to London. The train arrived late in the evening, and Philip hailed the fog, and smoke, and Babel-sounds which greeted him, as so many familiar friends. He was quite in good spirits during dinner, and laughed and talked with all his old manner. They had found scores of invitations awaiting them; for himself, notes from his old acquaintances, theatrical announcements, communications from his publishers; he seemed to have returned to life.

"You look tired, Clara, after your journey," he remarked, kindly, when they returned to the drawing-room, "and are not equal, probably, to the fatigue of going out; otherwise, there is a new opera to-night."

"Shall you go?" she asked, with a faint indication of surprise.

"Well, dearest, I have so much news to hear, that I must just go down to the club." Although only married a month, a marital intuition made him feel that it was as well to suppress, "and to the opera afterwards."

"Then good night," she answered, with abrupt coldness; "I am tired, and shall retire to rest at once."

She left the room without another word. One look of entreaty—if she had thrown her arms round his neck, and whispered, "Ah! Philip, do not leave me so soon," he would have stayed; but her cold, almost insulting, manner of wishing him good night, stung him deeply.

"She wishes to treat me like a boy," was his thought, and he went off to his club.

Clara heard the street door shut loudly after him, while she was still slowly ascending the staircase. She felt really weary and sick at heart, and when she entered her room, did not ring for her maid. She wished to be alone, and seating herself before the dressing-table, she gazed long at the reflection of her own face in the glass; she looked pale, tired, and not youthful.

"And thus begins my new life!" she said, at length, aloud. "Married to a mere boy, who took me from pity, and, after a month, leaves me alone to seek his former amusements on the first night of our return; without love in my own heart, and loathing myself for having married him; these are the conditions of my existence—my prospects for the future. But you succeeded, mother; you have married me to Miles Earnscliffe's heir."

She nerved herself proudly, and, turning from the glass, walked up and down the room, while her lips trembled, and occasionally her hands clenched involuntarily. Few who knew her in the world would have believed her capable of passionate emotion like this; but though worldly and selfish, she had still some of a woman's deepest feelings left. Little as she cared for her husband, his carelessness to her, on the first evening of their return home, had aroused all her pride, and with it the never-dying thoughts of her first lover —that recollection which was the avenging ghost of the youth and love she had so pitilessly crushed in her own bosom. She saw herself as she was—her ambitious plans successful, married to a man whom every girl in London had been anxious to win; and then thought what she might have been, had she, eight years ago, followed the honest dictates of her heart. It was a bitter thought.

Suddenly she paused in her hurried walk, and unlocked a case which stood upon the dressing-table. Within lay a perfect mass of jewels—diamonds, pearls, emeralds—the costly wedding presents, mostly given her by her husband and his uncle. They only reminded her that for them, and the wealth which bought them, she had married Philip; and she pushed them aside with disgust, paused a few seconds, and then touching, with a somewhat faltering hand, the spring of a hidden drawer, drew from it what appeared, from the care with which it was preserved, to be a treasured relic. It was only a little sprig of mountain heather, now colorless and withered with time, but worth more to the unhappy woman than a thousand such glittering heaps as lay before her. For it had been plucked by Harry Douglas on the first day he had ever spoken to her in love, in that lonely Highland glen, whose rocks and heath-covered banks she had never been able to forget; and, once more she heard the throstle singing, and the wild bee humming past her, as on that very summer morning. She looked long at it, with that eager recalling look, such as a mother may bestow upon some relic of the babe she lost in her youth; but yet she did not raise it to her lips, or utter one pleasant word. She tried to remember that she had herself discarded him; and was now the wife of another man; and at length with a supreme effort, but still tearless eyes, returned it to its hiding-place.

Then she seated herself in a chair before the fire, and covered her face with her hands. She remained long so, thinking again and again that humiliating thought, "He took me from a feeling of pity, not of love, and forsakes me already." She traced clearly her future position in the world—unattractive, sick (her health was delicate), without interest in anything, and married to a man five years younger than herself in reality, but a whole life-time in feeling—a man sought for by all London—brilliant, fond of excitement and society, all that she had wearied of and outlived. She remained long motionless, then rang for her maid, and retired to rest composed, but tearless. But when midnight passed, and she heard the early morning hours strike, one by one, and still Philip did not return, her calmness at length forsook her, and she burst into a long and passionate flood of tears.

Philip found a warm reception everywhere. At the club he made a dozen engagements, most of them to bachelor parties; although he at first said, laughing, he could not think of accepting them now that he was a married man; heard all the newest town gossip; and then went off with some of his friends to the opera, where they were still in time for the two last acts. As he took his accustomed place in the stalls, he was greeted with smiles from all quarters of the house, for his marriage had only spoilt him in the eyes of a few manœuvring mothers and their daughters, and, with this exception, all his fair friends were as delighted to see him as ever.

A new dancer was to make her first appearance that evening, so Philip had not the courage to leave before the ballet, as he had otherwise intended. He thought he would just wait to see her, and then return home. The *debutante* was charming, and Philip's applause unbounded; he forgot time, and home, and Clara, while watching the exquisitely graceful movements of this young girl, who was of surpassing loveliness; and he almost started when, at length, the ballet terminated in a flood of rose-light, and he was reminded that it was long past midnight. Of course, now that all attraction was over, Philip at once prepared to be off; and he was attempting to pass quickly through the crowd, when in the lobby one of his friends approached, and shaking Earnscliffe' hand, gave him a little, delicately-folded pink note.

"In your old luck, Phil!" he whispered. "Upon my word, it is rather soon for a bridegroom to receive such wicked-looking missives. I suppose La Thionville spied you out from behind the scenes, for she wrote this note in great haste, and begged me, with tears in her eyes, to deliver it to you without fail. However, you may set your conscience at rest; there is nothing wrong in it, for Celeste read it to me as she wrote."

The note was written in a small, rather illegible, hand, in French, and was as follows:—

"CHER M. EARNSCLIFFE,—Although you are married, I suppose you will not desert all your old friends. Lord B——, Neville, and a few others will sup with me to-night; we shall only want our poet to be complete. Do come to us. Votre amie, CELESTE."

Philip hesitated. "Not to-night," he said. "Make my excuses to Celeste; another time——"

"Nonsense," returned Neville; he was a rising young artist, and an old school-friend of Philip's. "If we once allow you a precedent, we shall be always losing you, on the score of your new duties. Celeste tells me that she has got F——, and B——, and little Fridoline herself. We shall be a delightful party—not one stupid person—and you know you are not obliged to stop late." And taking Philip's arm, he led him off—it must be confessed a not unwilling victim. They drove in Earnscliffe's cab to La Thionville's pretty house in the Regent's Park, where all the guests were already assembled.

"I know I am welcome," said Neville, on entering the drawing-room, "but not for my own sake. I have brought back an old friend to the land of the living."

The Frenchwoman gave a theatrical start on seeing Earnscliffe; then welcomed him with real delight. She took his arm as they went down to supper, and said in a low tone, "Ah, Philippe! I am so surprised and glad to see you. With all your English ideas, I feared we should not have you among us again, for a year at the very least."

The party was brilliant; but Philip could not at first feel quite at his ease. He knew that it was not the sort of society for him to make his first appearance in as a married man; and the remark of Celeste had unintentionally strengthened this feeling, so for a time he remained silent and constrained. But he was among people who would not let him long continue so. After trying in vain to make him talk, Celeste laughed maliciously, and asked if he was mentally composing a poem on the happiness of married life, to account for his silence.

"If he is," cried little Fridoline, in her pretty English, "Monsieur Earnscliffe's face is quite proof enough of his theory, without troubling himself to finish the poem!"

Celeste, then, looking at the time-piece, inquired till what hour he was permitted to remain, as she would not suffer him in her house to stay one second longer; and it soon ended by Philip, who tried in vain to be dignified, becoming as merry as his two fair neighbors.

It must be allowed that his position was a somewhat dangerous one. Celeste, on whose right he sat—she always reserved this place of honor for Philip—was a sparkling, animated brunette, of some age under thirty. She was not a first-rate singer; but her acting was excellent. She was always natural except off the stage—never over-strained—never vulgar—indeed, it was said Celeste was, by birth, a lady; or, at least, in her early youth, had moved in good Parisian society. She had lived long in Italy while studying her profession, before she appeared in England; but she was French by birth, and had all the liveliness of her countrywomen, softened down by a slight shade of romantic sentiment, which, as she said, she had "learnt" in Italy. Doubtless, she had only "learnt" it; but it became her mightily; and when her naturally laughing lips trembled a little, or her dark eyes filled with tears, Celeste was unquestionably fascinating. She always appeared well-off, and piqued herself greatly upon her house, her parties, and, above all, her wine, which, wonderful to say for an actress, was really good. She liked to collect, at her little suppers, all the cleverest men in London; for, though she never read anything herself but her roles, she liked to be spoken of as patronising genius; and, having once discovered that authors preferred talking of anything else better than of each other's books, she was never afraid again of being bored with their conversation.

Among books, however, she made one exception. She read Philip's. Perhaps she understood them; more probably she did not, for her knowledge of English was very superficial—but, at all events, she read them. She had made him write her name on the title-page of each, always had them lying on her table with many of the least remarkable passages marked in pencil; and once or twice she told Philip she had "much weeped" over parts he had rather intended to be the witty ones of the story. Celeste had always cherished a very romantic sentiment for the young author, and was quite cut up at his marriage, thinking that her parties would probably lose their best lion by this event, through some of those "detestable British prejudices." His re-appearance, however, so soon at her house put her in the highest spirits; and Celeste had never been more charming than she was that evening.

On Philip's other side was "little Fridoline," at that time a very celebrated actress and one whose mysterious appearance, and subsequent career, had become a subject of universal interest in London. The success of this girl in one year had been, indeed, almost fabulous. Coming, no one could say whence—very young—without friends, or even acquaintances—she had been engaged at the French plays to act minor parts. But her extraordinary conception of character, and the original coloring she threw over the most trivial *role* she played were such, that, in a few weeks, hundreds crowded every night, merely to see Fridoline acting as a *soubrette*. The manager saw that he had had a lucky find, promoted her at once, with a good salary, to first-rate characters, and her success in one season nearly made his fortune. Although her French was excellent, and her pronunciation of it so true as to be sweet even to a Parisian ear, she was not a Frenchwoman. Some said she was German, some Danish, some Russian. When asked herself, she invariably answered that she had not the least idea—that she had no country, no relation, no other name than Fridoline; and the utmost perseverance could win from her no further reply.

In person she was small and fair, with a profusion of waving golden hair, and large eyes of the deepest hazel, with very black eyelashes. She was too singular-looking to be exactly beautiful, although it was a face of most peculiar and lasting attraction—a face that, once seen, could never again be forgotten, but haunted the memory like one of those old pictures which we see, for a moment, in some dark gallery, or in the dim aisle of a foreign church, and never lose again. She lived alone, at some distance from town, in a cottage of her own; and free, and strange, and untinged with any affectation of propriety, as was her conduct, no breath had ever been raised against her, no man's name was ever mentioned with that of little Fridoline! She seemed more calculated to awaken extreme interest and admiration, than any warmer feeling; and there lurked something in the mocking expression of her great, dark eyes, that would, unconsciously, make any man feel himself ridiculous, who attempted to speak to her of love. She went seldom into the society of other artists; La Thionville's being almost the only house at which she ever appeared. For Celeste had seen at once, with her natural quickness in discerning talent, that Fridoline would one day be distinguished; and this—and perhaps some kindlier feeling—had made her hold out her hand to the friendless girl, when she first began her London career, and show her many little attentions which Fridoline's ignorance of English life rendered most acceptable; once, even attending her in an attack of sudden illness. Now she was amply repaid. To say "Little Fridoline has promised to come," was sufficient inducement to make every one else come also; and any party was sure to go off brilliantly when she could be persuaded to attend. For Fridoline possessed a fine and subtle wit; the most cutting powers of sarcasm; and, at times, but rarely, an unexpected and passionate pathos, which made her conversation unlike all others. And in her society grave men of genius were silent, in admiration at the ever-changing fancy and brilliant language of this gifted little being.

She liked Earnscliffe; perhaps, because he had never attempted to pay her any of the *fades* compliments which she detested; perhaps, because—although knowing no more of her history than did others—something in his own heart recognised Fridoline's high and extraordinary nature, and made his manner to her, while perfectly respectful, kind and sympathizing beyond that of mere acquaintance. This evening she was in her liveliest vein; every word that fell from her lips was sparkling; every idea seemed unusually fresh and original, even from her; and Celeste, without in the least imitating Fridoline, was scarcely less brilliant;—even more desirous to shine. Her green-room stories of the last two months—her excellent repetition of the *bon-mots* of others—her delicate mimicry—and her art of hitting off a character in about six words, had never appeared so amusing to Philip before. No wonder that, in such society, he felt like a person suddenly descending from the frigid Simplon into sunny Italy, after his courtship and icy honeymoon; and that the hours struck unheeded, which should have recalled him to his bride. He had, himself, regained all his usual spirits; and when, at length, the new dancer was discussed, grew animated in his praises of her exceeding beauty.

"I am slightly acquainted with Miss Elmslie (for, with all her grace, she is an Englishwoman)," said Celeste; "and shall invite her some evening, next week, to my house.

Of course, I need not ask you to meet her?" she added, maliciously, to Philip.

"Certainly not," he replied; "I shall need no invitation."

Celeste looked very bright. "And you, mademoiselle," she continued to Fridoline, "will you also meet the young *débutante*?"

Fridoline assented, after a slight hesitation; and then inquired if any one knew the particulars of Miss Elmslie's history before she went on the stage?"

"I do," answered Neville; "she comes from my own country; although not from the same neighborhood. I think I have heard that her father was a clergyman; he was, at all events, a professional man, and, dying suddenly, left this girl, then about fourteen, quite alone in the world, and without money or protectors. Her extraordinary beauty and grace—I remember once seeing her when she was a child—were exactly of that order best suited to the stage; but into whose hands she fell, and how she came to adopt dancing as a profession, I have never found out—indeed, it is only a few days since I discovered that the 'rising star,' about whom we have all heard so much, was no other than little Rose Elmslie."

Fridoline seemed greatly interested in these few words of the girl's history. "Yes," she said, turning to Celeste, "I shall be glad to meet her. What evening are we to come?"

Celeste considered. "Well, after 'Fidelio,' on Tuesday, if you are free. I know she does not perform that night." Fridoline was also disengaged, and Neville and the two or three chosen friends, "honored" by a place at Celeste's table, were invited and accepted. Lastly, she turned to Earnscliffe—"And you," she said, "will you really come again so soon?"

Philip had a vague recollection that on Tuesday was to be a grand entertainment at some of his wife's relations; but to meet Fridoline, and the lovely Rose Elmslie, and half-a-dozen of his own intimate friends, at Celeste's house, was to him temptation irresistible, and he accepted.

At an hour of the morning not to be mentioned, Neville drove home with Philip to his house in Park Lane, and noticing his friend's timid knock at his own door, congratulated himself, as he went off, that he was still a bachelor. The sleepy servant looked rather surprised, as he admitted his newly-married master at such an hour; but Philip was too much occupied with his own reflections to notice the man's face. Taking a light, he proceeded up-stairs as noiselessly as he could, hoping Clara was long since asleep, and would not hear him come in.

When he entered the room all was quiet—she lay motionless; the fire had long since burnt out, and the whole room seemed dark and silent. Shading the light with his hand, he approached the bedside, and glanced at his wife. She was not asleep; but—long and bitterly though she had wept—the marks of tears were now carefully effaced from her cheeks, whose ghastly whiteness formed a striking contrast to his own face, all flushed and animated. "Clara—not asleep?"

"Not asleep, Mr. Earnscliffe; yet, I believe, it is past four o'clock!"

"Clara, I am indeed sorry; I was detained by so many old friends—the club——"

"Stop, sir!"—and, as she rose a little, her face grew exactly like that of her father's in its expression. "You are, of course, at liberty to choose your own companions, your own hours; stay out as late as you like—live as you will—I am indifferent to it all; but do not, at least, stoop to the meanness of a falsehood. You have not been at your club until four o'clock in the morning. No, allow me to continue,"—for she saw the indignant words were ready to burst from Philip's lips. "Another time, you will, perhaps, have the goodness to sleep in your dressing-room, after remaining out half the night. My health is feeble, and will not admit of my being thus disturbed;" and she turned away from him.

In those few minutes she had completed their estrangement for ever. Philip stood one second irresolute—then turned, and, without a syllable in reply, left the room.

When he came home, he felt that he had acted unkindly towards Clara, in leaving her thus on the first night of their return; and at the sight of her pale face, kind words of excuse were rising to his lips, but her harsh reception of him had undone all. She had accused him of meanness—of falsehood, and had herself made the proposal that they should, in future, occupy separate apartments; his pride was galled to the very quick. From that moment he knew that an eternal barrier was raised between them, and a bitterer feeling than, in all his young life, he had yet experienced, arose in his breast. He threw himself down on his dressing-room sofa, and with a strange calmness, reflected what their future existence would be. He felt that love—even if its shadow had ever existed between his wife and himself—was entirely over now. Only four weeks ago they had stood together before God's altar, and taken those solemn oaths of love and truth, "till death should part them;" and already both had failed in their contract. Clara had openly acknowledged her indifference to him that night, and he, a dozen times, had bitterly repented his marriage, and already chafed impatiently under the yoke.

"I will live for the world only, then!" he exclaimed, at length. "She has offered me my life apart, and my freedom, and I accept it. In the society of Celeste and Fridoline, I am not likely to miss that of my frigid wife"—and he laughed, but with a forced, unnatural sound.

With all his faults, Philip had, unfortunately for himself, a deep and affectionate heart, and he felt an aching void when he recalled Clara's harsh, unforgiving words, and contrasted them with old Miles's kindly greetings at the breakfast-table, and ready excuses of his late hours.

The lights, the laughter, the gay voices of Celeste's party were still whirling in his brain; but a look of inexpressible sorrow stole over his young face, as he felt that for him the word "home" had henceforth no meaning.

CHAPTER VIII.

PHILIP and his wife did not meet the following morning. Clara afterwards went to spend the day with her mother; and, in the afternoon, Philip rode down to see his uncle. It was a fine winter day, the air ringing and elastic; and, as he cantered on at a quick pace, his spirits rose under the influence of exercise, and the pure, healthy atmosphere.

He found Miles at home, occupying himself, as usual, about his grounds. His face grew radiant when he saw Philip in the distance, riding up the long avenue which led to the house. He had not hoped to see him on the first day after his return, and advanced to greet him with as earnest a welcome as though they had not met for years.

"It was kind of you, Phil, to remember me so soon. I wanted you especially to-day. That idiot of a head-gardener has positively proposed that I should throw down the old wall by the kitchen garden, and extend the shrubbery as far as the stables on the other side, shutting out the distant view of the river. You don't think it would be an improvement?" He spoke quickly, and Philip knew well that he had branched off into another subject only to conceal his pleasure at seeing him.

"We will talk it all over, uncle," he replied; "for if you will have me, I intend remaining to-day, and dining with you."

"If I will have you, boy? I am only surprised at having you so soon. As a rapturous bridegroom, I never expected you would remember me. However, I must say, that even in your honeymoon you were not forgetful of me. You write capital letters, Phil."

A servant now came up and took his horse; and Miles, linking his arm in Philip's, walked him off to see the projected improvements, and hear his opinion upon them; and thus engaged, the short winter afternoon passed only too quickly to the old man.

Philip did not approve entirely of the gardener's plan, but proposed another, by which the shrubbery could be extended without interfering with his uncle's favorite view of the river; and he promised to draw the plans, and come down and superintend the work himself, as soon as the weather was favorable for commencing.

"I knew Duncan was wrong," said Miles, "although I could not improve upon his plan myself. I wanted your taste and quick eye, Phil."

"I am afraid I shall lose my old gardening tastes now," replied Philip. "London will henceforth be my home, with the exception of three months' shooting in the Highlands, or an excursion abroad every autumn; and I shall forget all the familiar lore of planting, and planning, and grafting, that I have studied in this old garden, under Duncan, so many years. You cannot tell how pleasant it seems for me to return here, sir; although I have been only away four weeks, I feel like a wanderer returning home."

"And how often shall I see you, Phil!" asked Miles, abruptly, when they sat together in their old places, after dinner, just as they had done for more than fifteen years. "I suppose, with all your grand friends, and your parties, and your wife, I shall stand a poor chance."

"You do not really mean that," returned Philip. "As far as engagements go, they cannot be much more numerous now than they were before I married; and, doubtless, my wife will be able to spare me a few hours occasionally, when I wish to visit you."

Something in his tone, as he said the words "my wife," made his uncle look at him more closely. Then he noted that Philip, without being either paler or thinner, or in any way altered in feature, looked already much older. In a few weeks, the indescribable expression of youth was gone, and his face had already the look of a man who has lived and suffered. It was a painful thought for Miles; and, changing the subject, he inquired if Philip was writing anything?

"Not at present, uncle. You remember our plan of going into the country, for me to think and breathe before beginning another book—well, I believe my new life will work, although in a different manner, a somewhat similar result. After a few months of matrimony, I shall take up my pen."

"Oh! where is Clara, to-day?"

"Clara? well, I believe she is at home—no—I recollect, at Lady St. Leger's."

"Indeed! Well, what do you think of my Yorkshire property, Phil?"

"It is a beautiful place. I wonder you have not been there more frequently yourself. The time of year was unfavorable for seeing it to advantage; but I was never tired of wandering about with my gun, over the moors, or among those wild hills, and in the deep recesses of the forest, covered although it all was with snow."

"Warm work for a honeymoon!" muttered Miles.

Then they began speaking of other things; old interests in which both were connected —old scenes—old times; Philip's literary projects for the future. They seemed, by tacit consent, to avoid any mention of the present; and Philip, especially, turned away from all subjects that bore upon his marriage, or the St. Legers.

When eleven o'clock came his horse was ordered round, and he was preparing to wrap up for his cold ride, when the old butler came in, and said it was a fearful bad night for the young master to ride up to town. It had thawed, and then frozen again in the course of the evening, and the ground was like ice; while the first flakes of an approaching snow-storm were beginning to fall.

"I don't like taking the horses out at night, when I can help it, Phil, as you know," said Mr. Earnscliffe; "but I will order the carriage round, sooner than that you should run any risk of breaking the mare's knees. Marcus and Anthony are so steady, they would not fall on ice itself. Besides, you are not half warmly enough clad to be exposed to such weather."

Philip saw that his uncle never even thought of asking him to stop all night; and he rather hesitated at making the proposal himself, though he knew Clara would not be anxious at his absence (after the manner of most young wives), and he really preferred remaining where he was, to riding through a snow-storm.

"Well, the fact is, uncle, I should not like to take out your horses; and it is certainly not a night for my skittish Gulnare. If my old bed-room——"

"Why, of course, boy. I am only too glad to keep you; but I thought your wife would be anxious, and I did not like to propose it."

"Oh, I dare say Clara will guess where I am."

So Philip's old room was prepared for him; and, as he was tired after his last night's vigil, he soon bade his uncle good night, and went off to bed.

"For the thousandth time in my life I thank Heaven that I never married," said old Miles, devoutly; when the door closed after his nephew. "Here is another specimen of wedded bliss, and after only four weeks' experience! When I think of all the talk there was of his honor and her happiness for life, I repeat it," he added, with increasing fervor; "thank Heaven, I never married!"

When Philip returned home at noon, next day, he found Clara reading in the drawing-room. She laid down her book on his entrance, and greeted her husband with the same polite ceremony she would have shown to a stranger. Her manner at once prevented Philip from volunteering any explanations of his long absence; nor was she likely to ask him any question after their recent scene on his return from Celeste's party.

"Are you engaged to-day? I have an

invitation for you to accompany me to my father's to dine."

The St. Legers, according to the usual plan adopted by people who are utterly ruined, were giving a whole series of expensive entertainments. Philip hated all grand dinners; and he felt that those of his pompous father-in-law would now be more than ever distasteful to him. He took out his note-book, determined not to go.

" I am sorry I have an engagement for to-day; it is one of long standing—a dinner given to B——, by some of our members, that it would be impossible for me to miss." Clara's lip curled.

" The Duke and Duchess of C——, the Marquis of W——, Prince N ——, and a dozen others, will dine with *us*," she said.

" It is almost a kindness in Mr. Philip Earnscliffe to give up his place; for the dining-room in Grafton Street is so unfortunately small."

The sarcasm was meant to hide her wounded feelings; but her lips quivered a second when she thought of appearing for the first time, as a bride, without her husband. She knew that a club dinner was really no engagement, and that Philip's answer was but a tacit acceptance of the liberty she had herself offered him.

" How brilliant you will be!" he remarked, sauntering towards the door. " We shall have only L——, and T——, and D——," naming some of the most distinguished literary men in London. " Pray remember for me a few of the Duke of C——'s best *bon mots*, and a little of the caustic wisdom of the noble marquis; and, in the meantime, *au revoire.*"

He smiled gaily as he left her; and she felt that her actual life had begun in earnest.

Clara dined alone at her father's; Philip at his club. But, as is usual in such cases, he was in high spirits, and enjoyed the evening immensely; while his wife had a martyrdom to encounter in the half-pitying looks of her dearest friends, and the still more trying after-dinner questions of her own female relations. A man feels no slur upon his pride in the world's thinking that he is not particularly happy at home; but to every woman the mere suspicion of being neglected in her marriage is in itself a humiliation.

" Well, my dearest Clara," said one of her cousins, as she sat in her bridal satin, turning over listlessly the leaves of some annuals; " I am glad to see you looking so bright and well. But where is Mr. Earnscliffe? Surely he must be here; and yet I have not happened to see him."

" Philip was engaged to a literary dinner," answered Clara, shortly.

" Ah, yes! Well, one cannot expect authors to be like other men; these great geniuses are so seldom fond of home, and Mr. Earnscliffe is *so* young."

" Your married happiness has at least, then, been spared the trial that is in store for mine, dear," replied Lady St. Leger's daughter, smiling calmly. " If genius is required to make a husband undomestic, Sir Harry is undoubtedly safe; " and she glanced at her cousin's husband—a stupid, heavy-looking young man, with elaborate whiskers, and a very small head, but who, nevertheless, had not the reputation of being excessively fond of his wife's society.

The lady colored scarlet, and Clara felt her small triumph. She began talking with more animation to the people around her, listened with apparent interest to Prince N——'s bad English and worse wit, and the inane dullness of the Duke of C——, and gradually her spirits rose with her desire to appear happy. But, when it was all over, and she was driving back to her lonely home, her cousin's words recurred to her in more than their first bitterness. She felt that numberless similar remarks upon her appearing alone must have been made that evening; that at every succeeding party to which she went without her husband these remarks would be confirmed and multiplied; and the pride of her nature revolted angrily against such an existence. Lady Clara forgot that this was but the commencement of the life of liberty she had herself offered to Philip—that, in all the flush of his youth and popularity, her harsh words had thrown him back upon his old world—his old associates—merely because her own pride had revolted at one evening's absence.

" And this forever!" she thought, as she entered her sleeping-room, and looked round at its costly luxuries, which seemed to mock their solitary possessor. " Oh, that either of us could die!" But people do not die in this world because they have made foolish marriages, or the human race would not be long in diminishing sensibly from the face of the earth; on the contrary, the fact of their having done so generally appears to add some years to the natural term of existence. Philip and his wife lived on just as they would have done had they been any happily assorted couple; and weeks and months passed by, while each in its course only deepened their mutual estrangement, and lessened any prospect of their re-union. It had become an established thing for Philip to associate, as usual, with all his old bachelor friends, and for Lady Clara to appear without him at the opera, or among her own circles; for, since his marriage, Philip had cared far less for balls and dinner parties, and more for that society in which it was impossible to meet his wife or her relations.

He had conceived a feeling closely bordering upon hatred for both the St. Legers. Of the way Lady St. Leger had beguiled him into his marriage with her daughter, sorely for his uncle's wealth, he had no longer any doubt; and for that good deed he felt exactly the amount of gratitude which was natural towards his mother-in-law; while in his sentiments for her husband was mingled a proud contempt that he was scarcely able to conceal. Lord St. Leger had, from the first, treated him with a sort of fawning affection, which coming from such a man, Philip knew could only cover some latent design; and very shortly after his marriage its nature had been revealed. St. Leger tried to borrow money of him. Philip affected the first time to treat it as a mere joke, saying he had not ten pounds of his own in the world; but when a few days having elapsed, St. Leger again assailed him—Philip having in the meantime attained his majority—and endeavored, with a great deal of soft plausibility, to induce him to endorse some bills (knowing well that any paper bearing the signature of Miles Earnscliffe's heir would be readily discounted by those among the fraternity of Hebrew money-lenders who already looked with suspicion upon his own noble autograph), Philip turned away from him with disgust.

"You are altogether mistaken in me, Lord St. Leger," he replied, haughtily. "I have no property whatever of my own; and it is, therefore, impossible for me to become security for others. The allowance made me since my marriage, by my uncle—although a most liberal one—is not more than sufficient for my own use. I shall consider it right to give it up entirely when I am enabled to live upon the fruits of my own exertions; and, in the meantime, I must entreat of you not to place me in the painful position of having to refuse you again."

When he was stern, Philip's face could assume an expression not unlike that of Miles; and in his dark eye and compressed lip, St. Leger read a cold, unalterable determination. He was foiled a second time by the nephew, as he had already been by the uncle; and, from that day forth, made no more affectionate demonstrations to his son-in-law. They detested each other mutually.

CHAPTER IX.

FROM his wife's relations, and the world in which they moved, Philip turned with undisguised pleasure to his artist friends, and the easy, unrestrained intercourse of their life. Especially between himself and little Fridoline, a feeling of friendship had of late arisen that soon bordered upon intimacy.

The world in general scoffs at the posibility of mere friendship between a man of Philip's age and a young girl, especially if, like poor Fridoline, she chance to be an actress; and, in the generality of cases, the world would be right. But Fridoline was so entirely apart from everybody else, in her odd, secluded life, and undisguised avowal of her preference, that even she was allowed to have Earnscliffe for a friend, and no tongue be found to whisper an idle word against her. He constantly met her at rehearsal of a morning, and when the weather was fine, and Fridoline walked, would accompany her home. She lived in a cottage on the very extremity of Hampstead Heath, an extremely inconvenient distance from the theatre, but which she had chosen from her love for the country, and because it was away from the noise and smoke of London. She could walk any distance without fatigue, and seldom took a cab in the daytime, when the weather was at all fine. One day, after the rehearsal of a new and difficult part, of a more tragic nature than she generally performed, Philip volunteered his escort home, and was, as usual, accepted. She was flushed when they left the theatre, but by the time the interminable streets were traversed, and they had gained the open heath, her cheeks became very pale, while her step flagged and she looked wearied. Some felled trees lay by the road-side, and Philip proposed she should sit down and rest awhile. She did so silently, and he took a place by her side. It was a sweet, breezy day early in June, and the country was covered with tender green. A few fleecy clouds flitted slowly over the blue sky; the swallows, newly returned, wheeled round in playful circuits, and the air was sweet with the scent of violets from a neighboring garden, mixed with the hawthorn-blossoms of the hedges.

"The world is fair," said Fridoline in a low voice, and as if addressing herself more than her companion, "but stained and blotted out with sin!"

"Of which you, at least, have known little," added Philip gently.

"Of which I have known much," she replied, turning round her wearied face to his. "Much,"—she went on, almost vehemently —"more than any other girl of my age; or, at least, I have felt it more than any other can have done—have had it crushed down in all its hideousness upon myself; ay! upon my own flesh and blood—until the whole earth has seemed to me a black and festering mass of corruption——"

"How old are you, Fridoline?" interrupted Philip, with a feeling almost of horror at the girl's unnatural manner.

"Nineteen," she replied; "and to-day is my birthday."

Philip took her hand, touched at the humble, mournful tone of her voice, and pressed it, as he wished her some kindly birthday congratulations. She scarcely heeded him, though she tried to smile.

"Nineteen," she went on; "and to know all that I do! I cannot believe I am so young. It is only four years since I woke from my childhood, and knew what I was, and the terrible darkness of my life? Oh, come away!"—she rose hastily, and as though suddenly recollecting that she was thinking aloud—"come home! I have need of my home and rest.

He gave her his arm, for she trembled violently, and they walked on during the remainder of the way in silence. Philip felt that, in her excited state, it was useless for him, ignorant as he was of her former history, to attempt anything like consolation; and Fridoline, pale and agitated, never opened her lips. She seemed scarcely conscious that she was not alone.

They stopped before a pretty cottage—one of the old country cottages that, a few years ago, were still to be found on Hampstead Heath; this was Fridoline's home. Roses and creepers grew almost entirely over the front, and covered the little entrance porch of rustic wood, where, happy in the sun, lay a rough, wiry terrier. He started up with an angry snap at his own sleepiness, when he heard approaching steps, but bounded forward the moment he saw his mistress. She stooped to pat him, and the creature looked up into her face with an expression of such love as, for the first time, brought tears into her eyes.

" You are glad to see me, poor old Karl !" said Fridoline; and she entered the little garden.

Philip had before accompanied her to the gate, but she had never invited him further, so he prepared now to take his leave.

"No; come in!" she cried. "You shall be my birthday guest."

Her manner was so earnest, that Philip saw she really wished it, and they walked together towards the house.

Karl looked with extreme suspicion at the first male intruder he had ever seen in his mistress's domains; and, as he followed them up the path, suddenly relieved himself of these feeling by giving an angry bark, and seizing the skirts of Philip's coat in his teeth, shaking the cloth from side to side with great ferocity. As he did so, he was almost lifted from the ground, and his hind feet scratched angrily in the gravel. Philip naturally turned at the unexpected assault, so did Fridoline; and, in a second, by one of those instantaneous transitions peculiar to her temperament, the sense of the ludicrous mastered every other feeling. The expression of old Karl, snarling and scratching, and rolling his sharp eyes with rage, yet still holding fast, while Philip, with great dignity, attempted in vain to shake him off, was too much for little Fridoline, although her eyes were actually suffused with tears at the moment, and she burst into peals of laughter; not one merely, but peal after peal of a clear, ringing, childish laughter, that at length brought the solitary maid-servant to the door, to see what it was all about. She was a dark, foreign-looking woman of

middle age, and harsh features; and her expression was not pleasant on seeing Philip. However, when she perceived how matters stood, she darted out at once to his relief, and by dint of pulling and threats, and, at length, a few vigorous blows, Karl was mastered, and carried off, to vent his remaining fury in captivity. Little Fridoline` only laughed the more at this conclusion of the contest, and when, at length, she was able to speak, and apologise to Philip for Karl's inhospitable mode of welcome, her usual spirits had completely returned, and every trace of emotion disappeared from her sunny face.

" We are so unused to visitors in my *ménage*," she said, "that you must forgive poor Karl. He looks upon all intruders as his natural enemies; and I see I must be more careful in introducing you to the other members of the household, for I have two large cats and a tame hawk, who could all be formidable if they chose."

" You are fond of pets, Fridoline."

" Yes, I am fond of Karl, and he loves me —the others are my amusement. It makes my greatest distraction to collect the animals together, and watch them, when my head aches after learning some long *rôle*. The cats are friends in appearance, but not in reality, except as regards their hatred to Karl—principle, perhaps, of many a human alliance; and it does me good to see the hearty spite with which they occasionally give vent to their feelings, and claw each other's ears. Karl looks down upon them with sovereign contempt, as if aware of his power; but in another quarter, he is a mere hen-pecked coward. My hawk, Old Bess—there she is, making rushes after worms on the grass-plot —is his household virago; and, by making unexpected descents on him from behind dark bushes in the garden, and peering fiercely down and hissing from impossible places when he thinks he is just going to have a quiet, noonday nap, makes his life a constant uneasy watch. The canaries are, compared with the others, stupid things; but even their rage, when the sparrows dare to come near their cage in the garden, and pick up their discarded dainties, is almost human."

And all this little nonsense, in Fridoline's foreign English, and told in her own lively way, sounded pretty. She led Philip into her small drawing-room, and the simple, good taste of its appearance struck him at once, compared to the glittering grandeur with which Celeste, like most actresses, loved to be surrounded. The furniture was all in the cottage style, and the curtains of plain white muslin; but, altogether, it had the air of a room inhabited by some young and innocent girl. A small piano stood open; work, and books that looked well read, lay on the table; and bouquets of fresh flowers were everywhere.

" Poor Hulda brought me all these flowers for my birthday," said Fridoline, "and told me, as she had no taste, I must arrange them for myself. She loves me as her own child, and has been with me all my life."

It was the first time Fridoline had ever made so distinct an admission of belonging to humanity, and Philip thought he might improve upon the opportunity.

"Your servant does not look English, from the slight glimpse I had of her," he remarked.

"No, Mr. Earnscliffe," said Fridoline, slily, "she is not; neither is Hulda an English name."

"Her face is not French."

"She is not a Frenchwoman."

"Nor German?"

"Nor German, nor Danish, nor Swedish."

He was silent. Fridoline's eyes laughed, though her lips did not.

"What do you think of my house?" she asked.

"It is a charming little place for the summer. How do you like it in winter, when the snow is on the ground?"

"Ah, that is not the question. You should say, rather, in those long months of mild, drizzling rain which make up your English winters. Well, I must confess, it is not so pleasant then as in June, though I am always too occupied to be dull. When we do have fine, hard frost and bright sun, and the trees and bushes bend under their load of snow, I love it!" (she looked animated)—"I wish it would last for months. It reminds me of our real, long, glorious northern winters——" Here she stopped short, and looked rather afraid she was going too far.

"Long, glorious winters!" said Philip; "but not those of France or Germany. Fridoline, I shall find out your secret soon."

She rose laughing, and cried, "I know your thoughts well; but I shall have no pity upon your curiosity; and, to punish you, you shall remain alone while I take off my bonnet, and ease Hulda's mind as to your appearance in my house, for I am afraid, at present, she is rather of Karl's way of thinking on the subject."

When Fridoline had left the room, Philip approached the table, and began to examine the numerous and well-read books, in all languages, that were scattered there. With the exception of a few volumes of poetry—a Dante, Goëthe's "Faust," some of Oehlen Schläger's smaller poems, and a volume of Shakspeare—all the books were of an abstract and somewhat gloomy nature. No works of lighter literature, no modern fictions, such as the generality of girls of her age would delight in, were there; but abundance of subtle philosophy upon human nature, and devotional books of the sternest, most austere description, such as might be fittingly placed in the hands of a criminal stained with the blackest guilt. She seemed

to have chosen all that bore on the darker side of our existence, or that analysed deeply the enigma of the human heart under the influence of sin, as though her young life could already need the solution which few care to seek for till they have themselves tasted fully of the bitter-after fruits of passion.

One large book seemed particularly well read, and Philip opened it. It was in striking contrast to all the other—the illustrated edition, in German, of "Grimm's Fairy Tales." He turned over the pages so loved in his own childhood; saw Hans once more, sitting under the rock with a lump of gold as big as his head; the musicians of Bremen defending, with their unearthly music, the lonely house against the robbers; the happy elves trying on their nether garments, made by the shoemaker's grateful wife; the mayor and burgomaster jumping into the pond after the reflection of the clouds, which they take for flocks of sheep; and at last Philip grew so interested that he seated himself, and began the perusal of some of his old friends with much zest.

In the meantime Fridoline had changed the dark morning-dress, in which she always went to rehearsal, for a little white muslin frock, and re-arranged her luxuriant golden hair. Then she ran off to Hulda, in the kitchen, and explained to her that Mr. Earnscliffe was to be looked upon with no mistrust, being a poet, and unlike other men, and a very kind friend of her own; during all of which Hulda continued her cooking with great sternness of expression, and did not look the least convinced in her own mind. Then Fridoline added, "And he will stay to dine with me, dear Hulda; so I shall have a guest on my birthday, and you must give us one of your best dinners."

After this she went out with Karl, whose temper was somewhat restored, into the garden, to look after a very early moss-rose she had been watching for some days past. The bud had just half-broken into blossom; and Fridoline plucked it, and ran up to the glass door which led from the garden into her sitting-room. She saw Philip reading, and, entering noiselessly, stole up, and leant over his shoulder, before he was aware of her presence.

"Oh, wise philosopher!" she cried, suddenly. "With a table full of deep and subtle works, I find you poring over Hans and Gretchen."

"Well," returned Philip, "the wonder is, not that I should read them, but that a person like Fridoline should permit such childish stories to repose among her sage books."

Her face grew grave directly.

"It is strange that I should like anything belonging to the innocence of children," she answered; "but, though I cannot care for novels, it delights me to read those wild German stories that I have known all my life. They have the same effect upon me as my animals; they take me altogether from the world, and the people I belong to; while novels are still mimic representations of our existence—only seen through falsely-colored glasses. No! if I read of human beings and human hearts, let me study them as they are, in their stern, unaltered reality; and then, when I want amusement, turn to the honest love of Karl, and the innocent vices of the cats, or the dwarfs and fairies of old Grimm."

"What an early rose-bud, Fridoline!"

"It is for you." She placed it in his button-hole. "For two birthdays I have had no companion but Hulda, and I am so glad, to see you here to-day, and to offer even a poor flower to some one who will accept it on my birthday."

"And I have nothing to offer you, Fridoline," replied Philip. "You should receive, not give, presents on your birthday."

"You can give me something I should like," she returned. "Write me a few lines —not like those you write to Celeste, full of compliments and sentiments you don't feel— but the simple expression of some feeling connected with this sweet June day—something that I can keep to remind me of my nineteenth birthday, in England, when I have returned to my own country."

"It is difficult to write lines, addressed 'To Fridoline, on her nineteenth birthday,' without being complimentary," Philip answered, looking up into her earnest face as she leaned over him; "however, I will try. But you must promise not to look at me as I write, or 'those deep, dark eyes' will be sure to be introduced, much to your indignation."

The slightest flush rose in Fridoline's cheek as she stepped back from his side; and, seating herself by her work-table, she took up some half-finished embroidery that lay there. But, as Philip began to write, the work fell from her fingers, and she watched him intently until he finished—watched his mobile features, that lit up with every rapidly-succeeding image of his own fancy— his high, fair brow—his careless, poet-like attitude; and thought—what did poor little Fridoline think?

"It is done, Fridoline; but I am afraid you will not like the lines. They are very common-place, after all. Shall I read them?"

"No; I would rather read them for myself."

She took the paper, and, turning towards the window, read the contents eagerly. Could Philip have seen her face, he would have discovered a slight shade of disappointment, when she finished; however, she turned quickly towards him again, and said, with a smile, "the lines were beautifully written, and that she should value them much," placing them, as she spoke, in a writing-case on the table.

"And the sentiment," said Earnscliffe— "does that not please you?"

"Yes—only you alluded to my theatrical success—you could not, even for to-day, forget that I am an actress. Come out. now," she added, "and see the extent of my wide domain. It is too fine to remain within doors."

They went out together into the garden, and sat down under a pink hawthorn in full flower on the little grass-plot. Fridoline's borders were redolent of early sweets, for Hulda was a good gardener; and, with directions from her mistress, kept everything in perfect order. She was 'a remarkably plain woman, and had always had an extreme dislike for the stronger sex, even in her own land; and this feeling, when extended to Englishmen, amounted to open enmity, that afforded Fridoline much amusement. So no man was ever admitted upon the premises, except for those needful operations of cutting and pruning, which were beyond Hulda's powers; and, in the early summer mornings, she even rose and mowed the lawn, to the great risk of cutting off her own feet, and the unbounded pleasure of all the small boys who gathered round the gate, however early she began, and, thrusting their snubby noses through the bars, made remarks detrimental to the "blessed old furriner's" science.

There was a hay-field close to the garden; the scent of the new-cut hay mingled pleasantly with that of the flowers, and Philip and Fridoline sat talking in the fresh air until three o'clock, when Hulda appeared and waved her hand at the porch; this Fridoline understood to be a signal for dinner, and they entered. Philip did ample justice to the simple meal, and never enjoyed a grand dinner party half as much as his tete-a-tete with Fridoline, who chatted and laughed merrily, but did the small honors as gracefully as though she were a countess. When dinner was nearly over she said—"I am sure Hulda must have taken a fancy to you, for she has given us two of our national dishes, and nothing is a stronger mark of favor."

"I should think the attention was more probably paid to your birthday than to your visitor," returned Philip. "The few glances I have caught her giving me have certainly not been loving ones. It is a pity she understands so little English, as I have no opportunity of paying her any compliments on her excellent dinner."

Fridoline conveyed this speech to Hulda in a whisper, whereupon, without any reply, she walked stiffly out of the room, shutting the door very loudly in her retreat.

"She is quite delighted," said her mistress, "but that is her peculiar mode of showing it; I know her so well, poor creature! Is it not strange how any one can live in a country for months and months, as she has done, without learning to speak? I could make myself understood when I had been in England six weeks.

"But every one has not the talent of little Fridoline——"

"*Fi done!* Monsieur Earnscliffe. You must be thinking of Celeste, or Miss Elmslie, to-day, or you would not pay compliments. You forget you are talking to me."

"Indeed I do not, mademoiselle."

A stranger might have thought this long day, spent in each other's society, rather a dangerous one for them both; but Philip, much as he admired and was interested in Fridoline, could never entertain anything but a friendly feeling towards this wild, uncertain little being, so unlike all other women; and every thought of hers was too strained upon one deeply-engrossing object, for her to run any risk from human love. At least, Fridoline believed so.

"I have still another room to show you," she said, after dinner. "This one has a western aspect, and when the summer is over, it is cold and dark in the morning; so I have fitted up one up-stairs for my winter study, where the early light shines fuller, and I have a pleasant view over the common."

She led the way up the old-fashioned staircase, warning Philip to beware of the projecting beams over head, and showed him into her winter study. It was almost a prettier room than the lower one—more light and cheerful; and though very plainly furnished, made artist-like by some plaster casts from the antique, and one or two excellent engravings on the walls. Philip asked, as he examined them, if she was fond of pictures.

"I love them beyond everything," she replied. "Painting is the noblest branch of art after all, and must be by far the sweetest to follow. Authors must toil with pen and paper, and bring out their glowing thoughts through the cold medium of words, which, you know, are not understood by everybody; untaught people and little children, for instance, the two classes I should like best to please, only see that books are printed paper. But the painter's words are like those of God: the sky, and flowers, and trees; and he speaks to all. How could the touching truths of religion ever have been realised to the common people before printing was invented, but for painting? The abstract idea of Christ as a teacher, delivering lessons of wisdom and morality, could never have been brought home to them; but they saw Him ministering to the poor—healing the sick—giving life to the dead; saw Him suffering—crowned with thorns—dying on the cross; and they loved and believed."

She spoke in her usual rapid manner; but her eye dilated, and Philip saw that it was a vorite subject.

"Poets and painters each have the same high mission," he answered: "to embody those true and beautiful thoughts that lie in the hearts of most men; but which they require another, peculiarly gifted, to express for them."

"Yes; but poets have more power of making you feel with their feelings, and see with their senses, than painters, and that is why I prefer painting. A sunset of Claude's, a Madonna of Raphael's, is only a faithful representation of the highest earthly beauty, from which each mind may derive its own unassisted delight, as it would do from Nature herself."

"I am convinced," said Philip, "that painters themselves are the happiest of men. Writers of all kinds, or, at least, the large majority of them, soon grow hardened by rough contact with the world, harsh criticism and literary jealousies. But an artist has little of such discipline; he dwells abroad with Nature, or in his studio with Art, hanging over his darling picture with the love of a mother over her first-born, with far tenderer feelings than an author ever felt for the blurred, unsightly manuscript he is committing to the printer. His work is so exclusively the painter's *own;* he has watched it from the first moment of its conception, through all the dawning shades of development, until its perfection; and he feels that that individual picture will exist and speak of him long after the hand that painted it is cold. And however poor the work, this golden delusion is the same. No disappointment, no poverty, ever mars the love of the worst painter for his pictures. But your own art, Fridoline," he added, gently; "let us speak of that also."

"Mine!" she answered, mournfully; "oh! you know well that the greatest singers have only their one 'crowded hour of glorious life,' and are then forgotten; while all other genius leaves some permanent creation for the future. An artist, who can live only through his physical powers, has no future existence—our memory dies quicker than the flowers flung at our feet on a farewell-night. Mine is the lowest art of all. I doubt if the first actor who ever lived, really ennobled human nature, or raised one fallen spirit through his genius. Everything about the stage is so false: the light and the paint, and the actors themselves, who are scarcely off the scene before they sink down again from the noblest character into their own debased lives. Why, the very air of the theatre has something unnatural in it—an association of mid-day darkness and tinsel splendor at night, that I can never shake off. Do you know, Mr. Earnscliffe," she went on, wandering from the original subject, "I never seem to breathe after rehearsal or performance, till I feel myself again in the fresh air of the country?"

"You have chosen a pleasant spot," said

Philip, as he seated himself at the open window; " one well suited to your simple natural tastes."

She took a low stool and placed herself near him. " Are you perfectly happy?" she inquired, at length, after a pause, and lifting her eyes earnestly to his face.

" Is any one so?" he replied, while a slight shade crossed his features. " I am certainly not less happy than the generality of men. I have plenty of interest in life; I enjoy society—have ambition to fulfil—bright prospects for the future."

Fridoline shook her head. She had heard rumors of Philip's hasty, ill-assorted marriage, and his reply told her that his pleasures were not in his home."

" I see," she remarked, and asked no more questions. They went on quietly conversing upon subjects unconnected with themselves, and, at last, among other names, that of Celeste was mentioned.

" Poor Celeste!" said Fridoline.

" Why do you thus pity her?" returned Philip.

" She seems so perfectly contented—so really happy in her life. You smile at my reason, but you do not know Celeste as I do. When I was utterly friendless in London, I was taken ill, a few days after my first appearance, with an inflammation on the chest —the effect, I suppose, of excitement and exposure to night air. Celeste heard I was alone, and visited and nursed me, and gave up her gay parties to make my sick-room cheerful. Then I found out what a good heart and kindly feeling lie beneath all her little false affections; and I am sorry now to think that Celeste should, after all, be so perfectly contented with the life of an actress."

" Celeste is very entertaining," said Philip. " How charming she was the night we first met Miss Elmslie, at her house!"

" Oh, how do you like Rose Elmslie?" cried Fridoline, suddenly, scanning Philip's face as she spoke. She thought she detected a slight change of color there.

" There can be but one opinion," he replied: " she is surpassingly lovely."

" Of course—do you like her?"

" Really, Fridoline, I cannot say that I dislike Miss Elmslie. Poor thing! one must regret that, young and beautiful as she is, she has chosen a life so full of temptations as hers."

" Temptations!" echoed Fridoline, scornfully. " Yes, you are right. Our life has temptations to such as Rose Elmslie, though to me they are horrors. Well, as you will not be candid, I will. I was interested in that girl's story, and wished to know her; but the moment we met I felt an ' éloignement '— I don't know your word in English—towards her, that I have never lost. Her beauty is extraordinary; but when I look at her fixedly, she grows hideous to me. Either what she is, or what she will be, makes me shrink away from her."

Philip thought Fridoline harsh, and could not at all agree with her opinions of the poor little dancer, and gradually their conversation turned again to other things. Fridoline talked of her childhood (an unusual confidence for her), in a quiet old country house, where they had seven months of bright intense winter, and five of summer and flowers; and where, until she was fifteen, she had never known more of the world than going on Sunday to the village church, three miles distant; or more gaiety than the midsummer's night festival among the peasants in the mountains. Then she made Philip tell of his own childish days; and her eyes glistened when she heard him regret that he could only just remember his mother.

" You are happy," she murmured, " very happy in that remembrance of her. Would God I had the same!"

" Have you no mother, Fridoline?" He was sorry for the question, when he saw the spasm of agony which suddenly contracted her features.

" None," she replied, with a hoarse voice and bloodless lip. " Let us speak of other things;' I know not why I spoke of home, or of my childhood."

And, with a wonderful effort over herself, she began speaking upon some indifferent subject; and, in a few minutes, had regained her usual lively strain. The hours passed by unheeded; for no one ever remembered time in the society of Fridoline. All that in usual conversation is tame and common, vanished away in the light thrown over the most trivial subjects by her brilliant fancy—her wit—her quick insight—and the natural eloquence, which, even in a foreign language, could find words always expressive—always ready. And Philip, who detested what are generally styled clever women, forgot that he was listening to one in little Fridoline. At length the western sun threw long, slanting shadows across the heath, and he began to think that he ought not to trespass longer on her time, of which every moment was so valuable. He was just preparing to say so, when a sudden noise arose in the household, and Fridoline sprang to her feet.

" Excuse me for a minute," she exclaimed; " Hulda is distributing some of her hourly injustice among my creatures, and I must interfere. She sits at work in the kitchen, and hears a low, ominous sound under the table, without deigning to notice it. The sound deepens—then comes Bess's well-known hiss —then screams from the cats—and when the hawk is flapping his wings with passion—the cats locked in a perfect embrace of hatred— and Karl flying round and round, gnashing his teeth at everybody, Hulda rises, and, with the nearest weapon that comes to hand, chastises them all round, and then turns them into the garden. But I never permit it when I am at home; for it is impossible they are all wrong and they know when they are punished unjustly."

She ran lightly down stairs, and Philip soon heard her in high discussion with Hulda, in some foreign language, which, spoken by Fridoline, sounded musical. Then the voices became fainter, as they went off into the back-garden—probably, after the banished creatures—and, finally, Fridoline remained away so long, that Philip thought he would himself go in search of her. There were two doors, both on the same side of the room, one leading into the passage, the other to Fridoline's sleeping-room; and, not having noticed at which he entered, Philip accidentally opened the wrong one. He instantly drew back; but the momentary glance he caught, was of something so white and fresh, that he held the handle of the lock irresolute, and, finally, took a fuller view of the little room. It was plain as her sitting-room, and as unlike the apartment of an actress. There were no untidy remains of finery—no cheval glass—no filigree bottles—no signs of theatrical costume. On the dressing-table a cup with violets in it was the only ornament: on the other side of the glass lay a large clasped book. A white French bed stood in one corner of the room, and immediately opposite, so that it was the first and last object upon which the eyes of the young actress must daily rest, hung an exquisite copy of one of Guido's pictures: the head of a dying Christ.

Philip felt strangely moved; and, impelled by a feeling that he could not withstand, he walked softly to the dressing-table and unclasped the book, which bore marks of being better read than any of those down stairs. It was a New Testament, and on the title page was written, in French, " Fridoline—on her tenth birthday." A slight knowledge of northern languages enabled Philip to discover that the Testament was written in Swedish, and printed at Christiania; so Norway, after all, was Fridoline's country. A black book-marker worked at one end with a cross, was in the book, and Philip turned to the page where it was placed. It was the story of that repentant Magdalene from whom He, in His perfect purity, did not turn away, and the leaf was actually worn and blistered with tears, as though daily read and wept over. Philip closed the book, and quickly retreated from the poor girl's room, with a feeling of compunction at having thus unwittingly discovered one of the secrets of her life—then he descended to join her in the garden. But in those few minutes his interest in her was increased tenfold, for he knew that, whatever had been her history, whatever her knowledge of vice—whose recollection still seemed to weigh so heavily upon her—Fridoline was now a pure and sinless being.

When the sun had set, and the moon was just rising over the trees, Philip bade her good night at the little garden gate.

"May your next birthday prove as happy to you, dear Fridoline, as this one has been to me," were his last words when they parted.

She stood long watching his figure till it was lost in the deepening shadows of the heath. Then she prepared to enter; but the cottage looked very dark.

"To work," she said, and an almost stern expression came over her features. "To work; I have nothing to do with such feelings. My life has henceforth only one object—to work, and toil, and win money." And all the youthful beauty was gone from her face, as she entered, and passed quickly into her study. Long after midnight the light still shone from Fridoline's window, while she walked up and down the room, with her eyes heavy, and her whole frame wearied, but still patiently learning her long *role* for the morrow.

CHAPTER X.

THE London season drew to a close—that sweet time of early summer, when Nature is in her youngest beauty, and every hedge and field laden with freshness, but which English people choose to spend in town.

Philip was going on in his usual life: he was, however, thinking earnestly of beginning another work, and was undecided how and where to spend the summer. He longed for quiet—to be away from the St. Legers, and even from his own friends for a time; but still he hesitated what plan to adopt. He always treated his wife with courtesy, and would himself make no proposal of actual separation, although their life together had virtually long been one; and the most deadly of all, a separation under one roof. A circumstance, however, occurred at this time which rendered him and Clara both more independent. Although the earl was himself irretrievably ruined, in a younger branch of the St. Leger family there was no lack of wealth. It had entered it by the marriage of one of their house, some years before, with the daughter of a retired manufacturer, and was now enjoyed by a cousin of Lord St. Leger—a widower, with an only son of about fourteen. It was in the power of the possessor to will the property to whom he chose; and this circumstance, as well as the two young, strong lives which stood between him and the succession, had prevented Lord St. Leger from ever speculating on any contingency that could affect himself. He was not on good terms even with his cousin. and the latter had a whole host of his wife's relations ready to become his heirs in the event of the death of his own son.

One morning, however—a few days before the time when Lord St. Leger had fixed, in his own mind, that exposure could no longer be avoided, nor angry creditors kept at bay—he found, on his breakfast table, an ominous-looking letter, with immense black edges, and directed in a lawyer-like hand. As his eye glanced at the post-mark, a strange, nervous tremor came over him, and he could scarcely break open the envelope. Like all gamblers, he was superstitious; and an unusual run of luck at hazard the last few days gave him a foreboding that his good star was in the ascendant. He was not mistaken. The letter was from his cousin's solicitor, informing him of the melancholy death of his two relations, who had been drowned together by the upsetting of a boat on one of the Highland lakes; and it went on to state that his cousin, having made no provision for an event like the fearful one which had just occurred, Lord St. Leger as heir-at-law, inherited the whole of the property. The father, in his will, had left everything to his son, with the proviso that, should the latter inherit, and die before attaining his majority, the money should then be divided between several of his late wife's relations, who were named. The catastrophe, however, which ended both lives, had been watched by a knot of spectators from the beach; and there was ample testimony to prove that the boy disappeared, never to rise again, on the first upsetting of the boat, while his father, who could swim, was seen for several minutes vainly battling with the waves, which at length overcame him. The son, therefore, had never inherited; and through this slender point of law, Lord St. Leger found himself, at the very moment when his reputation was about to be blasted to the world, suddenly possessed of a large, unincumbered property.

Earnscliffe, without any latent thought for himself, was undisguisedly glad at this sudden turn of events. He had long known that ruin and disgrace were hanging over his father-in-law, and this had made him considerate to Clara far beyond what her open and almost insulting coldness towards himself deserved. But with this new accession of wealth in her family, everything was changed, and, with no feeling of self-reproach, he might now see his haughty wife return to the protection of her parents. Clara's pride, however, still revolted against any open separation; and, miserable as was her married life, she could not determine upon so grave a step as herself proposing to leave her husband's house. Soon after their cousin's death, the St. Legers determined upon going abroad to spend the remainder of the summer and autumn, and her mother invited Clara to accompany them to some of the German baths—for Lord St. Leger's

first use of his wealth was, of course, to renew his acquaintance with Homburg and Baden-Baden. With so plausible an excuse, for her health was really delicate, and being under the protection of her own parents, she felt that the world, or even her friends, could say nothing about this temporary separation, and she really longed for any relief from her present life. Accordingly she made the proposal to Philip, and read in his brightening face his ready acquiescence.

"I trust you will derive benefit from the change, Clara," he replied. "My own autumn will be passed in some quiet spot, where I can enter undisturbed upon my new work. In the winter we shall meet again."

They parted coldly, but as friends; and when Philip heard the last sounds of the carriage-wheels which bore away his wife and her parents, he gave a sigh of intense relief, and felt "I am free."

In the afternoon he went to call on his friend, Neville. He found the young artist in unbounded spirits; his large picture in the exhibition was sold, and he had, that very day, received orders for two more of similar size.

"Congratulate me! I am now on the high-road to fame, Earnscliffe!" he exclaimed, as he shook Philip's hand heartily. "In another year I shall have realised enough money to enable me to go to Rome; two years I shall remain and study there, then return to England, and, I firmly believe, be one of our first landscape painters."

Philip warmly entered into his sanguine hopes, and sat long with his friend, who, with his accustomed energy, was already sketching the outline for one of his new pictures.

"Yours is a happy life, Neville."

"Yes; some of my lonely hours, when I have been working at my pictures, and my recent ones of success, I would exchange with no man. But I have had years of toil —bitter toil and disappointment—before attaining to even my present fame. There is so much mere mechanism for a painter to acquire before he can express his ideas. Look at yourself now: you are five or six years younger than I am, but your first book—written, as you have told me, without an exertion—made you celebrated."

The remark reminded Earnscliffe of Fridoline, and he repeated some of her observations on art to Neville.

"She is a gifted little creature," he replied; "but beware of these long, lonely conversations, Phil. A woman like Fridoline would be the very devil to have in love with one."

"There is no risk," said Philip, gravely. "Fridoline is not a girl to inspire any light sentiment, nor likely herself to fall in love with a married man."

"Ah, true! I beg both your pardons. The fact is, I never remember that you are married. How is your domestic bliss getting on?"

Philip mentioned the departure of his wife.

"And what are you going to do with your summer and your freedom?" asked the artist; "not waste them by staying at country houses, I hope."

Philip said he wished to live in perfect solitude for some months while he worked at his new book.

"Then I have it all," exclaimed Neville, throwing down his pencil, and seizing both Philip's hands; "we will go together, old fellow. I will take you to my wild quarters among the Highlands, where I spent last autumn; and if you do not find them retired enough, you must indeed be fond of solitude. You can write—I sketch—and both forget, in the mountain air, and with nothing but Nature round us, our feverish town life, our friends, wives, aye, and Fridoline herself!"

"I am ready," returned Philip. And they entered so eagerly into their new plans that Neville soon abandoned his pencil, and, after changing his painting-blouse for a coat, proposed that they should walk out together in the Park. It was a hot, bright day, and all London seemed there. Carriages and equestrians crowded past in an unbroken stream; and Earnscliffe's hat was off repeatedly.

"Hold it in your hand, at once," said Neville. "How can you be at the trouble of uncovering every second, for all these people?"

"It is one of the evils of society, I admit," said Philip; "but, still, unavoidable. Let us turn into one of the side-walks, where we shall be less disturbed."

At that moment a very dashing little equipage, with two showy black ponies, came along, clearing its way dexterously among the interminable labyrinth of wheels by which it was surrounded. It was driven by a lady, whose perfect *sang froid*, and dress, and remarkable beauty, drew every eye upon her. She was unaccompanied, a diminutive page only sitting behind, but did not seem the least disconcerted at the admiration she attracted.

"Rose Elmslie, by Jove!" said Neville. "Well, she is getting on. Who paid for all that, I wonder, Phil? Count B——, I suppose, out of his Derby winnings."

Philip's eye marked her coldly, and he bit his lip, without answering. When she was quite close she perceived them, and colored scarlet, as she bowed. Philip took his hat off to the ground; Neville nodded.

"Well, hang it, Phil! salute your own friends if you will, but I cannot understand taking off your hat to a woman of that kind, as though she were a duchess."

"I am only just beginning to think that she *is* a woman of that kind," said Philip, in a low voice.

"Why, what should she be?—poor, lovely, and a dancer—bah!"

Earnscliffe took his friend's arm, and they walked on to a retired part of Kensington Gardens, where they sat down to discuss their plans for the summer quietly. The artist continued in excellent spirits, but Philip seemed somewhat depressed, and even more anxious to get away from town than his friend.

"Are you 'thinking of an absent spouse?'" remarked Neville, at last. "You seem to be very much out of spirits all at once!"

"Not I. I am in remarkably good spirits, on the contrary."

"If it were possible—but no; the sight of that worthless young thing cannot have had any effect upon you."

"If you mean Miss Elmslie by your polite term, undoubtedly not. Miss Elmslie is nothing to me."

"And will continue so, I trust. She is of a worse description than Fridoline, or even Celeste. Tell me what your next book is to be about. Do you sketch the entire outline before commencing, as one does for a picture, or write on where your fancy leads you?"

"Oh! I shall write very differently this time. My two first books have succeeded as much from accident as merit—as much from their vices as their virtues. Now I must begin writing for real fame—for solid criticism."

And the afternoon passed by while they talked over their mutual hopes and projects. They dined afterwards at Philip's club, and in a few days were *en route* for Scotland. The remainder of the fine weather passed happily to them both. Each pursued his own occupation, absorbed and uninterrupted; but they had the companionship of kindred thought when they needed it, after work, and would wander for hours together among the mountains in the calm summer evenings. On Philip the change was most beneficial. He had a softer and more pliant nature than his friend, and his mind had lost more of its tone during its contact with the world, from the ready way he fell into the life of those around him. But this difference was merely one of temperament. He had more real genius than the artist; and after a few weeks spent among this grand, still nature, Philip wrote with a fervor and inspiration far surpassing that in either of his former works.

Neville studied fore-ground, noted atmospheric effects, and thought, as his sketches multiplied, of the pictures they would form, and of his own fame. He had exactly the organisation of a man who is to succeed in this world. Sufficient genius, untiring industry, energy that no failure could damp, an iron frame, and a boundless ambition. With Philip, to gaze at a golden sunset or mountain storm, was to unloose a flood of unconscious poetry in his heart; and afterwards he simply wrote down his thoughts as they existed, without labor, often without a single alteration, and always forgetful of himself or his own success. With him the artist was lost in the art, and both at times in the source from whence come poet and inspiration alike. With Neville this was never the case. Possessing an exuberant fancy, he was not for one moment himself under the influence of his own imagination. He could conceive wild and beautiful pictures, and for his art had a really passionate love, but it all seemed unconnected, as it were, with his own personal existence; and the artist ever remained a consistent, practical citizen of the world. He was the best friend and adviser possible for Philip, who, although he had conformed much more than Neville to the life of society, plunged into numberless follies, from which the other had continued free, was yet a very child at heart, compared to the artist, and still possessed a hundred illusions which Neville had lost in his boyhood. For instance, bitter as had been his own short experience of married life, Philip had still a firm belief in the existence of pure and faithful love; a point on which his friend, if not sceptical, was cold and sarcastic, and in his new works wrote with enthusiasm on this subject, in spite of Neville's criticisms. And often, when they walked silently under the starry summer night, he felt the mysterious workings of youth and love that were so strong within his own heart, and asked himself if they were never in this world to be satisfied—while he wrote of love and imagined it for others, was his own life to be spent only between the world, and the cold, dull tedium of his loveless marriage? But this was a theme he never entered upon with Neville.

The autumn passed quickly away. The hills, from bright golden, had become brown, and the purple was gone from the heather; but at the beginning of November the friends still lingered in their Highland cottage, endeared to them both from the glowing thoughts of pen and pencil which had there had birth, and neither of them was anxious to return to town. The days were, however, now very short, and the weather so uncertain, that they at length unwillingly departed; Neville to his London lodging, and Philip to pay his uncle a long-promised visit. The St. Legers had not yet returned to England.

During the autumn Philip had received occasional notes from his wife. They were, like herself, cold, abrupt, and uninteresting, and he did not read them twice; but in the one which awaited him on his arrival at Miles Earnscliffe's, the first lines arrested his attention at once. Lady Clara announced that they would all be in London during the course of the month, and reminded Philip, at the expiration of the present term, to take on their house in Park Lane for the coming season. So his wife had still no wish for an open separation!

CHAPTER XI.

AGAIN the London season was at its height.

Philip and Clara had met with a tolerable show of friendliness, on her return from Germany, but he had soon merged again into his old life; and Clara, whose health appeared little improved, became more gloomy and taciturn than ever. Her father's unlooked-for accession of wealth had only added to the bitterness which rankled in her heart about her marriage. She felt that, as the heiress of an immense fortune, she might have been spared the humiliation of stooping to win her young cousin, for the sake of his merchant-uncle's money; and her mother came in for the full share of thanks, which she merited, as principal promoter of the marriage; and had to bear many a cold taunt from her daughter on the subject.

In time, Clara went rarely even to her own parent's house, more rarely still into society. She shrank, with a morbid feeling, from the scrutiny of her old friends; and her life was passed in hugging to her heart her disappointment and loneliness. She had no child to break the tedium of her long hours, and open the one warm spring of happiness left to many a deserted wife; few mental resources; no religion, beyond that of appearing in her pew every Sunday, to listen to some fashionable preacher; while, week after week, she became more fully sensible of her husband's indifference, and the life of eternal dissipation he was leading. His new work was in the press, and great things were expected of it. Philip himself felt that it was far superior to either of his former ones, and his own opinion was confirmed by the friendly criticisms he had received on the manuscript. He had much to do in correcting proofs, and so on; but still found ample time for society, especially that of the coulisses, which now appeared to possess a renewed and powerful fascination to the young author.

Neville, meantime, was working, during every moment of daylight, on his pictures. He gave up parties of all kinds, and scarcely even went to the theatre, that his head might be more clear, his hand more steady, for his morning's work; and every afternoon after dusk he took long walks into the country, for the sake of his mental and bodily health. Everything he did was subservient to one object—he must complete his two pictures before the exhibition, be paid for them, and start for Rome; and not every pleasure in London could have drawn him aside from the steady execution of his plans. He had not seen very much of Philip since their return from Scotland. He had himself no time for visiting; and every moment of Earnscliffe's life was so taken up with some new excitement, that his visits to his friend's quiet studio were far less frequent than formerly. Besides this, Neville, on the plea of his seniority, always gave Philip quiet lectures about the way he was frittering away his time, which the latter did not at all relish, especially as he himself well knew the truth of these remarks.

One evening, Neville was returning from a long, quick walk on Hampstead Heath, his step firm, his head erect, and his arms folded, as was his wont, when he saw a figure some fifty yards ahead. He thought he recognised the slight form, the slow, graceful walk, and quickened his pace. It was Earnscliffe.

"Good evening, Phil."

"Hallo! Neville—what, you here?"

"Aye, '*que diable faites vous dans cette galère?*' I suppose you mean to say. Well, I have been doing as you should—walking alone on the heath to cool my head, after the day's work. And you?"

"I?—I have just been walking home with Fridoline," answered Philip, hesitating a little. He did not much like talking about her to Neville.

"Oh! how is she getting on, by the way? I have no time for theatres and actresses, and such things now."

"Fridoline is, as usual, working hard at her profession, looking paler and older, I think, and more strange and lonely in her life than she ever was."

"Only diversifying it by twilight walks on the heath with Philip Earnscliffe," added the artist. "Poor philosophic little Fridoline! Well, I don't think you are in any danger from that quarter, whatever she may be."

"In danger from her!—none, I should trust," returned Philip, with a short laugh, and seemingly quite disposed to change the subject.

"I hope not, I am sure. But, independently of Fridoline—who is about the best of them—you are wasting your fine energies among all these people, when you should be thinking of your art alone. That worthless young Elmslie, now—"

"Neville——"

"Don't be in a rage, Philip, or I shall really think badly of you."

"I am not the least in a rage; but I will not hear you speak in those terms of poor Rose. She was brought up to a life she now hates, when a mere child; she is lovely, young, surrounded with temptation, and therefore you condemn her."

"Not in the least. I think her conduct is excessively natural, and like that of every other dancer in the world. I made use of the word 'worthless' only because, for her

age, she possesses a really unusual amount of deceit, in addition to her beauty, and temptation, and sorrow for the life she leads. Well, it is wonderful how these women all pitch upon you for the repository of their pious compunctions, and how you believe them. First Fridoline, now young Elmslie; I suppose we shall have Celeste herself next upon your list of penitents. What an absurd world we live in!"

Although Philip defended Rose Elmslie so warmly, it pained him to hear his poor little friend Fridoline classed with her. He felt that the distance between them was immeasurable; but feared provoking Neville's sarcasm by saying so.

"How is Rose deceitful?" he asked, after a pause.

"Only in talking sentiment, and regretting her life with you in morning, and receiving bracelets from Count B—— in the afternoon, while she really laughs at you both with somebody else afterwards. But think as you like, you know; I shall certainly retain my opinions too."

Earnscliffe got rather angry, and again began defending Miss Elmslie with all the vehemence of a champion who really doubts the right of his cause; but Neville interrupted him.

"Let us change the subject, Phil; you are a perfect boy, still, and cannot learn experience as quickly as I did; however, you will buy it at last—and, in the meantime, do not quarrel with one friend for all the actresses in creation. Towards the end of May, I think I shall start for Switzerland, and shall then remain two years in Italy; so I shall not see much more of you. But write sometimes, and tell me how all this life of yours ends, and which was right you or I."

Philip's annoyance was quickly over, and Neville was soon talking eagerly of the progress of his pictures. Then he inquired how soon the new book would appear.

"In about a month," returned Philip. "It is far better written than either of my former ones; consequently, I ought to have good hopes of success; and yet—I know not why—I have a sort of foreboding that it will be, not, perhaps, a failure, but, at all events, very differently received to the two first."

Neville tried to reason him out of this feeling, and they parted, with their accustomed friendly shake of the hand, at the Regent's Circus, where their roads separated. Neville went off, happy, to his dark, comfortless lodgings, and Philip returned home to dinner. By some extraordinary chance he dined *tête-à-tête* with his wife, almost for the first time since their honeymoon, and they both felt strange in each other's society.

"Have you an engagement for this evening, Clara?" he asked, during the course of dinner. She looked up astonished.

"None. You know I have almost given up going out, now that my health is so bad."

"You will not go to the opera, then?"

"Certainly not." She felt positively bewildered at this sudden interest in her movements.

"Well, you are right. It is a stupid opera this evening, and there is no ballet; though, perhaps, you do not care for that."

Clara made no reply; and her husband, after one or two languishing attempts at conversation, became silent also.

After dinner Philip's cab came round almost immediately. Clara was in the drawing-room, and happened to be standing at the window, which she had just opened to place a bouquet of flowers on the balcony, in the fresh air, at the moment when Philip left the house. She saw him jump in, and then, without any intention of listening, accidentally heard him say to the servant, "Oh, just go back for the latch-key, I have forgotten it; and no one need sit up, of course. The opera will not be over till late." The groom returned directly, and, a second afterwards, the cab drove off. Clara then drew in her head and closed the window;—there was a slight tinge of color in her cheek. "So he is going to this stupid opera without a ballet!" she thought. "I wonder what gave him such an extreme wish to know if I intended being there." She inherited a good deal of Lady St. Leger's sharpness in drawing unfavorable conclusions from a word or a look; and, after considering a few minutes by the fire, felt certain that Philip had some hidden reason for his inquiries. She rang the bell. "I shall require the carriage in half an hour," she said to the servant who entered; "I am going to the opera this evening." Then she went up into her dressing-room, and ordered her maid to dress her quickly, as she was going to the theatre. Her plain toilette was soon completed, and in less than half-an-hour she was again in the drawing-room, walking up and down with an agitated impatience, that she could not have explained to herself, for the announcement of the carrriage.

The second act was just beginning as Clara reached the theatre. She was dressed plainly in a high pearl-colored silk, without ornament or flowers in her hair, and looked altogether so like an invalid, that her entrance was unnoticed, and no glass directed a second time to her face. Only a few of her old friends, when they happened to remark her, said "How awfully dear Clara was changed!" And one or two of her husband's acquaintance who knew her by sight, exclaimed, "Good heavens! can that pale woman, wretched-looking woman be young Earnscliffe's wife?"

Exactly opposite to her was the St. Legers' box, and Clara saw her mother, all diamonds and pink satin, and looking quite young and smiling, as she talked to Prince N——, who was by her side. A bitter sense came over her of the contrast between Lady St. Leger and herself, and she thought, "It would be better for me if I had been like her. With her jewels, and dress, and Prince N——, and all the world seeing her, my mother is perfectly happy; though her husband is playing away his very life at the hazard-table, and her only child made miserable by her own plans. I hope she may not see me to-night!" For, sensitively alive to her own deserted position, and her pale, worn cheeks, Clara shrank almost with a feeling of shame from recognition.

Her eye glanced stealthily among the stalls, where she had generally seen her husband, but he was not in his accustomed place. "I shall see him by the side of Lady N——," she thought; and she swept with her glass the long tiers of boxes—brilliant with flowers, and toilettes, and fair faces; still, she saw him nowhere. Lady N——, in all her jewels and beauty, was quietly talking, wonderful to say, to her own husband!—and at length wearying of the vain search, Clara gave it up for the present, and directed her attention to the scene. Philip had called the opera a stupid one, but it contained some of Meyerbeer's most wild and spiritual thoughts; and Clara, who had a natural love for music (though, like everything else, it had been as much crushed as possible by "education" and having to practise on the piano for four hours a-day during eight years of her life), now forgot herself for awhile, in listening to the notes of the great master, and the sweetest of all human voices—that of Mario.

The second act terminated; and, in the interval, Lady Clara again sought her husband among the crowds of faces which thronged the vast building. She thought every one in the theatre seemed unusually smiling and gay, and that she was the only neglected woman there. As she looked, one by one, at the young men in the pit stalls, thinking that Philip might perhaps be among them, although he was not in his accustomed place, she observed that numbers of glasses were upturned to one stage-box—the opposite side of the house, and on so high a range that Lady Clara had not even thought of lifting her aristocratic eyes in its direction—and that many smiles and significant looks seemed to be called forth by its occupants. A feeling of curiosity made her raise her own glass to this box, where she saw a face of such surpassing loveliness as even arrested her own cold admiration—a face which, in all that crowded house of high-born beauty, had no peer. After scanning the features for a few seconds, it occurred to her that she had seen them before; and she then remembered that they were those of Miss Elmslie, the new danseuse, whom she had twice seen perform. Miss Elmslie was talking gaily to some one beside her, but her head concealed the face of her companion from Clara. She felt her gaze strangely fascinated to this girl's box—although not connecting it in the least with her search for Philip—and waited patiently to catch a glimpse of its other occupant. Rose was dressed in pale blue, with camelias and silver in her bright hair, and a little white silk opera-cloak falling back over her shoulders. She was, at this time, about twenty, but scarcely appeared so old—her slight form, delicate features, brilliant complexion, and large blue eyes being all of that cast which generally give an appearance of extreme youth. She held a profusion of rare hot-house flowers in her hand, and appeared very animated—smiling and blushing, and repeatedly hiding her face in her rich bouquet at her companion's remarks. Suddenly she half stood up to look at something in a distant part of the house, and, after a minute, reseated herself with some slight change of attitude, so that the face of her companion was left fully visible to Lady Clara. It was her husband.

So this was the cause of his inquiries about Clara's movements! She had long known that Philip was more than indifferent to her, that his life was the careless and dissipated one of most young men of his age; but that was all. Now she saw him publicly in the company of a dancer—and to be an actress of any kind, was, according to her ideas, for a woman to be utterly worthless—with all the world seeing him, and remarking, as she thought, with malicious pleasure, upon the scene. At that unfortunate moment some people in the next box began talking about Earnscliffe. They were perfect strangers to her, of course, and probably not even noticed their pale, sickly-looking neighbor.

"Oh, yes!" said an old gentleman of the party, in answer to some remark she had not heard; "he married a daughter of Lord St. Leger, and dearly she must pay for her folly in marrying a genius. Such a dissipated life as he leads—always among actors and those sort of people! There, he is at this moment sitting by Miss Elmslie, the dancer, while his wife, poor creature! is probably watching it from an opposite box."

"Oh, where is he?—where is Philip Earnscliffe?" asked a young girl, leaning forward; "I should like so much to see him."

The gentleman pointed out Earnscliffe, and some one remarked on Rose Elmslie's great beauty.

"And how handsome he is! and how animated he looks!" said the young voice. "Is his wife pretty, I wonder?"

"Oh, no!" answered another lady. "I saw her once at a concert. Quite a pale, passée-looking woman, and such a very discontented expression of face!"

The blood seemed to grow like ice at Clara's heart, and her cheeks were white with wounded pride, as she listened. But she did not leave the house; she sat through-

out the whole remainder of the opera, unnoticed, alone; with her cold hands clasped tightly together, and her eyes fixed upon Philip's handsome, animated face. She watched his attentive manner, his attitude, and could fancy the very words he was saying; and then—but with a less deep scorn—she scanned the exquisite features of his companion, and the half-averted, half-smiling way she listened to him.

The performance went on. The fullest chorus, and the whole united strength of the orchestra, were joined in the finale scene; but Clara heard it not. Those few hateful remarks which she had caught, alone rang in her ear; and among all the hundreds of human beings around her, she only saw two faces—Miss Elmslie's and Philip's. No woman ever went through a truer martyrdom than did Lady Clara, during that evening.

To do Philip justice, he was incapable of willingly outraging his wife's feelings; and, had he seen Clara, would that second have quitted Rose Elmslie. But he believed her at home as she had told him she would be, and had never even glanced towards the box she occupied. And Rose was in her most charming, winning mood, talking so prettily and innocently, and saying she detested Count B——, and how much she wished she could leave the stage for ever. No wonder Philip's attention was fully taken up, and that he forgot all Neville's odious suspicions. He was looking on one of the loveliest forms ever given to a woman, and trying to believe that it inclosed a similar soul.

The opera concluded without Clara being aware of it, and as there was no ballet, every one rose to leave. Then she saw Philip help Miss Elmslie to draw her little dainty cloak over her white shoulders, and hold the bouquet for her while she fastened her glove—paying her all those nameless attentions which are more galling to a jealous woman when actually witnessed, than it would be merely to *hear* of some open dereliction on the part of her husband. Finally, they both left the box together, and she was reminded that she too must leave and go home. She stood up; but her head was giddy, and her limbs felt weak. An elderly person, who had once been her governess, and still lived with her as companion, had accompanied Lady Clara to the theatre, and she was forced to lean upon her arm for support; but she trembled so that her attendant inquired if she were ill.

"Let us wait here until the crush is over," Clara answered, reseating herself where the shadow of the box prevented her from being seen. "The heat has overcome me, and I am not well this evening."

They remained for nearly a quarter of an hour, while Clara called all her pride to aid in the struggle to nerve herself; and then, when there was less chance of meeting any one she knew, she drew the hood of her cloak over her face, and with a firmer step entered the lobby, which was now nearly vacant. She got to her carriage unnoticed, and drove home. On their way she spoke to her companion about the opera in a cheerful voice, and her hand no longer trembled. Every sign of weakness was over. When she reached the house she went up to the drawing-room, and ordered tea to be brought, with her usual calm manner; and when the servant re-entered, he found his mistress seated at the table, reading. She drank a cup of tea, and attempted to eat, but the food seemed to choke her; and, after a sufficiently long pause had elapsed, she again rang the bell. Then, when her attendants had finally left her alone, she placed herself near the fire and warmed her death-cold hands, while she brooded over the cruel shock her pride had sustained.

That she would leave him—never remain another day under Philip's roof—was her first fixed resolution. Many wives, even where previous affection existed, might, in all their heat of wounded feeling, have resolved the same. But Clara's was not a nature ever to swerve from a determined course; and as she sat thus alone, and thought of all the remarks that Philip's open devotion to an actress must have excited among her own friends that evening, her feeling towards him strengthened into actual hate, and her lips grew blanched and rigid in their stern expression.

At length she went up to her own room, and rang for her maid to undress her, as usual; but when the girl had left the room, she rose again from her bed, and, quietly locking the door, lit her candle, and partially dressed herself in a loose morning wrapper. Then she began opening her drawers and cases, and drew from them, one after another, everything of value that she could consider as in any way belonging to, or connected with, her marriage.

One or two notes from Philip, written during their courtship, a locket containing his hair, and a miniature of him, she laid together, and gazed at them silently for a few moments. Something softer came over her face as she recalled that evening when he had generously sacrificed himself for her in the impulse of boyish kindness, and she paused, and thought of her childish days when her cousin had been her only friend. But then she saw him again as she had done only an hour before—flushed and animated, and whispering to Rose Elmslie—and rising abruptly, she flung all the little relics of his false love upon the fire. The flames danced and crackled over them in a second, and she watched with a bitter laugh the last sparks die out in her husband's love-letters before they became a mere cloud of grey film. Then she turned to her other work. The bracelets, the tiaras, the rings—all the valuable jewels that she had received from Phil-

ip or his uncle—she divided from her own trinkets, and, making them into a package, directed them to " Philip Earnscliffe, Esq.," but without note or explanation of any kind ; and after this she lay down in her bed and watched.

In an hour or two she heard Philip's quiet step ascending the stairs, and the door close of his dressing-room. Her face grew a shade whiter as she murmured—" Yes—for the last time." And then she turned her head upon her pillow, and waited for the day.

CHAPTER XII.

LITTLE thinking of all the next twelve hours had in store for him, Philip went down early the following morning to call on his uncle. He had not seen his wife, who was indeed still in her own apartment, ripening the project which she meant in the course of the day to carry into execution—that of leaving Philip's roof for ever. When Clara's passions were roused, they were like her father's. Her jealousy of the previous evening—grown even more bitter during the long watches of the night—had deepened her former indifference to her husband into actual loathing ; and she longed for the moment when she could disclose her scorn for him with her own lips. Still Clara had no wish to play the *role* of a mere jealous wife ; and she had turned over in her mind a dozen different ways of announcing her intention, without fixing upon one that should sufficiently wound his pride, yet not lower her own. She shrunk, too, from the idea of again returning to her parent's house and the companionship of Lady St. Leger, although she felt it was the only alternative she could look forward to on leaving her own home, and that even this was better than remaining longer with her unfaithful husband.

Meanwhile Philip rode slowly along into the country. It was a grey cold day ; leaden masses of clouds covered the whole sky, borne slowly along in an English east wind, and the trees and distant country seemed one uniform tint of brown. It may have been the influence of the weather, or perhaps the natural after-effects of the previous evening's excitement ; but Philip's spirits were unaccountably depressed this morning. He seemed unable to throw off the weight that was upon him, and did not once urge his horse out of a walk until he reached the lodge of Miles Earnscliffe's place, where, for the first time, he attempted to rouse himself a little, and cantered up the avenue. He found old Miles confined to the house. His illness was not serious ; but still it was enough to make him fretful and impatient.

He was so used to a life of activity, that it galled him to remain idle in his easy-chair, instead of being out and busy in his grounds; and his reception of his nephew was not particularly amiable.

"Well, Phil, I thought you were never coming near me again; every week I see less of you now. But you knew I was ill, and therefore it was your duty to come, whatever your inclination prompted."

"I have been really much engaged, uncle," returned Philip. "My new book, you know, is in the press, and I have a great deal to do in correcting proofs, and so on: when it is out I shall have more leisure time."

"Um—well, I hope you are always as profitably engaged, though I doubt it," answered Miles. "I suppose your wife takes up a great deal of your time, too?"

"Not much of that, sir, I think." Philip saw his uncle's humor, and prepared himself for a pleasant day of it.

"Oh, I am sorry to hear it. As you would marry at your age, you should have tried to make her happy. How is Clara?"

"Much the same, thank you: she is never very strong, and stays so entirely at home, that she has no chance of getting more spirits or color."

"Philip," said Miles, sternly, and rising himself up grimly on one elbow, as was his habit when in a bad temper, "I believe your wife is a miserable woman, and that it is all your fault. You are just as dissipated, and worse, than you were before you married. I know more about you than you think, and I tell you frankly, I don't admire your conduct!"

"I am perfectly aware of my folly in marrying so young, sir," returned Philip, bitterly.

After a pause, Miles went on—

"I never saw such a changed face as Clara's. She was never particularly blooming, but now she looks ten years older, and so wan and indifferent to everything. What is the matter with her Philip? Perhaps there is a prospect of my having a grand-nephew, eh?"

"God forbid!" said Philip, hastily.

"Well, a mighty pious aspiration, certainly. People in general are pleased at the idea of having children."

"Aye, sir, when there is a home for them to be brought up in!"

"And have you no home, Philip? Do you want a larger house and establishment, or are you too proud to call yours a home, because you merely maintain it upon your allowance? You know well that my money will be all yours at my death, and that whatever you or Clara want you have only to ask for."

"No," answered Philip; "you are already too generous. I require nothing more in the world that money can purchase. When I spoke of home, I meant that union

of heart and feeling which never has been, and never can be, between my wife and myself. If Heaven had given me a child, it would have been, of course, brought up by its mother, and taught from its birth to be as indifferent to me as she is herself—indeed, I sometimes think Clara's feelings toward me are now those of actual dislike—"

"And whose doing is all this, Phil?" inquired Miles. "She may be cold, I don't deny it; it is her nature; and you know that you were marrying the daughter of Lord and Lady St. Leger. But it is not Clara's fault that, as a married man, you continue your old bachelor life, and are always philandering about after actresses and such rubbish, when you should be at home with her, or coming to see me. Hugh! hugh!" He coughed dismally, and plunged the poker into the fire, before returning to the charge; but, greatly to Philip's relief, who did not relish the tone of his uncle's lecture, was interrupted by the entrance of the servant with newspapers.

"Shall I read to you?" he added, taking up the *Times*.

"Yes. I am getting so blind I cannot even read for myself now"—(he had wonderfully good eyes for his time of life, but could never be prevailed upon to use spectacles)—"and try to find something worth listening to."

Philip accordingly began, and had read the leading-article half through, when Miles interrupted him with—

"Can't you find anything but that political stuff, nephew? What do I care about Lord John, or Lord Aberdeen, or which of them gets the head place in the mismanagement of the country! Do find something of general interest."

"The parliamentary report?"

"Worse still? There is meaning, at least, in what the *Times* writes, but none in those endless speeches; and, besides, I hate all that sickening trash of 'the honorable member to my right,' and 'my noble friend in the opposition.' Read me the city article."

"Stay, sir, here is the arrival of the Indian mail," said Philip, as he turned the paper.

"Well, then, read that, of course. Why did you not find it at once?"

Philip glanced his eye rapidly down the column before commencing aloud, and after some unimportant paragraphs, some name arrested his attention. He began to read, and his hand trembled a little, then he flushed deeply, but, as he went on, every particle of color left his face, and he became deadly pale.

"What ails you, Phil, that you change color so?" said his uncle, rising, all his kind manner returning in a moment.

"You are ill, my boy," and he advanced towards him.

Philip grasped the paper tighter, as though to prevent the other from reading it, and, looking up in his face, faltered out—

"Uncle, there is news—bad news—from Bombay——" Here he broke down. Miles's face grew white as his nephew's, and an instinctive presentiment flashed across him. But the old man's brave nature did not falter.

"Give me the paper, Philip," he said, in his usual firm voice. "I can read it myself."

Philip let him take it passively from him and covered his face, while Miles read the fatal paragraph. It was the intelligence of the failure of one of the largest Bombay banks, in which the greatest part of Mr. Earnscliffe's immense capital still floated, and Philip knew that he was comparatively ruined. He dared not look up, but kept his face still buried in his hands, without the courage to speak, when a sound made him start in terror to his uncle's side.

It was a fearful sound—half sob, half groan—wrung from the bosom of an iron man in his first moment of despair, and Philip prayed that he might never hear the like again. He looked in his uncle's face: it was white, and drawn as though paralysed, and under a hideous apprehension, Philip cried—"Oh! speak to me—one word dear uncle—only one word!"

"It is all gone," said Miles, in a low, hoarse whisper. "I am a beggar; help me to a chair, and leave me. I would be alone."

Philip obeyed him instantly. He knew that strong, proud nature would shrink from any eye being upon him in his agony, and having assisted him to his chair, he walked to the deep bay window of the library, and remained there silent for almost an hour. During all this time Miles Earnscliffe never moved—once only did he groan. He sat alone in his ruin, as he had been in the weary road to success, and the iron entered into his soul in silence.

And Philip—in that terrible hour, what were his thoughts. His own fall from being Miles Earnscliffe's heir to poverty — the taunts in his own household—the falling off of friends—did all this cross his mind? Not once. Even had he cared for money, he could have had no selfish thought then. He only saw the old man's bowed head and clutched hands; he only thought of his generous protector humbled from his high estate, and in his old age brought to the poverty he had always loathed; and slowly large tears rolled down Philip's pale cheeks, as he stood silently gazing at his uncle.

Suddenly Miles looked up.

"Come here, boy." He was at his side in a second. "You may well weep, you that were to be my heir. You are a beggar, Philip."

"Oh, uncle! I do not think of myself; I

think of you only. You have been my protector, my father—you have done all for me; and I would have given my life to save you from this."

The old man's stony gaze softened a little at Philip's warm and loving expression.

"Shall you still care for me, lad, in my ruin?" he said, helplessly.

Philip was on his knees, and seizing the cold, withered hand, he pressed it to his lips—

"As God is my Judge, I will, sir! I may have been selfish—careless of you in my own hour of success—but you shall now know all my affection for you. You received me a friendless little child—"

"Aye; but I turned from your father, Phil," he interrupted, huskily; "and I have never seen Herbert's face so plainly as in the last hour. I mind well the letter he wrote me in his distress, and how I answered it—how I scorned his honest poverty, and insulted him and his wife. Since then, I have shut my heart to the poor in my pride of wealth, and now—I am judged."

"You have not forgotten the poor of late years, sir," answered Philip. "You have built hospitals—you have founded schools; and many a widow and orphan have learned to bless your name. And, oh! whatever self-reproach you may feel with regard to any former action towards my parents, that action is more than cancelled by all you have done for their son. You have given me education, and I can now make my own way in the world."

He spoke so warmly and hopefully, that old Miles's features gradually lost something of their frightful rigidity; and clasping his hands, he thanked Heaven that, amid the wreck of all his worldly fortunes, there was still left to him his nephew's noble heart.

"God bless you, Phil!" he said very softly.

They remained long together, talking—not of the storm which had just burst over them, but of old happy days; of the summer excursions they had made together; of the thousand little events of Philip's boyhood. There is a strange proneness in human beings to take refuge, under the first shock of any sudden calamity, in the peaceful remembrance of the past; as though, in that brief hour, the heart tried to concentrate all that life has known of sweetness, before attempting to confront the stern and present reality. And this is especially the case when, as with Miles Earnscliffe, no vision of the future can offer anything half so bright again.

But this passed, after a time. He relapsed into vacant silence, and then starting up, as though the truth had only just burst in all its fulness upon him, exclaimed—"I will not believe it! What, all gone!—the labors of thirty years! Read it again, Phil; it is false, a newspaper lie; I am not a beggar. Read it, I say!"

And he fixed a look, almost of fierce hope, upon his nephew, as he again took the paper, which went to Philip's heart.

"There is no doubt of its correctness, sir, I fear," he replied, in a low voice, after reading the paragraph once more. "And we must not buoy ourselves up on any frail hopes of that kind. But neither will you be, by any means, brought to what the world calls poverty. Your estate in Yorkshire, and this very house, form in themselves a fortune that to many a man would seem riches."

"I shall not be an actual beggar, nephew, I know," answered Miles, bitterly. "But think what I was; dukes glad to sit at my table; even royalty smiling at me; an earl proud to marry his daughter into my family. Good God, Philip!" he exclaimed, the thought crossing him for the first time, "what will those people say to my ruin? and your wife! Ah! there lies the deepest of my humiliation."

Philip felt this, too, fully as deeply as his uncle; but he said little on the subject, and merely observed that it was not unlikely Clara's character might shine out in his adversity far more brightly than it had hitherto done. "It was woman's nature," he said, "to become more soft and gentle in time of trial; and after the unvarying kindness shown to her by his uncle, it was impossible for her to entertain any feeling but that of sorrow for him now; and as to the St. Legers," added Philip, "it matters little to us what they do or say. They will merely follow in the track of the other worldly acquaintance who will fall away at the first breath of our altered fortunes."

He stayed long, and his kindly consolation was some comfort to Miles, who gradually became more natural in his manner, less helpless, and more bitter, which, for him, was the best possible sign; and at length the unyielding spirit which, through years of drudgery and disappointment had never flinched, again began to rise with an elasticity wonderful in so old a man. By the time Philip left him he was deep in accounts in his study, calculating upon the wreck of his fortunes, and, with his old business habits, already writing letters to his different agents, and planning for the realisation of the small sum which remained to him.

"Well, good bye, Phil!" were his last words. "And if your wife and grand friends cast you off in our ruin, return to me. I shall still have enough for both of us."

CHAPTER XIII.

It was dusk when Philip returned to town; but this time he rode on fast, and lingered not on the road. The storm, whose distant coming he had instinctively felt that morning, had burst; and now, with his head erect, and something of the same feeling in his breast which as a boy had made him love to battle with the waves, he prepared to stem the real sea of life under its new aspect.

Totally apart from his sympathy with his uncle, it would not be too much to say that Philip's feeling were happy ones. His existence had hitherto been barren of many deep emotions—for his age, he had had too few struggles with difficulty—all that he had wished for he had won. "Now," he felt, with a thrill of conscious power in himself, "my life begins in earnest. I am Philip Earnscliffe, the author, not Miles Earnscliffe's heir. I must depend upon myself alone, and fight my own battle." And his eye dilated at the thought.

He rode on, and was soon on the streets of London, where the man of fortune, or beggared outcast, become alike, in the immense surge of human life, an unnoticed unit; and Philip thought that everything around seemed altered. The yellow lamps struggling through the dense fog—the confused roar of life in which no one sound predominates—the shops with their gaudy windows and sickly apprentices behind the counter; but, above all, the aspect of his fellow-men about him, struck him differently to what it had all done hundreds of times before. He looked at the miserable beings on the pavement—the common street-beggar, the greasy pickpocket, the black-coated hypocrite with tracts, the drunken lad of seventeen—men, lounging idle and desperate, who should have been, like himself, in the very prime of life—little children with the expression of premature age upon their stolid features, and attempting to extort alms with the whine of already-practised imposture; and, worst of all, girlish faces, where the lingering traces of youth and womanhood were all blurred over with bold vice, or sunken in the approach of a hopeless death. And Philip felt—"And I, with all these fallen beings around me, and the intellect and powers God has given me, how have I fulfilled my mission, or attempted to raise the lot of one fellow-man? By writing books for society, and verses for albums! It is indeed time some shock should come, to rouse me from my wasted existence!"

Then he looked at another class of men; clerks from the city, artists from their studios, professors from their lectures, who were all hurrying to their homes through the dusky streets; and he felt with pride, that he should now be one of them—one of those who work, and in some way contribute to the general good of the world.

The magnificent horse he rode did not seem his own; when he arrived at the door of his house in Park Lane, he felt that it was his home no longer, and almost rejoiced in the thought. "I was born to work," he said, "and all the false advantages of riches and position have been only bars to my success."

He enquired in a cheerful tone for Lady Clara, and, on hearing that she was in the drawing-room, and alone, proceeded at once up-stairs. But the bravest man in the world is not always so in his own household: and every step that Philip ascended, he seemed to feel his courage ebb in an inverse ratio. By the time he reached the first landing, he had painted Clara to himself, in one of her coldest, most cynical moods; and when he got to the drawing-room door, would sooner have announced his fallen fortunes to every acquaintance in London at once, than in this *tête-à-tête* interview to his wife.

He opened the door, and saw her. Not cowering before the fire as usual in the dark; but seated at the table, very erect, very well dressed, and writing; and Philip took this as a bad omen.

Clara had made all her arrangements during his absence, and had had a long conversation with her mother, after which—much against Lady St. Leger's will—it had been decided that she should return that evening to her father's house. Lady St. Leger hated the vulgar *éclat* of such a proceeding, and was also by no means anxious for her daughter's companionship.

"You are acting madly, Clara," she urged, "and will bitterly repent this false step. You say you do not love Philip; well, I suppose you never did, but still he is your husband, and some day will inherit his uncle's fortune. Now, you know that you have no settlements, and therefore, in leaving him, you at once forfeit all chance of benefiting by the old man's death—for it is not likely Philip would ask you to return to him *then* —and besides, all these things are bad in themselves; anything approaching to a scene or publishing her domestic grievances to the world, should be avoided by a woman of good taste. Your husband's talents secure him a place in society, and your position as his wife is far better than it will ever be, as Lord St. Leger's neglected daughter. Young, handsome, and rich, every one will be on his side; and to me falls the ridiculous *rôle* of chaperoning a married daughter—and you really have aged terribly lately—who could not agree with her own husband."

"You may set your mind at rest, mother," answered Clara; "I shall never appear in society, or interfere with you in any way. I only ask a place in your house, instead of living alone; at which the world, I suppose, would cavil, old and plain though I have become. But you seem to overlook, entirely," she added, bitterly, "my reasons for leaving Mr. Earnscliffe."

"Not in the least: and it is that which makes it more absurd. You see your husband at the opera, in the same box with an actress, or dancer, or some person of the kind, and you immediately draw all sorts of conclusions from this trivial circumstance, and then decide upon the grave step of a separation. What can be more natural than for a young man of his age to be led into such society? what more usual? Why, half the wives of London might leave their homes for such a ridiculous cause: and your not caring about Philip, makes it doubly incomprehensible to me, why you should be jealous! If you had gone more into the world, as I advised you from the first, and formed friendships and amusements for yourself, you would have been happy without troubling yourself about his proceedings. Look at me, Clara! do you think I should look as I do now, if I had worried myself at every neglect or indiscretion of my husband as you do? Yet I was much more attached to your father than you are to Philip!"

Clara did look at her mother's still fresh, well-preserved face; and she answered with a compressed lip, "Yes, it would have been far better for me to be like you, but I am not!"

No arguments of Lady St. Leger having prevailed, it was at length decided, much to her annoyance, that she should expect her daughter that evening; and Clara awaited Philip's return, to communicate her intentions to him personally. He remained away so long, however, that she at length thought he would not return for the day, and had just begun a letter to him, when she heard his knock at the door. She felt a momentary tremor at the sound; but quickly recovered her composure and was completely nerved for the approaching scene, when Philip entered the room. The opening of the attack she left to chance, having failed in planning any to her own satisfaction. She had quite resolved he should never know that jealousy of a dancer was the immediate cause of her resolution: and she would therefore be obliged to urge it on the general grounds of his neglect and her indifference.

"Good evening, Clara."

She laid down her pen, and looked at him. He was very pale; and his features were set as though under the influence of some strong emotion.

"He actually cowers before me!" she thought; and, with a scornful half-smile, returned his salutation.

"If she has any of a woman's best nature left, she will soften now," thought Philip; and advancing to her side, he stooped and kissed her forehead. But she turned haughtily from his caress, which to her seemed only a mean attempt at conciliation, and remarked—"You look agitated, Mr. Earnscliffe; to what am I to attribute all this sudden outbreak of affection?"

The chilling tone of these words, and the look that accompanied them, froze back Philip's half-awakened feelings of kindness. He seated himself on the other side of the fire and remained silent, considering how he should best announce his uncle's ruin to his cold, worldly companion.

" I have been to the Oaks to-day, Clara." She did not answer. " My uncle is not well, and is confined to the house ; he made many kind inquiries for you."

" Really, I am greatly indebted to Mr. Earnscliffe. And these kind inquiries you were doubtless able to answer fully, as you know so much of my health and life."

" Oh, Clara ! " said Philip, suddenly looking very full at her as he spoke ; " do not reproach me to-day ; I have had much to bear already."

" Indeed ! May I ask you not to communicate any particulars of your trials to me ? they must be of a nature in which it is impossible for me to have any interest ! " and half-rising towards the light, she looked at her watch.

Philip was stung with this assumption of indifference, and answered—" They are of a nature, Lady Clara, in which you *must* take an interest, and, if not told you by my lips, you will hear them from a hundred others to-morrow."

" Oh ! perhaps your new book—you have been writing one, I believe—is a failure ; if so, the event, of course, is not so serious to the world and to me, as to yourself."

He did not answer : but fixed his eyes—more in sorrow than with a harsher feeling—upon her face for a few seconds.

" It is strange," he said, at length, and as though to himself, " that she should have fixed upon this day as a fitting time to declare her indifference to me." And, even as he spoke, something in the soft tone of his voice thrilled through her heart. But the better feeling soon passed.

" As well this day as another," she returned. " The fact has long been so—why should I conceal it any longer ? As you have thrown off the mask, so may I."

Philip scarcely heard her words. For the second time in his married life, the image of his rough, unpolished uncle rose up brightly before him, compared with that of his highborn wife ; and he remembered how, amidst his own anguish, the old man had still spoken kindly to him.

" Clara," he resumed, " I have no wish to deny any of my errors, or that you have grave cause for complaint. But remember one thing, whatever my conduct has been, my uncle has ever felt kindly towards you ; and even this morning——"

" And what have I to do with Mr. Miles Earnscliffe's kindness ? " she interrupted, haughtily ; " and for what object are you wasting these sentimental speeches upon me ? You mistake me strangely, sir, if you think that I care for your uncle's regard, or his wealth either ! "

" And you mistake *me*," cried Philip, starting to his feet. " You mistake me strangely if you think that for my own sake I am endeavoring to soften a heart like yours. I was preparing to tell you, madam, of the ruin of an honest man. You need sneer no longer at my uncle's wealth—he has lost it. Yes, it is true ; and I, Lady Clara, am no longer the heir you married, but a poor struggling author." And folding his arms, he looked her full in the face.

She turned very pale, and did not answer. For only one second her better nature made her long to fall upon his neck, and return to him in his hour of trial—then the impulse passed. She was incapable of judging a generous nature like Philip's ; she had known none but people steeped in worldliness from her very cradle ; and, in his altered manner, she only saw some selfish project upon her father's wealth. Now, she thought, she could reject him—wound him to the very quick—without betraying her own jealousy, or lowering herself. And with her most cutting smile she remarked—

" Oh ! then this is the cause of your returned affection, Mr. Earnscliffe."

" Hear me, Clara," said Philip, with grave dignity. " Under my fallen prospects, I feel that, in spite of the cold unnatural way in which it has been your choice that we should live together, you are still my wife. You married me under different circumstances, and for your sake, next to his own, I grieve most at my uncle's ruin. You never loved me ; and it may appear hard that your unhappy married life should be deprived also of the prospect of wealth, under which it was undertaken. These considerations, I confess, gave me a return of warmer feelings towards you which you reject ; and if you see in this any subject for ridicule, I can only pity your own hard nature, not be ashamed of my motives."

But Clara only heard his allusion to her marrying him for money, and her eyes flashed fire.

" You do well," she cried, " to remind me, now, in your ruin, of my marriage with you ! You do well to remind me of my motives, now that they are rendered fruitless ! Yes ! I married you, as I thought, to save my father from disgrace—although in that, too, I was mistaken, for I know how you have turned from him in his difficulties. I married you simply and exclusively for money. I never loved you—no—not in the moment when I consented to become your wife. You have heard it all, now ! "

" And I, Lady Clara," replied Philip, stung out of all generosity ; " do you know why I married you ? "

" Tell me," she answered, her blue eyes filled with lurid rage. But even yet he forbore.

" No, madam, I will not ; your mother will do so far better than I can. I will say that, even in my marriage, the most bitterly regretted act of my life, I would not exchange the motives which prompted me for your own."

"Go on, sir," she cried, scarcely knowing what she said; "go on—and tell me that, deluded by my mother's falsehood, you married me from pity. I will hear all that you have to say, and then—then you shall hear me."

"Clara," returned Philip, and he advanced a step towards her, his face softening once more, "still I ask you to forbear. This is not a time for recriminations; now, if ever, we should remember all that we have once vowed to each other. I have erred against you—I have neglected you—and I confess it. Forgive me——return to me—return to me in in my poverty—and forget the first cold year of our married life!" and he held out his hand to his wife.

She recoiled from him, and, with all the expression of concentrated scorn that could be thrown into look and voice, replied, "Stay, sir, do not degrade yourself by any more mean attempts to conciliate me. I understand your object well, and scorn it and you. Hitherto, in your pride of plebeian wealth, you have not cared to court me for my father's money; but now, in your ruin, you—aye, and your uncle too—will both fawn and cringe, and lick the dust before the very woman whom you insulted yesterday with your neglect. Your uncle——"

But Philip's iron grasp upon her arm arrested her. Every gentler feeling was dead for ever in his breast towards her; and his dark eyes kindled again with passion at her taunts.

"Stop, madam," he said, his voice low and ominously calm; "I command you to stop and hear me. You have just uttered thoughts that could only have had birth in the heart of Lord St. Leger's daughter; and you know that your imputation is untrue. As you won, so you discard me—with a falsehood; and it is a worthy ending of our hateful union. My uncle, Lady Clara, and myself, are men of honor, and would both of us sooner starve than accept money which had been tainted by passing through the hands of your father. You can return to him, and to his wealth, at once. From this moment you are no longer my wife, even in the eyes of the world; and the day of my fall from fortune will be the sweetest of my life, as the last of my connection with you!"

They were the harshest words ever spoken by Philip to a woman, and could only have been wrung from him by Clara's insult to his uncle—but his blood was on fire, and he heeded not what he said. Both remained silent for some seconds; then Clara rose.

"Do not think, Mr. Earnscliffe, that you are the first to propose this step," she said. "My arrangements are already made for quitting your house; and my parents are prepared to receive me this evening. Before I heard of your beggary, I had resolved to separate from you for ever, and to leave you to your own course of life, and your own associates. In this case"—she pointed to one on the table—"you will find all the jewels I have received from your uncle or yourself; and if you have any further communications to make to me on business, you will have the goodness to do so through my father's solicitor. And now, I presume, I can leave your house at once. There can be nothing more for you to say, or for me to hear." And she moved towards the door.

"Nothing!" echoed Philip—"nothing. Thank God, no child of mine can call you mother! and that, in this moment, I have no one softer feeling—no duty pleading for you in my heart. Go, madam! return to your parents' house; you are far fitter to be their daughter than the wife of an honest man!" And he turned away, and buried his face between his hands.

In another moment the door closed after her. The carriage, which was ordered to convey her to her father's, was already waiting, and in a quarter of an hour she had left the house, and Philip and his wife were parted for ever.

CHAPTER XIV.

EARNSCLIFFE little knew, at first, the full extent to which his uncle's losses would affect himself. With all the romance of his character, he had pictured his new life as merely freed from the artificial trammels of society, and more like that of his friend Neville's, and had felt a sort of pleasure at the thought. The reality was such as he never dreamed of. All the world had hitherto been on his side on the point of his domestic grievances. Lady Clara, in her gloomy seclusion, had had few supporters; while all—ever her own relations—had smiled on her young, handsome, and rich husband; and had their separation taken place a month earlier, it is probable that every one would have pronounced in Philip's favor. But the news of Miles Earnscliffe's ruin, and of Clara's return to her father's protection, fell on the greedy ear of the world at the same time; and the feeling awakened by the first intelligence greatly influenced the verdict upon the latter.

Philip had so long been the universal favorite—the fashion in London—that people looked upon his fall from wealth as a sort of insult to their own judgment. The failure of Miles Earnscliffe was a thing the probability of which had never been admitted by even the most suspicious; indeed, it was generally believed that the old merchant's fortune had been long withdrawn from the uncertain field of speculation, and vested in

English securities. When, therefore, the sudden news of his ruin was made known, the general feeling towards him was one of pity, but indignation. From unfounded remarks arose reports; these quickly strengthened into facts; and in a few days Miles Earnscliffe was successively pronounced an unprincipled speculator, a man who originally amassed his fortune by fraud, and had now lost it through the discovery of the swindle. For the directors of the Bombay Bank, whose failure had ruined him, were in truth by no means clear from the imputation of dishonor; and the world, merely confounding the sufferer with the delinquent, decreed that old Miles was not only ruined, but infamous!

Philip, it was admitted, had nothing to do with this; but he was a coxcomb, a *parvenu*, and a bad husband; while, by a natural conclusion, Lady Clara was soon elevated to the position of an injured woman, long suffering angel, and a martyr. And Lady St. Leger, who had so strongly opposed her daughter's separation from Philip, was agreeably surprised at suddenly finding herself quite the fashion in consequence of this event.

Clara, however, received the advances of her friends with even more than her accustomed coldness. She would go into no society, and kept as much aloof from her own mother as was possible; above all, she hated to hear her husband's name, or that of his uncle mentioned before her. In her own heart she had felt, after the first burst of passion was over, the falseness of the accusation she had made to Philip. Now that they were actually parted for ever, she began tardily to acknowledge to herself the real nobleness of his character; and—with strange, yet not uncommon inconsistency—half believed she loved her husband, now that it was too late. She remembered his youth—his generosity in marrying her—how unsuited her character, in its utter worldliness, must have been to his own—and she framed a thousand excuses for his love of more congenial society; and even for that last open dereliction which had been the immediate cause of their separation.

In her long sleepless nights she recalled their parting interview, and saw herself harsh, unwomanly, unforgiving; taunting him on his uncle's affliction, and imputing sordid motives to himself, while he had forborne so long, and still tried to reconcile her. She thought of him now, the world turning from him as it should have done from guilt, not misfortune, and her proud, misguided heart—which might have been a gentle and loving one, had she been differently educated—throbbed for Philip in his loneliness, as it had never done in his popularity and success; and often in tears and self-reproach she longed to be at his side. But he never knew this. Clara would have died sooner than reveal to human ear that she repented

her own act; and through all her after-life Philip Earnscliffe never heard again from his wife.

The house in Park Lane was, of course, given up at once, and Philip returned to his uncle's for the present, until the future plans of both should be decided. Miles, though no longer a millionaire, was after all, very far from being a ruined man; and on the proceeds of the sale of this Yorkshire estate, he found that he might still continue to live in his present house—a great consolation to the old man, to whom his home was endeared by all the recollections of Philip's childhood. His tens of thousands had been reduced to hundreds; but he had an income even now, which, although poverty in the eyes of the world, would to his brother Herbert have appeared riches.

"I shall not have to lessen your allowance more than half, Phil," was one of his first remarks after the winding-up of his affairs. But the burning flush which rose in Philip's cheek, as he refused to receive one farthing more in the way of assistance from his uncle, was too sincere a proof of his sentiments for Miles to press the subject.

"I am fully able to work for myself," he answered. "And for my own sake, I am thankful that it is my lot to do so. I abhor the very mention of riches, as I do the people who have cringed to us for them so long." Philip had heard more of the evil reports about his uncle than had come to the old man's own knowledge, and his disgust was consequently bitterer against the world where they were circulated. He shrank with almost morbid sensitiveness from any mention of money; and innocent though he felt himself, conscious of his uncle's entire integrity through his whole lifetime, he yet could not bear to be seen by his old associates, while the imputation of dishonor was upon their name, avoiding even the society of the few friends he possessed, who really sympathised with him in his trial. Poverty would have been nothing to Philip, but the falsehood which was now current in the world was so unexpected a blow, that he staggered and felt powerless under the shock. It was his first great trial, and he felt it with all the keen and passionate grief of youth. But there was still more awaiting him.

His new book was now ready, and he determined that it should come out at once, though his friendly publishers, with a truer knowledge of the world, and a real regard for his interest, entreated him to delay its appearance until another season, or, at least till the present tide of public opinion had somewhat turned. Philip firmly refused to do so. "What have my private affairs to do with my writings?" he argued. "Or how can it affect the merit of a book, that the author has suddenly become a poor man, and that his wife and friends have chosen to leave him! No, it shall appear, and stand or fall upon its own worth. I am sick of success that I have not really won for my-self." And the publishers were forced to comply.

The book did appear, and was a dead failure. Only the few grave and honest critics who had warned the young author of the faults in his second work, acknowledged the real genius and increased powers of his present one, and encouraged him to proceed. The fashionable papers, by one accord, and also many of the literary journals, abused the book without measure. It was stupid, frivolous, impertinent; without talent and without principles; and one evening paper went so far as to say, "The work was only what might have been expected from such a pen, and was literally unfit for a drawing-room table."

Philip read all these criticisms, of course; it was his principal employment to do so in his loneliness and dispppointment; but when he glanced over the one last alluded to, a bitterer expression than usual escaped his lips. He remembered the two columns of fulsome praise upon his second book, which had appeared in this very paper, at the time that he was in the zenith of his popularity—praise which then had disgusted him, from its excess, and total want of discrimination—and contrasted them in his mind with the few lines of malevolent abuse bestowed now upon his last and far superior work. "It is well," thought Earnscliffe, as he laid down the paper. "These gentlemen are doing me a far greater service than even the few kindly critics, who have tried to stem, in my favor, the tide of fashionable opinion. My next book will be one that shall seek its success in the *world*. It shall be written, not for the flimsy praise of May Fair, or the ap-plause of evening papers, but for the people —the working and honest people—of whose wrongs, I will become the advocate, while I expose that society whose leaders have now cast me off." And Philip fulfilled his words.

He took an obscure lodging not far from his friend Neville (for he had a longing to be perfectly alone), and began working with a fervor and perseverance astonishing to the artist, who had hitherto only seen in Philip a gentle, indolent boy, with genius, but scarce-ly ambition enough to become really great. Now, in a few weeks, he seemed transformed into a hard-working, untiring, practical man. H s style altered with his character. It lost the old careless diction, the sunny enthusiasm, the *youthfulness*, which had constituted the peculiar charm of his earlier writings, and became earnest, manly, more forcible. The veins of sarcasm, that merely ran lightly through his first works, and scarcely tinged them, had now grown caustic and bitter, col-oring his whole thoughts. He showed up, with no sparing hand, the vices and foibles of those few hundreds of persons in Belgra-via who call themselves the world, sketching

many a well-known character with a few terse words of ridicule that yet rendered the like-ness to perfection, and were more biting from their brevity. Above all, he laid bare that hideous Mammon-worship which lies at the very heart of English society, making the fairest and first-born among us bow down with smiles before a railway schemer, who has succeeded through dishonesty, or a pro-fligate Eastern monster, whose atrocities are as well known as the number of his lacs of rupees. It was a subject on which Philip felt keenly, and about which—although with some pardonable excess of bitterness, .and slight exaggeration—he wrote well. But it was not one to win back his lost popularity among his former friends. In his second volume he turned to another class of English people, and dwelt eloquently upon the long sufferings, the patient-abidings, the wrongs of the laboring poor, whose masses make up the real bulk of society, and from their ranks the main characters of the story were taken. It was emphatically a book of, and for the people; and not all the critics in London could have prevented its becoming popular. But, if it had appeared with another name, few could have suspected that its author, and the author of the graceful tales and ballads which had adorned so many a silken boudoir was the same.

Neville watched his friend's progress with undisguised pleasure. He had always re-gretted the kind of life into which Philip had been so long drawn by his position; and he would now frequently say, "Ah Phil! the best day in your life was that when your un-cle's smash came, your great friends with-drew, and your wife was good enough to leave you. It was really far better luck than you deserved." Philip always tried to agree with him; but every week he looked more worn and old. Although energetic when under the influence of some strong excite-ment—as was now the case—his tempera-ment was not suited for battling with disap-pointment and rebuffs, like the artist's. He had no natural "genius for plodding," as Neville called it; and while his book pro-ceeded rapidly, he grew paler in his confined lodgings, and sometimes wondered within himself if he really were born for this kind of life, as on the first evening of his changed fortune he had decided.

Meantime, Neville's pictures were finished and sold; and as he had nothing more to detain him in town, his small arrangements were speedily made for his departure to the Continent. Philip went to his lodgings the evening before he was to leave, and found him, as usual, in his close room, his one port-manteau and his painting-box standing pack-ed under the table, and the artist himself seated at the solitary window which over-looked a sultry back street and a greengro-cer's shop, but with a more radiant expres-sion than Philip had ver remarked upon his face among all the glories of a Highland sunset.

"Here you are, Philip!" he cried, gaily, as his friend entered. "I thought I should see you this last evening; and, by Jove! I only wish you were coming away with me tomorrow—that is, of course, if you were as free as I am. I am not much given to bursts of enthusiasm, as you know, but I do feel singularly happy to-day, and should like to think we were to spend the coming summer together, as we did the last."

"You *look* happy," said Philip, as he possessed himself of the artist's other chair, and gazed half enviously at his bright countenance. "The world goes well with you, Neville."

"Yes, I make it do so! It is no surprise at unlooked-for success which makes me in good spirits this evening, but merely a feeling of contentment at finding how things turn out precisely as I intended they should; how singularly we can rule our own destiny! You know how I have slaved for the last seven months upon those pictures; they are now completed and sold exactly at the time I had fixed; and to-day, the thirtieth of June, as I thought, I am sitting for the last time in this room, where I have worked for four uphill years, and am closing the first period in my life. My old easel I have presented to my landlady for firewood; and to-morrow I start (without a regret, Phil, except that I shall not see you again for two years), and shall spend the summer sketching in Switzerland; next winter in Rome."

"Yours is a happier organism than mine," replied Philip. "I should feel a regret at sitting at my window for the last time, and giving up my easel for firewood, after it had been my friend during four years."

Neville laughed aloud. "It is not in my nature to create sorrows," he answered. "I am not a poet, and have no poetic tendencies whatever; and I am happy to think that you are fast losing yours. Just retain as much sentiment as is wanted for the tender part of your books, and discard all the rest from your own life; you will find quite enough to regret in the world, without wasting your sympathies on old easels. By-the-bye, what are Fridoline, and Rose, and all those people about? Have you given them up, as well as the grand world?"

"They at least have not given *me* up," returned Philip. "I have seen little of Fridoline lately; indeed, I have had time for nothing but writing, but I hear she is progressing wonderfully in her profession, and receives an enormous salary at St. James's. You would scarcely believe, Neville, how much feeling some of 'those people' as you call them, showed when I lost my expectations of wealth and my literary reputation at one blow. Celeste, poor thing, shed tears over the criticisms in some of the papers,

which she managed to understand, and Fridoline—"

"And Rose?" interrupted Neville, in his old tone.

"No, Neville, thank you," said Philip, reddening; "we will not broach that subject if you please. You know that I am not a fit person to listen to Rose Elmslie's detractors; and also that I have too few illusions left to be desirous of sacrificing any more. Against my own senses, I shall retain my former opinion of Rose, and therefore would rather not speak to her of you."

"Well, taking that view of it, you are acting rightly," returned Neville. "Like the nobleman who paid his valet three hundred a year to cheat him openly, you say to yourself that you are a happy man, and shut your eyes when you see Rose driving in Count B——'s pony carriage. How far have you advanced in your book?"

"Oh! it is half finished. In a month I shall go off to the seaside, and complete it there, for I am actually ill in this hot, close air of London. It will be published by next winter, and I will write and tell you of its success—ill or good."

"Do so. No one will be more interested in it than myself, and I shall be delighted if you would join me in Italy afterwards."

"I shall like it extremely if I were able, but—"

"Well, I don't see what there is to keep you in England. You say you hate parties and theatres now. Your wife is certainly no longer the attraction: surely you will not begin writing another book directly. It would be much better for you to give your brain a rest, and come to Italy for a stock of new ideas. I am positive the artist-life in Rome would suit us both."

"Yes—" said Philip, hesitating. "It would be very pleasant; but you see I have ties to England. My uncle is an old man, and has none belonging to him but me; for his sake I feel myself in some measure bound—"

"A convenient excuse!" exclaimed Neville. "I wish it were the real reason. However, the longest road has some turning, and I am sure your present weakness cannot be eternal. When that is over, you will find that you can make up your mind to leave your excellent uncle for a year, or even two, without the separation breaking anybody's heart!"

"But you forget that I am a poor man now. It is an expensive thing travelling in Italy."

"Oh you always talk as though you were actual beggars, when at this moment Mr. Miles continues to live in a house I consider a palace, and you have nearly finished a new novel, for which you will have six or seven hundred pounds, at least."

"Or half, or a quarter the sum," interrupted Philip. "After my last dead failure publishers will be rather shy of offering to purchase my works."

"Then publish on your own account; your new book must succeed."

They talked together until past midnight. Then Philip, after a hearty farewell, took his leave; and by five o'clock next morning Neville was driving along through the interminable streets leading to St. Katherine's Wharf, where he embarked for Rotterdam.

Philip felt a heavy sense of loneliness when he was gone. He missed Neville's cheerful face more than he had expected—his friendlessness oppressed him. There were long weary hours when his brain refused to work, and his eyes were hot and heavy; and then he longed most for youthful companionship, and so gradually took refuge more and more in the society of poor Rose. She was always ready to smile upon him. Without much real depth of feeling, the innocence of her country life gave her a tone unlike other women of her class—she was gentle, often sad; for the sentiment she really bore to Philip (the only approach to a true one in her whole existence) made her at times hate herself and her life, and when she was with him her eyes would fill with tears, and her voice tremble. In an hour after he had left, the momentary impulse was gone; and in the society of Count B——, or at the gay suppers after the ballet, Rose was again the light, reckless, high-spirited actress. But while her softer mood was upon her (and that was as he always saw her) it gave her a charm in Philip's eyes greater even than her beauty, and every day this fascination increased.

Still, Earnscliffe did not love her. There was something within him which instinctively made him shrink from loving any woman in her position. His naturally refined taste, and poetic notions about what woman should be, had made him from his boyhood feel differently to other young men on such subjects; and he knew that the moment in which he was *forced* to see Rose as she really was, he would leave her for ever. But, in the meantime, her beauty attracted him irresistibly. Amid his desolation and disappointment, he would gaze on her sweet young face, and listen to her low voice, and try to persuade himself that his Egeria was really found. While still, in his own heart, he knew that it was a false one.

CHAPTER XV.

Towards the middle of October Philip's book was finished. He had spent the summer at a quiet watering-place on the south coast, accompanied by his uncle, who seemed unwilling to part with him for a single week. The loss of his property had strangely softened the hard character of Miles. Nothing now gave him such pleasure as to walk up and down on the beach, listening to the waves, and watching the children who played with them, and gathered treasures by their side; or in stormy weather to sit at the window, which overlooked the sea, and gaze out at the scene before him. He would remain thus for hours patiently, while Philip was writing in another part of the room, not speaking for fear of interrupting him, and seeking no employment for himself; but when Philip at length, would say—"Now, sir, I have done work for to-day," the old man's face grew bright in a second; and when his nephew came and sat by him to read aloud something he had written, or talk over old times, he was happy for the remainder of the evening.

Philip was glad to see his uncle in this altered state of mind, but to himself the quiet monotony of their days was often galling. In the prime of youth and energy, he longed to cast himself again into the throng of life, and, by some new and brilliant success, wipe out the remembrance of his failure, and the stigma upon his uncle's name. It is only after a certain age, that solitude can be welcome in grief and disappointment; it is never so in youth. After the first blow, the first shrinking from the world is over, the natural reaction must always be to face the struggle again, and win back the lost object, or forget it in the pursuit of a fresh desire.

They returned to Miles's house in November, and in due time the book appeared; but neither of his earlier productions had met with success such as awaited this one. Philip was himself astonished at it. Edition after edition was called for, and in a few months Philip found his popularity established upon a far surer base than it had ever been before—the general good opinion of the middle classes. He had become one of the favorite writers of the day. Still, he felt in his own heart that the first pleasure in success was gone. He had fulfilled his desire of brilliantly effacing his literary failure; and the fickle voice of the public had already recanted, under the influence of his new triumph, the former base reports about old Miles; but the zest—the freshness of life was over. He did not doubt the sincerity of his friends, but he wished to be free from them and the whole world. Having achieved the victory, he cared not to wear the laurels; and he began seriously to think of joining Neville, or, at least, of going abroad for a time. He had often wished to visit the wild parts of western France—where the artist had once spent some months, and which he had described, in all its savage loneliness, to Philip—and he now thought he would like to spend the summer in accomplishing this, and afterwards go to Rome for the winter. The extraordinary success of his last work had supplied him amply with means for travelling, and he felt that a long rest and perfect change would be necessary for his over-worked brain, before writing again.

Only two objections weighed against this project: the first was leaving his uncle. The delight of Miles at his newly-arisen fame was far greater than his own. It had cheered the old man more than anything that had occurred since his own losses; and the first tears Philip had ever seen him shed, glistened in his eyes as he read over the different criticisms upon his boy's book. He thought Philip would now be contented and happy, and willing to live quietly with him, as in his young days; and when one day he distantly hinted at his idea of going abroad for a year or two, the look of bitter disappointment which crossed his uncle's face, touched Philip deeply, and he resolved to say no more on the subject. But when, day by day, he still looked paler, while his spirits did not improve, Miles himself began to think it might be really well for him to have a change of scene for awhile; and striving to forget what his own loneliness would be without him, he at length told Philip he thought it would be better that he should go abroad—for the summer, at least. And Philip, not realising to the full the sacrifice these words cost Miles, felt glad that the old man was reconciled to parting with him, and that only one more inducement to remain in England still existed. This inducement, however, was a strong one; and Philip had wavered again and again before he could resolve upon going abroad, when a circumstance occurred, which, although trivial in itself, had the effect of disenchanting him for ever with his last illusion (as he termed his feeling towards Rose when speaking of it to the artist), and indirectly influenced much of Philip's after-life.

One bright spring morning he went, at his usual hour, to call on Miss Elmslie. She was always glad to see him; but he thought he detected on this occasion a slight embarrassment in her manner when he entered, although she strove hard to conceal it. She was seated at an embossed and gaily-colored writing-table, near one of the windows, and, immediately closing the portfolio before her, she rose to meet Philip—not however, before a glance had shown him that she was writing one of her familiar little pink-colored notes, which, from another opened envelope and note by its side, appeared to be in answer to one just received.

"I am interrupting you, Rose," he remarked; "were you writing to me—par hazard?"

"Oh, no! how could I possibly have anything worth saying to you? I was merely writing to my milliner. Tiresome creature! my new dress for to-morrow is hideous, and there is scarcely time to make me a new one. Where will you sit? this horrid sun has nearly blinded me!" and closing the curtains, she threw herself into a chair, with her back to the light. "Tell me what you have been doing this last age."

Philip thought her manner somewhat forced, but replied quickly—"I am glad you consider three days an age, Rose! however, it is not my fault that I did not see you yesterday. I called, and you were engaged. Are you really growing so artificial"—he went on—"as to call this bright sun horrid? After all the winter fog, and the yellow glare of gaslight, I should have thought you would like the return of spring."

"Ah, that is where it is!" she replied, with a pretty sigh. "I am so accustomed to the false glare, as you call it, of my gaslit life, that I am losing my pleasure in all old things. The sunshine makes me miserable, and I hate the smell of violets, which they are selling in the streets; you know, until I was fourteen I lived in a country village, and I think I would rather never be reminded of my early life. But you have not seen me in the new ballet; and I am perfect in it. Do you know the whole thing was composed expressly for me, and they say the last flying scene is my chef d' œuvre, and little C—— is mad with jealousy at my success!"

"I do not go much to the opera now," replied Philip. "And, besides that, you know that I do not care to see you dance. I like to think of you as you are now, Rose—quiet and lovely, and with me—not gazed at, and commented on by half the men in London in your stage dress. In fact," he continued warmly, "I hate ballets; I have hated them ever since I knew you. I cannot bear to think of you continuing this public kind of life for years. Do you think you could be happy if you gave up the stage, Rose—could content yourself with the quiet, every-day happiness of an ordinary woman?" He seated himself by her side, looking very earnestly in her face, as though reading her reply more on her features than in her words.

Miss Elmslie's color came and went. There was something in Philip's manner which actually made her own heart beat a little, and, under the impulse of the moment, she would have gladly given up her beauty, success, admiration—all that constituted the sum of her existence—to be once more innocent, and able really to love, and be loved by, a man like Philip Earnscliffe. At least, she thought so.

"Give up my profession!" she replied, averting her face. "Oh, it is too late! I have nothing to return to now—I have no friends, no relations—and without something to fill my heart and time, I should soon weary of quiet, and only long the more to return to the excitement and forgetfulness of my present life—and it *is* delightful to be so much admired! But," she continued, softly, and this time she was really not acting when large tears filled her eyes, "if I had earlier met some one to care for me, to warn me of the dangers of my position, and save me, I should have hated to be a dancer—now it is too late!"

"Rose," began Philip, in a low, grave voice, "it can never be too late."

She shook her head; but he persisted. He, too, was carried away by impulse—the girl's beautiful face, and touching contrite manner had never so affected him before; he began talking about a quiet cottage in the country, and a life apart from the whole world; and, Heaven knows to what further extent Philip was about to commit himself, when, at that moment, a discreet knock came at the door of the room, and immediately afterwards, his guardian angel—in the shape of Miss Elmslie's very diminutive page—entered.

"Please, ma'am, is the note ready?" said the child—he ought to have been better trained, but Rose had only had him a few days in her service, the former boy having outgrown the fairy-like dimensions of her carriage. "The Count's groom says he has got so many ladies to call on this morning, he thinks he can't wait any longer."

Her face turned crimson with mingled shame and anger at the boy's stupidity, and Philip, with the feeling of one who has been rudely awakened out of a pleasant slumber over the brink of a precipice, rose to his feet.

"Tell him," stammered Rose, "to wait—I mean there is no answer—no—I will send one—in the course of the day."

The page withdrew, to comment on his mistress's odd manner and the young gentleman's face to the Count's groom, and left Rose and Philip once more alone. But in those few moments an immense space of time seemed to have elapsed. She was the first to speak.

"It is nothing," she hesitated, "only an answer to an invitation—Count B——, you know—" Philip said nothing—"has a party to-night—only a musical party, I believe—and—and—he wished me to join—Celeste will be there—and—but I shall not go," she added, glancing at his face.

"And you were doubtless writing a refusal when I came in," answered Philip. "Or did you say *that* was to your milliner?"

"It really was, I assure you."

"Let me see it."

"Do you not believe me?"

"Let me see it."

"Oh, you are too hard upon me," she answered, and burst into tears.

It was her best move. Philip never could stand the sight of tears, and his tone softened.

"Let me see your reply," he said, again; "I have surely a right to require that."

She rose very slowly, and after visible hesitation, drew a little key from her watch-chain, and prepared to unlock the case.

"Do not ask me," she said, once more, as she paused irresolutely, her head bent down, and her slight figure leaning in an attitude of excessive grace against the writing table.

Philip's eyes were intently fixed upon her, and she was so lovely at that moment, that he could scarcely feel angry with her for anything; but he answered——

"You have deceived me, Rose; however, as you object to it, I do not ask to see the note. You have a right to keep your own counsel. For the future, I will not attempt to interfere——"

She flew to his side. "I have deceived you!" she cried, her cheeks burning brightly, and her eyes swimming. "I have deceived you—and I confess it! I told you I was writing to the milliner when you came in because, I knew you would think me wrong to go to a party at Count B——'s; but I really was to go with Celeste, and we both meant to come away early—I am so sorry now—so truly sorry—only let me write a refusal to that horrid man, and—forgive me!"

As Philip had told Neville, he had too few youthful illusions left for him to be willing to part with any of those which still lingered; and with Rose's imploring eyes and flushed cheeks before him, it must not be greatly wondered at that he did forgive her. He saw the note written and sent, and tried to believe that she had accepted the invitation at first merely through her childish love of gaiety. They were reconciled at once; and Rose made faint attempts to renew their former conversation; but Earnscliffe could not at once get over the shock of this little incident. Count B——'s shadow had darkened the prospect of a country cottage, and he left Miss Elmslie's house in an hour's time without having returned to the subject which had, so happily for himself, been interrupted.

"Come to-morrow, and you will see how fresh I look after my early hours to-night!" were her last words as her hand trembled in his at parting.

CHAPTER XVI.

PHILIP felt in an unsettled mood after he left Rose. He had no particular engagement for the day; and when he had looked in at his club, and wandered about the streets for a time, he grew weary, and directed his steps homeward. The whole of this time his mind was dwelling on the occurrence of the morning.

"Is it possible, after all, that Neville was

indeed right?" he thought. "And is she—
not merely light and childish—but false?
She deceived me so coolly about the invitation, when she first saw me, and then afterwards—still, I suppose if Celeste is to be at this party Rose might think it a fit one for her too—poor child! He must invite a different class of guests now, by the way, for Celeste never used to go to such houses as Count B——'s!" He paused. "I wonder if Celeste *is* going to-night, after all?"

This doubt once awakened, Philip could not rest till it was satisfied. He turned his steps at once in the opposite direction, and an hour afterwards was seated in Celeste's drawing-room—all perfume, and *ormolo*, and rose-colored light —and listening to the lively little Frenchwoman's affectionate greeting, until he almost forgot the object of his visit. She had not seen much of "*ce cher Philippe*" lately, and was enchanted to be able to talk over his recent success.

"At length they begin to appreciate you," she exclaimed in French, as she made him take a seat beside her, on her dainty satin sofa. "These monsters! You will be one of the first writers of the day—indeed you are so already—you are immortal, and I—in my humble insignificance—I shall always retain the happiness of feeling that I was one of the very first to recognise your young genius, and to give you my small encouragement." Poor Celeste! she quite thought that her little supper-parties had some way or another assisted Philip in the literary world.

"And I," returned Earnscliffe, kindly, "shall always gratefully remember your zeal and warm sympathy with me in my failure. I have many to congratulate me now; but you were one of the few who stood by me through everything."

Her eyes softened. "Ah, Philip! you have a long and brilliant career in store for you," she cried: "and in your celebrity and your active life, you will have no time to think of old days. But I shall not forget you. As Fridoline says, you are the only man in the world with whom one can forget that one is an actress; and, you know, it is pleasant sometimes to think that we belong to the same humanity as your own sisters and wives. Poor little Fridoline!" she continued; "do you not think she has been looking pale of late?"

Philip, with some feeling of compunction, was obliged to confess that he had not seen her for a long time; he had been so fully occupied.

"Yes," interrupted Celeste, "I know all about that. But your book has long been published, and your present occupation is not of a nature worthy enough to make you forget your old friends; and Fridoline and I both used to consider ourselves among the number."

Philip was silent. Something in Celeste's tone struck him as more than mere wounded vanity, or feminine jealousy, and it reminded

him of the object of his visit. He shrank, however, from approaching the subject; and, after a short kind of laugh, went on inquiring for Fridoline.

"I shall never understand that girl," replied Celeste. "Her whole life is a perfect mystery. She works on, as I never could, at her profession; she improves wonderfully, and receives—*mon Dieu, quel salaire!* yet I believe every day she hates the stage more and more. Her greatest triumphs only give her a gloomy, unnatural pleasure, which arises neither from gratified vanity, nor any other feeling that I can understand; and, with all her money, would you believe that, instead of buying toilettes, or ornaments, or a carriage, or giving parties, she still lives in that dull old cottage, with her one servant and her beasts, and will not spend a shilling on a cab in rainy weather? And yet she is no miser; for she will give freely to any unfortunate being she meets in the streets. She goes nowhere but to the theatre, and to see me; in short, as I said, her life and herself are mysteries!"

"You know more about her than any one, Celeste. What do you really think is her early history? for, of course, little Fridoline did not actually drop from the clouds, when she first appeared in London?"

Celeste shook her head. "I know nothing—or next to nothing," she replied. "Fridoline is like a child in telling me all the incidents of her present life; but, if anything happens to lead her towards the past, she becomes suddenly silent and confused, and evidently shuns the subject. Two things I *do* know," she added, hesitatingly, "and certainly I would confide them to no one but yourself; however, I know you are so unlike most of the world, that, if I told you, her secret as far as it goes would be safe, and also that you would not judge Fridoline by mere appearance."

"And these circumstances?"

"Well, they are these." Celeste drew a little closer, and lowered her voice. "The first, perhaps, you may think unimportant; Fridoline, though she always speaks of herself as an orphan, has a mother living, and not very far distant. This I know for certain; for when she was ill and delirious——"

"And you nursed her, Celeste."

"She more than once spoke of her mother, wildly and mournfully, but in terms which showed that she had only lately parted from her. The second clue is dark, and to me incomprehensible; and often and often I have thought over it, and vainly tried to connect the circumstance, I am about to tell you, with Fridoline as she now is. You shall, however, judge for yourself. When Fridoline had been in London some months, she chanced one day to be sitting with me when an old friend of mine from Paris—a relation of my own, in fact, who had just arrived in England—came in unexpectedly.

The moment he saw Fridoline I was sure he recognised her, and his surprise was unequivocal; while she, on the other hand, bowed when I introduced them, with the perfect *sang froid* and unconcern of a stranger, and soon afterwards rose and took leave. The door had scarcely closed when my relation exclaimed, ' Where, in Heaven's name, did you pick up that girl? '

" ' I do not know what you mean by picking up,' I replied. ' She is Mademoiselle Fridoline, the most rising actress in London, and a particular friend of my own.'

" ' Oh ! ' returned my cousin ; ' so that is little Fridoline. Well, I am glad you like her, and perhaps you can tell me something about her past history.'

" I was obliged to confess that I could not, as there was considerable mystery attached to Fridoline, and it was not even known to what country she belonged.

" ' Then,' he answered, ' I can give you some slight information on the subject,—at all events, of her life in Paris.'

" ' I never knew she had been there,' said I.'

" My cousin smiled. ' My apartment at home,' continued he, ' happens to face the house of a certain Russian prince '—he told me his name, but it was so hard and hideous that I have forgotten it—' and sometimes, when I am tired after my day's work, I amuse myself a little by watching the visitors of my princely *vis-à-vis*. As to the men, I have seen, of course, English lords, French peers, German princes, by dozens, enter the hotel ; but the women, bah ! all of one class, and the worst.'

" ' Go on,' I said, impatiently. ' What has all this to do with Fridoline? '

" ' Well, only this. That on three different occasions last winter (and she may have been there scores of times before) I saw that girl descend from a fiacre, towards dusk, and enter the Hotel Danon.'

" ' Impossible ! ' I cried.

" ' But I would swear to it,' he answered. ' Her's is not a face to forget. Twice, certainly, I only saw her from my window, and I grant that I might have been mistaken ; on the third occasion, however, I happened to be passing the porte-cochère of the hotel exactly as she was entering, and the light falling full upon her face, I saw her as plainly as I do you now, and she and your friend are the same.'

" His manner was so odiously positive, that I was convinced of his truth in spite of myself ; but I tried to account for the occurrence, by observing that, allowing it was true he had seen her, Fridoline might have some humble friend among the prince's dependants whom she went to visit.

" ' Wrong, madam,' he replied (I hated him for his coolness) ; ' this young person did not stop at the Hotel Danon to visit any humble dependant, as I will show you. After my rencontre with her I returned to my apartment, and as it was a fine winter evening, I seated myself for awhile at the window and began watching the passers-by, and the opposite house ; but certainly not thinking of the young girl who had just entered it. I had a particularly good view of the interior of one magnificent salon, the curtains and blinds of which were still unclosed, and, as the twilight was deepening and the room lighted by a blazing wood-fire, I could discern all the objects within with perfect distinctness. My eyes had not been long fixed upon this window, when a figure, crossing before the fire-place, arrested my attention ; it crossed and re-crossed, evidently pacing up and down the room, and I at once recognised our little friend of the fiacre. She had removed her bonnet and shawl, so that I could remark the extraordinary quantity of fair hair which fell round her neck and shoulders, and this, together with her small figure, gave a childishness of appearance that, seeing her in such a place, made me pity her. She was apparently waiting for some one, and in a state of the greatest agitation, her hands clasped together upon her bosom, her head bent down as she walked. It struck me at once she was some young girl who had been seduced by the prince, but of whom he had afterwards tired, and that she had now come to make a last appeal, to his honor or generosity. And this conviction was subsequently strengthened by the fact that I never again observed her enter the hotel. Well, after about ten minutes' waiting, I saw her suddenly stop in her hurried walk, and another figure entered and crossed the room towards her. For a moment the girl seemed to hesitate and shrink back ; then she raised her head, and, stretching out her arms, fell upon the neck of her companion, in a long and apparently passionate embrace. After this, the two figures moved away to a darker part of the room, and I saw no more of them, for in a few moments an attendant entered and closed the curtains. I cannot be actually positive that the other person was the prince, it was about his height, and in my opinion it was he ; but I could swear in a court of justice that the young girl I saw that night in the Hotel Danon and your friend are the same.'

" I hated my cousin," proceeded Celeste, " for his story, and told him so. However, this did not prevent me from being convinced of the truth of what he said. He is a matter-of-fact person, this cousin of mine, a Paris advocate, and not likely to be deceived by imagination. But how deeply it grieved me I cannot tell you. For a time Fridoline's austere life seemed to me only hypocrisy—with her cottage, and her flowers, and her pets, after the life she must have led in Paris—and I could have hated her for her pretended innocence. However, perhaps I was to blame. The recollection of my cousin's story gradually wore off, and at last I have ceased to think of it; or rather, I am now convinced that, if Fridoline would, she might explain away this occurrence, mysterious though it appears."

"And did you never give any hint to show that you were acquainted with something of her history, and thus lead her to speak of it herself?"

"Oh, no," answered Celeste, with true delicacy, which might have done credit to a duchess. "As *she* wished to conceal her past life, I could not let her know that I had become possessed of any clue to it. I have never even asked her if she has seen Paris."

Philip felt strangely depressed by what he had heard. Though far from believing to the full the evil that had been reported of Fridoline, he was now forced to doubt her; and it seemed to him that he was just beginning to discover the falseness of every human being he had ever liked or admired. This thought naturally led him back to Rose, and the immediate object of his visit; and, after a pause, he remarked, with an air of assumed indifference, "Well, Celeste, I must confess I have left off attempting to understand any of your sex. One after another all my early prejudices are vanishing."

The actress opened her great black eyes. "(So, he has found Rose out!) I hope you do not mean that I am changed?" she added, aloud.

"No—" replied Philip, "but you have certainly altered in some things: for instance, a year ago I don't think you would have gone to one of Count B——'s supper parties."

"Count B——'s supper parties! I enter Count B——'s house!" cried Celeste, in a burst of outraged innocence. "And who tell you dat I go near dat monstre? I enter into his house!" In her indignation she tried to talk English.

"Don't be angry, Celeste," said Philip, but his own cheek was very red; "I was told that you were to be at his house to-night, and I believed it. Forgive me."

"Mon Dieu!" said Celeste, resuming her own language, "what could induce people to invent such wicked scancal? I, who am so exacting in my tastes, who unite under my roof all that is worthy and distinguished—I go to one of Count B——'s disgraceful parties, with chorus singers and such people! No, Mr. Earnscliffe, that is not the society I frequent; and I did not think so old a friend as yourself would have believed such infamies."

At another time Philip might have been amused at Celeste's excessive tone of injury; but he was too much taken up with other thoughts to heed it now.

"I beg your pardon," he said, rising to take leave. "I little thought of offending you when I made the remark. I am out of spirits, and scarcely know what I am talking about this morning."

Celeste's anger was short-lived; and as she held his hand at parting, she looked very full in his face, and said, "Pauvre ami! I believe I understand your feelings far better than you do yourself."

The rest of the day lagged wearily to Philip. Proofs of Rose's treachery seemed to confirm all that Neville had ever said of her, and once or twice he thought: "It would have been better to let her accept Count B——'s invitation, and break with her at once. Rose is not the first that has been false to me, and I could go abroad and forget her." But then, again, her young face in its sorrow for her fault arose before him! He could not believe her to be worse than childish, and almost longed to rush to her house and ask her forgive to him for his suspicions. Philip's own nature was so frank, that he shrank with actual pain from the idea of being deceived; and he turned away from any thought of another's unworthiness, until it had strengthened into certainty. Confiding, sensitive, and withal somewhat indolent, he was exactly a man to be deceived, not once, but dozens of times in his life, and Rose, with her beauty, and guileless manner, was just the kind of woman most likely to deceive him.

He dined at his club, and spent the evening there with two or three old acquaintances. One of them had just returned from Italy, and having seen Neville in Rome, had much to tell Philip about his friend, whose genius and cool eccentricity were creating quite a sensation among the English in the Eternal City.

"From some caprice," he said, "people want Neville to be the fashion, and a lion; but it won't do. He says he has gone to Italy to work, and refuses nearly all invitations. Some fair Roman, I was told, even fell in love with his bronzed face (he looks like a Spaniard after all his wanderings), and contrived to let him know the tender nature of her feelings, but his answer was characteristic,—

"'Signora, I have no time!'

"Yet there was nothing churlish or selfish about Neville; on the contrary, he is one of the best fellows in the world. One object, one desire, has taken hold of him, and he can never lose sight of it, or be drawn away by pleasure either of the soul or senses. He will be a great artist!"

Philip asked if he had done any large pictures lately.

"No, he was only studying, spending the entire days in the different galleries, and in fine weather sketching in the Campagna or among the ruins round Rome. He seems thoroughly happy, your friend Neville, and told me he hoped you would join him by next winter."

"Perhaps I may," returned Philip. "I am very undecided at present, whether to go abroad for a year or two or not."

The conversation now turned into other channels; and about twelve o'clock Philip started to walk home. It was warm and starlight, and he enjoyed the beauty of the night in the quiet, undisturbed streets. He sauntered along slowly, but when he had nearly reached his own lodging, a sudden fancy made him wish to extend his walk, and scarcely heeding which way he took, he went on towards the Regent's Park. He felt calmed by the influence of the stillness around, and his mind recovering its usual frame, he thought less about Rose Elmslie than he had done all day. Gradually he fell into one of his old reveries, and walked on and on, entirely lost in himself, and thinking of his starlight walks at Harrow, and the boyish poetic dreams which *then* filled his heart, until he was suddenly aroused by loud bursts of laughter, and a stream of light across his path. He looked up, and to his surprise became conscious that he was exactly opposite Count B——'s villa. The occurrence was purely accidental. Philip was incapable of attempting to watch the movements of Rose, even had he still doubted her; and when he discovered where he was, his first impulse was either to pass the house quickly, or retrace his steps homewards. Some after-thought, however—perhaps one of those unaccountable presages of evil which every one must so often have experienced in his own life—made him pause.

" I shall go home happier," he thought, " when I have seen the kind of a party from which I saved poor little Rose ! ".

But he had a nervous feeling all the same. The party was now at its height; and, to admit cool air to the heated revellers within, the curtains were withdrawn, and the windows on the ground-floor thrown wide open, so that where Philip stood he had a full view, through the shrubs in front of the house, of the interior of the supper-room. It was brilliantly lit up with groups of wax-lights, wreathed round with artificial flowers, and the night air was laden with the scents of costly viands, and wines, and perfumes. But this voluptuous refinement was confined only to the externals of the feast; the peals of laughter, and the tawdry theatrical dress of the female part of the guests, left no doubt about the class to which they belonged. The men seemed mostly friends and associates of Count B——'s, gamblers, *gentlemen*, swindlers, and doubtful foreign noblemen.

The uproarious merriment waxed louder and stronger, when suddenly, amidst those bold laughs and coarse jests, a sweet young voice smote on Philip's ear, and made him turn pale. He took hold of the iron rail by which he was standing, and listened. Again and again he heard it, clear and joyous, the voice of Rose; and, with a desperate resolution, Philip resolved to stop, and know all.

Changing his position slightly, he saw her at the head of the table, on Count B——'s right hand, flushed and animated, and lovlier than ever. She was dressed in a little ballet-looking pink dress, her exquisite arms bare almost to her shoulder, and glittering with gems and bracelets, and a bouquet of white roses (the same which Philip had that day given her) in her bosom. There was not the slightest shade upon her features; she looked as she felt, radiantly happy, in her beauty and her jewels, and the admiration she awakened, and forgetful of that morning, and everything else besides. Count B——, evidently under the influence of his own champagne, was talking to her in low whispers, his arm over the back of her chair, and his eyes fixed upon her face. The rest of the guests were too fully occupied with themselves to observe them much; but Philip noted his earnest manner, and her low answers and averted eyes—noted them, as Lady Clara had once done before, when he, not Count B——, was the recipient of her smiles and blushes, and, whatever Clara had then felt, she was certainly avenged at the moment.

Philip's of course was not the anguish of a boy robbed of the first pure love, or of a man suddenly awakening to a knowledge of his own dishonor. Rose had never been anything but a dancer; and there was, perhaps, in this last discovery of her true character, nothing to be wounded but Philip's vanity. Still, amidst his disappointments, his own fancy had raised her to the place which should have been held by a worthier object. He had believed her erring—never lost; and now, as he saw her in an atmosphere whose very breath was corruption, surrounded by women from the lowest grades of her own profession, and receiving with smiles the whispered flatteries of a world-hardened sensualist like Count B——, a sense of mingled disgust and regret came over him, which, without being agony, was very bitter.

Suddenly there was a pause; and the Count, striking on the table, announced to his guests that Miss Elmslie was going to sing. Rose had a very sweet voice, and had often sung to Philip when he was weary and miserable.

" Bravo ! " cried a pale young Frenchman opposite her. " A song from la belle Rose! Attention ! " And every one listened.

" What shall I sing ? " said Rose.

Several songs were proposed, but she turned to Count B——, as though appealing to his preference.

At first he scarcely understood her, then mentioned, as it chanced, a favorite ballad of Philip's, and the one she had oftenest sung to him. He saw her face change a little.

" Not that," she said : " any but that."

" And why not ? " returned the Count; " if I wish it, why not that ? "

" I have forgotten it," pleaded Rose.

" But I have it," he went on with the pertinacity of a half-sober man ; and then he whispered to her something which made her smile.

"Well," cried Rose; "if I must; but give me some champagne first, my lips are too dry too sing."

He poured her out half a tumbler-full, and she drank it off, and began. Her voice faltered at first, then steadied; and except that it was louder and less modulated than usual, she went through the song well.

Philip heard her till she had finished—listened to the loud applause that followed—watching her smiling thanks, and Count B——'s low praises and increasing warmth of manner; and then he turned away homeward. He had seen enough. He walked about a hundred yards away from the house, until the last faint sounds of the distant revel had died away, then he stopped. His arms were folded, and the dim light of the stars fell full upon his grave face.

"And among such people," he exclaimed, "I have spent my existence! and to that very woman I was this morning ready to give my love, and even, in some measure, bind my future life. Good God! what a fool I have been! and how have I wasted all my hopes and energies! Well, the last illusion is over now; this little dancer has brought the finishing stroke to my belief in any human being, and I am free. Yes," he went on, passionately; "as free as a man without an affection or tie of life can be. It is all the same—fortune, friends, wife, mistress—all faithless!"

The next day he left England.

CHAPTER XVII.

WHEN Philip awoke on the following morning after his arrival at Kersaint, the sun was shining brightly into his room. For a few seconds, he could not remember where he was, or disengage his adventures of the evening from the dreams of the night—dreams in which, it must be confessed, Marguerite had still held a prominent place. Gradually, however, his full consciousness returned; he recalled the quaint furniture of his sleeping-room, and the murmuring of the sea without, and he rose and began to dress.

His toilet was just finished, when he heard a merry young voice immediately under his window, in conversation with another, whose high, loud tones he soon recognised as those of Manon; and drawing back the old-fashioned bolt of the casement, Philip opened it, and looked out.

It was a sweet May morning; every trace of the storm of yesterday had disappeared and only left the grass and trees more brightly green than before. The air came in fresh from the sea, which Philip now saw at the bottom of the garden, blue and sparkling, but still bearing small crested waves upon its bosom. The sea-gulls were floating happily among them, or skimming towards their nests among the rocks; the pigeons wheeled in circuits round the manoir, their varied colors gleaming as they flew in the red morning sun: and a perfect chorus of blackbirds and thrushes arose from the orchard, which, thick with pink blossoms, lay on the left side of the garden. The white sails of some fishing-boats, making their way up the Channel before the western breeze, and the tolling of a very distant church bell, were all that belonged to humanity in the scene, until Philip, leaning somewhat through the open window, looked down; and he then saw his little friend of the previous evening and Manon—both so intent, however, in watching the damages done by the rain to some of the garden flowers, that for the last few seconds they had been quite silent.

Philip gazed at Marguerite intently; and, if he had thought her lovely the evening before, his admiration now was enhanced tenfold. She had been for an hour or more in the open air, and her cheeks were in a perfect glow of health and freshness; her long hair—rather disordered, for she never wore a bonnet in the garden—hung about her face, and caught a thousand wavy reflections in the sunshine; her full, graceful figure showed to perfection in a close-fitting holland dress; and, as she held it high out of the damp gravel—an unnecessary precaution, for it was already short enough—Philip remarked that not even the thick country-made shoes could conceal the symmetry of her little feet. In one hand she held a bouquet of such flowers as the rain had spared; and Manon's basket of parsley and salads showed that they had already visited the kitchen garden.

"Do you think he will be very late?" cried Marguerite, suddenly.

"The English monsieur?"

"Yes, of course."

"I hope so, poor gentleman! after such a wetting as he had yesterday, there is nothing like a long night's rest. I remember once, when I was a girl—it will be just six-and-thirty years next All-hallows—my father was returning from Quimper, one stormy night, and——"

"Yes, good Manon," interrupted Marguerite, "I remember all about it; and he was *not* drowned, you know. How disappointing it is," she resumed, to herself, "to think that he will not be down for hours, perhaps! and I was up and dressed before five, in case he should wake early and want to see the garden. I hope the curtains of his room are not drawn, and then the sun may shine in, and wake him. Let us see!" and, running back a step or two, Marguerite looked up.

There—leaning forward, so that he must have overheard every word she said—was the stranger. He bowed to her, and smiled, as their eyes met,; but Marguerite blushed deeply, and thinking she had done something wrong in talking so loud under his window, the called hastily to Manon, and, without returning his salutation, ran away. Philip followed her with his eyes until she disappeared on the side of the orchard, and then, after nodding kindly to Manon, who all the time had been giving him a series of bows and smiles, he prepared to descend. This was, however, not quite so easy a matter as one might think at first; the passages were so intricate, the turnings so endless, that Philip, at length, almost despaired of finding the great staircase, and he was just making a third effort to do so, when he came upon a small, dark flight of winding stairs, communicating with the lower part of the building, and down these he proceeded at once. At the bottom he met Manon, who was hastening to the kitchen with her basket of vegetables, and her dignity was greatly wounded on discovering that monsieur had descended by the servants' stairs. She half proposed to accompany him again to his apartment, and conduct him down by the legitimate mode of descent; but Philip interrupted her with a smile, and said he was glad to make acquaintance with all parts of the chateau, " which," he added, " from the difficulty I had in finding my way, must be a very large building."

" Ah, monsieur?" returned Manon, " it is a noble and beautiful place, and you would think so, could you have seen it in former days; I mean when we first came to live here. Now it may seem a little lonely, with only my master and mademoiselle, and not a servant save me. But it is *his* wish, you see," she added, confidentially; " he cannot bear a number of attendants about him, and one must not thwart the fancies of an invalid." It was Manon's grand object in life to conceal her master's poverty, and she took this early opportunity of accounting to the stranger for the scantiness of the household.

" I fear Mr. St. John is far from well," remarked Philip.

Manon looked very grave. " He is greatly changed in the last year," she replied; " and unless he improves much during this summer, he will never get through another such a winter as the last."

" The climate must be severe here," said Philip.

" Well, it is not very cold—not nearly so cold as in Paris, for example, where I lived with my dear mistress for two years after her marriage—but it is damp and foggy, and so much exposed to storms, that it is almost impossible for an invalid to get out from November till May. It does not hurt those in health—my young lady is as blooming as a rose in the dreariest weather, and of course nothing can hurt me, a Breton peasant—but for my master, Kersaint is no good place."

" His daughter seems unaware that Mr. St. John is in any danger," observed Philip.

" And may the bon Dieu forbid that she should be otherwise," returned Manon, hastily. " She will have sorrow enough when he is gone, and she is thrown upon strangers, without having trouble forced upon her now. I like to see her smiling and joyous, my poor child; and I am glad, monsieur, very glad, that you have arrived to bear her and my master a little company. There are none in this neighborhood fit for them to associate with."

Philip quite won Manon's heart by his evident interest in her master's health; and, after a few minutes, she volunteered to show him round the garden. " Mademoiselle is there," she said, " and as my master will not be down quite yet, perhaps monsieur would like to walk for half an hour on the terrace before breakfast."

But Philip said he should find his way perfectly this time, and, leaving Manon to proceed to her kitchen duties, he went out through a low archway into the garden. The good order of the flower-borders struck him immediately as contrasted with the desolate-looking house, broken flights of steps, and the disordered state of the walls and fences. He judged rightly that the little fairy of his night's dreams presided over this portion of the garden, and he looked on all sides in search of her; but she was nowhere visible. Then he walked to the further end, and reached the terrace, from whence he could see over the adjoining orchards and meadows —but still no Marguerite.

" Can she really be offended," thought Philip, " because I overheard her talking of me? No, she is too child-like for that." He took a few turns, every moment expecting to see her, but when a quarter of an hour passed on, and she did not appear, he grew impatient; and, spying a flight of moss-grown steps, which led down to the sea-side, he resolved to go and walk by the sea-side for an hour, and forget this capricious little lady. He sprang down, three steps at once, and suddenly discovered Marguerite, seated at the bend of the wall, on a projecting slab of granite, and making up bouquets from a heap of spring flowers in her lap. Philip stopped short.

" Good morning, mademoiselle."

" Good morning." She turned her face quite away from him, with a feeling of shyness she had never before experienced in her life. Had she really said something so wrong when he overheard her?

" I thought you were lost, and have been searching for you all over the garden." No answer. She could not confess that she had run away from him.

" Ah!" said Philip, next; " I see, you are very angry with me for overhearing you; but it was not my fault. I opened my window, to listen to the birds, and I could not help it, if your voice was amongst them—indeed, at first I did not distinguish it from theirs!"

Marguerite looked up at him quickly, and the expression of his face showed her her mistake: he thought *her* offended. Young as she was, this idea gave her pleasure, and, to keep it up, she tried hard not to smile; then—shaking her curls so as to conceal her face—bent down again, and went on with her bouquets. Philip seated himself on the step, at her feet, and began watching her very gravely; but Marguerite could not get on half so well with her work now, as she had done before he came, and once or twice the flowers slipped from her hands as she was fastening them.

"Well," said Philip, at last, "I am sure I could make up bouquets better than you do. You place all the wrong colors together;" and he took the scissors from her hand, and some of the best flowers from her collection, and laying them on the steps beside him, began very leisurely to arrange them. He had naturally a good eye for harmony of color, but he now, purposely, assorted them as ill as he could. Yellow primroses he placed by pink hawthorn, violets with the bright blue hepatica, so that the color of each was destroyed by its neighbor; then he tied them in prim, regular bunches, each stalk exactly the same length, and with no mixture of green leaves, but all the time preserving a countenance of the most perfect seriousness, as though he were performing the task to the best of his ability. Marguerite looked at him from under her long eye-lashes, and tried hard to repress a sly smile at the hideous little bouquets, and Philip's air of satisfaction with himself. But it would not do, and at length she was forced to cover the lower part of her face with one hand. Philip looked up, and saw her eyes laughing.

"I flatter myself mine are arranged with taste," he remarked.

Here Marguerite could hold out no longer; clasping her hands together in her lap, she went into such a long fit of childish laughter, as did Philip good to hear. It was a minute or two before she could speak; at length she cried, "So that is English taste! and those are English nosegays! Oh! I am glad I have seen them." And again she broke into a clear merry laugh.

Philip looked astonished.

"Is it possible you do not admire them?" he said. "Well, I thought they were perfect—so neat and regular; but, of course, you are right. Suppose you give me a lesson: I want to know how everything is done in Brittany."

He cut all the strings, and, mixing the flowers together, returned them into Marguerite's lap. This little scene had made her feel perfectly at her ease with him again; and, believing that he was quite in earnest in his wish to learn, she gathered up the flowers in her frock, and, seating herself on the step close beside him, said she would teach him. The lesson began, and lasted long. Philip was very slow to learn, and Marguerite had to give him a thousand practical instructions, which he never could master until the second or third trial. She was quite interested and serious, and her impatience was great when her long bright curls would fall upon their work and interrupt them.

"Am I very slow?" asked Philip, as Marguerite was trying to bend his fingers to their task.

"Well," she answered, "not slow—but I think you a little——"

"What? I like to hear my faults."

"A little perverse. Your hands do not look awkward, and yet you *will* not learn to hold the flowers more lightly. Now, let me show you once more, or you will make it look like another English nosegay;" and she knelt on the step beneath him, in her earnestness guiding his hands with her own, and every minute looking up and smiling in his face.

"You have made that last one beautifully!" she exclaimed; "better than mine!" I believe, after all, you only pretended to take a lesson, and have been arranging flowers all your life."

"Well, it is so very pleasant to learn!" answered Philip.

"Is it? Ah! not always. I do not like my irregular verbs with Monsieur le Curé, par example; but I might like to learn from some people."

"From me, perhaps?"

"Y—es, perhaps."

"A very hesitating answer. I am sorry I look so bad tempered."

"Oh! it is not that, I assure you, for I told Manon I never liked any face so much as yours before. But, then, you are too young for a master. Just when you meant to be very severe, I should look in your face and—laugh."

"Then, I must not offer to give you lessons in English pronunciation, as I had intended."

"Yes, yes, you may; only, you must promise not to be too severe, and not to be offended, if I sometimes forget to be grave."

At last all the flowers were gone, and they had finished four bouquets.

"One for my father, one for you, and one a-piece for Manon and me."

"And who is this for?" he asked, taking up the one in which Marguerite had collected all the most delicate and sweet-scented flowers, even to a rose-bud, which she had discovered under shelter of the terrace.

"That is for father, of course; but you shall have the next best."

"And which for yourself, Mademoiselle?"

"Well, Manon must choose, and whichever is left is for me. Do not call me mademoiselle, please. Father says, as long as I am a child, every one should call me Marguerite."

" And are you only a child still ? "

" Oh ! " she answered, smiling. " I am, indeed. I often wish that I were older and wiser, for his sake; but in two months I shall be sixteen, and that, you know, is getting on towards being grown-up. Shall we go down to the beach before breakfast ? "

She ran lightly down the steps, and they were soon close to the sea. It was now low water, and there was a wide expanse of shining dry sand, stretching far away before them. Philip felt a new sense of youth and life as they walked, and Marguerite, holding her flowers, her up-turned face more blooming than they, and her hair dancing about over her shoulders, was soon talking to him with all the unrestraint of the previous evening.

She possessed a rare charm—one with which he had never before chanced to be thrown in contact—that of perfect innocence. And Philip, who, a few weeks back, had pronounced his last youthful illusion over, now became conscious—while he gazed into this young face and read, through all her child-like manner, the deep, tender nature of Marguerite—that the true illusion of life —the first love which bathes the whole earth in golden glory—had for him never yet dawned.

CHAPTER XVIII.

PHILIP's childhood, after his parents' death, having been passed exclusively among his own sex, he had never, as a boy, known the sweet love of mother or sister; and, as he grew up, the women with whom he had been most intimate were Clara St. Leger and her mother—the one a mere woman of the world, the other cold and unnatural from her education. In society he had certainly met hundreds of young ladies—many of them, lovely, all, of course, innocent and interesting, and ready to become excellent wives—but these were uniformly " young ladies," well trained, well paced, well looked after, and they had been trotted out in rotation before Philip without one of them effecting more than the awakening of a passing fancy in his mind. The miserable failure of his married life had been his next trial of what ought to be love, and the society of actresses the crowning stroke of his experience.

No wonder the companionship of Marguerite seemed something far apart from all he had known before! No wonder, as they walked along, Philip forgot the wide gulf which, in reality, separated them. He already world-stained and weary, and bound by a tie which must for ever shut him out of the pale of all pure love; Marguerite, with the holiness of childhood yet upon her forehead, and no knowledge of life, except that the sky was blue above her, and that God was good. He only felt that a sinless nature was, at length, before him, and that the true love he had written about, but never found, would some day awaken in Marguerite's heart—for whom ?

" You look thoughtful, monsieur; that is your grave look now."

" I believe my looks are always grave."

" No; not when we were tying up the flowers. Then you looked very happy."

" Are you often grave, Marguerite ? "

" Not very often; but sometimes I am more than grave. When my father looks so pale, and begins to speak of my mother, and that it would be far better for him to be with her, I come out, alone, on the shore, and feel something here,"— she laid her hand on her heart—" which I cannot describe—a thick, dull weight it is—and then I almost wish to die. I seldom feel this great pain, however, except when it is connected with father; but often of an evening, when the sun is down, and the stars are coming out one by one over the sea, and I sit by the window alone, or, in summer, down on the terrace, I feel, not unhappy—that is not the word—but I miss something, you understand, and then I am very grave; and the more beautiful the sea and the stars look, the more I feel lonely. I never felt this when I was younger, only the last year or two; and yet I have my father and Manon with me just the same now as formerly. Did you ever feel the same ? "

" Yes, years ago, when I was your age," replied Philip.

" But you are not very old now."

" Old enough to gaze at the stars without becoming sad."

She looked at him quickly to be quite sure he was not laughing at her; but there was no smile on his face.

" Have you any mother ? " she asked, softly, and touching his hand with her own.

" She died when I was a young child."

" Or sister, or——"

" I have no one," answered Philip, shortly.

" Ah ! "—and the little hand closed upon his—" and I have no one but my father! But when you have one person to love, you do not wish for any other. It must be dreadful to be quite alone." After a pause she resumed timidly, " Did you say you would remain half the summer in Bretagne ? "

" Yes," replied Philip ; " what I had already seen of it made me wish to stay ; but, since yesterday, I have quite determined upon doing so."

It was one of those accustomed compliments which pass current, and mean nothing in society ; but Marguerite's heart actually throbbed. " That is since he has known me," she thought. Then she added, aloud, " I shall think I have a brother while you are here."

They had now wandered to some distance on the sands, and a clear, wide stream of fresh water, running towards the sea, formed a barrier to their further progress. They were just hesitating about fording it, and Marguerite was saying she had done so dozens of times before, when one of them happening to turn, descried Manon, barely visible on the terrace, in the far distance, waving her arms and throwing up her apron in a wild state of excitement. The breakfast was ready, and poor Manon for some minutes—with feelings none but a cook can appreciate—had been watching the guest walk further and further away from his meal, and feeling herself powerless to recall him. When they halted, her hopes of being seen revived; and she soon thankfully perceived that they had understood her signals, so she ran in to keep the coffee hot, and to tell her master that they were coming.

Mr. St. John was seated in his library—the room in which they were to breakfast—wrapped in a loose dressing-gown, and with a book already in his hand. This room was the warmest in the house, being smaller than most of the others, and with a southern aspect; and here the invalid generally spent the entire winter. The walls and ceiling were all of oak panelling. Scarcely any of the former, however, were to be seen, for well-stored bookcases stood on each side of the room. An English carpet covered the floor, and the worked cushions on the window-seats, the footstool and warm easy-chair, and a dozen little home-constructed luxuries, bore witness to the female care which presided over the occupant's comfort. The window opened upon the garden, and Mr. St. John soon saw Philip and his daughter descending from the terrace, both looking animated, and Marguerite laughing merrily at something her companion was saying; and as the invalid watched them, evidently so well pleased with each other, a thought arose which caused a faint smile to wander across his face. Perhaps, had this vague hope been rendered into words it might have been—"After all, it is possible that I may leave my child with a protector!" Their entrance, however, dispelled any such dreams for the present, and, after a cordial greeting, the trio were soon seated at their cheerful breakfast.

Philip did great justice to Manon's provisions, all of which were excellent. Clear strong coffee—such as he had vainly wished for with his own grand English cook—fresh eggs, broiled fish, caught that morning in the bay, butter of Manon's own making, constituted the staple of the meal. Mr. St. John smiled at the hearty good-will with which his guest attacked his breakfast; and then turning to Marguerite, asked her why she ate so little. She could not reply that she was too happy to be hungry, which was the truth, but said Manon had cut her such a huge tartine early in the morning, that she had no further appetite.

"Perhaps, we walked too far," added Philip.

"Oh!" said Mr. St. John, "'too far' are words unknown to Marguerite. She spends the whole of her idle life out of doors, in summer, and, I verily believe, never experiences such a thing as fatigue. Where did you get all these flowers, little one?"

"I had such a hunt for them, father! The rain has beaten down the best, and I could only gather those which grew in very sheltered places. Do you see that rose-bud in yours?—the first this summer, petit papa."

"But you should have presented that to your visitor."

"No, no! The first rose is always for you. But I have given Mr. Earnscliffe a lesson in bouquet-making this morning. It was so pleasant sitting on the terrace steps in the warm sun; and do you know, father, just when we finished, I found out that he had only been pretending, and could make them as well as I all the time? N'est ce pas qu'il est méchant ce monsieur?"

The conversation went on merrily, and Mr. St. John appeared in such good spirits, and so animated, that Philip thought he must have been mistaken in considering him dangerously ill. They talked much about the inhabitants and antiquities of Brittany, and Mr. St. John's invitation of the previous evening, to remain, at least for some days, at Kersaint, was repeated, seconded by an eloquent look from Marguerite, and cordially accepted by Philip. He felt that he was with old friends already.

After breakfast, when Marguerite had retired to confer with Manon on domestic matters, Earnscliffe began to notice his host's extensive collection of books, and led him on gradually to speak of them, and of himself.

"My books have been my sole friends, except my child, for sixteen years," said Mr. St. John; "and I have grown so accustomed to look upon them in the light of human beings, that I scarcely now am conscious of the absence of other companionship. At your time of life, such an existence as mine must appear a kind of living death. It is only after a man has outlived ambition, and lost the ties of domestic life, that he can find in himself a happier resting place than in the world. Are you anything of a bookworm like myself? If so, in this case, nearest the fire-place, there are some rare works likely to interest you; and should we have wet weather during your stay at Kersaint, you might find a day's employment among them."

Philip thought that Marguerite's face would be better reading than the somewhat ponderous volumes alluded to by her father. However, he entered with animation into the subject which formed the one interest of the invalid's life, and they were soon deep in literary talk. Mr. St. John had been so long absent from England, that he was anxious to hear about all the new writers of the day; and had also numbers of old friends to inquire for, most of whom were now either dead or retired from their active life.

"Then, who is the most popular writer of fiction now?" he asked, at length.

Philip knew that his own was one of the rising names in the field of romantic literature; he replied, however, by naming several others of the more distinguished authors.

"And of poetry?"

"Well, that is easily replied to—none. Since the galaxy of poetic genius, which arose in Germany and England early in this century, the race seems to have died out. Writers of poems we have many, and one whose thoughts, when not utterly obscured by affectation, are so sweet—his word-painting so true—that one is half tempted at times to call him a poet. Still, not even his will be a lasting fame. We have no collossal genius now that, like Shakspeare, or Dante, or Cervantes, can create at once and for ever an absorbing interest—take fast hold upon the hearts of all classes of readers, and become a familiar household god beyond the power of fashion to cast down. Wordsworth and Moore, certainly, still live; but they belong to the past. England has now no great poet.

"And France in my opinion, has never had one. Fond as I am of some portions of French literature, their artificial, monotonous verse—with the single exception of Beranger's songs, perhaps—sends me to sleep. But every day I make my little daughter read aloud to me some of our own Milton or Shakespeare; if she is too young fully to understand them, she can yet read well; and would you believe, sir, that hour is pleasanter to me than the remaining ten of my own studies—so fond are we all of anything which seems to connect genius with ourselves? and the child's voice makes me actually feel those glorious thoughts my own more than all the annotations upon them that ever were written."

Philip said he could well believe this, and after a minute or two added, simply—"Your daughter is very lovely, sir."

"Is she so?" returned Mr. St. John, almost starting. "Well, I never thought about it before. Of course, she is fair in my eyes; but I have not yet considered that she would be called beautiful by others. It is possible," he added, dreamily, "she is like her mother."

His face relapsed into its habitual melancholy at this recollection—it always did so at any allusion to his wife—and Philip began to think that her death must have been the origin of Mr. St. John's disinclination for the world.

"Shall you venture out to-day?" he inquired, hoping to change his thoughts.

"No I thank you. The ground is still damp, and the wind too uncertain for me. But you must not remain in the house this fine spring day on my account. See, Marguerite's is already in the garden, doubtless, expecting you to join her for a walk."

Philip saw that the invalid preferred being alone, and he was soon by Marguerite's side in the garden, helping her to tie up some flowers that had suffered from the rain. When they had finished, she proposed a long walk; and, crossing the orchard, they started through heaths and forests to some ruins about a league distant.

Marguerite did not care much for wet paths, and, in taking Earnscliffe a short way of her own discovery, sprang lightly over streams and bushes in a manner rather surprising to eyes only accustomed to London young ladies. A little straw bonnet, which the wind blew incessantly from her head, and a scarf round her throat, were the only additions to her morning dress; and yet, thus attired, and running wild in the wildest parts of Brittany, no stranger could have met Marguerite without being struck by her easy, high-born carriage, and the natural grace which made everything she wore becoming. She was in high spirits at having to conduct Philip, and pointed out to him, as they went along, all her favorite summer haunts.

After traversing a forest of fir trees—whose peculiar odor in the warm sun struck Marguerite on that morning as more than usually fragrant—they reached a wide tract of heath, an angle of which must be crossed before reaching the gentle eminence where stood the ruined chapel. It was a scene rendered grand in its flat monotony by its utter loneliness. As far as the eye could reach, there was no habitation, no trace of man, nothing but the purple moorlands, until they faded away into blue distance, or enormous tracts of untrodden fir forests. Life, however, was not wanting—that mysterious life, which rejoices everywhere, and is most exuberant where man is not. Myriads of gossamers floated on the golden air in their perishing fairy craft; wild bees murmured amidst the gorse: the grasshopper called joyously from his bed of wild thyme; and the lark hovered high in the pure space above, and unburdened his little heart of its melodious gladness.

When they were about half way across the heath, Marguerite pointed out to her companion a singular-looking heap of stones, which she told him were Druidic remains, and proposed that they should rest there awhile and look about them. "For," she added naïvely, the walk will be too quickly over if we get on so fast."

Philip said he should enjoy nothing better; and they were soon side by side on the highest stone of the pile, which formed a kind of throne among the others. Bello, who accompanied them, but had lingered behind in the forest (where, on the score of old recollections, he was fond of taking private excursions after game, on his own account), now came up, and extended his grisly length at their feet, shutting his eyes in the sun with luxurious enjoyment of its warmth, and forgetting in his happiness to bestow any more surly looks on the stranger.

"How fair it all is!" said Marguerite, at length.

The words recalled to Philip that day when he sat on Hampstead Heath by little Fridoline, and she had made use of a nearly similar expression, and he contrasted in his own mind the immense difference between these two young creatures; one so happy in her ignorance of what is called life, and the other already weighed down under a premature knowledge of sin.

"Everything must be fair to you," Marguerite.

"Why so?"

"Because you see everything through the medium of your own mind."

She paused. "Then everything is fair to you?"

"No, that is different."

"Tell me why. Do you not see things through the medium of *your* mind?"

"Certainly I do. But—"

"Then they must be fair to you, likewise."

"I am afraid not; their beauty is more in the heart which looks at them, than in themselves."

She shook her head. "You know better than I do, of course; but still I think the sky must be as blue, and the air as fresh, to you as to me."

"Everything seems fair and fresh this morning, Marguerite," he replied softly.

"Does it? I am so glad," and she turned her sweet face to his, with an expression which made Philip withdraw his gaze, and determined to make her no more pretty speeches.

"What do you do at home?" she asked next. This was a trying question; for few of Philip's pursuits had been such as he cared to disclose to Marguerite. However, she was unsuspicious as a child, and listened with interest to all he chose to tell her—of dinner parties and balls, and the opera and the parks, and what people did at all these places.

"And what is London like?" she inquired, when he paused. "Is it at all like Quimper? I have been there twice to the fair, and that is a very large town, too."

Philip tried to describe a great city. She listened with wondering eyes to his accounts of brilliant shops, and streets, and carriages, and thought, on the whole, that it must be better than Kersaint. However, she quickly retracted this opinion on hearing that the air was generally too foggy to allow you to see the blue sky, and that there were no birds or flowers, very few trees, and those black.

"I will never go to London, then," she cried, "or at least not to stay there. Bretagne is better."

Poor child, as she said these words, seated by Philip's side, with the May sun on her cheek, and the delicious feeling of youth and freedom at her heart, how little did she dream where and how her future life was to be passed!

———

CHAPTER XIX.

"How long have we been here, I wonder?" said Marguerite, at length. Philip looked at his watch, and replied that it was two hours since they left home.

"And we are not half way to the chapel yet, and have part of another forest still to cross!" cried Marguerite, jumping lightly down. "You always make me forget the time, monsieur. Come, Bello."

Philip was quickly at her side, and once more they proceeded on their walk. Every object on the way, a stream glittering over white pebbles, an azure butterfly hovering upon some wood-anemone, a solitary primrose at the foot of an old hawthorn—afforded perfect pleasure to Marguerite; and Philip, who had been bored to death, dozens of times by affected enthusiasm on such subjects, delighted in listening to her childish admiration of all the common things of nature. Marguerite possessed the rare gift of language—not book language, she had read too little for that, but an unusual and even poetic turn of expression, when speaking on ordinary subjects, which prevented anything she said from sounding common-place; and her slightly foreign accent and sonorous voice only added to the charm.

Once or twice this morning, Philip had already felt that they both would be in danger by the continuance of this intimate companionship. His own heart whispered that he could not long remain unmoved at the gaze of her clear eyes, and the pressure of her small hand; while for Marguerite, her excessive youth and innocence made it only too likely that her first and natural love might be awakened for him. Philip was strictly a man of honor, and he said to himself, "This walk shall be the last." But he could not now restrain the happiness of his companion, or assume a distant manner towards her, while he remained a guest in her father's house; he could only resolve for the future, and be content with the present; and he was—perfectly content.

They had walked for nearly a mile, when the ground began to rise, and solitary groups of trees stood out here and there, as sentinels of the forest which they were now about to enter. Bello bounded off with a low bark after some wild animal, whose track he had suddenly discovered, and was soon lost among the deepening shadows; while Marguerite conducted her companion to a small bye-path, along which, and through the densest part of the forest, lay a near way to the ruins.

"There are no gamekeepers to interfere with Bello's amusements?" remarked Philip.

"Gamekeepers?" echoed Marguerite.

"Yes; garde chasses, as you call them."

"Oh! I believe there are some; but the forests are so large we never meet them, and besides every one knows my father, and would not hurt his dog. But do look round," she cried, "and tell me if there are forests like these in England."

The mass of foliage around them was indeed singularly beautiful in its variety and early summer freshness. Ash predominated among the larger trees, but there was also a thick undergrowth of cherry, aspen, buckthorn, and wild apple, the latter now rich in scent and blossom. They walked on noiselessly upon the thick, long moss, enjoying the peculiar sweetness of the forest air, and the sounds of existence with which they were surrounded; the cooing of the wood dove, the measured cry of the lapwing, the happy song of the thrush, and the confused hum from thousands of unseen insects. For, again, in this solitude, so rarely trodden by human foot, might be heard, even more audibly than upon the heath, the beating of that immense pulse of life which eternally proceeds from and returns to God, unknown, uncared for, save by him.

After a time, Marguerite pointed to what seemed more a deer-track than a path, upon the left hand, and saying that was their nearest way, she led Philip still further into the recesses of the forest. So dense, however, was the chaos of vegetation, that their progress was frequently impeded, and at every step the scene grew more wildly grand. Here and there some huge oak, overthrown half a century before by age or storm, lay, still supported in its ponderous decay by the stems of the surrounding trees; while bright young creepers, on which the midday sun now glistened, interlaced its trunk in a thousand graceful festoons, that formed airy bridges for the birds and squirrels; and in some places the earth itself appeared to have been convulsively rent asunder at some former period, and was traversed by numerous ravines, whose fissures were now partially overhung with briars and huge projecting rocks.

Suddenly an opening amidst the bushes discovered, almost at their feet, and at some distance beneath them, a large sheet of water, completely studded over with water-lilies. The wood-pigeons were skimming across it, the kingfisher sparkling like a gem amidst the flag-rushes on its banks, while one solitary heron sat patiently watching for prey

among the lightning-scathed boughs of a distant willow.

"This I call my lake!" cried Marguerite, pointing to the dark blue water. "I discovered it first when I was quite a child; and like it better than all the others in the forest. There are not water-lilies anywhere but here; and when it is very hot weather, I come and sit for hours by that large mossy rock—"

"Surely you do not come alone to this wild spot?" interrupted Philip.

"Why not? it is too far for my father to venture; and when Manon does take a walk, which is very seldom, except to church, she prefers going into town, and does not care for my walks. She says there are so many snakes in the forest, and especially by the lake—fancy being afraid of the beautiful blue and gold water-snakes!"

"And do you never fear to meet any one in your wanderings?"

"Oh, I am very glad: par example, if I meet Guillé and Bon Affût, the wood-cutters. They lay down their axes, and always have a chat with the 'little queen,' as they call me. And if I meet robbers, why I have nothing to lose; and you, old Bello, to protect me," and she stretched out her hand to the hound, who had rejoined them. Philip looked in wonder at this fair young girl, with her noble bearing, and innate grace of soul, who wandered alone through these forests without an idea of danger, and thought it a great pleasure to chat with Guillé and Bon Affût—leading a life of companionless, unchecked freedom, and yet with a refinement in her face and manner a duchess might have envied. He was right when he said Marguerite would be a new study for him.

"We must not linger," she exclaimed; "the sun already darts across the silver beech; it must be three o'clock." Quitting the side of the lake, they once more began to ascend; and a quarter of an hour's walking brought them into a beaten path which led to the ruins. When they were within a few yards from what appeared to be a sudden opening among the trees, Marguerite cried, "shut your eyes, monsieur, and give me your hand."

Philip, as may be supposed, willingly obeyed; and she led him on (her face lighting up with the expectation of his surprise) into the ruined chapel, which the trees had hitherto entirely screened from their sight. Then placing him by the window that she considered the best point of view, quitted his hand abruptly, and told him to look around.

"You are indeed a fairy!" was Philip's first exclamation. "A moment ago we were in the gloomy depths of the forest, and now" He looked around before finishing the sentence, and then acknowledged that a fairer scene had seldom been spread before him. The little chapel, which stood considerably elevated in the very centre of the forest, although entirely in ruins, still retained some traces of its former beauty in a few delicate columns and pointed arches, and one exquisitely-carved rose window. The accumulation of soil within the walls amounted to eighteen or twenty feet, and in one part enabled a good climber to reach the highest fragment of the ruin; and Marguerite had placed Philip close beside the eastern window, which commanded an extensive view of the surrounding country. At their feet lay, first, the forest itself, its different hues of foliage blending softly in the slanting sun; beyond that, wide tracts of purple lowlands, dotted over with an occasional church tower, or the remains of some old feudal castle; while, as a background to the whole, rose the sea, rivalling and exceeding in its intense blue the cloudless sky above them.

As Philip still gazed upon the prospect without speaking, an immense sea-eagle floated slowly past, ignorant of the presence of man so near his habitation, and adding a strange sense of wildness to the whole scene. After hovering a few seconds, so close they might almost hear the movements of his graceful black wings, he suddenly made a swoop upon the forest beneath them, and reappeared, holding his prey in his talons. Marguerite pointed out his nest upon the summit of a high oak, whither he presently flew with his prize, and added, "I know him, and his mate well, and often sit here and watch them. The young will be fledged next month. But we must now go to the very top of the ruin, and you will see Quimper Cathedral, if the distance is quite clear. I hope you are a good climber."

She flew with the lightness of a young roe up the loose stones and broken parapets, and Philip was quickly beside her. The kind of platform upon which they stood was only a few yards square, and on one side there still remained a low crumbling wall, three or four feet high; on the others it was completely unprotected: and it required a clear head to look down upon the deep gulf of rocks and foliage beneath.

"You can just see the cathedral," said Marguerite, "like a silver dot in the distance. But you are looking at me again; you must follow the direction of my finger:" and she made him bend his head to the level of her hand. Philip was almost as slow in discovering Quimper Cathedral as he had been in learning bouquet making; however, he succeeded at length, and he then praised the whole fair landscape in terms that delighted Marguerite.

"It is so pleasant here," she cried; "I wish we could sit down for a time and rest, but I am afraid the ground is not dry enough."

"Most assuredly it is not," returned Philip; "but what should prevent you, however, from resting upon the wall?"

"Well"—Marguerite hesitated—"I think it is rather dangerous. Father tells me never to lean over this parapet."

"But if I hold you?"

"It would tire you too much."

"Try at all events."

Philip lifted her on the wall, which, though decayed, was still perfectly safe and firm, and supported her slight waist with his arm; while Marguerite, her bonnet discarded, and the fresh breeze playing in her hair, seemed drinking in the beauty around her with as much pleasure as though she saw it all for the first time, and only fearing occasionally that she was tiring Monsieur Earnscliffe.

After Monsieur Earnscliffe's wise resolutions of an hour ago, this near neighborhood was certainly a somewhat inconsistent stroke of policy! Marguerite—never having learnt propriety—had no more idea of indecorum when Philip's arm supported her, than has a London young lady while waltzing at a hot ball with eighteen consecutive strangers; she liked to enjoy the view,—she wished to rest, —it did not tire her companion to hold her, and that was all. But with Philip it was different. The soft touch of Marguerite's long curls, as they floated across his hand, her warm breath upon his cheek, her eyes turning every moment to his with their child-like caressing expression—all made, his heart beat, and brought to him a bitterer sense of the never-ending tie which bound him to Clara than he had hitherto experienced. With all his knowledge of the world, a few hours in poor little Marguerite's society had already taught him more of the great secret of our existence than he had ever yet learnt.

"Would you not like my life better than London?" she asked, after both had been for some minutes silent. "Confess that you would."

"*Your* life, Marguerite? I should indeed."

"Then why not choose it?"

"We cannot always choose what we prefer. Do you not wish for anything beyond that which you now possess?"

She considered a moment. "Nothing, but for father to be better."

"You are perfectly happy then?"

"Certainly. I have everything I could wish for in the world—I am well—I am free."

"And what would be your idea of misery?"

"I do not know; I have never considered. I think, for me, perhaps, the greatest unhappiness would be, to be separated from my father, and confined in some close house in a town—in London, for example."

"My home!" remarked Philip.

"Well, you acknowledged yourself, that you liked our forest better."

"For a time, yes. But you, Marguerite, will not be a child forever. Some day you must learn to be a grown-up woman, and obey some one not your father, and give up wandering with Bon Affût, and sitting by the water-lilies."

Marguerite opened her eyes wide at this programme of futurity. "And why must I do all this?" she asked.

"Is there not a time when the existence of every young girl changes, and she becomes dependent upon the will of another—when,"—her full gaze troubled him—"when she marries?"

Marguerite went into a merry laugh. "Marry—I marry! Oh! that is too good. Why, I never saw any gentleman yet, but father! Am I to marry Bon Affût, or the Black Eagle, my only friends?—unfortunately, both have mates already." (Poor Philip, how those unconscious words stung him.) "No, Kersaint is not a place for weddings. I have only seen two—and those were among the fisher people—in my whole life!" and she laughed on at the ludicrous idea of any one being married from Kersaint. Young ladies in general blush when they speak of marriage; but Marguerite, being uninformed on this point, seemed to think the subject very amusing.

"And you have never any visitors?" went on Philip.

"Never, except the cure. My father has invited a cousin of ours once or twice in the summer, but he has not come yet."

Philip immediately disliked this unknown relation; and remarked, "Ah! it is the cousin, I see, who will rob Kersaint of its little queen."

"The cousin? why he is older than father, and has had two wives already."

"Oh, but you may have chance visitors, you know—a young artist, or a traveller, for example, suddenly benighted, like myself, and seeking shelter at Kersaint. He might stay on and on, and in time you would not dislike him, and of course from the first he would admire you—and then——"

Was the sun too bright, that Marguerite abruptly raised her hand to her eyes, and shaded her cheek? It could not be that, for she turned her face full towards the west, and away from Philip; and he felt that she was blushing. It was the first blush of womanly feeling that had ever dyed her cheek—and for him! In after years they neither of them forgot that moment.

"I think we should go home," said Marguerite, timidly, at last. "It is time now."

He lingered, still supporting her, and with an unusual emotion in his dark eye, as though a struggle were passing within. Then he replied, "Yes, it is time," and lifted her gently to the ground, without looking at her face again.

They took a different homeward route through the forest; it was even more beautiful than the other; but Marguerite spoke less now of the birds and flowers than when they came. She walked by Philip's side,

and he was very silent. But around her the whole air was golden. The waving branches of the trees were kindly arms held out to her as she passed; the very wind, as it swept freshly by, had a kiss for her cheek, and the turf rose lovingly under her feet. Could it be the same lonely path she had so often trod before?

When she reached home, her father said she looked flushed, and must be tired; and, glad of an excuse, she ran up quickly into her own room; while Philip remained conversing with Mr. St. John upon the beauties of the walk, and the wild grandeur of Breton scenery in general.

By her open window, with tearful eyes, Marguerite raised her face to the blue sky, and thanked God for the new-born happiness within her heart.

———

CHAPTER XX.

During the remainder of that day, Marguerite continued somewhat silent. She related to her father at dinner what a delightful walk they had taken, but she was not eloquent; it was greater pleasure to her to be still and think. Philip, however, conversed much with Mr. St. John, who was every hour better pleased with his guest. Between these two men—dissimilar though they might have appeared in many things—there was yet in reality sufficient resemblance to give them a harmony of ideas and feelings. Both had, in a certain measure, wearied of the world; both had been disappointed in domestic life; the one through death, the other through a miserable marriage; and in both was the same natural perception of the beautiful, and the power of appreciating keenly all true excellence in art or literature. Marguerite —without fully understanding the whole of their conversation—listened with delight. Her father's voice (the only one except her nurse's which had murmured love over her cradle) had been the gladness of her sixteen years of life, and the stranger's—low and dangerously musical—was already sweeter to her ear than she dreamed of.

"Have you remarked much of the singularly deep religious feelings among the Breton peasants; or, as some would call it, of their superstition?" asked Mr. St. John, in the course of conversation.

"I have observed that the churches are generally crowded," answered Philip; and when I have entered them during service, the people appeared to me earnest in their devotions."

"Yes; but their devotion does not end with the service. In every action of a Breton's life, from his birth to his grave, religion holds a prominent part. A wild religion it s, mixing up the dogmas of the Catholic church with the weird traditions of their Celtic forefathers, in a manner that is certainly more poetic than orthodox. They will frequently, for instance, after attending mass on a saint's day, conclude the evening by gathering round the mystic ring of some prophetess or soothsayer, and listening with the greatest reverence to her visions of futurity—the maidens seeking for knowledge of their married life, the wives for the success and safe return of their sailor husbands. The priests, of course, discourage these practices; but they have too much tact—and, indeed, some of them too much sympathy with the people—to run violently against old-established prejudice."

"Father," broke in Marguerite, gravely, "many of old Anaïk's prophecies come true."

"Oh," said Mr. St. John, smiling, "if you acknowledge to all your superstitions, Marguerite, you will make Mr. Earnscliffe think you a complete little Bas Bretonne. You take Manon's tales on too easy credence."

"What I could tell, is no tale of Manon's," she replied.

"May we not hear it?" asked Philip. "I should like to become acquainted with some specimens of Anaïk's powers."

"Well," said Marguerite, looking away from him as she spoke, "one evening, late in autumn, Manon and I were hurrying home from town. There had been violent storms for several days, and we did not care to linger on the road; but as we passed through Rosnareu—a little hamlet on the coast—a stream of light from one of the cabanes made Manon peep through the window, and she called me to look at a filerie—"

"Which—being translated?" interrupted Philip.

"Is a party of women who meet together to work and talk. Well, about a dozen of fisher wives were seated round a reed fire, spinning and chatting merrily, and Jean Bruzec's young wife was among them with her baby in her arms. Several other little children were sleeping before the fire at their mother's feet, and they formed such a pretty group in the flickering blaze, that I liked to stop and look at them in spite of the cold.

"Suddenly the door opened on the other side of the cabane, and a gaunt, tall figure entered. Manon knew her, and crossed herself; it was Anaïk the prophetess. She was dressed in rags—a sort of wallet of red serge upon her shoulders, and her long grey hair falling about her face. The women all rose and gave place to her on her entrance; but without noticing them she walked up to the fire and warmed her long bony hands over the flame; then turning round to poor Louison, who was bending over her child, she screamed to her in a voice that made me

tremble, and with the most fearful look of pleasure upon her face—

"'Louison, wife of Bruzec, listen to me! Once, last winter, when the snow was falling fast, and the very birds of the air had found shelter, old Anaïk was out in the cold, blighting blast, without a roof to cover her. Anaïk asked money or bread of Jean Bruzec, and he called her a groac'h—a drunken witch—and said she had bewitched his mother with her spells. And Anaïk swore that Jean should never see another winter himself. Her words have come true! The last leaves of autumn still hang upon the trees; but among Carnac rocks lies Jean Bruzec, cold, and stark, and dead, and his child is fatherless!'

"One shriek burst from poor Louison, and she fell senseless with her babe upon the ground, while Anaïk, laughing loud, left the cabane. We were so horrified that we ran on home; but next morning Bruno brought us word from the village, that Bruzec's companions had returned without him; he fell overboard in a gale, two nights before, and was never seen again."

"And a coincidence like this, my child," said Mr. St. John, "strengthens old Anaïk's reputation fourfold; and the dozens of times that she has prophesied falsely are forgotten. You believe even your own songs, little one——"

"Do you sing these Breton tales as well as narrate them?" asked Philip.

"I sing sometimes," answered Marguerite; "but I have never learnt, and I hear no music except at church."

"Yes, that is poor Marguerite's only music lesson," said her father, "and, as nature has really given her a somewhat remarkable voice and ear, I am glad for her to have even this opportunity for improving herself. The service is extremely well performed at N——, and the organ far superior to what you generally meet with in a remote country town."

"To-morrow is Sunday," said Marguerite stroking Bello's head, and looking away from the table.

"But you need not go to-morrow."

"Oh! not unless"—she glanced at Philip.

"I should really like to hear the service," he said. "And if you will allow me to accompany you—"

"Of course," returned Mr. St. John, quietly. "Marguerite is only too happy to exhibit all our wonders; but I fear they cannot give so much pleasure to any one else as herself. And now, as we have finished dinner, let us turn round to the window and look out awhile. I could bear the open air this soft evening. And do you, Marguerite, sing some of your Breton romances to Mr. Earnscliffe."

They were dining in the large salle, one of whose bay windows faced the west, and overlooked a kind of inland gulf, formed on this side by the sea. The setting sun threw its slanting beams upon Mr. St. John's pale face, when they had wheeled him, wrapped up in a cloak, to the open window, giving him, for the time, almost the hue of health; Philip, somewhat apart, stood leaning against one of the deep stone embrasures; and Marguerite very flushed at having to sing for the first time in her life before a stranger, was seated on a low, old-fashioned ottoman, in the centre of the group, tuning her guitar, and not daring to look up at Earnscliffe. She played almost entirely from ear, for her father understood only enough of music to teach her the names of the notes, and excepting a few Scotch airs, which she had picked up from him, her songs were mostly wild Breton romances. She hesitated a little when all the strings were tuned, and turning to her father, asked what she should sing to Mr. Earnscliffe.

"What you like, darling. What was that I heard you singing to Manon yesterday morning in the garden?"

"Oh, that was only part of a dirge that I heard the peasants chanting for poor Loubette, but it is very melancholy."

"I should like to hear it," said Philip, speaking for the first time; "I know none of these Breton songs."

Without reply Marguerite struck a few wild chords, and then, gradually subsiding into a low murmuring cadence for accompaniment, she began. Mr. St. John said rightly that nature had gifted her with no common voice. It was full, deep, and remarkably powerful, and had all that exquisite freshness which belongs only to the very young. She was utterly untaught; but her ear and taste were alike so faultless, that Philip, fastidious though he was in music, soon listened to Marguerite's singing with undisguised pleasure. He had rather dreaded hearing her, thinking it likely her father's opinion was partial, and that a very mediocre performance would take somewhat from the charm of her beautiful face; but he was now forced to acknowledge that of all Marguerite's gifts, her voice was infinitely the greatest.

As she sang she lost the slight timidity which had made the first few notes tremble, and forgetting everything but her theme—half of which was an improvisation of her own—her cheeks glowed, and her eyes filled with tears. The words, which Marguerite translated into French, although wild, and with scarcely any rhyme, had yet no lack of real feeling, and with the plaintive monotony of the chant, possessed a singular charm. The young girl for whom it was sung had been drowned in waiting for her lover among the rocks; and the distant beating of the sea, blending with Marguerite's voice, gave a reality to the little romance which was simply told in the funeral dirge.

When she finished, somewhat abruptly, she placed the guitar beside her, and turned round to her father. She was afraid to read in Philip's face what he thought of her music; for she was as unconscious of her extraordinary voice as of her own beauty, and felt rather ashamed at performing before him—"he, who lived in London, and must be such a good judge!"

"Will you sing again?" said Philip, in a low voice, after a minute or two's pause. He was not in a mood to flatter, but the expression of his face showed what he felt, and the invalid was delighted.

"There! Marguerite, our guest wishes to hear you again," he said. "Suppose you try something in your own language now—some of our old Scotch ballads."

With one look towards Philip she obeyed. This time she chose a favorite song of her father's—"The Land o' the Leal," and the deep pathos her voice gave to those touching words was indescribable. Mr. St. John's lips quivered as she sang; for Marguerite's voice was like her mother's, and that song always reminded him of the great sorrow of his life; and Philip felt he would rather listen to her ballads than to the finest opera in the world. She went on from one to another, until the last red rays of the sun had disappeared from the oak carvings round the window, and the freshening breeze warned Mr. St. John that it was already late to be near the open air. Marguerite sprang up hastily, and then, assisted by Philip, she wheeled her father's chair towards the hearth, where Manon had already laid the logs ready for a cheerful blaze.

"But you have not read to me to-day," said Mr. St. John, softly, to his daughter. "I must hear you for half an hour, darling, if Mr. Earnscliffe will excuse us."

Marguerite went at once to the library in search of the sacred volume, which always furnished their evening reading; and Philip, thinking they would probably wish to be alone, said he would enjoy the fresh sea air, and stroll out into the garden with his cigar.

The sun had now completely set. Only one faint streak of light lingered over the horizon, as loath to quit the blue sea upon which it rested; a few stars had already risen; and the wind, which during the day had blown freshly, was sunk into a whisper. Nothing but the gentle plash of the waves—now close beneath the terrace wall—broke the stillness; everything in external nature seemed calm and at peace. But Philip's heart was not so! He walked on to the terrace, and there paced up and down—his arms folded and his lips compressed—and unconscious of the whole scene around him.

Love, after a day's acquaintance, is generally a somewhat doubtful feeling; but Philip's was just a nature, quick, impulsive, irreflective, in which it could be genuine. He already felt for Marguerite St. John more than he had ever felt for any woman before, and it cost him a bitter pang to reflect that, in his position as a married man, only one right course was open to him—to leave her at once. He said to himself that there was dishonor in remaining one more day under her father's roof in his assumed character; for although he had not said so in words, he had certainly given Marguerite to understand that he was a single man, and her own warm blush, that morning among the ruins showed, Philip well knew, that his own manner had already gone too far.

" Should he then disclose his true position at once to Mr. St. John, or leave Kersaint ? "

From the former course he shrank morbidly. He had resolved on quitting England, to forget his former life as much as possible; he wished neither his fame as an author, nor his private history to follow him; and had chosen Brittany as the spot on earth where he would be least likely to be recognised. Merely to mention to Mr. St. John that he was married must naturally call forth other explanation, which would lead him back to all his recent trials. And, besides this, there lurked in his heart a feeling that he would rather quit Marguerite at once than stay near her in a different character to that under which she now knew him.

" Then he would leave Kersaint directly. No, that would be too sudden; one more day he must stay, and then speak of going. And in the meantime he would avoid being alone with Marguerite, or even thinking of her. Yes, he had resolved rightly, for a short time longer he would stay."

Philip had an excellent heart, and a sensitive regard to honor; but—and this was the mainspring of all his life's errors—his will was weak, his resolutions wavering. He would torment himself for days upon some point of conscience, which to another man would appear trivial; yet when a broad path of duty lay before him as was now the case, he did not enter upon it boldly and at once. The struggle was over in ten minutes; but on those ten minutes depended the whole after-coloring of Marguerite's life.

The night deepened: millions of worlds began to glisten, like tears in the blue eyes of heaven, over the deep space above, and all the reproaching holiness of nature was around him. Philip turned hastily towards the manor, where already a bright fire was glimmering through one of the lower windows, and he could trace the outline of Mr. St. John's drooping figure, as he and Marguerite read together. Poor father, ignorant that already another voice than his was sweet to his child's heart!

And once again Philip's conscience smote him.

CHAPTER XXI.

THE next day was Sunday, and they went to church together; the next, some other little excursion was planned, and so it went on . each day, until Philip had been a week at Kersaint, without ever speaking of renewing his travels. He had faithfully guarded over his manner with Marguerite, during this time, and there had been no recurrence of any conversation like that among the ruins. But, although he spoke to her on indifferent subjects, and scarcely ever called her Marguerite, she felt that his eyes sought hers, that his voice softened when he spoke to her, and her whole heart was full of joy.

She was innocent beyond what we in our ordinary life ever meet with—innocent beyond any young creature just leaving the school-room or convent, with cast-down eyes and regulation modesty. True innocence was the state of Eve before she had tasted of the tree of knowledge and learnt to assume, and such was Marguerite's. The blush on her cheek, when she met Philip's gaze, was as natural as the red glow on a flower which is kissed by the sun; and she could neither reason it away, nor make it come at her bidding. A new feeling was dawning upon her existence, and she felt within her an unwonted and delicious trouble, though she could not analyse the cause. She knew not that her childhood was dying, and the stronger, deeper, woman's life awakening. She had never read a novel, had never spoken to any one of love; and had she heard that Philip was married, it would have been a far less shock to her than he imagined. What did she know of marriage, or how connect it with herself?

The love of a very young girl is, I believe, a subject no man can really comprehend. Grosser from their very cradles, men's whole lives are such as sully their ideas of love; and the purest feeling that was ever felt by one of them, is as clay compared to the pure silver of hers.

With her father's image another now rose before Marguerite at her evening prayers—another to be remembered in her petitions; and if the prayer for the stranger was warmer than that which she had breathed from her infancy, she knew not that it was less pure. She liked to be with Philip, to lay her hand . timidly on his, to sing to him, to listen to the poetry he repeated to her, to see his face grow each day less gloomy when with her, and to hear him say he could not bear to leave them. Nor was her evident pleasure in his society concealed. Mr. St. John—though by no means clear-sighted, and so much in his study that he rarely saw them together, except at meal-times—had suspicions that Marguerite and the visitor liked each other well, and the thought pleased him. He was greatly attracted towards Philip himself;

his whole manner and tone of mind were precisely what he admired most; and, without really knowing anything about his history, he thought that his child's happiness would be safe in his keeping.

Only one thing more was wanting to complete his predisposition in favor of his visitor, and this shortly occurred. On the eighth morning after Philip's arrival at Kersaint, they were all seated at the breakfast-table when the post came in. Not in a uniform and with a double knock, as may be supposed, but in the sudden apparition at the window of Bruno—an uncouth-looking and only half-witted personage, who professed to take care of the garden and poultry, and was sent to N—— to market, when Manon was too busy to go herself. In one sense he performed this office well; that is, he knew the value of sous and centimes as well as the sharpest market-women on the "place," and bought provisions as cheaply as Manon could herself. But he was obtuse to the last degree, in understanding that he had no legal right or share in his own good bargains, and always appropriated so large a tithe to his capacious mouth on his way home, that Manon now rarely trusted him when anything had to be bought that it was possible for him to consume. Even here, once or twice, her judgment had failed her, and half a package of starch and a quantity of raw salt fish had severally fallen victims to Bruno's indiscriminating palate.

On the morning in question, however, he had been despatched at four o'clock, Manon's hour for rising, to call at N—— about a new kitchen table that had been ordered, and which Manon rightly conjectured would be safe from his appetite, even were he required to bring it home on his shoulders. Having performed his commission satisfactorily, i. e., by calling at the carpenter's, and ascertaining that the wood was not yet sawn, which should one day form the stage for Manon's art, Bruno, his great hat slouched over his forehead, and his sheepskin dangling round his ungainly figure, was shambling along through the streets homeward, his stolid eyes fixed intently before him, yet in reality, observing every one he met, when, as he passed the post-office, he heard his own name shouted. Stopping with a jerk, he gazed on all sides but that from whence the sound proceeded, with his mouth wide open, and a look of the most hopeless imbecility upon his face.

"Bruno—dolt—idiot!" reiterated the voice.

Bruno shook his head slowly, as though the person spoken to could not possibly be himself, and then pursued his road.

"Bruno!" called the voice. He did not turn.

"Monsieur Bruno—Monsieur Bruno!" now sounded faintly. A grin distorted Bruno's wide mouth, and chuckling to himself at his new title of dignity, he turned and beheld the post-mistress, her head outstretched through the small window of the bureau, which also formed her sitting-room, and holding something in her hand.

"A newspaper for M. St. John," she explained as she approached. "Just take it with you, good Bruno."

Good Bruno was aware that Kersaint was distant more than one league from N——, and that, by taking the paper, he saved the post-mistress or her son from walking that distance, and he made no sign of receiving it.

"Bruno is no postman," he muttered in his most stupid manner. "Poor Bruno!" pointing to his forehead.

"But that does not signify," urged the lady. "Come, take it at once; your master will wish to see it,"

"And if Bruno won't take it?"

"I must send it, you"—fool, she would have added, but refrained until her point was gained.

"And who pays you?"

"Pays me? why government; only you don't know what that means, and little enough too!"

"And who pays Bruno?"

"Oh! that is it, is it?" returned the post-mistress. "You think you must be paid like anybody else;" and with a great show of generosity, she produced a five-centimes piece. "There, take this, and be off."

But Bruno shook his head; and not until he had stood out for half an hour, and finally obtained ten centimes, would he receive the paper. Then he started at a quicker pace than usual, his face beaming with the double delight of having to tell Manon that her table was not yet begun, and that he had realized ten centimes for himself. After this fashion the post usually came in at Kersaint.

The newspaper was sent by "the cousin," Mr. St. John's only remaining correspondent in England, who wrote to him about once a year, and sent a paper every six months. It was merely intended as a sign that he was living and well; and was generally a month old when it reached Kersaint. Marguerite, however, always hailed its arrival as a kind of event, and would read aloud the advertisements of new books to her father, and wish she had got them all.

"May I open it, father?" she asked, when she had finished her colloquy with Bruno through the open window, and he had related with great glee, in his Breton patois, how he had outwitted the post-mistress.

"Certainly, child," and he went on talking to Philip.

Marguerite knew where to find the literary advertisements, and turning to that part, began reading them over to herself. Suddenly the color rushed into her face, and she exclaimed aloud—

"Mr. Earnscliffe!"

" What have you found Marguerite? " said her father.

She rose, without replying, and pointed to the part which had called forth her astonishment. It was the announcement of " A new edition of Mr. Philip Earnscliffe's last successful work." Mr. St. John looked a little surprised, and read the notice over twice without speaking, then he turned to Philip—

" My daughter has found out a literary namesake of yours, Mr. Earnscliffe; the name is so uncommon as to make this coincidence somewhat remarkable," and he handed him the paper.

Philip colored as his eye glanced over it. This was certainly the part of his history he cared least about revealing; still, he would have been better pleased had the discovery not taken place. Now he could conceal it no longer.

" I must acknowledge," he said, " that Philip Earnscliffe the author, is no other than myself."

" Oh, father!" burst from Marguerite " he is a great author, after all."

" And a modest one," added Mr. St. John. " Few men of your age, Mr. Earnscliffe, like their fame to pass incognito, even among such simple people as ourselves."

" Well," replied Philip, " the fact is, I have been so often wearied to death, when listening to other writers talking about their own works, that I resolved to adopt the other extreme, and never speak of mine at all "

" And you have kept well to your resolution. Still, though you never told me you were an author, I have more than once suspected that your talents had not lain idle all your life, and the other day was nearly questioning you on the subject. You seemed so thoroughly *au fait* of all literary matters and people, that I could not but think you were one of the fraternity yourself."

During the time her father spoke, Marguerite read and re-read the advertisement, and then looked long at Philip, trying to connect her kind, simple companion with the successful Mr. Earnscliffe. She felt rather awed at seeing a living author; and thought with shame how he had listened to all *her* childish conversation, and of the immeasurable distance there must henceforth be between them; she so ignorant and he in all the dignity of acknowledged authorship.

" What are the books about, father? " she whispered, at length, not daring to address Philip.

" Why do you not ask Mr. Earnscliffe? " he replied, aloud.

She turned away her face.

" Marguerite is afraid of you in your newly-discovered character, I believe."

" I hope not," replied Philip, " or I shall indeed regret that my secret is known."

Marguerite glanced at his face, and felt that there was no fresh gulf between them; and all her confidence returned.

" What are they about, then? " she cried, returning to her chair, which she drew quite close to his side. " Are they poetry or stories? Have you written many? And please tell me their names."

And Philip, when he once began to reply, was cross-questioned with such earnestness for a good half-hour, that Mr. St. John, although nearly as much interested as Marguerite, at length told her that she would tire Mr. Earnscliffe.

" Well," she pleaded, " only one thing more then; may we see any of your books? "

Philip replied that he had not a copy with him, and her countenance fell.

" But if you would really like to possess some of them, I will write a line to my publisher, and ask him to send them in a packet to Kersaint. They will remind you of me when they arrive, and I am gone,"

" Gone!" echoed Mr. St. John and Marguerite together, in a tone that spoke the sincerity of their surprise.

" Oh! do not go," the latter softly added. " Father, do not let Mr. Earnscliffe go ! "

" I thought you were to remain in Brittany half the summer," urged Mr. St. John.

" But not trespassing on your hospitality," Philip replied.

" My dear sir, you are conferring a simple favor upon an invalid like myself in remaining here; and Marguerite, for the first time in her life, has the pleasure of being with a youthful companion, and listening to another voice than mine. We have so little to attract you that I cannot press you to remain; but it will pain me to bid you farewell."

His manner was even kinder than his words. Philip felt that the invalid really wished him to stay with him, and it coincided but too well with his own desire. Conscience, however, once more urged him to leave Marguerite, and he faintly pleaded something about his wish to visit the remoter parts of Brittany.

" Of course, you should do so," returned Mr. St. John; " but you could not choose a more central spot for this object than Kersaint. Have your luggage sent here from Quimper," (where Philip had left it), " and make this head-quarters. You can take excursions without end, and return every few days to rest, and give us the pleasure of your society."

Marguerite did not speak, but she watched his face. He paused irresolutely, a sense of duty still warring with inclination; then he said, hesitatingly—

" I really do not like, stranger as I am, to accept your kind invitation—"

" If that is all," interrupted Mr. St. John, " your objection is at an end. I do not consider you a stranger already, and besides, all the world may claim to know a celebrated writer. I look upon you as our promised visitor for many weeks to come.

And Philip, overcome by Mr. St. John's warmth, and his own wishes, accepted. The note was written that morning, and despatched to his publisher; and Marguerite counted the days that must elapse before the books could by any possibility arrive. Philip said his last work was for her father, but the earlier ones, the poems and tales, were for her. And when he added, "Will you accept them as your own from me?" she could scarcely answer for delight..

CHAPTER XXII.

THEY generally walked together by the sea for an hour or two at sunset; and on the evening of this day Marguerite had more than usual to say. She was never weary of asking Philip about his writings, trying to make him repeat aloud any passages he could remember, and only discontinued when she at length saw he really did not relish the subject. But she wondered extremely how he could prefer their usual strain of conversation, to speaking of what engrossed all her thoughts. "It is because he thinks me so childish, and that I am not able to understand him," she said to herself.

After wandering for some time, they rested upon a high rock, which stood somewhat apart from its fellows, and watched the tide come in. Although the weather was still fair, there was a good deal of wind, and the waves were high, each bearing a wreath of foam that the sun converted into flame, and which formed a singular contrast to the cool, pearly green of the water beneath.

"I like to feel the spray upon my face," said Marguerite. "How can people be happy away from the sea?"

"Do you not like the country better?"

"You mean the fields and forests? Well, I like them too, and I could not bear to leave them; but I love the sea! Trees and flowers are merely beautiful, but the sea is living, and it has been my companion all my life. It has a thousand voices and expressions that I can understand: it can smile like a human face in the sunshine, or moan and wail like no other voice, when it casts up the drowned fisherman on the shore: it can break and surge over the huge rocks, and even uproot them from their resting-place, as it did yonder Kernot cliff last winter. Yes, the sea is full of life and power, and I love it! Think how dull it would be here in winter without the roaring of the waves!"

Philip smiled. "Do you consider that a cheerful sound?" he asked.

"Not cheerful, it is grand: and when we have clear frosty weather for a few weeks, and the waves are still, it seems quite lonely." She sang a note or two from an old ballad, then was silent. After some minutes Philip said, abruptly—

"Sing to me, Marguerite! I feel ill at ease this evening, and I should like to hear your voice in the open air, with only the fall of the waves for an accompaniment; sing something low and melancholy."

After pausing to select what would please him, she began one of her plaintive, old Scotch songs. Her voice sounded unusually sweet, and Philip leant back against the rock, his hat pulled forward to shade his eyes from the slanting sun, gazing at her profile, and listening to her rich tones with a perilous keenness of delight. His poet's temperament made him subject to a thousand temptations from which another man would have been free; and a soft half-hour at sunset could at any time turn into nothing his strongest resolutions.

"That was delightful, Marguerite!" he whispered, when she had finished.

"Was it?" she replied. "Does it really give you pleasure to hear me? I suppose my voice must be good, then."

"In all London I never heard a voice like yours, off the stage. If you took lessons for two years, you would be a first-rate singer. Would you not like to be courted and sought after in society for your extraordinary talent and beauty?" He wished to see if any desire for admiration—that strongest feeling with most women—lay dormant in the girl's heart.

"No," she returned, after thinking a little. "I am quite sure it would give me no happiness. I should not care for all the people at those great parties you tell me of, and I should not value their praises: how can it signify what strangers think of you? The praise of one or two would be sufficient for me. I should like to be beautiful and loved, I confess; but I would rather not be celebrated."

"You are right!" said Philip. "Fame is wearisome in the pursuit, unsatisfactory in possession."

"Oh, you should not say so!" Marguerite interrupted. "I only meant that, for myself, I could not value it. If I were a man I should be ambitious; and I should like my brother, if I had one, to be very celebrated. I could glory in his success."

It was a dangerous remark. Philip's eyes softened as they rested upon Marguerite's glowing face; and he remembered Lady Clara and her sympathy with him.

"What might I have been," he thought, "if I had had this girl for my wife? What might I still be, if I were now free to choose? Could you not extend this feeling to any but a brother?" he went on, aloud. "If at any

future time, for instance, you hear that I am
a very celebrated writer, will it give you no
pleasure?"

She drew nearer to him, and replied, looking up kindly in his face, "It would give me
more pleasure than anything in the world.
Except my father, you are my only friend,
and I should like to hear of you as though
you were really my brother. But that will
never be," she added, mournfully. "When
you leave Kersaint, I feel it will be for ever,
and I shall not even hear your name again."

"You are wrong, Marguerite; I shall return here next summer, if I live."

"Will you promise that? It will give
me something to hope for during the winter."

"If you are still here, I promise it," Philip replied; but he felt too truly that by another summer Marguerite might be an orphan.

"I hope I shall be improved," she resumed, timidly: "my father is going to teach me
so much next winter, and I shall have a
greater interest in learning now. How do
you think he has looked the last day or
two?"

"I think he varies much," answered Philip, evasively. A week's observation had
convinced him that Mr. St. John was wasting away under the slow, sure influence of
consumption, and that his occasional good
spirits and heightened color were merely
symptoms of his treacherous disease.

"But on the whole he is better?"

Her wistful tones, as though she half feared his answer, smote him.

"I trust your father may be long spared,"
he replied. "But I think his state requires
the greatest care."

"He is so melancholy," said Marguerite,
"and when we are alone I find it difficult to
cheer him. He thinks more than ever of my
mother now."

"She must have died very young," Philip
remarked.

"Yes; I believe before she was twenty;
but Manon could tell you better about her
than I can. She died directly after I was
born, and they say she never saw me. But
I wish I had not been told that; I cannot
bear to think that I was never—no, not for
a minute—in my mother's arms; it makes
me unlike all other children!"

Philip took the poor little hand as it wiped
away her tears and pressed it. "Do you
like to speak of her or not?" he said gently.

"Yes, I like it, but I never do so to my
father; it makes him look so wretched; and
Manon will not say much of her either. But
on my birthday she always will—it is my
treat, the greatest of all the year—and then
we sit together in my own room, and Manon
tells me of my beautiful young mother, and
shows me some of her things. She died of
some complaint of the heart; and, do you

know, I have often thought I shall die of it
also! They tell me I am like her in everything; and at times I have a sudden, painful feeling—here—which makes me feel there
must be something wrong. Do you think it
is likely?" She looked at him very earnestly.

Philip drew her to his side, and pressed
his lips upon her long, shining hair. The
action was involuntary, and the feeling which
prompted him innocent. At that moment
Marguerite was a perfect child, and he would
have done the same had she been six, and
not sixteen; but it was a fatal precedent.

"You should not give way to these
thoughts," he replied; "they might really
injure you, and are without foundation.
Both of my own parents died young of decline, yet you see I am strong and well; and
you, Marguerite, have the very bloom of
health upon your cheek. You must never
indulge these fancies again."

"No," she answered. "I will not, after
what you say. But I never mentioned it
before to any one, though I have often
thought of it. I should be sorry to die,
now that my father seems getting better,
and that you have come to us."

She had not shrunk from his side, and
there was no blush upon her cheek now.
Speaking of her dead mother, and of her
own secretly-cherished forebodings of an
early death, the feeling of timidity which
she occasionally experienced towards Philip
was forgotten, and he might in reality have
been her brother—at that moment. And so
they remained, until the sun was fairly set,
and the features of each grew less distinct
in the twilight, and they drew closer together as the fresh night-wind rose from the sea.
Then Philip could hear the quick beatings of
her heart, and her tremulous breath amidst
his hair, and his own pulse grew unsteady.
The delicious dawn of first love was upon
them both. That time when to breathe the
same air—to be silently at each other's side,
is in itself happiness all-sufficing—that time
which is the last remnant of Eden still left to
us—the only passionate delight that bears no
trace of the serpent.

At length Marguerite said it was time for
her evening reading with her father, and she
must go.

"Stay," said Earnscliffe, still holding her
hand, "another moment. Marguerite, I
have something to say to you."

What words were those which hung upon
his lips? Fresh words of cruel tenderness,
or a tardy avowal of his marriage? For
that time, at least. Marguerite did not hear
them. She had turned as he spoke towards
the distant manoir, and saw her father standing at one of the lower windows. She rose
to her feet.

"Not now; he is waiting for me. Tell
me to-morrow morning, before you set out.
I shall be up very early, and we will come

out on the terrace together; but I cannot keep him waiting now." And she ran quickly towards the house.

Philip followed her slowly, and was soon pacing up and down, with his cigar, on the terrace—his usual evening walk. He had already planned to start on the morrow for an excursion of several days, and he felt now, more than ever, that it was time for some change—that every hour he remained was perilous. It was in vain that he argued with himself how pure were his feelings towards Marguerite, and that, were he free, he would gladly make her his wife, and give up all the excitement of his past life for quiet domestic happiness. He was *not* free. Each pressure of her hand, each whispered word to her, were so many derelictions, faint, but progressive, from the path of honor; and Marguerite's ignorance of wrong, and her father's perfect trust in him, made his position the graver.

"If I had Neville's strong will," thought Philip, "with my own conscientious scruples, I should have left them at once. He might see no harm in the passing deception, and treat it all as the amusement of a few summer weeks; but at least he would act honestly up to his conviction, whilst I "—his reverie was here interrupted by a footstep advancing from the garden, and turning round, he distinguished Manon's square, solid figure as it approached him in the dusky light.

Manon held the opinion common amongst French persons of her class, that to be alone is the summit of human misery, and as the supper did not then require her attention, she had purposely joined Philip for a little conversation. She had an immense liking for the handsome young Englishman, but he was so engrossed all day with Marguerite, that she had rarely a chance of speaking to him alone.

"It is a dull evening, monsieur; I am sorry to see you by yourself."

"And you have kindly come to bear me company, Manon; I have not seen you all day."

"No, you have been on the beach, or away with mademoiselle, as usual. Poor child! it does my heart good to see her with a companion, after her life of solitude."

"She was talking to me, for the first time, to-day, of her mother," said Philip.

"Was she so, monsieur? Yes, it is her favorite subject, but I do not allow her to dwell much upon it; it is not well for the young to brood over death and sorrow. Her mother! she grows more like her every day." Manon raised her brown hand to her eyes.

"Was she as beautiful as her daughter is now?" Philip asked.

"Yes," returned Manon, "and as sweet and loving. Ah, monsieur! hers was a sad young life—so sad, you would not care to hear it told."

"On the contrary, I should feel the greatest interest in it. In anything concerning Mr. St. John," he added.

"Well, monsieur, if it will pass away the time for you, I will tell it. I am sure I may confide anything to you with safety; but you will see, without my asking you, that it is not a subject for you to mention again to my master."

She seated herself on a low bank at one end of the terrace, in the attitude consecrated from time immemorial to the teller of a story—her head erect, and her hands crossed—while Philip leant against the balustrade at her side, and prepared to listen.

The sky was now overcast, and the occasional cry of the owl, and the mournful beatings of the sea, formed a fit prelude for the history of Marguerite's mother.

———

CHAPTER XXIII.

"I WAS just sixteen," said Manon, "when I first entered into the service of Monsieur le Comte de Josselin. He was one of the oldest seigneurs in Brittany, though no longer rich; indeed, the vast possessions of his family had dwindled down, they said, to scarcely more than the old chateau and estate of Beaumanoir, near Quimper, where he lived with Madame la Comtesse and their only child Mademoiselle Lilla.

"I was her foster sister; and next to her own parents, she loved none so well as me. When we were both children, she saved all her treasures and dainties to share them with me, and she would leave all her companions to come and play with me and our goat upon the moor. I can see her now, in her little white dress, plucking the marguerites de pré, and the coquelicots, to hang them round Mimi's neck!

"Well, when I was sixteen, and mademoiselle a few months younger, the first grief of my own life came—my mother died. My father, who was old and infirm, was henceforth to live with my married sister; and I was, in a manner, cast upon the world. But Mademoiselle Lilla entreated her parents with such earnestness that I might be taken into the chateau, that they at length consented, and I became her own maid—or rather her companion, for she always treated me as a sister—and, in the happiness of being with her, my grief for my mother's death gradually diminished, and we were again like children together.

"She was at that time the most beautiful creature I ever beheld. Her hair was more golden than Marguerite's—her eyes of a softer blue; and her whole face and figure had something reminding me of the picture of Our Lady in the cathedral, as it looks in the moonlight.

But, though she was fragile and delicate, mademoiselle had high spirits; and it would have done your heart good to hear her merry laugh ringing through the gloomy rooms of the old chateau. Her parents doted on her —I have never denied them that—but they were both proud and fond of money—Madame la Comtesse especially; and, when they looked at their daughter's sweet face, I believe—God help them!—they thought more of the grand marriage it would enable her to make, than of anything else.

"When my foster sister was just seventeen, her cousin, the Marquis de St. Leon, came to stay with us. He was about six-and-twenty, slight, fair, with dark eyes, and a low voice—a voice not unlike yours, monsieur—and I saw, from the first day, he would love her. Soon his eyes never left mademoiselle; and, as they all walked up and down under the charmille, in the summer evenings, I could see him continually at her side, and I knew how it would be.

"Shall I confess to you that a feeling of jealousy crossed me at the idea? I knew that it was wicked, that of course she must marry some day, and I become nothing to her; but still I felt it. She was all I had in the world, and I could not bear that she should take any of her love from me.

"Gradually I saw a change come over her; she no longer cared for our childish games, she was silent and thoughtful and would blush whenever her cousin's name was mentioned. At length, one day she ran hurriedly into my little room where I sat working, her face all flushed and tearful, but so happy, and told me that the Marquis had proposed for her, and had been accepted. Even in her new joy she did not forget me; but said I was her dear sister still, and that I should continue to live with her after she married; and I was ashamed that I had ever felt jealous of her cousin.

"He was believed to be rich; for a good patrimony was said to have descended to him a few months before, on his father's death, and my master and his lady appeared well satisfied with the engagement. Our bishop—Monseigneur, at Quimper—wrote off to the Pope of Rome for a dispensation (because they were first cousins): they were soon formally betrothed to each other, and then the Marquis returned to Paris to arrange his affairs, while at the chateau preparations for the wedding were begun at once.

"It would weary you to tell the excitement and bustle we were all in. Mademoiselle Lilla was the gayest of us all, and her cheeks bloomed brighter than they had ever done before. It was not a marriage like most others, do you see, merely made up between parents without consulting the children's hearts: she loved her cousin truly, and looked forward to a life of quiet happiness with him when she should become his wife.

"The Marquis had been gone about three weeks, and we now expected him back for good in a few days, when the wedding was to take place. Mademoiselle got a little paler as the time drew on, and appeared more thoughtful again. I believe the near approach of a great happiness makes one tremble, or perhaps a secret foreboding of coming evil might have hung over her; but, however this was, all the preparations went on as usual, until one morning, when two letters arrived from Paris by my master, and put an end to all our joys and hopes.

"He was walking on the terrace with Madame la Comtesse when they were given to him; and mademoiselle and I were watching them from the window of her own sitting room, where we generally spent the forenoon together. The reading of these letters seemed to produce an extraordinary effect on the Comte and his wife, yet it did not exactly appear that they had received bad tidings; on the contrary, after consulting long together, there was a triumphant look upon the face of my lady when they returned towards the house which made me shudder without any real reason, and my foster sister threw her trembling arms round my neck, and said she knew her mother's smile boded no good to Henri. She never personally liked him, and I believe, although she accepted his suit, she thought her daughter ought to have married a prince at least.

In about an hour's time, a knock came at the door, and a *femme de chambre* entered, and told mademoiselle that Monsieur le Comte wished to speak to her in the library. Her hand, which was fast clasped in mine, turned as cold as ice at this message; however, she immediately rose to obey, and telling me to remain there until her return, she walked slowly from the room.

"I waited long—so long, it seemed to me like hours—before she came back, tormenting myself with thinking of all that could have happened; but when at length the door opened, and she tottered in, I felt sure none of my fears had been bad enough. Monsieur, did you ever see a young face gain the expression of years of misery in one day? if so, you can imagine how Mademoiselle Lilla looked. She was not pale, she was ashy; and there was a look—a fixed, hard look—upon her soft features, which made her seem positively old. It was the first time I ever saw anything of her mother in her face.

"'Oh, mademoiselle!—oh, my darling!' I cried; 'what is the matter? Is Monsieur Henri dead?'

"She seated herself without speaking, and remained so for several minutes; then she turned and said, in a harsh and altered voice —'Manon, never mention his name to me again. Dead, no! a thousand times worse; would, God, he *were* dead!' She moved about that day and the next like a thing of stone; on the third, she told me to come with her and walk. I remember when it was, a mild autumn day, and we wandered through the woods until we reached a small kind of temple that stood by the lake, at some distance from the château. She had used to come here with her cousin when they were engaged; but after he left, we had had no leisure for walking, and this was the first time she had visited it since. 'Let us rest,' she said; 'I am weary.'

"She looked very pale, and I opened the door of the temple for her to go in. There, upon the rustic table, lay a bunch of withered flowers—they had gathered them in their last walk together among the woods, and afterwards forgotten them in their happiness—and close beside them was one of Monsieur Henri's gloves. For a moment she stood still, her lips drawn tightly together, and her hands clenched; then, with a stifled cry, she seized the glove, pressed it to her lips, her bosom, uttered a thousand tender words over it, and burst into a flood of tears. They were the first she had shed; and I believe those tears saved her reason. When slowly she recovered, the unnatural firmness had left her face, and of herself she began speaking of her cousin. Still holding his glove in her trembling hands, she told me her father had discovered accidentally that he was unworthy of her; that he was leading the most wild and dissipated life, and at the very time of their engagement had made his profligacy and his intended marriage with her, alike a boast and a jest among his companions. 'And I wrote him,' she went on—' I wrote him a letter at once; my mother dictated it, I could not think for myself; but I know that I gave him back his false love, and told him from that moment he was free, and that I thanked God I was so too. I could not write it now,' she added, softly; 'for though I would not be his wife, I forgive him everything; and, Manon, Manon, I love him still!' She carried back the withered flowers and the glove. Ah, monsieur! she never parted with them again, as you will see.

"Winter set in early and severe; and mademoiselle grew so pale and thin, that I feared greatly for her health. Her parents, too, at last took alarm. I think her mother must have felt some pangs of self-reproach when she looked at her child's face, and knew it was her own work; she was, however, entirely taken up with a new scheme, and perhaps that prevented her from seeing Mademoiselle Lilla as others did.

"It appeared that one of the letters on that fatal morning, was a proposal of marriage from a gentleman of great riches, but about three times her age, who had seen mademoiselle at a country fête some months before; and either was, or pretended to be, ignorant of her engagement to her cousin. They had written to him without consulting their daughter, but, as she afterwards told me, begged him to wait for a few months, on account of her extreme youth. Madame la Comtesse judge rightly, that it would be well to let her first sorrow pass away before speaking to her again of marriage. When at length, however, she thought the time come, and *did* ask her consent to marry this new suitor, she was surprised at mademoiselle's decided rejection of him. 'I shall never marry Henri,' she said, 'but I will have no other—at least, not yet. Give me one year, mother, before you speak to me of those things again.'

"Madame la Comtesse was proud and grasping for wealth; but still she was a mother, and she could not withstand her poor child's mournful face, so they unwillingly wrote and told this gentleman, that their daughter's health was too delicate for her to think of marrying at present; and shortly afterwards we all went to Paris for the winter. They had several grand physicians for my foster sister, and they all said she had as yet no positive disease; but that she had a disposition to something of the heart. I forget what they called it, it was a long word; but I knew what the complaint was better than they, and could have given it a shorter name —her heart was breaking.

"She went to parties and balls—' she must be amused,' they said, ' and forget the past ; ' but, when she came home each night, weary and pale, and would weep upon my breast, in all her silks and flowers, I thought she would have been better sleeping quietly in her grave. She never met her cousin; for, immediately he received her letter, we were told he had gone right away to India, or America—I don't rightly know which—so, at least, she was spared the pain of seeing him again.

"Well—I must not keep you in the cold too long—when we had been in Paris about four months, mademoiselle met an Englishman in society, who pleased her better than all the gay young men she had known as yet; and that was my master—Mr. St. John. He was pale and quiet even then, but had, I used to think, a look of her cousin, which may have struck her too. At all events, she liked him; and when after a few weeks he proposed to her, she said to her mother, ' Let me marry Mr. St. John?'

"I was in the room at the time—for they kept nothing from me—and she never blushed or cast down her eyes, as she had done for the marquis; she was quite earnest, but cold and quiet. I believe she chiefly thought of leaving Paris and all these gay parties; and she did not remember, poor child! that she had no love to give with her hand.

"It was a dreadful blow to her parents, after all their schemes. The doctors said, unless they allowed her to marry as she liked, and at once, she would die; and they had no choice but to consent. Mr. St. John, however, was not a rich man, and did nothing but read and write books; so, after all, mademoiselle made what is called a very poor marriage, although, God knows, she gained a true and faithful heart in my master.

"After the wedding, her first words to her husband were, 'Let me go back to the country.' And he took a pretty place not far from Paris, where they passed the first year of their marriage. I remained with them, you may be sure; and when at last a fair little daughter was placed in my darling's arms, I thought her old smile had come back for good, and that she would grow really well and happy. My master loved her beyond everything on earth; he thought of nothing but her—and she was so sweet and gentle that it was only natural he should believe she loved him in return, for he had never heard anything about her former engagement with the marquis.

"When the baby was a few months old, a distant relation of her mother's died, and left this property of Kersaint to my young mistress. I believe it was very acceptable to them; for her father's estate, as he had no son, would go to an uncle on his death; and he had nothing but that to leave. And, besides this, Mr. St. John, who was too book-learned to understand money, had lent nearly all his to a relation to be put out in business, and he had just failed at the time of the child's birth. So they decided for the present to come and live quietly at Kersaint.

"They had many friends in Paris; and though neither of them cared about society, they were persuaded to go there for a few weeks before starting for Bretagne.

"That was a fatal delusion, monsieur.

"They were invited out a great deal; and one evening they had gone to a grand fête at some foreign ambassador's, and I, as usual, was sitting up to undress my mistress on her return, when I heard the carriage enter the port-cochère of the hotel an hour or two earlier than I had expected. I ran out with a light into the great corridor to meet them, and after waiting some minutes I saw Mr. St. John supporting his wife with difficulty up the stairs. She was just as white as the day when she broke off with her cousin, and had something the same expression on her face.

"'Eh, mon Dieu! I cried, 'what has happened?'

"'Your mistress has been taken suddenly ill,' replied my master, quite calm, though he too was very pale. 'Get her to bed, good Manon, and watch with her through the night; it is best for her to be kept perfectly quiet.'

"He left us at the door of the sleeping-room, and I did watch with her through that dreadful night. At first she was faint and unconscious; but that soon passed, and the worst was then to come. All she said I could not tell you; but I gathered from her delirious talk that in the middle of the ball she had suddenly seen her cousin, whom she believed far away in America. He had spoken to her and asked her to dance; instead of that, however, they had gone into another room alone, and there for the first time she heard the truth.

"The letter which her father had received, on the same morning with the fresh proposal for her hand, was from Monsieur Henri, saying, that on looking into his affairs, they were not so straight as he believed: his father in fact had been extravagant, and the money did not all come clear to the marquis. But in the letter he had asked for time, and said he would start gladly for foreign parts, and try to win more money for himself, if his cousin would only wait for him.

"'And they never told me this,' she cried. 'They deceived me, cruel father! cruel mother! they deceived me, and I wrote him that letter! I thanked God that I was free! when I would have died for him, when I loved him—when I love him still.' And she took his glove from the place where it always lay with the withered flowers, and wept over it till I thought she would die from weeping. I never saw such grief before, or since, and I think it was the worse coming from one so gentle as my mistress.

"Towards morning I bethought me of something that might soothe her; and as I had now persuaded her to lie down in her bed, I crept from the room to the baby's nursery, and wrapping it in a shawl, I brought it back sleeping, and placed it in her arms. For one moment, monsieur, she shrunk back from her child. It was only a moment, however. The next she covered it with kisses and hugged it to her heart. It woke; and seeing its mother, gave a soft cooing cry, and held out its hand to her breast; the little touch I suppose recalled everything to her, that she was another man's wife and a mother, for she attempted to check her sobs, and I could see that she was praying over the child.

"She was long dangerously ill; but as soon as she could be moved, we came down to Kersaint. When I think of my master during that time, I believe I pity him most of all. I was afterwards told that at the ball when my mistress fainted, he overheard some of the guests saying to each other 'Ah! Madame St. John has met her old lover—poor husband!' And this was the first he ever knew of her former engagement. At all events he never looked the same after that night.

"The sea air and change seemed to do her good; and she tried so hard not to repine, and to be thankful to live, that her husband could not but forgive her—indeed, he was soon more devoted to her than ever. He is unlike all other men; and when from herself he heard the whole story, and how she had been deceived, he forgot his own disappointment, and only tried to make up to her with his love for what she had lost.

"A year passed by; and, though she was

not worse, I could see that she did not really gain strength. At times her color was high, and she would rally, and sing to him, and play with the child; but suddenly, her hand would be pressed to her heart, and the faint shade round her lips told me she was suffering inward pain. At the end of that year the child died—died of croup—in the night, when we all thought she had fallen asleep in perfect health; and, from that hour, I knew we should lose my mistress. She showed no passionate grief—she scarcely wept for the child; but, when she hung over the little body in its coffin, she smiled; and I could see she was only parting with it for a short time. It was the last thing that kept her to life.

"And now she faded rapidly; every day I saw a change; but what made it worse was, that she expected soon again to be a mother. She liked to be carried out by my master to the terrace, and would sit there for hours, watching the sea, with a kind of dim look upon her face, but seldom speaking. When I tried to rouse her, for the sake of the unborn babe, she would only say, 'Pray God, Manon, that it be not a girl! I do not wish to bring another sorrowful life into the world.'

"While she was able to sit up, however, she embroidered a little cap for the child —I have it now, monsieur—Marguerite would sooner look at it than at all the treasures on the earth—and said, when it was finished, 'This is all I shall ever do for my child.'

"She knew she should die at its birth— and she was right. She never even rallied enough to hold it in her arms. But, on the morning of that day, she said to me, 'Manon, be faithful to my husband, as you have been to me, and never leave him and my child.' I promised her, and I have kept my word. Monsieur, I feel the first drops of a thunder-shower, and it is supper-time."

CHAPTER XXIV.

MANON's prediction was right. A violent thunderstorm broke that night over Kersaint; and, when Philip prepared to depart at an early hour the following morning, the weather was still dark and lowering.

"You had better not go," said Marguerite, as they sat alone together at breakfast (Mr. St. John having taken leave of his visitor the previous evening), "I am sure there will be another storm, and one day can make no difference."

Philip, however, knew that each day *did* make a difference; and, for once, he remained firm. He went; and Marguerite felt that her whole life had become a blank.

The days succeeding his departure were dark and gloomy. Mr. St. John, who was affected by every change of weather, was not so well, and kept to his own room, and the lonely silence of her home struck Marguerite as it had never done before. She could not take the old interest in her birds and flowers, but she was too restless to remain within doors; and, except at those times when she was with her father, spent the entire day wandering near the sea, listening to its soothing, familiar voice, and dreaming those first dangerous dreams which further the progress of an absent lover, far better than his own presence.

Philip was away more than a fortnight, exploring among the wilds of the Menes Arres hills, and the Loc Mariaker lakes. The lone grandeur of the scenery, and the character of the people among whom he passed, really interested him; he needed a strong contrast to his soft, artificial life, and here he found it. But in his wanderings, with no companion save his own thoughts, he had unfortunately, quite as much time for dreaming as Marguerite; and he returned to Kersaint with his heart fuller of the little "wild daisy" than when he started.

During his absence the packet of books had arrived from London, and were opened, as Philip requested they should be, by Marguerite. In addition to the copies of his own works, he had ordered several new books which he thought would interest Mr. St. John, and one or two of a different nature for Marguerite. But all of these she laid aside; they were not his, and she scarcely thought of them again. The name of Philip Earnscliffe upon the title-pages of his works, had, for her childish eyes, a charm beyond everything she could have imagined. She made her father scrupulously reserve to himself the one bearing the latest date, which Philip told her was for Mr. St. John, and read and re-read the volume containing his early tales and poems with more deep interest and admiration than had ever been bestowed upon them in his time of first success. There were no faults for Marguerite; she enjoyed the fresh beauty of the style, without perceiving its irregularity, and entered into all the young poet's glowing visions of life, without knowing they were false. But to Mr. St. John the perusal of Earnscliffe's last work laid open a page of the author's own life. He knew that such exceeding bitterness against one peculiar class of society could not flow from the pen of so young a writer if it were really a principle; and felt sure, from his own experience of human nature that some great personal disappointment gave a latent tone to his writings. But of the true nature of this disappointment he could not even surmise. The idea of Philip being married, of course, never presented itself. Young and handsome, it was not likely that he should already have made shipwreck in love; and his literary career appeared to have been successful. So Mr. St. John, who was naturally somewhat apathetic about the concerns of others, simply conjectured that his guest had passed through some one of the great trials of life, and troubled himself no further on the subject.

When Philip returned, his host's true and measured criticism upon his works, and Marguerite's undisguised admiration of them, afforded him more real pleasure than any incense to his author's vanity which he had yet received. He remained some days at the manoir, then made another more distant excursion; and in this manner two or three months passed quickly by. Mr. St. John and his daughter grew accustomed to his frequent absence, but they always awaited his return with renewed pleasure. Philip Earnscliffe was becoming a part of their existence—hitherto so barren in events—and they neither of them would even speak of the inevitable time when he should leave Brittany, and they return to their old monotonous life. An intellectual companion had roused Mr. St. John from his habitual melancholy, and given him once more an interest in the things he had cared for in other days; while Marguerite—poor little Marguerite!—every week made her feel the more that her whole earth was now concentrated into Philip's presence.

All this time he had guarded himself well. Constantly associating with Marguerite, watching all the dawnings of her young mind, reading but too truly the varying color of her cheeks, and in the full possession already of her every thought (that first soul-possession which mocks at all other, and to which no future rival can attain), he had yet breathed no syllable of his own fast deepening passion; he had said no word that she might not have listened to from a brother—nothing which her father might not have heard. That one kiss, whose recollection yet thrilled through him a hundred times that day, had been the first and last:—if he took her hand, his own pressure was grave and calm; and Earnscliffe thought that he was in all things acting like a man of honor.

But the hour of awakening from this dream of self-reliance was very near.

"I think you should take Mr. Earnscliffe to the grotto of Morgane, Marguerite," said Mr. St. John one evening to his daughter. "There is scarcely anything more curious in the neighborhood; and, indeed, in Brittany. Do you think it would be too far for you in this hot weather? If so, Bruno must act as guide in your place."

Marguerite did not think it would be in the least too far. "They might start early, while it was yet cool, take a basket of provisions with them, and return at sunset, after spending a long day in the caves. She knew the way better than Bruno, and would be able to tell Mr. Earnscliffe all the different legends connected with the place."

Mr. Earnscliffe appearing equally anxious with herself that she, and not Bruno, should be his companion, the expedition was soon planned, and it was settled that on the following Monday they should start by seven o'clock for the distant grotto.

The next day was Sunday, and they went together to church; Manon having heard low mass at an earlier hour, in order to be with Mr. St. John during their absence, for his state was now so uncertain as to make her dread leaving him alone.

It was a great festival of the church, and the music was more than usually fine. The morning sun streamed through the Gothic windows, throwing a thousand richly-colored gems around the altar; the freshest flowers stood there, mingling their odors with the voluptuous sweetness of the incense; the notes of the organ stole in soft, prolonged whispers through each dim aisle and distant chapel of the immense cathedral; and when the priest, a tall and dignified-looking man, held aloft the glittering symbol of our salvation, and every head bowed before it in lowly reverence, Philip was carried away by all the poetry of the scene, and sank on his knees upon the pavement. He felt somewhat ashamed of his enthusiasm, when, on glancing at Marguerite, he saw her calm and unmoved at his side, evidently fully enjoying the music and beauty around her, but with no trace of devotion upon her face. When they were on their way home he recurred to it, and asked her if the solemnity and grand effect of the service never made her feel half a Catholic. She looked quite surprised.

"Do you not know that I am of my father's religion?" she answered.

"Yes," said Philip; "but it would be only natural if you had a leaning occasionally towards the only faith whose services you have ever heard celebrated."

"But it is not my father's faith," was her reply.

That answer was the key-note to her whole character. Sentiment, reason, religion itself must be derived with her from the person she loved. Hitherto this one person had been her father; and she could not even admit the possibility of temptation to feel otherwise than he had taught. Perfect trust in him was the leading article in her early belief, and she was now unconsciously extending this faith to Philip.

The following morning was hazy and full of promise, a true summer morning; and by a little after seven they had started for their distant walk. Marguerite was radiant with spirits, but Philip felt less inclined to talk than usual. The perpetual restraint under which he forced himself to act began to chafe him; and perhaps some internal warning told him that this long, lonely day together would not be passed through without betraying him into words that nothing could efface; while Marguerite's unconstraint and growing familiarity made his position only the more difficult to maintain.

Nearly their whole road lay by the seaside. For the first mile they kept on the sands; but then, as the tide was now in, they were obliged to ascend a high cliff intervening between them and the next bay, which at low water might be reached by the rocks. The road was steep, but Marguerite was accustomed to climbing, and as the sun was not yet hot they soon reached the summit, where a wide table-land lay spread before them. The scene was monotonous in the extreme, yet still possessing a kind of indefinable harmony which was not without its charm. The rocks festooned with heath in full flower—the mysterious Druid circles of stones—the silence only broken by the hoarse, measured whisper of the waves far beneath—all was in unison; and the sea-breeze, which at this height was as invigorating, as real mountain air, made Marguerite's young blood circulate in her veins with a feeling of actual pleasure. But Philip was still depressed. The view before them was just of that unmarked character which takes its coloring entirely from the tone of spirits in which it is seen, and the immensity, the solitude, the perfect repose, weighed upon him, while they stimulated his companion.

"Look!" she exclaimed, suddenly, touching his hand with her accustomed quick gesture—"a chase!"

He turned and saw, almost immediately behind them, two birds, whose cries had attracted her notice; one, a heron, who was still considerably a-head, and in pursuit of her one of the larger kind of hawk.

"Poor bird!" continued Marguerite; "I hope she will escape." And they stood still and watched this natural "hawking," which soon became so near a chase as to be considerably exciting.

The hawk gained gradually upon his prey, and was at length so close that they expected each moment to see him strike. He had, however, missed his aim, or in the ardor of pursuit forgotten his usual wariness, and instead of flying over the heron, and thus securing her at once, he passed about a foot beneath her, receiving at the same instant a vigorous stroke from her long beak, which made him turn over twice or thrice in the air with pain. At first it seemed as though he would descend to the ground; but then, giving a shrill, angry cry of defiance, he rose with redoubled energy to the pursuit. Meantime, the heron had profited by her temporary advantage, and taken a fresh turn towards a distant shelter of fir-wood, hoping this time to save herself by distance, not height. But the hawk saw the manœuvre, and cutting diagonally through the air with the rapidity of an arrow, he almost met her in her downward flight. The heron gave two or three screams of distress, and once

again attempted to escape by suddenly rising perpendicularly as she had done at first; her pursuer followed her hotly, and after some seconds the two birds had become like two mere black specks upon the pale sky.

"Will she escape?" cried Marguerite, quite breathless in anxiety for the heron's fate. "Poor bird, did you hear her cry?"

"No," returned Philip; "she will not escape. It is an unequal contest, the weak against the strong, as is usual in this world."

"See—see," Marguerite exclaimed, "the hawk is uppermost now, and listen to her screams!"

As she spoke, a long cry, just audible in its intense agony of distress, was again heard, and both birds began swiftly to descend. The heron now attempted no longer to defend herself; she sank rapidly, only answering to the incessant strokes of the hawk by her screams. Suddenly she folded her wings, and shot downwards like a stone. It was her last feint, but her antagonist did the same; and when she again attempted to take flight, a tremendous blow from his beak finally overcame her. She continued to fall, occasionally turning over in the air, and at the moment that she touched the earth, the hawk pounced down upon her with an exulting shriek that drowned her last faint cry.

The two spectators had watched the final scene with equal interest, and tears for the heron's death stood in Marguerite's eyes. But there was a singular expression upon Earnscliffe's face.

"The weak against the strong," he repeated, as they resumed their path.

Marguerite little knew that the unequal struggle between the two birds could have awakened any comparison to themselves in his mind.

"I have watched this kind of chase before," she said, "but never saw the weaker bird escape. How could the ladies in olden times, whom I have read about to my father, delight in assisting in such cruel sport?"

"It is an unnatural feeling for your sex," replied Philip. "In ours, the delight of hunting and destroying what is weak is inherent from our cradles. As school-boys we persecute every defenceless creature we come across; as men——"

"Well," said Marguerite, "why do you hesitate? Surely you were not going to say that all men are cruel! At least I know two exceptions: my father would not destroy a worm upon the path; and you, Mr. Earnscliffe, I am sure would protect everything weaker than yourself."

The unconscious appeal touched him.

"I believe I would, dear Marguerite," he answered. "But at least I am glad that you extend your favorable opinions of humanity to me." He looked down into her trusting face, and impulsive in everything, suddenly determined to tell her at once of his marriage. It was one of his better resolutions, and he gave himself no time to waver.

"Come, Marguerite," he continued, "we have still a long day before us; let us rest awhile on the heath under the shelter of yonder group of firs, and converse a little. I have something to tell you in which, I believe, you will take an interest.

They walked on about a hundred yards, to the solitary trees he mentioned, Marguerite's eyes dancing in expectation of the secret she was to hear, and she then seated herself, her head leaning against one of the fir trunks, while Philip took his place at some distance from her, and with his face averted from his companion.

"Now begin," she cried. "I am sure it is something very interesting.

"To me it is," he returned, "although I have no reason for supposing it should be so to others. It is about myself——"

"That is right," interrupted Marguerite. "Only yesterday I told my father I should like to know all the history of your life, and I even wished him to ask you; but he said you would tell us just as much as you liked, and I ought not to be so curious. Now, you will tell me all—and, first, why you are sometimes so sad."

She turned her large eyes upon him with a look of childish affection, that might again have made him irresolute had he seen their expression; but his own were intently fixed upon the tiny blossoms of the wild thyme at their feet, and with a sort of effort he began. He told her of his childhood, of his parents' death, of his uncle's kindness, of his schoolboy dreams, and tried to linger over all these early recollections, which delayed him, as it were, in his approach to the darker period of his life. Marguerite liked to hear every detail, and when at length he spoke of his first book and its success, she clasped her hands and exclaimed with pleasure. He then told her somewhat of his progress in great London; he mentioned Neville and one or two of his other friends, and at last he brought his lips to speak of Lady Clara.

"Was Lady Clara very beautiful?" she asked, timidly.

"She was not beautiful; she was pale and sickly, and rarely smiled."

"Was she young?"

"Older than myself."

"Was she—I mean—did your cousin like you very much?"

Earnscliffe only smiled bitterly at the question; and Marguerite was silent. Without knowing why, she felt her heart throb painfully, and an odd, stifled sensation at her throat. Had Philip loved his cousin without return?

"Marguerite," he resumed abruptly, "I can better describe my cousin's character when I have told you the real tie which binds her to me. Lady Clara is my wife."

"Your wife!" she stammered; "your wife! Are you married?" The words died away, and with it all the flush of youth on Marguerite's face. Married! She looked aside over the vast heath, at the grey curlews which circled round the Druid stones, and the fern leaves waving in the wind, and knew that it was all monotonous and dreary, though the sun shone brighter than ever.

"Yes," he went on with desperate resolution, "I have been married for some years; but my marriage has been misery to me. I have long been parted from my wife; I would give all in this world, yes, my talents, my hope for the future itself, to undo that miserable marriage. The recollection of it is so bitter to me, that on coming abroad I resolved to mention it to none but those already acquainted with my past history, and thus I have deceived you, too. Will you forgive me?" .

The sorrow on his face was so real that she forgot herself, and extended her hand to him. Earnscliffe pressed it, hesitated, then relinquished it abruptly, and went on with his story. He told her of his uncle's losses, of the failure of his own literary prospects, lastly, of his wife's leaving him; and if he spoke little of his own errors it was out of respectful feeling towards the innocent girl who listened to him, not from any idea of exculpating himself. "I have told you all, Marguerite," were his last words. "Now you must be my judge."

She looked at him irresolutely for a few moments without speaking; and during that time her thoughts were painful ones. Then all recollection of herself, or her own faintly-dawning hopes, died within her. She saw him forsaken, disappointed in his nearest ties and remembered him only.

"Philip," she whispered—she had never called him so before—"they have all left you. Will you let me love you, and be your sister?" and before he had divined her intention, she took his hand and raised it to her lips.

The reader (especially if a young lady), must again remember poor Marguerite's perfect ignorance of the world, before judging her too harshly. Of course, had she been properly educated, she would have at once returned home to her father on discovering that Philip was married, and have felt a fitting amount of indignation at so nearly being led into loving him! But Marguerite knew absolutely nothing of decorum; and she therefore stifled in her own bosom at once, and with a silent pain, those half-formed visions of the future which during the last few weeks had begun to spread their golden vista before her. And seeing Philip a lonely, and as she understood, forsaken man, she tried to comfort him with the same childish caress that had so often won a smile from the pale lips of her father.

He withdrew his hand hastily from her touch.

"Have I offended you?" she asked softly, but with no feeling of shame. "Oh, Mr. Earnscliffe! I wish I knew what to say; indeed, I should like to show how much I feel for you," and again she ventured to touch his hand. Philip started to his feet.

"But I am married, child! How can I talk to you of love? How can I suffer myself to receive your innocent kindness? Do you not hear that I am married?"

His voice had never sounded so harsh to Marguerite before.

"Yes, sir," she answered, looking timidly up. "But have I offended you? Will you not let me be your little sister? I am ignorant and childish, I wish you see how my father loves me, and if you——"

Philip took a few paces upon the turf: then he stopped short, and he was very pale; but for the present the mastery was gained.

"Marguerite," he said, "you are a child. You know nothing of life or human nature; and what you offer is impossible. There can be no talk of brotherly love between a man of my age and a young girl like yourself. You know not what you say when you ask it. Look upon me as your father's friend—as your own friend, if you will—but nothing else. I could not love you as a brother," he added, bitterly.

She rose to her feet. Not a glimmering of his real meaning had reached her. Her cheeks had never flushed at his words; and, in a saddened voice, she proposed that they should continue their walk. She only felt that he had rejected her affection; and her loving nature, not her pride, was wounded.

"Forgive me for what I have said!" she whispered, after they had walked some distance in silence.

Earnscliffe was only human; and when he looked down into that sweet, beseeching face, is it wonderful that warmer words than he intended once more found their way to his lips?

CHAPTER XXV.

"Are you not tired, Marguerite?"

"No; I am seldom tired, monsieur."

"You are paler than usual. Take my arm, child; the ascent is steep."

She looked at him wistfully as he spoke, and then accepted his proffered assistance.

Marguerite could not understand Earnscliffe that day, or interpret his changing mood—at one time so cold and formal, and then warmer than he had ever been to her before. But she thought the recollection of his marriage had, perhaps, made him fitful and capricious, and tried to render her own manner to him more kind than usual. Yet even as

she walked, and strove to speak cheerfully of the objects around, the painful feeling at her heart would return, and unbidden tears start into her eyes. Was it all sympathy for Earnscliffe? Marguerite knew not.

They had soon finished the ascent of the last hill, and were on the summit of the steeps of Morgane, which formed a boldly-jutting promontory of down and cliff; and the sea lay around them on all sides, save that by which they had approached. Blue and silent it lay; only dotted over by the tiny sails of the fisher-boats, or the black rocks, around which there was scarcely sufficient foam to whiten; and the sea-birds skimmed lazily over the quiet world of waters.

"Our path is here," said Marguerite, approaching to the very edge of the cliff; "but I have first a visit to make to my friend the gabarier. That is his house." She pointed to a rude kind of hut, built into a corner of the rock, about thirty feet beneath them, and so completely of the same grey color, as at first to be scarcely distinguishable. The roof was merely a mass of dried sea-weed, kept down by some enormous stones; and the smoke from the peat-fire, issuing through more than one aperture, showed that the mid-day meal of the family was preparing. The gabarier himself sat outside the door on the small platform of projecting earth, which formed the extent of his worldly possessions, employed in mending nets, and watching some four or five half-clad urchins, who were seated on the very edge of a precipice of several hundred feet, kicking their legs in the air, and trying to push each other off, in a manner which in no way discomposed their parent—these being the daily practices of the infant Blaisots, from the time they could walk alone.

Marguerite tripped down the steep path which led to the hut, and then suddenly calling, "Père Blaisot!" made the boatman start round with surprise. His harsh features lighted up on seeing Marguerite, who ran to his side and said a few words, which made him turn and uncover to Earnscliffe.

"We are going to visit the caves, père Blaisot. The tide is just right, is it not, and the weather too?"

"For the tide," he replied, in his rude patois, "you must wait an hour and a half. For the weather, you had best not go at all."

"Why?" said Marguerite; "the sky is clear, and the sea without a ripple."

"Nevertheless, there will be a storm before night," was the reply. "I have not lived alone for thirty years among the rocks, without getting to understand the signs of the weather. Take the *gentilhomme* to the grotto if you will; but return quickly, little queen. It will be no evening for such as you to be out."

Marguerite translated his words to Earnscliffe, who only smiled in reply, as he glanced towards the blue horizon, over which there appeared not even the faintest shadow of a cloud.

"He does not believe me," said the gabarier, resuming his netting. "Maybe he knows best—night will show."

"Nay, father," said Marguerite, "I believe you are always right in these things; and we will certainly return quickly from the grotto. Meanwhile, will you let one of the children carry our basket for us down the cliff, for we shall have enough to do minding our own steps; and, as we have still an hour to spare, we will eat our dinner among the cool rocks until the tide is down."

"Moser!" called the gabarier—and a sun-burnt imp of seven summers disentangled himself from the heap of small humanity which overhung the precipice, and ran up to him. "Where is your basket, little queen?" he added.

Marguerite gave it into Moser's hands, and his black eyes were already sparkling at the idea of purloining dainties on the way, when the gabarier snatched it himself, with a nod, indicating small belief in the good principles of his son. He then bound the lid strongly to the basket with a piece of fishing-line, and administered a hint to its bearer, that if he attempted to open it, his granddam should whip him; and the expression which this awful promise awakened on Moser's face showed that the threat was well selected.

"Be off!" cried the boatman; "fly!"

The child seized the basket, and appeared actually to bound across the edge of the cliff. Earnscliffe could hardly repress an exclamation of horror; but on approaching cautiously, he descried a kind of goat-track that, from above, seemed absolutely perpendicular, but down which the little rock-imp was already making fast progress.

"Is this our road?" he inquired.

"Yes," said Marguerite, "but it is nothing to what you will find it lower down. This is easy walking. Good bye, pere Blaisot; we will be sure to come back before the storm."

The path was certainly not so steep as it had appeared; still it required steady nerves and a light foot, and the dry weather made it somewhat slippery. Earnscliffe, in his boyhood, had been a fearless climber, and he thought nothing of the descent for himself; but he was astonished at Marguerite's perfect coolness, and the speed at which she turned the abrupt points overhanging the sea. She was so accustomed to these kind of walks, that it never occurred to her to look for his assistance, and she did not even turn round until they were more than half-way down. Here the path ceased altogether, and they had to descend an abrupt wall of cliff, several feet deep, at whose base was a bed of loose soil leading down to a perfect *débris* of broken rocks and stones. She paused.

"This is the worst part, and you must help me, Mr. Earnscliffe. I am not quite like the gabarier's children, who can climb up and down the bare granite like little spiders."

Philip swung himself down the rock, and then extended his hands to Marguerite.

"Come," he said, "I will lift you safely."

She was not fearful of danger, as he had seen; but for a second she shrunk back, and she felt that her face flushed crimson.

"I am afraid——" she began.

"Nay," returned Philip, gravely, "you are safe with me; come!"

She had to kneel before he could reach her waist, then he lifted her quickly to the ledge beside him; but Marguerite thought she felt that strong arm tremble.

"Can you walk along this narrow track alone, if you are so nervous at looking from a height?"

"Oh! I was not afraid of *that*," she answered, looking up so artlessly in his face that he could not forbear smiling. Marguerite could never be a woman for more than one minute together.

"You were afraid of me, then?"

"I did not like—I mean to say it would have been better——" But she felt she was again betraying herself; and, without finishing, ran quickly past, that he might not see her face.

There were more difficulties to surmount, however, more rocks to descend, and by the time they had reached the shining sands which lay at the base of the cliffs, all recollections of Philip's marriage, and the result produced upon both by its disclosure, seemed to be forgotten. They were just on their old friendly terms; and Marguerite's cheeks as bright, or a shade brighter, than when they left Kersaint.

They found Moser seated in the middle of some wet sand, the fierce sun streaming full upon his bare head, while with eager eyes and scent he vainly attempted to guess at the contents of the basket, through the wicker-work.

"Moser!" cried Marguerite. He sprang up detected, and, doubtless with his granddam's bony fingers already crackling in prospective over his ears, began pouring forth a voluminous mixture of tears and gibberish. Marguerite told him, however, he had performed his task well, and opening the basket gave him some fruit, and then a piece of two sous, which sent him home rejoicing, to display his spoils.

"Now where shall we dine?" she said.

They selected the shady side of a huge rock, where the sands were dry, and near which a trickling stream furnished them with cold, fresh water. Marguerite spread the snowy serviette, of Manon's providing, upon a small, flat rock on the sands, and laid out thier pic-nic upon it. And a merry meal they made! They had forgotten knives and

forks, of course, and she laughed heartily at
Philip's affectation, when he was obliged to
eat with his fingers; and they had only one
glass between them, and he would always
insist drinking after her, although she offered each time to get him fresh water from the
brook; and—oh, reader! if you are young,
I need not paint this happy two hours to
you; if you are not, you must remember at
least one such morning of your youth, and
not require my description.

"We are just like children," said Marguerite, at length, trying to call up a look of
dignity. "Here we are, wasting the whole
afternoon, when we have so much to see in
the caves; and, beside, we have forgotten
the gabarier's storm."

"Of which there are at present few signs,"
added Earnscliffe. "We are quite happy
here, Marguerite. You ought to sing some
ballad connected with the scene before I see
these wondrous caves—and I am sure they
will look better at sunset. I should like to
hear your voice first."

She sang to him, and they lingered yet an
hour before starting for the grotto. Both
seemed to have an instinctive feeling that this
was in some manner a farewell to their past
life together; everything they said was tinged
with the tone we adopt on the "last day."
They could neither of them have framed this
presentiment into language; but it existed:
and never had the presence of both possessed
for the other so deep a charm before.

At length they rose, and slowly pursued
their way. The caves were on the other side
of the creek, but at no great distance from
the spot where they had dined; and, after
traversing one or two short subterranean
passages among the rocks, they again emerged upon the sand opposite the entrance to
the principal grotto of Morgane, where they
stopped for a few minutes to remark the singular character of the cliffs among which it
lay, before preparing to enter. Huge red
pyramids shot up against the pale sky on one
side; on the left, slate-colored reefs of granite, piled one upon another, overhung the sea
in giddy, aërial galleries; while in many
parts the rocks were hollowed out by the
action of the waves into gigantic arcades,
now filled with swarms of grey curlews, whose
incessant cries might have told to more experienced bearers that a storm was not far
off.

The entrance to the grotto was so low that
they were forced to walk for some yards in a
stooping posture, and then found themselves
in such complete darkness as to be unable
for several minutes to distinguish any object
around them. Gradually, however, the
obscurity seemed to diminish, and a faint
bluish ray stole through the low aperture
they had entered, along the shining walls
and sandy floor of the cave, until, as the eye
at last became accustomed to this half-light,

the whole grotto rose before them like some
scene in a child's fairy book.

The roof was about forty feet in height
and was completely covered with a glittering
vitrification, extending down the sides to
the base. Long veins of the deepest red and
pale green marbled the dome, and gave a
softer beauty to the savage grandeur of this
natural palace. In the middle stood one
huge rock of rose-colored granite, rendered
smooth as marble by the constant washing of
the waves at high water, and at the extreme
farther end was a bank of bright-colored
sand.

Some of this sand Marguerite collected for
Manon, who thought it a great ornament to
the flower-pots in her windows, and afterwards she began picking up shells—of which
a variety in every shade of color lay profusely
on the ground—while Philip stood watching
the singular beauty of the scene, and thinking
how well Marguerite might have personated
Undine, in her little white dress, and with her
bright hair falling round her shoulders. Again
they forgot the time, until a sudden crimson
ray fell upon the green rock, just above
Marguerite's head, and made Philip exclaim
that there must be some opening on this side
of the cave, and that it was already sunset.

"And time for us to be going," added
Marguerite. "We will just explore this
new entrance, and then return at once."

Directed by the streak of sunshine, they
were not long in finding another egress, and,
after a little climbing, again emerged into
the open air. The altered appearance of the
sky struck both of them at once. Had they
noticed more closely, they would have observed, even before entering the caves, that
a few light mists had arisen over the western
horizon. Now the entire sky was covered
with masses of ominous-looking cloud, edged
with gold, and of a deep, inky purple, that
foreboded coming tempest. The sun shone
with a lurid crimson from out the dark bank
into which he was just sinking; the air was
oppressively heavy; the sea still quiet.

"The storm is coming," said Marguerite.
"Blaisot was right, after all."

"Yes," returned Philip. "I scarcely
think we shall have time to reach his hut
again before it begins. See, there are a few
drops already; we had better remain under
shelter of the rocks until it is over; it will
probably, not last long."

Philip had not understood the gabarier's
warning; and, observing the water still
comparatively low, and far away upon the
sands, he thought only of shelter for Marguerite
during the storm, and did not calculate about
the return of the tide. He was unaware of
the treacherous circles in which it rises on
these shores, often leaving a space of some
miles apparently still free, while its victims
have, in fact, been surrounded. So they
merely withdrew a few steps under the over-

hanging rocks, and watched the progress of the storm.

"Are you frightened, Marguerite?" he asked, for she looked pale.

"No, I am with you; I was thinking of my father."

"He will believe us safe at the boatman's cabin by this time. He will not know how we forgot the hour, like children, Marguerite."

She tried to smile; then drew closer to his side, and said, "But I know he will be anxious for me; and it will hurt him in his weak, nervous state. How I wish we had not lingered!"

The sun had now completely disappeared beneath the heavy ridges of cloud; and, as Marguerite finished speaking, a sudden flash of lightning almost blinded them. It was closely followed by a long peal of thunder, which echoed and reverberated through the hollow of the rocks, until another and a louder peal succeeded. Those who have not actually witnessed it, can form no conception of the unearthly character of a storm in such a position as that in which they were now placed. The echoes of thunder among high mountains are sublime and grand; but, given back by these rocks and caverns, they have a weird, terrific sound, like voices from chained demons in the earth, and can scarcely be heard without an unacknowledged dread of the supernatural. Soon the lightning was playing around them in all directions—the rain poured down in torrents—and, the wind having suddenly arisen, the distant waves were seen rising angrily above the sands.

Earnscliffe had still no idea of their perilous position; he merely thought that, should it come to the worst, and the storm had not abated as the tide rose, they would have to walk through the drenching rain to the gabarier's hut. He knew not that every lost moment was bringing them nearer to inevitable destruction.

"Lean on me, dear Marguerite; you are terrified."

"No! Mr. Earnscliffe; I see God everywhere around me; I am not terrified—but for my father."

"The storm may not be so violent at Kersaint; indeed, I think it is abating slightly, even now—the rain is already not so heavy."

"But the waves are higher."

"They will not harm us. As soon as the rain is over, we will get on before the tide rises higher."

"The tide!" repeated Marguerite. "Is the tide rising?"

"I should think it was half way in; see, it has surrounded yonder black rock, which seemed a mile from the sea when we first looked out. But we have plenty of time."

"We have not!" cried Marguerite, seizing his hand, while her own grew cold and damp with sudden terror. "The gabarier

told me not to remain in the grotto one moment after the tide had turned, and it is already half way in."

"Child, you should have told me sooner," was Philip's calm reply. "God grant it be not yet too late!"

He passed his arm round her slight form, and almost carried her back through the narrow opening of the rock—a few more seconds, and they had crossed the grotto. Then he placed her against the centre rock, and bade her wait for a minute, while he looked out at the weather.

Earnscliffe had a stout heart, but it quailed before the sight which awaited him. The water was nearly at the mouth of the cave, and already separated them from the mainland by a broad and increasing channel. Quickly it came on; each terrific wave bearing aloft a crest of whitened foam, and bringing death for them. They were waves no swimmer could have stemmed for many minutes, even had he been unburthened, and Earnscliffe knew that for their rescue his own powers were vain. Unless escape on the other side were possible, certain death was before them.

He returned into the grotto—whose shining roof and spangled floor might so soon be their tomb—and found his companion pale, but perfectly silent. One glance at his face told her all.

"We are surrounded!" she cried. "I hear the waves already."

"We are surrounded, Marguerite," he answered; "but our longest chance of life is at the point we have quitted. The sea will cover the sand at our feet in a few minutes."

He took her in his arms—she lay cold and still—and carried her quickly back to the distant opening, which was many feet higher than the floor of the grotto; and there, on the rock where they had watched the sunset, he seated himself; Marguerite still clinging to him, and her long hair falling round his neck.

Escape in this direction he had seen at a glance was hopeless. The high, bare rocks, which overhung the shore, were perpendicular, even could they have reached them; but a current through one of the many tunnels at the back of the principal cavern had already cut off retreat upon this side also; and the smooth granite which rose immediately behind them afforded not even clinging hold for the sea-weed which clothed the more distant rocks. Death was approaching them; not slowly, but with each onward surge of the waves—with every fresh gust of the tempest. In another half hour they must pass through a darker sea than the one before them; in another half hour they would be in eternity!

They remained silent. Marguerite had gathered from Earnscliffe's face the dread extent of their danger; no sound, however, escaped her lips—she was only deadly pale. But the full color of life was on Philip's cheek. It was a moment in which human passion would be supposed to die before the might of infinity around, and the certain approach of destruction; when the soul, paralysed to every other emotion, would be concentrated upon its own fate alone, and forget the tumult of earthly desire which it had experienced a short hour or two before. But with Earnscliffe it was not so. Life held no object for him so dear as the one to whom he was to be united in death; and he felt, with a strange rapture, that he might at length hold her to his heart, and disclose his passion to her without sin. He felt himself already freed from the chain of his marriage; and that, for the half-hour of time which yet remained, the only woman he had ever loved was his. His in a more perfect possession than life could have bestowed—his in her latest breath—in her death agony. He folded her closer still to his bosom, as though already preparing for the coming struggle, when the waves should essay to part them; he pressed his lips upon her lips; he poured forth such words of passionate love as no moment in real living life could have wrung from him; he thanked Heaven he might die with her.

"Speak to me, beloved, one word; tell me, now when God alone can hear, that if I had been free would you have loved me?"

Even at that moment of approaching death her face flushed more brightly than on the May morning when, full of life, he had seen her among the flowers.

"Oh, Philip! I *have* loved you. I have thought of nothing but you since I have known you, and I am glad to die with you—except for my father," she added.

He did not hear her last words, he only heard that she loved him, that she was glad to be his in death; and his brain turned.

*   *   *   *   *

The storm raged on, the wind moaned wildly around them, and the thunder rolled unceasingly along the cavern. But the conflict of human passion in Earnscliffe's bosom was fiercer. With his cheek bent down to hers, and his arms clasped round her as though to still the uneven beatings of her heart, he heard every whisper from her lips among all the tumultuous roar of the hurricane, felt every trembling breath she drew, and counted them greedily, for he knew their number was measured.

The waves drew on. Already he felt their spray upon his forehead. But he only pressed her more closely, and never raised his eyes from her face; when suddenly the throbbing of Marguerite's heart seemed to cease; a livid color gained round her lips, and her hands relaxed in their hold upon his —she had fainted. The mingled conflict of emotions had been more than she could bear; she lay cold and senseless in his arms.

A sudden revulsion came over Earnscliffe. As he looked into her pure marble face, passion left him, and only the nobler part of love remained. He did not even press his lips again upon those helpless ones, which so lately were all resigned to his; he parted back the hair from her forehead softly, as a mother might have done for her dying child, and then rising to his feet, he clasped her to his side, and in that awful moment prayed God to have mercy upon them both!

Mercy upon their souls only, the time was past for aught else. The next wave washed to Earnscliffe's feet; the next made him stagger slightly; the next, he was already breast-high. He retreated to the very highest attainable point; and there the waters from the interior of the cave were fast whitening through the opening. Another minute, and they and the sea without would be one!

Buffeted upon every side, he yet held his senseless burden aloft, and strove to keep her from destruction to the last; but in vain. Already Marguerite's long hair was floating on the water, and Earnscliffe, carried completely off his feet, was clinging with one hand to the only mass of sea-weed which grew upon the rock above them—the last frail stay which kept them from eternity—when, amidst the roar of the waves, a long, shrill cry fell upon his ear.

It might be only the shriek of a curlew that had lost her shelter; but to Earnscliffe the sound appeared that of a human voice, and it quickened his desperate hold upon the sea-weed, whose slimy, treacherous substance was already gliding from his hand. A wave higher and stronger than those which had preceded, broke over them at this moment, beating Philip against the rock with a force that almost stunned him, and causing him half to relax his hold upon Marguerite. But still, with the undying instinct of self-preservation, his other hand again sought the rock, and attempted to clutch at its surface. This time he failed. Nothing but the smooth, polished granite met his grasp; and another wave like the last must inevitably have sealed their doom, when again the cry arose, this time distinct and near; and through the blinding spray, and the dimness of his own bewildered brain, Earnscliffe descried, close beside them, a boat containing human figures.

His whole energy returned at the sight. Life, dear life, was before him. Still holding Marguerite to his side, with his right arm he battled against the waves as none but a practised swimmer could have done, striving to keep above water until the rescue reached them. And, though apparently close at hand, it was yet some time before the boat could near the rock, the height and power of the waves being such as to place her almost beyond the control of her crew; and once when they were within an oar's length of

Philip, and the cry of triumph had broken from the lips of the gallant boatman, a wild eddy again carried them back many feet from the fast-sinking forms they had risked their own lives to save. But they had stout hearts and strong arms, these Breton gabariers, and they gained the struggle! Half-senseless, bruised, fainting, Earnscliffe at length felt that a powerful arm had relieved him of his still inanimate burden, and in another second he lay himself in the bottom of the boat.

He knew not how long he remained insensible. When he returned to consciousness he found that they were still at sea; and for some moments the gigantic waves by which they were surrounded, the lightning-flashes across the lurid sky, and the harsh features of the boatmen, seemed to him only the recollections of some fearful dream, from which he was awakening. But he then became conscious of a soft hand clasped upon his own, of a pale, sweet face bending down and gazing into his with breathless anxiety, and all the past returned to his recollection.

Marguerite had quickly recovered from her swoon; and Earnscliffe had so well protected her, by placing himself between her and the rock, that she was scarcely injured, although numbed and faint from cold. When, from the hurried words of the gabarier, she learned how they had been rescued in the very moment of certain destruction, her first thought was of her father, and a fervent thanksgiving to Heaven for her own safety. The second was of Earnscliffe.

Amidst the strange chaos of memory, warm, passionate words re-echoed in her heart—words spoken by his lips—and she turned round timidly, expecting still to find him at her side.

He was there, extended lifeless along the bottom of the boat, his hair lying in dark, tangled masses upon his forehead, his lips apart and livid. Marguerite sank by him in a moment, and unmindful of the storm which raged around them—unmindful of the presence of the boatmen, she hung over Philip, chafing his hands with her own, and looking down into his face with an agony such as her life had never known before.

She loved him—she believed him dead; what was now her own safety to Marguerite? What would it have mattered to her if the eyes of the whole world had been upon them?

It was then that he returned to consciousness, and through long after-years of separation, Marguerite never forgot the rapture of that moment, when the first deep breath of life escaped his lips!

The night drew on apace. By the time they reached the shore they could scarcely see an object around them; and, although the storm had somewhat abated, it was a long and toilsome ascent to the hut of the gabarier. For, drenched and numbed with cold, Marguerite's limbs refused to aid her; and the path was a difficult one for even those stout men accustomed to live among the rocks, when it had thus to be surmounted in perfect darkness, with the burden of her form in their arms. And Earnscliffe, although his strong frame had already partially recovered from the shock it had sustained, was yet weak and unsteady, and required assistance in all the more perilous turnings of the path.

A bright peat-fire was ready burning in the gabarier's hut. When the storm was first threatening, and he could see from his look-out among the crags that the stranger and Marguerite were yet lingering in the caves, he had dispatched Moser to recall them; but the child, frightened at the sounds of thunder, or from mere wilfulness, had returned and hidden himself outside the hut, not daring to tell his father that he had disobeyed him. Nearly two hours afterwards one of his brothers had discovered him there; and the gabarier's rage was fearful when the boy acknowledged that he had never reached the young lady and the Englishman. He swore that, as their lives had been sacrificed through his own son, his should be also risked in attempting to save them; and dashed down the rocks towards the creek where his boat was moored, with an oath, and a set look upon his face which made his wife's heart tremble. Her own brother, a neighboring fisherman, happened to be in the cabin at the time, and she begged him so piteously to follow her husband and help, that he consented to do so, although he, too, had a wife and children dependent for their existence upon him.

As night drew on, and the storm continued, and still they returned not, the suspense of Blaisot's wife became agony. She looked on her five sleeping children, and knew that, if their father perished, they would cry for bread on the morrow, and in her heart she could almost have cursed the stranger, whose idle curiosity had been the cause of her husband's peril. But she loved Marguerite, who had used to bring fruit and flowers to a little lame child she had lost, the dearest of her flock; and when she thought of that, and of her kind, familiar ways with them all, she felt Blaisot had only acted rightly. She lit a large peat-fire, to be in readiness for them, *should* they return, and strove to pray and hope for the best. But every few minutes she would creep from the cabin-door, and make her way through the blinding wind and mist to the edge of the precipice, to listen, or gaze down the giddy path, lit up by the fitful gleams of lightning. At length a long, shrill whistle, through one of the lulls in the storm, made her heart beat wildly; it was renewed, and she recognised Blaisot's whistle. She flew back to the hut, falling over the children in her happiness; and by the time the party arrived, the fire was blazing cheerily on the hearth, and the few woolen clothes and blankets possessed by the fisherman's family were hanging, warm and dry for their use.

There was a rude out-house belonging to the cabin, and here Earnscliffe and the two men remained, while Blaisot's wife removed Marguerite's dripping clothes, and wrapped her up warmly in their own woolen garments, with many a kind word of rejoicing at her safety, and apology for the coarseness of the things that the "little queen" condescended to put on.

She formed a strange picture when Earnscliffe re-entered; her delicate figure swathed in this uncouth gear, seated close to the flickering fire, and her long, wet hair hanging to the ground over her shoulders. Her first thought was for him.

"You must require warmth and rest, too!" she cried. "Let Blaisot take me back to Kersaint; and when I am gone, you can make yourself comfortable here for the night."

"To Kersaint!" replied Philip. "It is impossible for you to think of leaving shelter again to-night. I will make my way on at once, and tell your father that you are safe."

Marguerite shook her head. "He will believe nothing until he sees me," she said. "I cannot delay another minute while he is in suspense." And turning to Blaisot, she addressed him in Breton. At first he was irresolute in his replies; but Marguerite implored with such earnestness that the wife came quickly over to her side. She thought of her own agony if one of their hardy imps was missing among the rocks, and felt for the poor invalid father. So Blaisot at length consented to start for Kersaint at once.

"But I am afraid I cannot walk," said Marguerite.

"I should think not," returned the gabarier. "Wife, bring my two strongest nets."

They were brought, and soon formed into a kind of litter, upon which Marguerite was placed—the two men preparing to carry her between them. Then she turned to Earnscliffe, but with downcast eyes—her manner had quite altered to him now—and bade him good-night.

"I am coming with you," he answered. "I am already warm, and nearly dry, and shall be better for walking."

She did not attempt to argue with him; and after bidding the fisher's wife a kind farewell, they again set out. The storm was now completely over; only an occasional cloud flitted across the deep blue above, and the stars were fast appearing. Already the angry roar of the waves was softening into their usual pleasant voice; already the wet herbage sent a sweet fragrance round, and the night insects were skimming through the air. For in so short a time can Nature forget the wildest of *her* storms, and return to

her own placid smile; while one half-hour of the conflict of human passion leaves traces on the heart of a man that a lifetime is unable to efface.

They proceeded in silence, Earnscliffe lingering somewhat behind the others, and striving to bring into clearer shape the visions which still thronged bewilderingly through his brain. At first the recollection of the storm—of the peril—the nearness to eternity—of the rescue of his own life—was dominant. The bravest man who ever lived must feel the horror of sudden destruction when he has escaped it, and then recoils from Death as he had never done when standing with him face to face. And Earnscliffe thanked God that had not called him, amidst the unatoned sins of his youth, into His awful presence! But soon other thoughts arose. The passion which he had strengthened in the moment of coming death, was only hushed for a short space now; and Earnscliffe reflected long and bitterly upon all into which that day had betrayed him. He had avowed his marriage, and afterwards his love—his love for Marguerite, a poor, innocent child who had been committed to his care; he had spoken words to her that no woman's heart could ever forget; he had strained her to his breast in the strong embrace of death; and, more than all, he had won from her own lips the secret of her love for him—and a cold shadow fell across Earnscliffe at these thoughts. He had tasted of that fruit whose flavor is like no other; he had just entered into that golden land which had been the longing desire of his life; and now—like a mother who gazes upon the face of the first-born son she had so yearned for, but to see him die—the hope had become darkness at its moment of consummation. Marguerite was lost to him for ever!

The future lay before him in its cold, dull reality. To-morrow he should disclose to her father both his marriage and his madness in speaking to her of love when a certain death seemed before them—for, as a man of honor, he could not shrink from this: Mr. St. John must know exactly to what extent his child was compromised; another day and he would have left Kersaint; another, and Marguerite would be among the things of the past; another, and he would return to his old life, his old pleasures, his old associates, and be again as he was before he knew her; and so on for life. His thankfulness for his safety was darkened. In the despairing thought that he must lose *her*, he forgot all the other prospects that life still held forth for him; he forgot his unfitness for death: and, with the impatience under disappointment which from his boyhood had characterised him, he clenched his hands together as he walked, and muttered, "Would God that I had died with her!"

And still the sky grew brighter, stars more

clear, the freshened grass more sweet; and Nature seemed to mock his real living anguish with the calmness of her eternally-reviving and unconscious beauty.

CHAPTER XXVI.

It had been a fearful evening for Mr. St. John. Although ignorant of the full peril in which his child was placed, and striving to hope that she and Philip were under shelter at the gabarier's hut, his parental love had yet conjured up ceaseless visions of evil which no reasoning could dispel; and as the night wore on, and still he received no tidings of Marguerite, the suspense grew almost beyond endurance. Powerless to act, or even to learn the worst, the poor invalid could only place himself by the window, watching the progress of the storm, and praying that each burst of thunder might be the last, while his usually pale cheek flushed deeper and deeper in the fever of anxiety, and his clasped hands became cold and clammy as death.

Manon would fain have consoled him, but her apprehensions were to the full as dark as his own; when she attempted to speak, her voice was thick and choked, and she sat somewhat apart from her master, holding her crucifix, and praying to all the saints for Marguerite's safety. At length, unable, like Mr. St. John, to bear the uncertainty in quiet anguish, she bethought herself of making preparations for them when they should return, lit fires in the bed-rooms, heated water, and even laid out supper in readiness. The action took her from her own thoughts, and she became more hopeful over her employment. But still the father remained in his old place, his face turned towards the darkness without, and his ear strained to detect the earliest sound of his child's arrival.

Suddenly Bello, who throughout the evening had been wandering about the room, occasionally licking his master's hand, and looking up in his face in token of his mute sympathy, gave one of his low, joyous barks.

"She is here!" exclaimed Manon, rushing to the door. "Bello would not bark so for a stranger."

Mr. St John rose to his feet, but he could only walk half across the room—the yet uncertain happiness, the longing to behold her safe, seemed to overpower him, and render his limbs powerless. What if it should not be Marguerite? what if it should be some messenger with dread tidings of his child? In another moment, however, he heard her voice calling, "Where is he? where is he?" Then came the well-known sound of her light footsteps—she was in the room—and he held her in his arms.

Philip held aloof during that rapturous moment of meeting, and the boatman, who had followed to the door of the library to speak to Mr. St. John, drew his hard hand across his eyes as he watched them, and thought that he was well rewarded for periling his own life. It was some time before either spoke; then Marguerite, in a few hurried words, told her father how they had been surrounded by the tide, how Mr. Earnscliffe had preserved her until his own strength failed, and how the gabarier had finally succored them.

"Where is he?" said Mr. St. John, for the first time remembering anything but her. "Let me thank Mr. Earnscliffe for what he has done."

Philip advanced, his heart reproaching him as he received the thanks of Marguerite's father, and felt the earnest pressure of his hand. Would he press his hand to-morrow?

"But you are still in your wet things," continued Mr. St. John; "Manon must take you at once to your room, where you will find a fire, and dry clothes. You, my child, seem better provided for. How did you come by this strange apparel?"

Marguerite told him of their reception by Blaisot's wife; and then Mr. St. John turned to the gabarier, and, shaking his rough hand, thanked him warmly for his services. Neither of the boatmen, however, would receive reward from Marguerite's father. It was part of their Breton character not to be paid for what they had done by a friend. But this scruple did not extend to the stranger, and they left the house each enriched with a present from Earnscliffe that would make their households wealthy for the remainder of the year.

Manon insisted upon carrying off her young lady at once to bed; Mr. St. John was so worn out by the excitement and suspense that he had experienced that he soon retired also; and Earnscliffe felt relieved that, for this evening at least, there was no room for explanation. Marguerite's manner with him was so altered in the last few hours, that he felt it would be impossible for her father to see them together without remarking it. She was constrained; almost distant; but her cheeks flushed, and her eyes fell to the ground if they met his—the very sound of his voice made her change color. And Earnscliffe felt that the scene among the caves, and the subsequent terror for his life, had deepened all her former love into passion—dawning, indistinct as yet, but which would grow with every hour of further intercourse. Certainly she knew he was married, but what was that to her—so ignorant of the world and its opinions? how frail a barrier to stay in its course the master passion of our nature! And Mr. St. John would see this, and from Earnscliffe's lips must learn that he was married; that, as a married man, he had declared his love, and, far worse, won the guileless heart of his child! He took a hasty supper alone, and then retired to rest, but he could not sleep for hours. Worn out though he was by bodily fatigue, the emotions of the mind overcame all inclination for sleep; and he dreaded the morrow and the disclosures it might bring, more than he had done the waves which had threatened him with instant death. In persons of his temperament, the moral is seldom equal to the physical courage; and the idea of forfeiting forever the good opinion of Mr. St. John was a pain to Earnscliffe of which those who knew him as a mere man of the world could not have conceived the extent—it even outbalanced, for a time, his grief for the approaching parting with Marguerite which he felt was inevitable.

At length, towards morning, he fell into an uneasy sleep, from which he awoke with a start when the early sunlight was streaming through the window. He had been dreaming over again the perils of the past day—the booming thunders, the eddying waters; and it seemed to him that, while he escaped himself, he had left Marguerite to perish; and that Mr. St. John, pale and ghastly, now stood beside his bed, demanding his child, and saying, in a hollow tone, "You have lost her—lost her—body and soul!"

The cold sweat stood upon his forehead when he awoke, and he rose at once, glad to exchange the dreams of the night for the day realities, painful though they might be. He opened the window, and the sweet air blew softly into the room. Everything out of doors was radiant in dew and sunshine, the sea once more unrippled; and Philip was reminded of that first morning after his arrival at Kersaint, when he had listened to Marguerite's young voice under his window. But now the tender green had become abounding verdure, and the scarcely open buds were full and gorgeous flowers. Like the progress of their own love, the changing, uncertain spring had deepened into the glowing maturity of summer. After he had dressed, he remained long standing at the open window, and in deep thought, when suddenly a fluttering knock came at the bedroom door. Somewhat startled, he went to open it, and saw Marguerite, in a white morning wrapper, and her face extremely pale. He knew that her father was worse.

"He is very ill," she said, with trembling lips. "He has had a violent fit of coughing, and broken a blood-vessel. What am I to do?"

Philip followed her without speaking a word, and at the door of Mr. St. John's room they were met by Manon. Her features had an awe-struck expression, but still she had not lost her presence of mind.

"Will you start immediately for N——,

monsieur," she whispered to Philip, "and inquire for Dr. Thibault? Bruno is not here, or I should have sent him at once. And make the doctor return with you—there is not a moment to lose."

"When was he taken ill?"

"Half an hour ago the bell leading into my room was rung suddenly, and on coming to my master, I found him speechless, and his pillows deluged with blood. It was the excitement of yesterday."

Philip glanced through the open door, and saw Mr. St. John, livid and exhausted, supported upon pillows, with his eyes closed; and Marguerite, who was again at his side, wiping the dark streaks tenderly from his lips, her face perfectly white, and her large eyes dilated with terror. He started, almost with a feeling of guilt, at the sight; and, after some more minute directions from Manon, stole quietly down-stairs, and was soon in the open air on his way to N——. He forgot the weakness of his own still exhausted frame and stiffened limbs in his self-accusing wish to be of service to the man whom he thought that he had injured; and in a wonderful short time had reached the town and found out Dr. Thibault's house.

The doctor had attended Mr. St. John during the preceding autumn, and he listened to Philip's account of the present seizure with an expression of grave concern, then he shook his head.

"Surely you do not mean that there is no hope?" Philip exclaimed, hastily.

"I cannot, of course, pronounce till I have seen him; but I have little hopes myself. He is too feeble to bear up against any loss of blood; and, from your account, one of the larger vessels must be ruptured. I have long known that any sudden emotion might be fatal to him in his precarious state."

The doctor prepared some medicines, and started at once on his pony for Kersaint, leaving Philip to follow on foot. He ran the greater part of the distance; and, when he reached the manoir, Thibault was still in the sick room, and Marguerite—too agonised for tears—was crouching outside her father's door, waiting to hear his verdict as he came out.

She looked up at Philip when she heard his step, but her expression did not change. He took her hand, and the cold, relaxed fingers lay lifeless in his own. This new, great sorrow had swallowed up every other feeling, and now that her father was in danger, he seemed again as entirely her whole world as in the time before she ever knew Philip Earnscliffe. The minutes dragged on like hours while they waited thus. At length there was a subdued movement in the sick chamber, and then the doctor noiselessly opened the door and came out. In his solemn face Earnscliffe read all—Mr. St. John was dying.

Marguerite sprang to her feet, and seized

the doctor's hands, but she could not speak; something in his expression made the words choke wildly in her throat.

"Tell me," she tried to articulate—"tell me ——"

"My child!" said Thibault, kindly (he, too, had a little daughter), "God is good, and you must pray to him."

She knew his meaning, but strove not to believe it. "What must I do?" she cried, her speech returning in her terror—"what must I do to save him?—tell me, doctor, and I will bless you, and pray for you all my life. Oh, save him, save him!"

His eyes softened! but he was a plain countryman, and he never adopted the cruel system of saying "Hope," when there is no hope. "My child," he answered, turning away his face, "your father must be kept perfectly quiet, the slightest agitation might terminate his life at once. If you remain with him, you must command your own feelings, and not permit him to speak; give him every two hours a spoonful of the medicine I have left, and keep his chamber as cool as possible. I will return in the afternoon to see how he is going on."

She asked no more questions. She had now something to do for her father, to watch over him, to restrain her own sorrow; and, without a word, she turned away, and re-entered the room.

"Can I speak to you monsieur?" said Thibault, when she was gone.

Philip led the way down-stairs, and they entered the library, whose air of cheerful home comfort seemed like a mockery now. The doctor closed the door softly, seated himself in Mr. St. John's easy chair, and took a pinch of snuff. He was a good and kind-hearted man naturally; but he thought it part of his professional duty to keep up a dignified calmness which he did not feel on these occasions.

"Is he dying?" said Philip, abruptly.

"Monsieur!" returned the doctor, startled by his tone, and the strange look in his face.

He repeated the question. Thibault paused.

"Well," he resumed, slowly, "I may as well tell you the truth at once. My patient is in the last stage of exhaustion; indeed, I may say, dying. His frame is already debilitated, and he has broken one of the largest vessels of the lungs. All the art in Europe could not save him."

"Will he last long?"

"That is uncertain: I really could not give an exact opinion. These things vary so much. When the blood proceeds from one of the greater arteries, you see, the chances are——"

But Philip rose, and paced impatiently up and down the room, and the doctor was silenced in his intended disquisition.

"What is to become of her?" broke from Earnscliffe at last; and, as though speaking to himself. "Who is to take her?"

All the doctor's silly pomposity vanished in a moment.

"Ah, monsieur!" he cried, "it is I who was going to ask the question. They have no friends here, and all the French relations of the mother's side, I am told, are dead. But as you are a friend, and a compatriot, I thought you would know what relations they had in England; or perhaps monsieur himself is connected with the family?"

Philip did not hear the question. He was now standing at the window, gazing out into the garden, without knowing what he saw. He felt that Marguerite, orphaned and alone, would be thrown as it were upon his protection; and the consciousness of his own weakness made him shrink from the trust.

"Doctor," he said, turning round suddenly, "do you believe that Mr. St. John is in *immediate* danger?"

"As immediate as a man can be to be alive at all. I do not expect him to live another forty-eight hours—his strength is ebbing fast; and, even if he should have no return of the cough, he will die."

There was another silence: then Earnscliffe resumed—"You are married, sir, I believe?"

"I am. I have a daughter rather younger than Mademoiselle St. John. Would you think it well for my wife to come over here?"

Philip knew enough of Marguerite's nature to feel that she would rather have no stranger to comfort her in her affliction, and replied that "he had not exactly meant that; but that Doctor Thibault being a married man, he would be able to afford Marguerite the protection she required, until some of her own relations were written to; for himself, he regretted that it would be necessary for him at once to leave Kersaint, as——" Here he hesitated, and Doctor Thibault gathered that the young Englishman wished as much as possible to be rid of any responsibility in the matter. And, considering how long he had been a guest of the dying man, the inference did not give the worthy doctor too high an opinion of English gratitude. He little thought the pain his own resolution cost to Earnscliffe.

"Are you acquainted with the address of a cousin of Mr. St. John's in London?" Philip inquired. "They have frequently spoken of him to me, but I have forgotten even his name."

The doctor was also ignorant upon this point; they agreed, however, that Earnscliffe should write a letter at once, saying that Mr. St. John was dying, and urging some of the relations to come over to his daughter immediately, and that he should learn the address from Marguerite later in the day. The doctor, having promised to call in the afternoon, then took his leave.

"A true Englishman!" he soliloquised, as he trotted quickly home on his pony. "With his haughty manners, and his cold heart, no more warmed by that girl's loveliness than if he were an iceberg. He must leave the house, forsooth! in his sanctity of virtue, the moment the father is dead, and hand over the poor child to my respectable protection! Yet there is no lack of fire in his face, either—*mais ils sont tous comme celà*—*ces Anglais—bah!*"

Earnscliffe was left alone for some hours. He wrote the letter, and afterwards remained unoccupied, standing at the library window. The actual presence of death had never so weighed upon him before. To meet it in peril and excitement was nothing, compared with this slow, lingering approach to eternity which one inmate of the house was now treading alone. And, besides this, a painful feeling of self-accusation was ever at Earnscliffe's heart, which made him shrink from approaching the dying man. Not the consciousness that he had in some measure been the cause of the previous day's catastrophe —in that he was innocent of intention—but the feeling that he had betrayed a solemn trust; and that to the last he should meet Mr. St. John's eye in an acted character. Slight looks and words were recalled which convinced him that her father had not been unmindful of his preference for Marguerite, nor unwilling that it should be so; and he shuddered at the idea of him dying in the belief that his child might soon have another protector.

"And all this would never have been had I acted honestly from the commencement!" was Philip's bitter thought.

The hours passed by, and towards noon Marguerite entered the library. She looked quite changed, and her childish face had become like that of a woman; but she was calm, and did not weep.

"How is your father, Marguerite?"

"He is asleep; and Manon wished me to leave him, and take food, that I might be more fit for watching afterwards. Have you breakfasted?"

"Oh! do not think of me; I require nothing."

"Manon made some coffee an hour ago; I will bring it to you."

She left the room with the same unnatural composure, and shortly returned with a tray and some breakfast. Philip poured her out a cup of coffee, and she drank it, and then strove to eat; but she could not swallow a morsel.

"You eat," she said. "I am not hungry."

Philip took some coffee, and then resumed his place at the window. Marguerite seated herself on a low footstool, and laid her head wearily against the arm of her father's chair; still, she never wept—she was only stunned

and bewildered as yet—the agony of grief was to come.

"Will you not come to the open window, my poor child? The air will refresh you."

Her lips trembled a little at his expression —it recalled her father—but she only hid her face. "No; I am better here," she answered.

Then Philip approached, and seated himself beside her. "I have been writing a letter," he said, gently, "which I should like to send by to-day's post. It is to your father's cousin, telling him of his illness, and asking him to come to you. Will you give me his address?"

An indescribable look of anguish crossed her face at his words. She understood why he had written, and it realised her position to her; already she was being given over to strangers!

"Ah, Mr. Earnscliffe!" she cried, wildly. "Do not write to him; they will take me from Kersaint, where we have always been together, and I shall not be near him when—when——" "he is dead," she would have added, but she could not utter that word. She raised her hand to her heart, where the old sharp pain had arisen, and looked piteously at Earnscliffe. "Do not send it yet; wait another day, until we know all. God is merciful! He cannot leave me so utterly alone. Oh, Mr. Earnscliffe! He cannot take my father from me yet! I have no one in the world but him." After a pause she continued—"I should like to hear all the doctor said to you—his exact opinion, word for word."

With averted face, Earnscliffe tried to break the dread truth. He did not deceive her; he rather strove to soften her grief, and make her weep; and, at length, he succeeded. Speaking of her father, he had dwelt much upon the excellence and beauty of his character, and of his fitness for death; and then added, when she turned away almost impatiently from that terrible word—death—

"But think of his gain, Marguerite—from a life of constant pain and sickness to the glorious life of eternity, and the joy of again beholding your mother."

Then the tears were unloosed; and she wept long and passionately, as a child of her age should weep, in natural sorrow.

"I am selfish to grieve so for myself," she said, at length; "but you can never know all that my father has been to me. What love can I ever find like his?—so forgiving to all my faults—so gentle; he has never once been angry with me in my whole life, and I have often been forgetful of him. Only yesterday—the last day, Mr. Earnscliffe—I was away from him so many hours, and thinking of my own happiness, while his anxiety for me has caused this dreadful illness——"

She could get no further for her tears;

and it was a difficult task for Philip to comfort her, with so much tenderness in his heart to be obliged to content himself with the usual common-places of condolence! He began speaking again of her relations in England.

"I know my father's wishes," she replied, mournfully. "Last autumn, when he was so ill, he told me I was to live with my cousin, in London. And I have never seen any of them; they will be perfect strangers to me. I would much rather remain at Kersaint, alone with Manon in these rooms, where I have spent all my happy life with my father."

"But you will act as *he* thought best, Marguerite?"

"Yes; and, after all, it will not matter much. What will life be anywhere, with no one to love or to care for me?"

Had she so soon forgotten her love for Philip? or was there, mingled with her passionate grief for her father, a recollection that *that* too was over—a thing that could never be?

"Think of my life, Marguerite! How few have any to really love them! But you are young, and may form new attachments."

She turned, and looked at him very full.

"Do you believe what you are saying, Mr. Earnscliffe?"

He hesitated. "I did not mean that a parent's place can ever be filled in a child's heart; but there are ties even more near!"

"Philip."

"Do not look at me so, child—*I* am nothing to you. When we separate it will be for ever, and your only thoughts of me must be pitying ones."

He tried to give his voice a firm tone, but it betrayed him in its quivering accents, and the hand which held hers grew very cold.

"Philip!" she replied, with a grave composure, that contrasted strangely with her usual manner, "you think me a child, you treat me as such, and I know that you misjudge me. You say rightly, that none can ever supply my father's place—none ever will. I may like my relations, but nothing more. Even if—I—had married you"—she brought these words out with difficulty, yet still with no change of color—"I should never have forgotten him; and it is not likely now, when I shall be for ever alone in the world. But why should you tell me that all I said to you yesterday was nothing? that I shall easily form new attachments? Mr. Earnscliffe, my father is dying, I speak to you solemnly, and in my great sorrow, and I am not ashamed to say it now—I shall never forget you. It is not in my nature to love many times, and when I *do* love, it will go with me to my grave. You are married, you have told me that I can be nothing to you, but you have made me love you—you have made me confess it, and I shall never forget you!"

She neither blushed nor trembled; but spoke all this in a fixed, gloomy tone, as though thoroughly convinced of the truth of her own assertion. Philip scarce trusted himself to reply. Even as she reassured him of her love, something in her manner made him feel how entirely they were divided; and the words, "you have made me love you—you have made me confess it," sounded like a fresh condemnation to him. By what right had he embittered this fair young life, over which the hand of God was laid so heavily? How could he attempt to offer consolation?

"Marguerite, can you forgive me?" he murmured.

"Forgive you?" she answered, gently; "you have done no wrong; like me, you are sorrowful and alone—my poor Philip. It will be my fate, like my mother's, to die young, and not be very happy in my life—but it is through no fault of yours. And now," she added, rising to her feet, "I will return to my father, I will leave him no more."

"And I?" hesitated Earnscliffe. "Will you not let me be with you in your watching?"

"Oh, yes! you may come towards evening, for Manon then will require a little rest, but now I would rather be alone."

She left him, and an hour or two afterwards the doctor arrived. He found his patient quiet, without pain, and composed, but sinking fast; he showed no inclination to speak; and as long as Marguerite was by him, and her arm round his neck, looked happy.

"He may last till to-morrow," said Thibault to Philip, when he came down again, "not longer. I shall call in very early in the morning, however, but it will be to see the child. I can do no more for him."

Philip told him of Marguerite's wish, about the letter, and they agreed that one day's delay could make no difference. She would have no reason for not sending it on the morrow.

"I do not fear any further rupture on the lungs," added the doctor. "So, if he shows a disposition to talk to his child, it need not be checked. Poor little creature! she will hear few words enough from him again in this world."

And Philip wrung the doctor's hand when he spoke so feelingly of Marguerite, in a manner that made him think he had somewhat misjudged the cold young Englishman that morning.

The day wore away without much change in the sufferer. Towards night, however, he spoke more, and his mind began evidently to wander. His voice was soft and low as ever, his eye calm—but his ideas were becoming confused. At one time he thought he was speaking to his wife—that she was dying, and he watching over her; then he re-

7

curred abruptly to his own state—to his anxiety of the previous day—to Marguerite, and who would take her when he was gone?—and then alluded to Earnscliffe, in a manner connected with her, which sent a thrill through the conscious heart of one of the listeners. Manon had gone to rest herself, that she might be better able for her duties when they were required; and Philip and Marguerite watched together during the early part of the night. She would not leave her father for a minute; she felt no fatigue in her constrained position and her hand never wearied of lifting the cooling draught to his lips, or wiping the fast-gathering damps upon his forehead. She seemed suddenly to have acquired the strength and composure of a woman. But Philip knew that the last scene would be a different one to this, and trembled for her powers of enduring it.

About two o'clock Mr. St. John fell asleep, and remained so for more than an hour. When he woke the watchers were still in their place; but Manon had returned, and forced Marguerite to swallow a cup of tea, and change her position, which she had not hitherto done for fear of disturbing her father. The grey light of early morning was already stealing through the closed curtains, giving a ghastly hue to the lamp by the bed-side, and revealing the ashy features of the dying man, and those, scarcely more life-like of his child. At the bottom of the bed, perfectly motionless, stood the old hound. They had vainly attempted to keep him from the room the previous day; but, as he was so still and silent, at length permitted him to remain. His great brown eyes never turned from his master's face for one second; and their expression of wistful sorrow and knowledge of the truth, was almost human in its intensity. When Mr. St. John woke he seemed quite calm and conscious; and his voice had resumed so much of its old strength that Marguerite's heart beat with a wild hope that he was better. But Manon's face grew more solemn, and she glanced at Philip.

"Still beside me, my little one; you must be worn out!"

"No, father; I am not tired. I was so glad to see you sleep."

"It has restored me, darling. I can tell you all I wish now. Put your arm round me—so. Child—I am leaving you."

"No—no, father! You must not leave me—I have no one but you. Do not leave me in this great world alone, father!"

"Where is Mr. Earnscliffe?"

Philip advanced to the bed, his face bloodless at the thought of what the dying man might say.

"I am here, sir."

"Give me your hand. Why, it is colder than mine—and clammy. Ah; you feel for my child. I have not known you long; but I am sure that you have a warm heart and

high principles. Will you be her friend when I am gone? She is worthy of you."

These words, and the fervent clasp smote Philip to the quick.

"I will do my best," he faltered—"I will endeavor to perform——"

Mr. St. John smiled faintly. He already thought that Philip loved his daughter; and his deep emotion—his hesitating accents—now confirmed this belief.

"I can die contented," he said, softly; a happy expression stealing over his face. "Now, little one, all I have to say must be to you. Nay," he interrupted himself, as his eye fell upon another weeping figure, "Manon first."

Manon took his weak, out-stretched hand, and kissed it with the reverence she might have shown to a saint.

"Oh, master! forgive me all my faults," she said, through her fast-falling tears.

"You have had none, poor Manon! You were faithful to my Lilla; you have been faithful to her child and to me. God bless you, my friend, and reward you as you deserve."

Then he turned to Marguerite. She bent down over him, and he spoke in low, loving whispers, so that only she could hear; while Philip turned aside, not to intrude, even by looking, on the last earthly communion of these two beings, who had so long been all in all to each other. At length a sudden exclamation from Manon made him look round, and he saw a change on Mr. St. John's face. His color had returned, and his eyes were brighter.

"Draw aside the curtains!" he exclaimed. "Open the window, and let me feel the air once more."

Manon obeyed him; and the fresh wind, laden with a thousand early scents, stole in, while a golden beam from the rising sun fell full across the bed.

"She died at this hour," murmured Mr. St. John; "and I am going to her—God remember thee, my child!"

"Father, do not leave me!" cried Marguerite, as his clasp slightly relaxed, and all the reality of death overwhelmed her. "Father, stay with your little one—father—father!"

But the ear which had never turned from her faintest wish before, was becoming dull, even to her voice; and, though he yet strove to answer, his lips moved only with an inarticulate sound.

"And he dies without the sacraments?" said Manon.

Poor Manon! She knew not that the single ray of God's sunshine brought more of his presence about the dying man than all the priests in Christendom could have done.

"Kiss me, darling—once more."

These were his last words. As her lips still pressed upon his cheek, his eyes brightened, strangely—then fixed; and, without another sound, he expired.

Marguerite started back in sudden terror, then looked fearfully round at her companions, then at her father's face. She seized his hand, it was already cold and damp, the chiselled lips had fallen; and with a cry—so long, so intense in its anguish, that neither of the hearers ever forgot the sound again—she sank heavily and senseless upon the ground.

CHAPTER XXVII.

At breakfast in his own house, in a quiet, dingy street neighbouring on Russel Square, Mr. Danby sat alone at his morning meal, his wife and step-daughter being persons too long accustomed to fashionable life to conform to his early habits.

The room was dark, the furniture old. It was the room in the house especially dedicated to Mr. Danby, and where no visitors were ever admitted; consequently, it was not thought necessary to introduce any of the light and modern furniture which, during the last few years, had found its way into most of the other rooms, and Mr Danby rather liked this arrangement than otherwise. Perhaps it allowed him occasionally to dream—when glancing at the stiff-backed chairs and horse-hair sofa—that he was still in his former life of tranquil widowhood; while the fanciful patterns and Frenchified ornaments in the drawing-room perpetually reminded him of his fanciful wife and her Frenchified daughter. However this might be, he always looked upon his breakfast as the happiest meal of the twenty-four hours; and on the morning in question—about four days after the event described in the last chapter—was eating his toast, and drinking his third cup of tea, with great appearance of repose and cheerfulness. It was a sultry July day. The house, however, being on the shady side of the street, no sun ever found its way into the rooms; so, through the open windows the inmates only partook of the glare from the opposite houses, and the stuffiness common to small London streets during the dog-days.

Mr. Danby had never lived out of London since his boyhood, and perceived nothing of this. True, when he occasionally went down into the country, and breathed the fresh air, and looked up to the blue sky, something in his heart made him feel that he liked it all, and might have been happier had he never left it; but the feeling quickly passed, and he always returned with pleasure to the associates, and habits, and old city faces, for which nothing can compensate a thorough Londoner, as he was. He had been in business the greater part of his life, business of various kinds, and none of which had answered remarkably well, although he had never actually failed. Danby was honest and industrious; but his nature was not one likely to do much in the world. He had neither sufficient courage for speculation, nor clear-sighted prudence enough when it was really required; and, to sum up all, he had been "unfortunate." Some one had always stepped in before him, just at the very moment when a fortune was to be made; and if he did undertake any larger risks, there was sure to be some unlooked-for depression in the very article he had speculated upon. In short, as all men who have the knack of not getting on say of themselves, he had been "unfortunate."

Mr. St. John was his first cousin on the mother's side, and, as the reader may remember, was induced about the time of his own marriage to embark almost the whole of his small capital in one of Danby's larger undertakings. "It was to make them both rich men, there was no risk whatever, it was unlike all his former speculations"—such were the arguments which persuaded Mr. St. John, who was like a child in business, to give over his money to his cousin. As usual it turned out "unfortunately." There were other persons in the transaction besides Danby, equally unsuccessful, but not equally honest, and at the end of six months, without in the least understanding how, Mr. St. John discovered that he had been swindled out of the whole of his money. He talked faintly at first about taking legal measures for its recovery, but soon abandoned the idea, and finally concluded that it was one of the usual risks of trade, and that poor Gilbert was more to be pitied than himself. As it happened, Danby was not involved to such a very great extent in the speculation—the failure at least did not ruin him—but the thought of having caused his cousin's poverty remained with him for life, and he could never hear his name mentioned without a certain pang of self-reproach. No ill-feeling towards Danby had rankled for a second in Mr. St. John's heart. They continued at intervals to correspond, and when his health began to fail, he appointed his cousin in his will as Marguerite's guardian in the event of his own death, and acquainted him at the same time that he had done so.

At that period Danby was still a widower. He had married quite early in life; but his first wife died within a twelvemonth after her marriage; and for thirty years the idea of taking to himself a second never occurred to him. When, at length, he had realised sufficient money to live upon in small independence, he left business entirely, and bought a house in Tavistock Street, where he lived comfortably enough, with an old housekeeper to attend upon him, until about two years from the present time, when his good—or some might say his evil—genius threw him in the way of his present wife and her charming daughter.

It was Mr. Danby's practice, every summer, to go down to the sea-side for a few weeks, Margate or Ramsgate being usually his choice, as cheerful and accessible from London, away from which he was never happy for many days together. Just as his housekeeper, one fine afternoon, was packing her master's portmanteau, in readiness to start for Ramsgate the following morning, one of his friends came in, and, in a fatal hour, persuaded Danby to change his plans, and accompany him to Boulogne. This friend was an old school-mate, and they had entered business about the same time. He had, however, been just as successful as Danby was the reverse, and old Mortimer, the stockbroker, was now looked upon as one of the most fortunate men on 'Change. He was rather younger than Danby, and still in business, although he had long since realised a large fortune.

"Come to Boulong, Danby. There is twice the amusement there to what there is at Ramsgate, and the best prawns I ever ate."

"But I don't know the tongue; I was never among Frenchmen in my life."

"No more you will be now. French isn't spoken at Boulong. The shops are English; the visitors are English; prices are English; and you have all the advantages of living in England, with the variety of being able to say that you are in a foreign country."

So the next morning, attired in that amphibious costume of large-check shooting-coats, short nankeen trousers, dust-colored shoes, and wide-awake hats, which elderly Cockneys deem most congenial to sea-side life, the two friends departed in a Boulogne steamer.

Danby liked the change immensely; and for the first fortnight he and his friend were constantly to be seen, linked arm-in-arm, walking about the sands of a morning, or up and down the pier of an evening—the arrival of the English boats, and looking out 'for new-comers forming one of their principal amusements. At the end of this time, however, the stock-broker, much to the regret of both, was recalled to town on business that would involve some delay, and Danby was forced to remain alone during the three weeks he meant yet to stay abroad.

"And I will just tell you what, Danby," said old Mortimer, as they walked together, late in the evening, on the pier, for the last time—" you steer clear of the widow when I am gone."

"What widow?" said Danby, innocently.

"Why, Mrs. Burgh, or De Burgh, or whatever she calls herself, of course! She has had her eye on both of us from the day we entered the boarding-house. She first found out I was richest, I suppose—they are the devil for their instinct in that, these widows; but when she saw it wouldn't do, turned her attention to you; and, as sure as faith, they want to get you between them."

"To get me! and what, in heaven's name, do they want to do with me?" replied Danby, aghast.

"Why, to marry you, of course! Tut, man! you need not be so unconscious of what widows mean when they lay themselves out to please men like you and me. Why, you get quite red with pleasure, as it is, when Mrs. Burgh singles you out to talk to before every one else at dinner. I believe the girl was after me at first, till she saw I wasn't the kind for them, and that disreputable looking Italian (who cheats young Greenwood every evening at ecarte) began to pay her attention. But the mother is after you—and for herself, too."

"And I hope she will like me when she gets me," added poor Danby, with a little dry laugh at the intended pleasantry.

"Now, Danby," rejoined his friend, "don't you go and be such a con—founded idiot (I beg your pardon) as to have anything to do with those women. If a man of your age, or mine, marries at all, he's a fool; but, if I ever *did* commit such an act of insanity—which I never shall—at least I would have something fresh and tolerably innocent, a farmer's daughter from the country, or some article of that kind—something, at all events, that should know rather less of this wicked world than I do myself. But one of these widows, or their daughters—it's all one—who have been here and there—one time in one capital of Europe, then in another—offered up and refused in every watering-place in England and out of it, and carrying on about a dozen such games a season as Miss Georgy is now doing with that moustachioed rascal at the boarding-house—I tell you what, my friend: I would quite as soon, or a good deal sooner, marry one of those fisher-girls who are carrying home their baskets yonder on the beach. One can, at least, feel pretty certain what *their* lives have been hitherto, and I defy mortal man to say as much for the others."

As Mr. Danby had a good memory, and Mrs. de Burgh afterwards became his wife, it is possible that his friend's words recurred to him with more distinctness than was agreeable in future days. However, for the present, he only answered—" He was quite safe from all the widows in creation; but, he must add, he thought Mortimer's strictures unjust regarding Mrs. de Burgh—a woman of good family and reserved manners, and who had always, from her own account, mixed in the *very first* society."

"Then what was she doing with her daughter in a Boulong boarding-house?" answered old Mortimer.

He went off early the next morning, and poor Danby was left alone to withstand the attractions of his new friends.

Mrs. de Burgh was the widow of an officer —of Irish police, it was believed—but she dropped the particular corps to which he belonged, and only spoke of him as the late Major de Burgh. It was also whispered that the gallant Irishman during his life-time, had been known under the name of Bruff, and that his widow, coi sidering that title plebeian, had changed it into Burgh, and subsequently De Burgh. These were, however, merely malicious whispers, to which so many others were added as made one think Mrs. de Burgh must, on the whole, be a very injured woman. She was now about five-and-forty, still good-looking, tall, slight, and unmistakably lady-like—for, whatever else was false, she *was* a woman of decent family herself, and her appearance was refined. She was rather die-away, and considerably affected ; but Danby, who was little acustomed to female society, thought her very elegant, and was quite dazzled at the number of " Sirs," and "Lords," not to mention a few " Dukes," whom she spoke of as intimate acquaintances. A thorough knowledge of the peerage, and an unblushing application of it, is always a characteristic of the class to which Mrs. de Burgh belonged.

Miss de Burgh, commonly called Georgy, was twenty years younger than her mother, and consequently already at an age at which the first timidity of girlhood may be considered over. She was tall, high-colored, with hazel eyes, black curls, and white teeth, and was of that style usually termed by middle-aged half-pays at watering-places, "a doosed fine girl." Of Georgy's inner woman it would be more difficult to speak with certainty than of her black hair and high color, a remarkable instability being, indeed, the leading feature of her character. In Switzerland, for instance, she sketched, rode, crossed torrents, climbed mountains, or was fast, to any extent which suited the college men who might be " reading " at Interlachen. At Heidelberg, the Kron-Prinz von II——, might have thought her the incarnation of German sentimentality as she talked of *ewige Liebe* with him under the lindens by moonlight (Georgy spoke all languages well,) and smiled as placidly as a German maiden should while he smoked in her face. And, if thrown accidentally with English clergymen, she could *à disposition* be high-church, cloth-embroidering, architectural, mediæval, catholic ; or low-church, world-adjuring, district-visiting, tract-dispensing, papist-hating. With the very young of the opposite sex she was ordinarily amusing, rather dashing, and not sparing of piquant anecdotes—boys like that style ; with the middle-aged she was giddy, perhaps, but guileless ; said the strangest things without knowing it, and, if her mamma reproved her, would show as much childish shame as could well be expected from a young lady of five-and-twenty summers—most of them spent on the conti-

nent—and who was perfectly well read in French novels.

With her personal attractions, her mutability of character, and her mother's aristocratic blood, it may seem surprising that this young creature should still have continued Miss Georgy after nine years of charming womanhood. That it was not her own fault, however, must be admitted, and also that instances are not rare in which the harder sex remain long untouched by the prospect of matrimonal bliss so readily and liberally held out to them.

On the present occasion, having soon seen that Mr. Mortimer was a knowing old card— Georgy could be very slang—and no go, she was deep in a flirtation with a handsome, good-for-nothing Italian (brother to one of the first singers in the world, by whom he is allowed a hundred-a-year to live out of England) just to keep her hand in. Young Greenwood, the only other Englishman in the boarding-house, was beneath her game for marriage ; and Danby she handed over to mamma. They believed him richer than he really was ; and, as the widow and her daughter were always extremely well-dressed and had such high connections, Danby also took t into his head that their means were not small.

He managed to keep clear of ' them for some days after Mortimer left. His friend's words had impressed him unpleasantly, and he had no deliberate intention whatever, of committing such folly as a second marriage. He was perfectly comfortable in his snug, old-fashioned way in Tavistock Street ; his housekeeper kept everything in order, and gave him well - dressed meals at regular hours ; he had his friends to dine with him occasionally, and dined with them in return ; what more could he want? But " *l'homme propose.*"

Four weeks after the friends parted on the pier, the stock-broker received the following letter:—

" DEAR MORTIMER,—I should have written to you sooner, but my time has been so taken up since you left that I have not had an hour to myself. Excursions, walks, boating parties, picnics, have been making quite a *young man* of me—and an old fool, you would add, at my time of life. Well, the fact is, my friend, Mrs. de Burgh's daughter (you remember Miss Georgy,) is naturally fond of these kind of amusements ; but her mother, with the reserve peculiar to our countrywomen, does not choose her to enter into them, even under her own chaperonage, unless escorted by some gentleman, in whom she can place confidence as more than a mere acquaintance ; and this circumstance alone has led me into habits so unlike my usual quiet ones. They (I mean Mrs. and Miss Burgh), are only waiting here a few days longer, until the arrival of Lord and Lady

Windham, their cousins, whom they will accompany to Paris; and about the same time you may expect to see me in London. It is already past the time at which I should be dressed for a *donkey exhibition* to some distant ruins; so I must conclude.

"And I am ever, dear Mortimer, your faithful friend,   GILBERT DANDY.

"JOHN MORTIMER, ESQ."

"Well!" said Mortimer to himself, as he finished the letter, "I did not really think my old friend would have turned out such a beastly idiot—at sixty years of age! 'Reserve'—'confidence'—'more than mere acquaintance'—faugh! Well, if the man is still to be saved, it sha'nt be my fault if he marries either of them." And, at considerable inconvenience, Mortimer left town that very afternoon, arrived at Boulogne by the evening packet. He walked in high dudgeon up the pier, a garcon, from the hotel he had always frequented before he tried that ——boarding-house, carrying his carpet bag behind, and when he was about half way up, whom should he see but Danby, with the widow on one arm and the daughter on the other, looking very red and foolish, and the ladies remarkably cheerful. Danby looked more red and foolish still when he recognised his friend; while the widow simpered, and looked conscious, in a manner that made poor Mortimer absolutely sick. His manner was none of the pleasantest when they all stopped for greeting.

"Quite an unexpected pleasure, Mr. Mortimer!"

"Quite so, ma'am, to all parties:" and he glanced at poor Danby, who felt like a detected school-boy.

"I hope you will stop longer this time than you did before."

"That all depends upon circumstances. I mean to stop until I take my friend back again with me."

Miss Georgy laughed; and, being in a child-like mood, remarked, "That he might have to escort a larger party than he thought for."

"Indeed, Miss Bruff! Who is to form the addition, if you please?"

Mortimer had heard the story about the change of name; and, being in a vicious temper, threw this in accidentally, as a chance shot t' at might tell upon some one. Mrs. de Burgh turned red, and clung to Danby's arm, while she whispered, somewhat hysterically, in his ear..

"Mortimer!" said he somewhat deprecatingly.

"Sir!"

"You seem unaware—that is—it might be as well——" His voice got quite gurgly.

"Sir!" repeated Mortimer, looking straight before him in a way not at all calculated to help his friend out.

Several persons had by this time turned round to stare at the irascible-looking, middle-aged gentleman, and the well-known widow and daughter. The garcon rested the back of his hand upon his mouth, and little French boys cried, "My God! Adolphe! regard then the English;" while Danby wished himself fathoms deep in the sea.

"It might be as well," he went on, in a low tone, "to let you know, as my oldest friend, the peculiar and delicate"—Mortimer smiled politely—"circumstances of the case. My happiness may appear to you sudden; but, the fact is, I am in a few days to have the happiness—I would say honor—of becoming, or rather of Mrs. de Burgh becoming, my wife."

Mortimer listened quite quietly to the end.

"Garcong!"—"Yes, sare."

"When does the next boat start for England?"

"De next boat!" The garcon looked at his watch. "Tide high in fifty minutes—in one hour, sare."

"Very good. Then carry back my carpet-bag to the landing, and wait until I return; I shall go by her."

"Yes, sare," utterly amazed, although accustomed to Britons. "Will monsieur not stop to the hotel, he has plenty of time?"

"And can look after himself, sir, thank you; which is more than every man of sixty can do," and he glanced at Danby, who seemed actually sinking with shame; for one or two idlers from the boarding-house had now joined the knot of lookers-on.

"My dear Mortimer, surely you will stay to witness——"

"I thank you, Danby. The time is gone by when farces interest me, or executions either. I wish you all the happiness you deserve, and your amiable future wife also, not forgetting her youthful daughter—*your* daughter, I should rather say—ha! ha! excuse my good spirits; and when the honey-moon is over, if you can spare an hour, I shall be still happy to see you in Portland Place, and hear how you are going on. Pray do not let me detain you; I have just time for a cutlet."

And with a gay nod, but really boiling over with rage, Mortimer passed on, leaving the bridegroom-elect in much the same state of feeling as a man who has received the last good wishes of his relations, before being hanged.

However, Danby had fairly done it. His friend returned the same evening to Folkstone; and in a few days afterwards the well-born widow became his wife. That he was not long in bitterly regretting his marriage, it is needless to say. What man of sixty ever found his happiness increased by marrying again, especially if his second wife be a widow, with a very grown-up daughter?

The new Mrs. Danby and Georgy were

mightily disappointed when they reached London, and saw the old-fashioned, hum-drum style of their future home. Nor was Danby less surprised on discovering the extremely small means on which these ladies had hitherto contrived to keep up a good appearance. And mutual recriminations ensued.

To overturn all his habits, and sneer at his dowdy friends, and introduce a thousand innovations into his household, were the first endeavors of the ladies. But Danby was no fool in general—although in one particular instance he had so egregiously showed himself one—and he would neither give up his house, his friends, nor his economical habits. He would have been as glad, after a few months of step-paternity, as most people, to get Georgy married. It would be one less, at all events. But he could not see how this was likely to be effected by following out the same false, flashy system which had signally failed for ten years already. So he resolutely set his face against balls and parties in his own house, and said—" If Georgy wanted to get a husband, she had much more chance of doing so by stopping decently at home, than by going to Hanover Square balls, and trying to hang on to the disreputable skirts of grand society." For he soon saw how far his wife's acquaintance with titled people was genuine; and that, while the majority of her noble friends were myths, the one or two broken-down lords and tawdry " Lady Somebodies," whom she had managed to get acquainted with at foreign watering-places, and hunted up again in London, were people whose character had long since thrown them out of their own rank of life in England.

Danby had now, however, been married for two years, and he had found out, like many wiser men before him, that his greatest chance of peace in allowing his woman-kind, as far as possible, to have their own way. They might go to their parties, and occasionally have their " reunions " at home, at which he seldom appeared, so long as they kept tolerably within bounds in money; and he dined with his old cronies, and occasionally had them to dine with him in return, generally selecting those days on which Mrs. Danby and her daughter were engaged elsewhere. Mortimer, when his first irritation was over, had become just as friendly as ever; indeed, it rather afforded that old bachelor pleasure than otherwise, to get Danby by himself to dinner and listen, with the grim cheerfulness of a friend, to accounts of his domestic happiness. And as every year made Georgy more alive to the necessity of keeping on good terms with all rich, single men, Mortimer usually received a very civil reception in Tavistock Street, in spite of that unpleasant manner of his on the pier at Boulogne.

***

CHAPTER XXVIII.

Mr. DANBY had just breakfasted as the postman came up to the door; and in another minute he was reading Earnscliffe's letter.

Percy St. John had been his last natural tie in the world, and he was greatly shocked at hearing so unexpectedly of his death. The recollection of their youth, of his cousin's unworldly nature—his ready forgiveness towards himself—the kindly letters he had always written in his varied difficulties—overcame him; and Danby covered his face with his hands, thankful that he received the tidings alone, with no wife or step-daughter to witness his emotion. After a time he took up the letter again, and read it to the end. " You are his daughter's guardian, and will, doubtless, at once receive her into your care," were the last words.

" Receive her ! Yes, poor child, that will I ! " said Danby, half aloud. " Would God it were a better home to bring her to. If I had not married again, she would have come like a child to me in my old age, for Percy St. John's daughter must have something of his nature in her, and I could have loved her. Now, she will have Miss Georgy for a companion, and become like her, perhaps ! Well, I must hope for the best. I wonder how Mrs. Danby will take it ! "

He rose, and paced up and down the room for nearly an hour; old and bitter remembrances thronging fast upon his mind, joined to his musings on the young creature, whom death had just thrown upon his care, and was so deep in thought, that he quite started when the door flew open, and Georgy, not in the neatest of morning costume, entered the room. She considered a dressing-gown, untidy slippers, and hair pinned up tightly on her temples, quite attention enough for her step-father.

" Morning, pa."

" Good morning, my dear. Is your mamma dressed ? "

" I really could not say," seating herself. " Coffee cold, toast tough : just ring the bell, pa ! "

He obeyed mechanically ; and as he did so, she saw his face. " Gracious ! how pale you are. Are you ill ? perhaps you ate too much melon yesterday. Hot coffee and toast ! "—to the old servant who entered ; " And are there no rolls ? "

" No, there ain't, miss," was the reply ; " the boy forgot them."

" Stupid wretch ! " returned Georgy, glancing fiercely at the old woman, and leaving it doubtful to whom the title was applied. " Everything is forgotten in this house ! Make some toast, at once." And she stretched back in her chair, and patting her knife up and down on her plate, discontentedly, forgot all about her step-father's pale face.

He continued to walk about the room, without speaking; and after a few minutes, Mrs. Danby entered. The greeting between herself and her daughter was not much more affectionate than had been that of the step-father.

"No breakfast ready!" said the lady of the house, peevishly, as she seated herself, without even looking at her husband.

"I have ordered some, hours ago," Georgy answered, "but, as usual, the rolls are forgotten, and now, I suppose the coffee, too: ring the bell again, pa."

"My dear, Wilkins has not had time to get it ready; besides, she does not like to be hurried."

Georgy tossed her head. "When I have servants, they must learn what I like," she said.

On another occasion, Danby would have retorted that Georgy must wait till she *had* servants: however, he wished now to keep them both in good humor, and rang the bell again. Wilkins came up immediately with half-done toast and bad coffee, and remarked "she had had no time to get the things better." It was singular what clear, strong coffee, and hot rolls, always graced the master's early breakfast-table, when compared with those which appeared at the late meal of the ladies.

"She is intolerable," said Mrs. Danby, almost before the door was closed. "I shall have some change in the establishment soon."

"There is likely to be one," interrupted Danby, stopping short, and catching the opening. "I have received a letter this morning telling me of my cousin St. John's death; and as his young daughter is left my ward, she will for the future find a home with me."

Like all nervous people, when Danby *did* bring out anything with an effort, he spoke quick, and told it abruptly.

"Oh!" exclaimed both ladies. "Has she money?" added the eldest one.

Danby winced. It was the one sore point on his conscience.

"Not much; but I suppose the sale of the old chateau where they live will realise something. However," he added, firmly, "she will want for nothing while I live."

His wife and her daughter exchanged looks; and Mrs. Danby hated Marguerite on the spot.

"He died quite suddenly," Danby went on. "Poor little child! how desolate she must be in that lonely place!"

"Oh! she is only a child, then?" cried Georgy; and the vision of a brat of five, who could live in the kitchen with Wilkins, flashed across her.

Danby made one of those elaborate calculations by which some persons find it easy to arrive at dates; starting with his own age, deducting ten, adding thirty, taking away

something else, and finally concluding that Percy's child must be about sixteen. "And indeed," he continued, "in one of his last letters, poor fellow! he said she was growing up, and was very like her mother. If she is so, and has anything of his features too, she must indeed be lovely; for I have heard that his wife was a very beautiful woman, and I never saw a more perfect face than Percy's."

There was an ominous pause.

"And you mean this Miss St. John is to live with you?" Mrs. Danby resumed.

"Undoubtedly," replied Danby. "Her home will be with me, so long as she remains unmarried, and I have a home to offer her."

His face had just the expression it always assumed when his wife tried to persuade him to dismiss his old servant, and she knew that he would be firm.

"It might have been as well to have mentioned all this sooner," she said, peevishly. "If I had known you were going to have cousins and people coming to live with you——"

"Yes, ma'am?"

"Yes, Mr. Danby, I say it would have been as well to mention these things before you married me."

"I don't suppose it would have made any great difference in your decision, Mrs. Danby." He was roused at last at her cold selfishness. "Besides, the question scarcely involves yourself at all. I intend to take one fatherless girl of sixteen into my house, and to treat her—God help me!—as though she were my own child. You need not trouble yourself about her, unless your own feelings incline you to do so; and the more she keeps at home with me, and the less she goes out into your society the better."

"Very well, sir. I am glad I understand the footing on which she is to be placed," said Mrs. Danby, sharply. "And as you will love her 'like your own child,' doubtless you will introduce her to your own circle of friends. When does the young person arrive?"

"Her father is not yet buried," Danby returned, quietly, "so I cannot say. Perhaps you would like to see this letter, Georgy? you are fond of distinguished people," he added, turning to her; for Georgy did not feel at all the same amount of spite as her mother on the subject, and was looking rather amused at the small fight. "After all," she thought, "the girl won't interfere with me, and, as she is half French, can help me in my dress, and keep up my accent." Danby saw that she was smiling, and thought he would try to win her over to his side.

"Would you like to have the autograph at the bottom of the letter?"

"Philip Earnscliffe!" exclaimed Georgy, in astonishment; "what, *the* Philip Earnscliffe?"

"I should suppose so; the name is not a common one."

She read the letter greedily.

"Goodness! and how intimate he seems! 'My excellent friend'—'poor little Marguerite!' How on earth did they get to know him?" She was much too *au fait* of all the scandal of London life, not to be perfectly *au fait* of Philip's private history; and, indeed, had seen him once or twice at the theatre, and thought him " a dear, interesting creature." Miss Georgy looked quite excited.

"I am sure I don't know how they became acquainted," said her step-father; "but I do know that any man of education or genius would be certain to take pleasure in St. John's society."

"And he must be actually staying in the house, ma? Perhaps he will come over with her. How I should like to know him!"

Mrs. Danby felt mollified at the idea of the St. Johns knowing Philip Earnscliffe, though she was too dignified to show it at first. However, she made no more unpleasant speeches for the present, and even condescended to say " she wished the child well, and if they had friends in their own rank of life, that made a great difference."

"I shall not be in time for his funeral," Danby went on, "even if I start to-day. Letters are so long coming from that remote part of France; but I must go over at once for the poor girl."

"Why?" said Mrs. Danby. She had been for some time meditating a trip to Brighton for her own health, and foresaw that Danby's journey to Brittany would just swallow up the money she meant to spend on carriages and doctors by the sea-side. "Why at once, Mr. Danby? Indeed, if you cannot be in time for your cousin's funeral, I do not see the object of your going at all. It is not likely Miss St. John would wish to leave the home where she has always lived immediately, and she must have some friends in the neighborhood to take care of her. At all events, you had better write first; express your sorrow, and so on, and take time to think over it. But act as you like. You know how the sea disagrees with you; and, indeed, that a long sea voyage is almost dangerous for you to undertake with your full habit of body. Act for yourself."

The last hint was not thrown out without its effect upon Danby. The sea really disagreed extremely with him, and if it were at all stormy, made him ill for weeks afterwards; and he had often heard from Mr. St. John how long and rough a passage it generally was from Southampton to St. Malo. So he thought, and wavered, and hesitated, between kindness for his little cousin, and his own dread of sea-sickness, until his wife saw how it would end.

"Think over it, Mr. Danby," she said, mildly; " think over it. Write the letter, you know; and then afterwards, if you think it really necessary to go for Miss St. John,

and that the voyage will not hurt you, you can do so."

"Well, it may be better to write, perhaps," said Danby; " it would be different if she had no English friends; but Mr. Earnscliffe appears so really interested in her—"

"Yes," interrupted Georgy. "And why can't Philip Earnscliffe bring her over to England, when she does come? You might propose it, pa; it would be a good introduction to him."

Danby promised to do so; and that afternoon wrote a letter to Earnscliffe, inclosing a few lines to Marguerite. They were kind and simple, and told her that, from henceforth, his home should be hers; and that, as far as possible, he would try to make up to her for her great loss. But Danby said nothing about her coming immediately, neither did he make any allusion to crossing the Channel himself. Mrs. Danby's hints about sea-sickness, and his full habit, had done their work; and the following week they all went down to Brighton, where Miss Georgy made and improved the acquaintance of a very long-coated young Anglican divine; and Mrs. Danby, who, since her marriage had thought it necessary to be an invalid, became a convert to homœopathy, and an extremely soft-handed, black-whiskered apostle of that faith.

CHAPTER XXIX.

To all the dreadful minutiæ of death. Marguerite remained, happily, insensible, She was very ill for many days; and when she could once more mention his name, her father was lying in the cemetery of N——. Although her illness was chiefly the effect of her sudden grief, the excitement and exposure to cold and wet, on the day among the Morgane caves, had produced actual fever; and for some time the good doctor thought very seriously of her case. Philip, who would otherwise have left the manoir at once and taken up his quarters at N——, could not find the resolution to do so now that Marguerite was ill, and remained on from day to day—his own pale and altered face bearing token of the suffering through which he passed.

Earnscliffe had had many trials already: disappointment, sense of injustice, wounded pride; but this was his first sorrow. In his nature was a store of deep tenderness that had never yet been called into action, and now, for the first time in his life, he utterly forgot himself in his anxiety for another. He wandered silently about the house; he took no food, except when Manon pressed it upon him; and when Marguerite slept, or during the time that she was insensible to all external objects, he would steal into her room and watch over her with almost a woman's tenderness, bathe her burning forehead, admit the cool air to her bed, and perform a thousand offices which all Manon's honest love could not have supplied. And Marguerite, unconscious though she was, knew the gentle touch, and received the water or medicine more willingly from Earnscliffe's hand than from the nurse.

One night she was delirious, and in her delirium called upon Philip's name repeatedly. From her lately-acquired habit, what she said was in English; but Manon could still detect the name, and her eyes stole searchingly to Earnscliffe's face as she listened. He could not become paler than he already was; but his lips quivered as he bent over Marguerite, and heard again her innocent love for himself told in the vague, unconscious language of delirium, ever mingled with her father's name and a dull remembrance of her recent loss.

"He loves me, dear father—Philip loves me. I shall be his little wife—no, he is married—that can never be. Lady Clara—he told me all, I must not love him. But then, the storm—the waves—father, I could not help it! death was coming, and I told him. It is over now—it is all over; he has left, and I shall remain with you. I may love you, father;" and she tried to raise her hands as though to clasp his neck. "Oh! not so pale—those dark, dark streaks, father; you are leaving me—this is death. The waves — Philip, save him — save us both!" and then the words came more wildly still, until he could not distinguish what she said.

Worn out by her long watching, Manon at length slept heavily in the large chair by the bedside; and throughout the remainder of that night Philip tended her alone. Again and again had he to listen to words such as those she had just uttered; hear his own name whispered with meek reproaches "that he had made her love me," then watch her parched lips writhe in sudden terror, as the recollection of the storm, or of her father's death returned, and vainly strive to calm her incoherent cries for help. In all she had a strange sense of his presence. If for a moment he quitted her side, her face turned beseechingly in the direction whither he moved, and she would extend her helpless hands towards him. It seemed to soothe her when he leant over her and whispered gentle words, although she could not have understood their meaning; and when towards morning, worn out by fever and delirium, she sank to sleep—the sleep which saved her life—Philip's arm supported her, and her flushed face was still upturned to his.

Her long hair had become unloosened during the night, and hung in damp and heavy masses upon her shoulders; one hand lay helplessly on the coverlid of the bed, the other was thrown upwards over the pillow in the child-like attitude of sleep. She looked so pure, so perfectly innocent as she lay thus, that tears rose into Philip's eyes, more like those of a father for his child than for a lover for a mistress. He was not a man easily moved to tears, but Marguerite had stolen into the inmost depths of his heart. He loved her as no human being can love but once; and as he bent over her through the silent hours of this night alone, the dim starlight that stole through the open window his only witness, the best emotions of Earnscliffe's nature were stirred. The sinless child whose head was pillowed upon his breast seemed to him as a symbol of everything pure and perfect; and as he bent down over her unconscious face, thoughts returned to him that he had not known for years.

He thought of his early childhood, when he too was innocent, and his young mother had hung lovingly over his little bed; he recalled her sweet face as she kissed him for the night; and thought with a pang, that no pure kiss had ever blessed him since. He remembered her love for his father—how they used to sit together by the evening fire, hand clasped in hand, watching him as he played at their feet—and felt that such a life would to him too have been happiness. "If she had been my wife," he added. And at that moment Marguerite stirred slightly in her sleep, and murmured "Philip!"

When she awoke at length, after many hours' deep sleep, the fever had left her. All that now remained was extreme weakness, and in a few days she was well enough for Manon to lift her to a couch by the window, where she might breathe the fresh air. As yet, she had spoken very little. Her mind was quite clear; and Manon could see that she was fully aware of her father's death, for she never alluded to him, nor to his absence from her room. She was conscious of that, and of everything; but we are mercifully organised that our own bodily weakness takes away half the poignancy from sorrow; and as Marguerite, feeble and helpless, lay thinking of her father's death, it was more with a feeling of thankfulness that he had gone to rest, and a wish that she too might follow him, than with anything of grief for his loss.

From the time of her improvement, Philip never entered her room; and on the second day after the fever left her he departed for N——, where he took up his quarters at the rustic country inn. If Marguerite missed his presence, she made no allusion to him; she asked no questions, she showed no interest when Manon accidentally mentioned his name—every kind of feeling seemed numbed within her. But about a week after her crisis, on a warm, soft August morning, her nurse had carried her to the couch by the open window, and the sight of the old familiar garden without, and the feeling of the fragrant air, laden with the sound of birds and insects, brought for the first time a look of life into her wan face.

"Support me higher, Manon, I wish to see my white rose." It had been her father's favorite rose, from which every summer morning she brought him a blossom. "How fresh it looks, *they* are not withered. I should like some flowers, I think."

"You have some already, *ma mie*; but you were not well enough to look at them. See;" and Manon brought an exquisite bouquet, which stood in water upon the table. "All fresh this morning."

A faint flush stole to the pale cheek. "Give them to me. Ah! they are very sweet." She placed them in her bosom. "Manon, are you quite sure that I shall die?"

"Die! *Ma mie, ma chérie*, why should you talk of dying? You have been very ill, but the fever has left you now; and the doctor said this morning that you will soon be as blooming as ever."

Marguerite turned away her face, and was silent; but the nurse saw large tears stealing down her cheek, and she let her weep on, for Thibault said it would be good for her to shed tears. After a time she looked at Manon, and said—"How worn you are, poor Manon! You look as though you had never slept for weeks. Have you watched and nursed me all alone?"

"Not quite alone, darling. When you were very ill, Monsieur Earnscliffe" (the trembling fingers clasped tighter round her flowers)—"Monsieur Earnscliffe would watch by you too, and during the worst night he never left you. *Ce pauvre monsieur!* he looks as pale as you, *ma mie*; but, then, he never had much color."

Marguerite was not pale now. The old bright flush came over her face when she heard that Philip had watched her in her illness; and, looking once more towards the sea, she said, softly, "I am so glad that I shall live."

Poor Manon was delighted at these words, and at her improved looks. Ever since her master's death she had been in hourly dread that her darling child was to be taken also; and now, in her sudden thankfulness, she almost forgot her late great sorrow.

"You will get strong, my child, quite strong. We will carry you to the terrace in a few days, and give you nourishing things, and make you so well and blooming—better even than you were before your illness;" and her honest face was all beaming with happiness. "See, there is monsieur on the terrace now. He told me he should remain awhile, when he gave me the flowers for you."

"Remain? where is he then? has he left Kersaint?"

Manon explained that he had gone to N——, but came over every day to inquire for mademoiselle; and then she lifted Marguerite on the couch, so that she could see the terrace. The old soft expression stole into her eyes as she watched Earnscliffe slowly pacing up and down, and the color lingered in her face.

"I am well like this, dear Manon. If you have anything to do, you can leave me awhile. I shall be happy alone."

Manon had much to do in her neglected household; and seeing the little invalid so refreshed by the open air, she thought she might safely go down-stairs to her work. She returned every few minutes, but found Marguerite each time in the same position, and saying "she was not tired yet." In about half an hour, however, Earnscliffe finished his walk, and returned slowly towards the house. He did not think of Marguerite being up, and never looked towards her window, little knowing how anxiously her eyes were following him. When he was quite out of sight she called to Manon: "I am weary of sitting up, the air feels so chilly, and the sky is cloudy—take me back to my bed." And when she was placed there, she turned her face upon the pillow, and did not speak again for hours.

That very morning, while Marguerite watched him, Earnscliffe had taken his final resolution, to see her once more, when she had sufficient strength for the interview, and then quit her for ever. No vain sophistry of staying to console her in her loneliness led him astray now. Her father had died asking him to be her friend, and, with the acknowledged feelings of both towards the other, the only way of fulfilling this request was to part from her at once. "She is too young for the wound to be very deep," he thought. Yet, even as he did so, her earnest face rose before him as she said, "I shall never change, I shall never forget you!" and—strange inconsistency of our nature—Earnscliffe felt a thrill of pleasure in disbelieving his own words.

He had told the doctor that he was married, during Marguerite's illness, thinking it right for her that their mutual position should be understood in the neighborhood; and something that he had either seen or guessed from Philip's manner made the kind-hearted Frenchman form conclusions not far from the truth; while he fully concurred in the propriety of Earnscliffe's leaving Kersaint. They both agreed that it would be well for Marguerite to remain for several weeks, at least, in her old home, during which time Thibault and his wife could watch over her, before going to her English relations. And, indeed, she was now so weak, that some time would be absolutely needful for her to recover sufficient strength for the journey.

Mr. Danby's letter arrived in due time, and Earnscliffe was not greatly prepossessed by its tenor. Although the note to Marguerite was kind, there was a constraint about it, and an absence of all expressions of sympathy from the women of the family, which made him augur ill for Marguerite's happiness in her future home. The letter to Earnscliffe himself was plain and business-like. "Mr. Danby regretted that he could not be in time for his cousin's funeral; and also that circumstances"—he did not mention what these were—"prevented him coming himself for Miss St. John; but that, as soon as she was able to travel, he hoped some of her friends would accompany her to St. Malo, and he would meet her at South-ampton." He then added that, in his una-voidable absence, he should be glad if Mr. Earnscliffe would read his late cousin's will, and make him acquainted with the contents. "Through an agent in Paris he should ar-range for the sale of the property of Ker-saint; and he remained Mr. Earnscliffe's obedient servant."

Philip flung down the letter upon the table. He formed a worse opinion of its writer than was altogether just; and pictured to himself Marguerite, after her free, unfettered life, and the sole companionship of one so refined as her father, living in some close London street, and associating with the family of a retired tradesman. For Danby's hand was a clear, round text; the paper he employed blue letter sheet; and the appear-ance of the whole epistle unlike any Philip had ever received in his life, with the ex-ception of duns or communications from his bookseller. "And I am unable to save her from these people," he thought. "Would God that I were free!"

Marguerite gained strength daily now; and in another week Manon announced to Earnscliffe that she was well enough to see him. The old servant's eyes had not been closed all this time; indeed, it was impossi-ble for any one to have seen Philip under the circumstances that she had done, without discovering his feelings towards Marguerite; and, ignorant as yet of his marriage, she fervently hoped that her darling might be-come his wife, and be spared the misery of having to live among strangers. Of herself she never thought. Of her loneliness, her poverty, when Marguerite should be gone—for she had no relations and had saved but little money—all this was nothing compared to Marguerite's welfare. She had always been so completely treated as one of the family, that she felt herself actually one of its members, not merely a hired servant, whom a death or a marriage could at any time throw upon the world—as was now the case.

"She will see you at once, monsieur; she is looking quite herself this morning."

Philip had shrunk from the interview as long as was possible. Resolving that it should be the last—he yet had not courage for the actual parting with the only being on

earth whom he had ever really loved, and when Manon proposed that he should see the invalid, had each day answered, "that he would rather wait until there was no risk of the excitement harming her." But now he could delay no more. Marguerite herself wished to see him; and as he followed Ma-non through the long winding passages, Philip's heart throbbed within him, as though he were some boy-lover awaiting his mis-tress, rather than a man of the world who expected an interview with a girl of sixteen!

"Violà Monsieur Philippe, ma mie!"

Marguerite was lying on a couch by the open window, dressed in deep mourning, which gave additional whiteness to her com-plexion; but at Philip's name the blood rushed crimson into her face for a second, then retreated, and she felt her whole frame turn cold.

"Marguerite!"—"Monsieur!"

Manon closed the door and left them, never doubting that when she returned they would be affianced lovers. There was a mo-ment's silence; then Philip threw himself upon his knees beside her, and kissed her hands.

"You have suffered, my child—you are pale and changed."

"Monsieur, he is gone."

"Call me Philip, Marguerite. This is the last time we shall ever meet—you must not be cold with me now."

"The last time! Not—not," she falter-ed, "the very last. Do not leave me yet. Think of my utter loneliness without my fa-ther," her voice choked. "Philip, think of his last words to you!"

"I have thought of them—day and night since the solemn moment when they were spoken."

"Yet you leave me! And he asked you to be my friend."

Philip released the little fluttering hand he held within his own, and then seated him-self by her side.

"Marguerite," he said gravely, "your words recall to me my own reproach. When your father spoke to me as he did, he was ignorant of my marriage; he knew only my admiration—my feelings towards you—for that it was impossible for me to conceal; but he knew not the grave dishonor of which I had been guilty in concealing my marriage."

"Dishonor! Oh, Philip, that is no word for you!"

"It expresses my conduct, and is there-fore, a fitting one. This dishonor——"

"No, no," she cried, eagerly. "You had told me of your marriage before—be-fore—"

"Before I spoke to you of love—yes. But I loved you from the first hour that I met you. And while your innocence, Mar-guerite, rendered your misplaced love blame-less, mine from the beginning was guilty. Nothing can exonerate me to myself, or lessen my own feelings of self-reproach: and the only way—a very poor one—in which I can carry out your father's trust, is that on which I have resolved—to leave you at once and for ever!"

He said all this very fast and resolutely, and Marguerite's eyes filled with heavy tears as she bent aside her head: then both were silent. Philip dared not trust himself to speak, scarcely to look at the sweet, sad profile turned away from him. A torrent of love was ready to burst from his lips, yet he must restrain it, and remember, now in her hour of desolation, that it was dishonor for him even to think of love; so he sat moodily, his arms folded, and his lips compressed with their sternest expression. At length, Marguerite reached her hand to some flowers Philip had sent her, which stood by her side, and raised them to her lips.

"I shall never care for them again when you are gone."

The mute appeal, the childish submission of her voice, were too much for Earnscliffe. He was on his knees, and his arm around her, in a second. "Oh, Marguerite! *must* I leave you?"

He looked up at her—his dark eyes softening, and his cheek flushed with all the passion of his impulsive nature; never was his face so dangerously beautiful to Marguerite before.

"It is hard, Philip. I have loved no one else in the world but my father, who is gone from me, and you. Must we, indeed, part? Think what parting is! Long years of life—cold winter days—sweet, warm summer; but not together! I can hardly bear to think of my life without you; it seems so long and objectless. If"—she glanced at him timidly—"I might be anything else to you—I know that I can never be your wife, but your companion, your friend—I should give no trouble; I would follow you—I would care for you when you were tired of the great world, and you would be glad to return home to your poor little Marguerite—Philip, may I be this? She laid her hand upon his arm, and leant forward for his reply, until her hair rested upon his cheek.

Had Marguerite been anything but what she was, Earnscliffe would never have passed through this fiery ordeal of temptation—for he was a man, and no faultless one. And, somewhat lax as were his conventional principles, somewhat undefined his religion, it is doubtful if an abstract idea of right would have prevented him from making Marguerite his, and thus seeking to drown, in the love of her fresh nature, all the past disappointments of his life. But her innocence, her absolute and entire ignorance of the import, even, of her own words, was her shield; and a stronger one with a man like Earnscliffe, than all the barriers with which society attempts to hem in the frail daughters of fashion.

"Marguerite," he answered, hoarsely, and as though with a strong effort over himself, "some day, when you are older, you will look back upon this moment and pity me. You know not the torture your own words cause me; you know not—God forbid you ever should!—the temptation through which I am passing. Alone in the world, thirsting for love that I have never found, you offer me yours,—yours in all the fullness of your youth and beauty; a very heaven is within my grasp, and I must reject it. And the after-recollection that I have acted with honor will ill efface the agony of this moment. You love me, as you can love, in your childish simplicity; you grieve to part from me; but you cannot understand the bitter sorrow of my breast—the strength of my love." And, burying his face in his hands, Philip sobbed aloud.

Marguerite trembled at this strong emotion. As Philip said, she was too young to fathom the nature of his passion; and the sight of that strong, proud man weeping like a child filled her with a kind of terror. She turned her face upon the pillow, and waited, cold and silent, until the paroxysm was passed. Then Earnscliffe uncovered his face, and rose slowly; he was deadly pale, and his features were set, almost hard, in their expression.

"Marguerite, good-bye."

"Not yet, Philip; I cannot bear it. At least you will write to me?"

"No; no half measures. You are not to be mine—forget me." His voice was quite stern as he turned away from her.

"And you leave me in anger?"

"In anger! my life—my love."

He caught her in his arms, he pressed her to his breast, he kissed her hair—her brow—her lips, he called her by names never to be forgotten until Marguerite's last pulse should beat. Then he tore himself away.

"Philip, I shall die"—every vestige of color had ebbed from her face, and her small hands were clenched tightly together—"I shall die without you. But if you think it right to leave me—go. Let me hear from you once—let me have one letter of yours to love and treasure—and I will be content. Promise me that."

He promised her. Again he held her to his bosom, and she threw her arms around his neck. She told him she would never love any other but him; that, distant, she would pray for him. She said a hundred things which, from any lips but hers, might yet have made Earnscliffe swerve. Then gently she quitted him!"

"Leave me, Philip; I am stronger now—leave me!"

He turned, and obeyed her without a word. She saw him leave the room, heard his hasty step as he descended the stairs, then the heavy house door open and shut after him, heard his steps still in the court-yard, then grew fainter and fainter, and was gone. And the sickening reality of her desolation overcame her.

"Philip, you have left me!"

Had he heard that tone—had he seen the anguish of her young face, the hopeless misery in which she sank back upon the couch, white, and cold, and tearless—even then his purpose might have failed him! But Philip returned no more; and that evening, when the twilight gathered over Kersaint, and Marguerite, attended only by her faithful servant, was weeping out her very heart in the same room where Philip left her, he was already far on his way to Paris.

CHAPTER XXX.

LOVE and its sorrows undoubtedly weigh more lastingly upon women than men. No man ever yet broke his heart for love, although some few may bear the scars of disappointment to their grave. The world, ambition—a thousand channels are open to turn the mind from what, after all, is more a pastime with most men than a serious occupation; and, in nine cases out of ten, other loves—lighter ones, it may be—spring up to replace the first and pure one. But women, in solitude and tears, hug this kind of grief to their hearts; and, from their lack of any other engrossing pursuit, think unceasingly upon the forbidden fruit whose taste once changed their life into a paradise, until it becomes even sweeter in recollection than reality. Men may feel as much, but they show it differently; and had Marguerite been able to see Philip, three days after he left her, at a large dinner in Paris more gay and sparkling than ever, she would certainly have accused him, and unjustly, of forgetting her.

Philip found many bachelor friends in Paris on his arrival—young London men, who contrive to form a society of their own there when all the Paris world is in the country—and he entered into their life with a feverish kind of desire to escape from himself and his own thoughts. The St. Legers, too, happened to be in Paris at the time; and the idea, in itself, of being near his wife was enough to goad him almost to madness in his present excited mood, and make him fly to any dissipation for forgetfulness.

Letters from England awaited him. He had given his address at Kersaint to no one; but a host of notes, left at his lodgings in town after his hasty departure, with one or two kind letters from old Miles, had been forwarded to the Paris agent of his publisher as he directed before leaving England. There were a dozen despairing notes from Rose Elmslie, full of regrets that he should have

misinterpreted her, and reproaches at his abrupt departure, *et cetera*; but Philip could scarcely read them through, and flung aside the last without finishing it to the end. Had he done so, a certain tone of sincerity in her hints at some desperate purpose might have struck him; but, after the love of Marguerite St. John, he was in no mood for the sentimentalities of Miss Rose; and even a few kind lines from little Fridoline were thrown, half-read, into the pile of letters, carelessly torn up, which lay on Philip's table the day he left Paris.

For it was in vain he strove to forget Marguerite. Her girlish figure, her sweet, loving face rose beside him continually; and after a weary fortnight of sleepless nights and heavy days, Philip started for Switzerland—pale, haggard, and out of health, and having offended all his old friends with his querulous moods and odd outbreaks of temper.

The resting place he chose was a little hamlet near Meran. It was now the time of early vintage; and in those southern nights, when the purple mountains stood in their clear softness upon the cloudless sky, and the silence so peculiarly solemn among mountains was around, Earnscliffe's thoughts became calmer than they had been for weeks. The anxiety and excitement he had gone through, during the time of Mr. St. John's death, and Marguerite's illness, had physically weakened him; but, as the mountain air restored his old elasticity of frame, his mind returned more into its habitual state, until, at length, he was able soberly to reason with himself upon his last and deepest disappointment, and look forward to life from this fresh starting-post; for every real disappointment is an era from whence a man must, in some measure, start anew, either for better or worse.

He lingered among the Italian lakes, still shunning every English person with whom he came in contact, and spending whole days, and often nights, in an open boat upon the water, alone, and silent; but, perhaps, once more happier then he would have chosen to believe. In the autumnal nights, the air heavy with voluptuous odors from orange and myrtle groves on shore, under the rich, deep sky of the south—and still with Marguerite in fancy beside him, and her soft hand in his—I am disinclined to think that Mr. Earnscliffe was utterly miserable. His youth was yet too strong within him for beauty, whether human or that of Nature, to have lost all its old power. Although his truest love was gone for ever, and the world and ambition were no longer what they had been, his temperament was still a poet's, and too keenly alive to external enjoyment for existence to be as really dark as he had pictured it.

At Milan he found a long, kind letter from Neville, full of busy projects for their ensuing winter together; and late one December night, Philip first saw the spectral dome of St. Peter's loom before him in the starlight.

———

CHAPTER XXVII

But with Marguerite life went differently. She wept for Philip until she could literally weep no more—wept with an intensity of grief unusual in one so young, and rendered more touching by her perfect gentleness and submission of character. The doctor wished to remove her from Kersaint to his own house for a few weeks prior to her departure for England, but this she so earnestly opposed, that he was forced to let her have her own wish and remain.

As the time wore on when she was to leave France, she scarcely spent an hour of the day within doors. Her bodily strength had somewhat returned, and she would sit alone among the rocks for hours, or wander over the walks she had taken with Philip, and pluck the few autumn flowers she could find to be dried and carried with her to England. In the evening Manon made her a bright wood fire in the library, as in old days; and she would remain there for two or three hours, never reading or working, but sitting on her low stool, gazing in the fire, her head resting on the arm of her father's empty chair, with Bello crouching by her side.

Marguerite had written several times to her cousin in reply to his letters; and begged that her father's books, and the old pictures might not be sold. "The only things I care to keep," she had said. And Danby promised they should be sent after her to England. But she looked upon her father's dog so entirely in the light of a friend, that it never occurred to her that he could be left behind, and had not even mentioned to Danby that she would bring a large deer hound to his house.

The evening before her departure arrived, and as she sat, tearless and wan, before the fire, thinking drearily of the morrow and of her long journey alone, poor Bello suddenly gave one of his quick, impatient barks, and licked her hand; looking up into her face at the same time, as though to show that he could understand and sympathise with her sorrow. "Bello," she said, laying her arm round his neck, "I must not forget you. You are the only thing left to me."

"And I, mademoiselle?" exclaimed Manon, who sat watching her with the devouring, eager look of a mother about to be parted from her own child. "What will be left to me?"

"My poor Manon! But, at least, you will not leave France; you will even remain at Kersaint until—until—the old place is sold,

and afterwards you are to live at Jean d'Aubret's cottage, where you will have the bright sea before you, and even see the roofs of Kersaint in the distance. Oh! you will be better off than me."

"Mademoiselle, you have been too generous, and by your noble father's recollection of me, and with my own savings, I shall be well off, and never require to work again. I am grateful to the bon Dieu for his mercy! But, child, what is this if I am to lose you? For sixteen years, little one, I have nursed and watched, and not one night or day been without you. Sixteen years—and after tomorrow I shall be alone. I shall never hear your voice—never look upon your face again. Oh, child! I did not think I was to lose you thus. If things had been as I hoped, and——"

"Manon," interrupted Marguerite, hastily, "I know what you would say; do not give me the pain of hearing it. Speak of nothing but your love for me to-night. God knows I need to be told of it! I am not likely to meet with such love again;" and, going to her side, she laid her head upon Manon's shoulder, and was silent. Her grief seemed now of that dull, heavy nature which cannot admit of the relief of tears.

"It pains you, ma mie," pursued Manon, "that I should speak of ce monsieur, but I will do so nevertheless. How can I tell that you will never meet him again, or others like him, in his own country? and I choose to warn my darling against such men. I am a poor, rough peasant; I know little of great people, and, Heaven be praised! less of love: but I could not be your father's servant for twenty years without learning what the honor of a gentleman is like—and Monsieur Earnscliffe was not so."

"Manon, you forget yourself!" interrupted Marguerite, starting to her feet, and drawing up her stately young figure to its full height. "You forget yourself strangely in presuming to judge of Mr. Earnscliffe or his actions! I knew long ago—of—of—that he was married; and, even if he had never mentioned it, how could it have signified to us? None but you, Manon, would have ever indulged in dreams of my becoming his wife! He dishonorable! you don't know what you are saying—you speak in your ignorance!".

She turned proudly away; but her heart throbbed painfully while she was speaking. A sudden thought flashed across her that there might be some truth in Manon's words, although she had always disbelieved Philip's self-accusations; and that thought was agony to her. She would rather have been guilty herself than have doubted him.

"Mademoiselle," returned Manon, meekly, "this is the last evening we shall ever be together, and for the first time in your life you have spoken harshly to me."

"You spoke against him, Manon!"

" Why should you care, *ma mie?*—he is married."

" I know it.; you need not remind me so often that I am nothing to him. But that does not prevent me from remembering Mr. Earnscliffe—with—with respect and admiration."

" Ah, mademoiselle, you are very young; forget him."

Marguerite bent her head, and gazed long upon the red embers. She was thinking of the evening when she and Philip stood, side by side, in the fire-light, and she had listened for the first time to that voice, whose slightest sound was afterwards such music to her. She thought of all that had happened since then—the new light that had opened upon her in his love, and her own—her father's death—Philip's departure. All passed before her vaguely and dream-like, but leaving a dull shadow behind each as it passed away, while she gazed in the red embers.

" Forget him!" she repeated, after a long silence, and startling Manon with her solemn tone. " Would God I could forget him!"

She reseated herself in her old place, and began speaking of other things. " Manon, while you are here do not neglect my flowers, and when strangers come to Kersaint, if there is any young girl among them, ask her to take care of my white rose-tree. And Manon, be kind to Bruno now, he will have no other friend left, and if I can, I will try to send him some money, poor creature! Tell Bon Affut I am gone, and wish him good-bye for me; and, above all, take the Blaisots the presents I have laid aside for them. Say to Monsieur le Curé, I had only a few books to send him, but I hope he will never forget me, nor cease to pray for me. And Manon, dear Manon, do not grieve too much for me when I am gone. We may meet again sooner than we expect, and I will write to you as often as I have anything to say; and if I am ever rich," she tried to smile, " you shall come and be my servant."

Manon strove vainly to repress her tears, and speak cheerfully of the future. Ever and anon a sob choked her utterance, as the reality of the approaching separation forced itself upon her; and at ten o'clock—glad of any excuse for action—she made Marguerite leave the study and go to rest, reminding her of the early hour at which she must start next morning. Then Manon undressed her, as in old days when she was a little child, and afterwards sat by the bedside, talking to her of her mother, and of long past times, until, at length, Marguerite's eyes grew heavy, and she slept.

But Manon watched all that night—counted every breath of her child as she hung over her in her sleep—saw, at length, the cold glimmering of the day that was to divide them; and not until she had kissed Marguerite for the last time in the diligence, and returned again to the solitary manoir,

did she give way to her own passionate outburst of sorrow.

* * * *

" *Est ce que cela vous gêne, monsieur?* "

" *Mais du tout, mademoiselle!* " with a polite smile, as Bello extended his length in the coupé of the diligence, and crushed up the feet of the Frenchman who was Marguerite's travelling companion.

" *Du tout!* Few things inconvenience me." And the speaker, a ferociously ugly little man, threw himself back in his seat, and began to sing. " You like music, I am sure, you must like it, with your face? Then your voyage will be a pleasant one, for singing is my forte."

His voice was worse than his face; but his utter, his appalling cheerfulness, so to speak, aroused Marguerite in spite of herself. Every small hamlet, every wretched clump of houses that they passed, her companion let down the window.

" *Conducteur*, how do they call this place? Ah!" evidently not hearing the reply, " very well. How near are we to St. Malo?"

" Half a league nearer than when monsieur inquired last."

" Just so—ah!" (Back in his place again.) " Pardon, mademoiselle! your dog does *not* bite, I believe; just so. ' *Le plaisir d' être un soldat.*' I never was in the army though, mademoiselle. It is right to tell you that; for my appearance is military, and might mislead. No, I have served my country in another way. *Conducteur, hola!* where does one breakfast?"

And so on for about two hours, until they stopped before the one hotel of a small dirty town.

" Mademoiselle does not descend?" as Marguerite declined getting out. " But it is unheard of—impossible—on this raw morning to travel fasting. I implore—I entreat——" But Marguerite was firm; and the little man, " desolated " at her refusal, ran in to breakfast alone. However, in a few minutes he returned with coffee and a roll—" Mademoiselle, I supplicate you to eat."

His ugly face was so earnest that Marguerite took the coffee to please him, and was better for it. The poor child had not been able to touch a morsel before leaving Kersaint, and was actually faint from fasting and all the tears she had shed.

" I am better now," she said, timidly, when they were once more on the road; " the coffee has refreshed me."

" Mademoiselle!" returned the Frenchman, solemnly, " you are very young, very young—sixteen years, perhaps; I am forty-two; an immense difference—a lifetime, in fact; permit that I give you a counsel. You are doubtless a young person of sensibility, so was I. You have had sorrows already probably, not greater than mine were. You love music, so do I. There is therefore a

similarity of disposition—of disposition only ;
I am aware of external differences, and also
of your thoughts at this moment. You probably consider me the most hideous person you
ever saw."

" *Mais, monsieur !* "

" Deny it ! "

" Oh, monsieur ! "

" Mademoiselle, you shrink from giving
me pain, when, in fact, your admission of
my ugliness would be the greatest compliment you could pay me. I hate to be like
other people, and, as I am not handsome, I
am proud of my plainness. It is a distinc-
t.on, mademoiselle, to be the ugliest man in
a society, which I invariably am—a very
great distinction." He paused, a little out
of breath, then resumed with sort of a jerk,
" Ah ! my counsel to you ; pardon me for
wandering from my subject ; you did not
know I had one, I have though. My counsel to you is this. In all your trials, your
sorrows, your disappointments—for, even
with your youth and beauty, you may have
them—eat and drink. When I was young, I
had a dreadful grief, a grief that went to my
heart's core (you can guess its nature, perhaps,) and at first I really thought I should
never get over it. But I happened at that
time to be staying in Perigueux, and to that
circumstance I owe my very life ; for a pate
de Perigueux accidentally taught me one of
the greatest secrets of man's existence.

" It happened on the third day after my
—bereavement, I may call it, I came down
from my room. I was living in an hotel, the
Chene Vert, at the time, pale and haggard ;
figure to yourself that I had eaten nothing
for about sixty hours. I entered the salle a
manger with no better intention than to have
one cup of cafe noir, and then go out and
put an end to myself. Well, as luck would
have it, neither of the garcons were there,
or answered to my call, and I was just leaving the room again, when my eyes fell upon
the most lovely little breakfast you ever
saw, laid out for one person on a side-table.
I think I see it now, a pate de Perigueux, a
cold capon, and a bottle of Chateau Mar-
gaux. Now, mademoiselle, the devil may
have put it into my head ; but when I saw it
all, although I knew it was for a fat old colonel of dragoons, who came there regularly
every morning to breakfast, I resolved to eat
it myself. ' As I shall be a corpse by noon-
day,' I thought, ' the old fellow cannot call
me out.' And with that I sat down and began.

" Ma foi ! I think I taste that pie now.
Never, before or since, have I eaten anything
so delicious. I finished the whole of it ; I
ate half the capon, and I drank the wine.
Then I looked through the window, and saw
the colonel coming along, stroking his beard
and clanging his sword as he walked. ' Place
aux morts !' I thought ; ' I shall so soon be
dead, that it is only fair a living man should

give me his breakfast.' So I jumped up,
took my hat, and got out just as my colonel
swaggered in, and the waiters all rushed up
to show him into the *salle.*

" Well, when I got into the streets, everything seemed changed. The sun was shining
on the old cathedral, the people in the market looked happy and cheerful, and by the
time I had got to the bridge that was to witness my death, I never felt in better spirits in
my life. I went back to the hotel, where
the old colonel was swearing eternal perdition
to the scoundrel who had eaten his breakfast,
and frankly confessed my delinquency, and
that it had saved my life. And from that day
to this I have always known that eating and
drinking is a sovereign remedy against bad
spirits or misfortune.

" But, mademoiselle, I have often thought,
from the look of his eye, when he heard my
explanation, that greedy old beast of a colonel would much sooner I had jumped off
the highest bridge in France, than have eat-
en his breakfast. Such is human nature ! "

Marguerite listened, and tried to smile at
her companion's stories, but she felt wearied
and spiritless. To be alone, and travelling
to unknown people, and a new home, was
enough in itself to depress her, even had it
only been for a visit ; but when continually
the thought arose, that she had seen Kersaint
for the last time, and that strange faces and
new scenes were henceforth to be her life,
the great tears rose in her eyes, and her wan
face became paler and paler. Late in the
day the diligence stopped at St. Brieux for
dinner.

" Mademoiselle ne descende pas ? " again
inquired the waiter, in astonishment, as Marguerite hesitated.

" Certainly," answered the little man at
her side, fiercely. " We both descend."

And Marguerite felt grateful for his protection, as they entered the large room, at
which the *table d'hôte* dinner had already com-
menced, and about twenty bearded faces
looked up in visible admiration at her as she
came in.

" Bring some hot soup," said her small
companion, when they were seated. " Soup
is what you want, mademoiselle," he whispered. " Wine would not suit you, and a
choking sensation in your throat prevents
you from eating solid food. However, as
you pay three francs, whether you eat much
or little, you can help yourself from the
dishes as they come round, and make over
what you don't want to your dog." For Bello, faithful to his old trust of protector, kept
close to Marguerite's side, and made angry
demonstrations, when the waiters tried to
turn him out.

" I think I shall have to pay for Bello,"
said Marguerite. " In the diligence they
made me pay a coupé place for him."

" Poor child ! " returned the little man,
kindly. " When you are en voyage you

8

must not pay everything they demand. Was no one with you when you paid for the dog?"

"Only Manon, and you know she does not understand travelling."

"Manon—oh, yes! I see. Garcon! la carte. Chateau Morgaux—La Rose—St. Julien—that will do. A half-bottle—ah!"

Marguerite thought the long dinner would never end, and was astonished at her little companion's powers of reception. Fish, flesh, and fowl, solids and sweets—there was room for all; and when the conducteur of the diligence came in to announce that the horses were ready to start, he emptied two or three dishes of walnuts and bonbons into his pockets, to amuse himself with on the way.

The shadows soon began to deepen, and in another hour it was night—night!—for the first time, and with strangers. Marguerite looked out upon the barren tracts of country through which they were passing, and over which a watery moon occasionally broke forth through the mist, and trembled as the cold autumn wind swept in upon her cheeks. The Frenchman, tired out at last, slept in his corner. Bello lay motionless at her feet, and only the cracking of the conducteur's whip, as they rattled through some solitary village, broke the monotonous rumbling of the wheels.

Sick and weary, Marguerite laid her head back in the corner of the diligence, and at length an uncertain and restless slumber overcame her. She was roused by a more vigorous cracking of the whip than usual, and the rattling of the wheels over rough pavement; and looking out, she saw that they were in a town, rolling along narrow, ill-lit streets, and rousing up the peaceful inhabitants from their midnight slumbers. They stopped suddenly before the Hotel de France, and the Frenchman awoke with a start.

"Sacre Mort! Where are we? Conducteur, are we here?"

"Monsieur, we are here."

"Dieu sait bèni! Mademoiselle, we are in St. Malo."

He jumped out with his little sac de nuit, his only luggage (it is wonderful with how few changes a Frenchman can travel), and then assisted Marguerite to descend. "How many pieces have you?" he inquired. "I will see after your baggage for you."

"Nous ne dechargeons pas le soir," said the conducteur, sleepily.

"But I start early to-morrow by the steamer for England," Marguerite interposed.

"All in time!" returned the man, who was now unharnessing the horses. "Entrez, entrez, mademoiselle."

"I hope it is all right," she said, turning to her friend. "Manon told me never to lose sight of my things."

"Do not fear. I will take care of them for you. At what o'clock does the steamer start to-morrow, garcon?" to the half-awaken-

ed porter, who, candle in hand, was impatiently waiting for them to enter. "Cinq heures et demie. Bon! show mademoiselle to a sleeping-room. I shall remain in the salle," the little man thought. "It is nearly one, now; and it is not worth paying for a bed for four hours. I can sleep sweetly on a chair."

CHAPTER XXXII.

"Cinq heures, mademoiselle. Vous n'avez qu'un petit quart d'heure pour le dèjeûner."

Marguerite started, and saw a rosy, good-tempered peasant-girl standing by her side.

"Where am I, Manon?" she exclaimed.

"You must not delay, mademoiselle!" called out a discordant voice in the passage; "the steamer starts precisely." The tone recalled to her the events of the past day, and after hastily bathing her face, and smoothing back her long, uncurled hair, she followed the bonne down stairs; and found her little travelling companion awaiting her in the great vacant salle, where some coffee stood ready on the table.

"Monsieur, I hope you have not risen so early for my sake?"

"Not at all, mademoiselle; in fact, I have not risen at all, for I perferred not going to bed. Take some breakfast, I entreat: if you are a bad sailor, it will not make you worse to eat; if you are a good one, it will save you buying it on board, where, as it is an English boat, the coffee will be execrable, and the price enormous."

Marguerite seated herself, but she could eat very little. "I wonder where my luggage is?" she suggested, timidly.

"Give yourself no trouble: I know," said the Frenchman. "Have you really finished? Then, mademoiselle, we had better start; the tide is low, and you must take a small boat."

Outside the hôtel stood a porter, waiting for them, with all Marguerite's luggage. The day was now just beginning to dawn, but the narrow streets were so dark, she would never have made her way without her guide, who gave her his arm, and assisted her over the rough, dirty pavement. At the harbor, a crowd of noisy boatmen assailed them, and attempted each to seize some of the luggage; but the little man waved his hand imperiously, and made his way to a better-looking boat than the rest, into which he helped Marguerite, Bello closely following.

The steam was just up when they reached the vessel, and the Frenchman had only time to run up the companion-ladder, and see Marguerite and all her things safely on board before the bell rang, and it was time for him to return.

"Monsieur, I cannot thank you sufficiently." Marguerite extended her hand. The little man touched it, then bowed low.

"Here is my card, mademoiselle," he replied, producing a very glossy one from his waistcoat-pocket; "and in the vilain pays to which you are going, I shall be too honored if *my* name is not forgotten in your thoughts—the last Frenchman, remember, to whom you have spoken before you exile——"

"Going with us, mounseer?" said a sailor, jogging his elbow.

"No, I dank God, sare. I not vis you."

"Well, you must look sharp, then; we're just off."

The Frenchman, with much dignity, descended the ladder, and in another minute the steamer was in motion.

Marguerite glanced at the card, on which was written, "Achille Jules Cesar le Grand, Marchand Tailleur," and then at the small hero himself, who was sitting in the boat watching her. She waved her hand kindly, and was ashamed to feel the tears come into her eyes. "This little tailor is perhaps the last person who will show kindness to me," she thought. Just then, another idea flashed across her—she had paid nothing in the hotel or boat, and of course Monsieur Achille would be responsible for all, "and he was too delicate to tell me of it!" she said, as the steamer swept out of the harbor, and he vanished out of her sight. "And only a tailor!"

Her further reflections upon her own forgetfulness were here interrupted by warlike sounds from Bello, who was resenting the attempts of two sailor lads to remove him from Marguerite's side.

"Blow the great ugly brute!" said one; "whoever heard tell of passengers bringing such as you aboard, before?"

"You had better not touch him," interposed Marguerite, in her soft, foreign accent; "he is so fierce to strangers! If he must not be here, I will go where you like to take him, and he will follow."

Both lads touched their caps. "We didn't know he belonged to you, miss; there's a regular place for dogs below, but it ain't fit for you to come there." However, Marguerite went with them, and saw Bello safely consigned for the voyage, and then returned to her place.

It was a fresh autumn morning, with a rising wind from the west; and the heavy cross sea soon sent the other passengers below. But to her the roar of the waters, and the cold spray dashing across her face was delightful, and she remained on deck, silently watching the coast of France until it vanished in the hazy distance. At about ten o'clock they reached Jersey, where they had to change into a larger steamer, and this time she was forced to see herself after the luggage and Bello: no pleasant task for one so young and timid, and with the consciousness

that she spoke like a foreigner. However, she managed pretty well; and though no English gentleman came forward to assist, the common sailors were all civil, and touched their hats when they spoke to her. Marguerite was dressed, of course, in the deepest mourning, and, according to the provincial French fashion, a long crape veil nearly reached her feet. But her fresh young face was one that black became; and a certain air of timidity, perfectly distinct from shyness, joined to her graceful and dignified carriage, told even the commonest sailor-boy that, though she was travelling alone, she was of gentle birth.

There was a great many passengers from Jersey, and some ladies seated themselves beside Marguerite. One of them was young and good-looking, and as the steamer passed along the varied coast of the island, Marguerite said to her gently, "It is beautiful, this little island, madame!"

The lady stared, and then laughed, and then, with the slightest possible bow, turned away and went on talking to her companions.

"Heavens! are these Englishwomen; can they be compatriots of Philip's?" thought Marguerite. However, this little incident served as a warning to her to speak to no more strangers; and she sat alone and silent the whole remainder of the day, eating only a few biscuits, and declining to go below to the cabin dinner.

It was quite dark when they reached Southampton, and, as she had forgotten to mention the exact day when the steamer sailed, no one was there to meet her, and she had alone to disembark and go to an hotel, where the enormous bill the next morning made Marguerite blush with shame as she thought of Monsieur Achille, and wondered if he had paid so much for her at St. Malo.

"Four shillings for my supper! I thought I had nothing," she ventured to suggest to the magnificent head-waiter.

"For D's supper, miss. Allow me to refer. Ah! your large dog; two more for his breakfast."

She paid without a word, but hoped, mentally, meat would not be so dear in London as at Southampton, or her cousin would have to pay a good deal for Bello's keep.

"Do you have a commissioner to clear your things, miss? He will bring them to the station, and save you all trouble."

"Oh, if you please."

"And a carriage for yourself?"

"Certainly." And with all these small expenses, together with similar ones in London, Marguerite reached her cousin's house with just sufficient money left in her purse to pay the cab, and very nearly dead with the fatigue and excitement she had gone through.

Danby met her himself at the door.

"My poor child, you are heartily welcome." The kind tone of voice was a pleasant surprise to Marguerite, who had pictured him to herself as very different; and a brighter expression came in her face, as she followed him upstairs to the drawing-room. "If you had told me what day you were coming, my dear, I should have met you at Southampton."

"Oh! thank you, sir. I should indeed have been glad to see you on my arrival; I felt so lonely travelling by myself."

Danby opened the drawing-room door; and, entering, Marguerite saw her future companions, Mrs. Danby and Georgy, both seated together on the sofa, and looking frigid and stately.

The room was not a large one; the windows were hung with rose-lined muslin curtains and gilded scrolls, and a rose-colored silk *portiere* replaced the old-fashioned folding-doors, communicating with the small back drawing-room (which, when the stained-glass window was open, overlooked the Tavistock Mews); endless trinkets, and gewgaws, and gaily bound books adorned the table; Chinese monsters of doubtful antiquity, stood on bracquets in the corners: a score of family miniatures (most of them picked up in Hanway Street) hung on each side of the mantlepiece; water-color drawings of Miss Georgy's graced the walls. But, in a moment, Marguerite detected the flimsy, bad taste of the room, and saw that neither fresh flowers, nor well read books, nor signs of occupation, gave it the look of home. She glanced at the De Burghs, and knew they were neither of them prepared to like her.

"Here is little Marguerite," said Danby, rather nervously. "Mrs. Danby, my dear! your new cousin."

Mrs. Danby extended three languid fingers to her "new cousin," and the expression of Georgy's face betokened anything but a hearty welcome. She had troubled herself very slightly about Marguerite, as soon as she found that Earnscliffe would not accompany her, and only expected to see an awkward country girl of sixteen, who would not be much in her own way, and probably some day go out as a governess; and when Marguerite entered in all her flush of striking beauty, and with as much grace of manner as though she had been accustomed to good society from her cradle, the surprise was by no means agreeable. She did not want a lovely girl, ten years younger than herself, to attract away the attention of the few men they managed to get at the house, and at once foresaw a desperate rival in Marguerite.

"How do you do, Miss St. John? You must excuse my surprise; but from your letters, we expected quite a little girl."

"Ah!" returned Marguerite, in her rich voice and foreign accent, "I express my English so ill; no doubt you thought my

letter childish; but I am, indeed, sixteen—sixteen and a few days."

"You look very much older."

"Yes? Oh! I do not look at all old without my bonnet."

"You have your father's eyes, child," said Danby, very kindly.

The little speech went to Marguerite's heart, and she turned and kissed the old man's cheek: "Oh, cousin! he so often spoke of you." she whispered, while the ready tears gathered in her eyes.

Mrs. Danby tossed her head, and Georgy said something about scenes. Marguerite looked very calmly from one to the other. She knew intuitively they did not like her, and drew nearer to Danby, as to her only friend.

"You must be very tired, dear," he went on, "after your long journey. Dinner will be ready in about an hour. Georgy, take your cousin to her room."

Very slowly Miss Georgy rose; and she was leisurely approaching Marguerite when the door burst open, and in flew Bello, nearly upsetting two great china jars as he entered, and leaving marks of his muddy feet upon the carpet. Danby was very timid with dogs—it amounted almost to a peculiarity with him—and he exclaimed as loud as the two women at the intruder.

"Poor Bello!" said Marguerite, quietly; "it is all so strange to him; but he will soon get used to you."

"Miss St. John," exclaimed Mrs. Danby, actually rising from the sofa with outraged dignity. "You do not mean that that monster is yours?"

"Undoubtedly he is, madame."

"And you have brought him with you to this house?"

"I have."

"My dear," interrupted Danby, "there must be some mistake! You cannot mean that you wish that very large hound to become my guest."

"Cousin, he was my father's favorite—his constant companion."

"Oh! was he? Ah, poor Percy! Well, we will see."

Danby fidgeted about, and winced as Bello glared savagely at him and showed his teeth.

"But, to tell the truth," he went on, more resolutely, "I am not fond of dogs."

"Not fond of dogs? Oh! sir, you must like Bello. When once he knows you well, he will be so faithful! It is his very sagacity that prevents his taking to strangers."

"Yes, exactly; but in the meantime—"

"In the meantime," interrupted Mrs. Danby, "you will recollect, Miss St. John, I don't allow such creatures in my drawing-room. What your cousin may permit in his sitting-room, I know not!"

"Perhaps Wilkins likes dogs," hesitated poor Danby.

"Perhaps something temporary might be arranged in the coal-hole," cried Miss Georgy, wittily.

Marguerite looked from one to the other of the speakers, her dark eyes dilating, and her lips parted. She really scarcely understood them at first. That any one professing regard for her father should hesitate at the slight inconvenience of receiving his dog, was something she could not believe; but at Miss Georgy's remark, and the sneer accompanying it, her cheek flushed crimson.

"Am I to have a room to myself?" she said, turning to Danby.

"Of course, of course, my dear, and——"

"Then, please may Bello come with me? He shall trouble no one else."

"That brute in one of the bed-rooms!" said Mrs. Danby.

"Oh, madame! would you turn him into the streets? He is old, and will not live very long, and he is all remaining to me of my home."

Mrs. Danby turned away coldly from the supplicating young face, and addressed her husband.

"Just settle all this as you like, Mr. Danby; but spare me any more scenes with this young person for the future. I am not in a state to bear these shocks on my nerves; and as it is, I shall be ill and unstrung for the rest of the day. And, Mr. Danby, sir" (her voice became prophetically shrill), "turn out that creature, that monster, and take away—the young person—I am fainting;" and this excellent woman sank back hysterically on the sofa.

So Danby himself showed Marguerite to her room, a very small one, overlooking extensive ranges of chimney-pots, with a distant glimpse of the Foundling Hospital, and a mews in the foreground. And here, with Bello crouching by her side, she wept like a child, as she was, at her first coming to her new home.

———

CHAPTER XXXIII.

"AND why did not Mr. Earnscliffe bring you!" was Georgy's first distinctly-addressed question to Marguerite in the course of the evening. "I thought, he was such a great friend, he would not have let you travel alone!"

The sudden mention of his name made Marguerite color up, and start, in a manner, that caused Georgy to fix her eyes searchingly upon her face, and draw all sorts of conclusions in a moment.

"Mr. Earnscliffe had left, he was only paying us a visit."

"Returned to England? Shall you know him in London, then?"

"Oh, no!" replied Marguerite, very quickly. "I shall not see him any more; he is going to Italy, to remain abroad some years."

"Ah! I never thought it would be much of an acquaintance!" said Mrs. Danby scornfully from her throne on the sofa.

But Georgy, with sharper eyes, saw that it *had* been an intimate acquaintance, and that Marguerite winced at the name. "Tell us what Earnscliffe is like?" she went on, happy in her power of making the poor child's face blush and her eyes fill. "I have seen him, but not near. Is he very good-looking?"

"Yes," said Marguerite, in a low voice, and gazing straight into the fire, round which they were sitting; "he is considered very handsome."

"Considered?—but what do you think?"

"I—I—hardly know, madame."

"'Madame!'" said Georgy, laughing rudely. "It is not the fashion in England to call young ladies 'madame.' How long did he stay with you?" she went on, relentlessly.

"Three months altogether."

"A visit of three months—goodness! What was there to amuse him?—had you any neighbors, or parties?"

"Oh, no," replied Marguerite, hoping to escape from speaking of Philip; "we knew no one but the curé and the doctor, and I never went to a party in my life."

"No one would say it from her manner," Danby ventured to remark.

"No; there are some people without any natural timidity," replied his wife; "and Miss St. John appears to be of them."

"But how did you amuse Mr. Earnscliffe?" went on Georgy, untiring in her sport.

"He never wanted to be amused; he was perfectly happy, conversing with my father, or wandering through our wild woods with me," replied Marguerite, turning her large, dark eyes full upon Miss de Burgh. "Our life was delightful to him after having had so much of society in London."

Utterly unused to what English young ladies term "quizzing," Marguerite had detected the bent of Georgy's inquiries; and her spirit rose at the idea of being cross-examined.

"Oh, how pastoral!" returned Miss Georgy, with a sneer. "From all I have heard of Earnscliffe, he must be just the kind of man for these innocent pleasures and companionships!"

"And who has educated you, dear?" said Danby, upon whom this little by-play was lost; "for educated I am sure you are."

"My father taught me in English for two hours every day," replied Marguerite, "while he was strong enough to do anything; and monsieur le curé has taught me in French from my infancy."

"Monsieur le cure!" interrupted Mrs. Danby. "I trust, sir," addressing her husband, "that you have not introduced a papist into this house?"

"You are not a papist, my dear?" said Danby, nervously—"surely you cannot be one!"

"Papist, sir?"

"Yes; a Roman Catholic."

"Oh, no! Much as I admire their form of worship, I have been brought up to my father's faith."

"Admire their form of worship!" exclaimed Mrs. Danby, with pious horror. "Idolatrous wretches!"

"Ma, I wish you would drop those expressions," interrupted Georgy; "they are so wounding to the feelings of persons of Catholic spirit."

"Oh, Lord! if they have begun *that*," ejaculated Danby, his head sinking hopelessly between his hands. "Marguerite, do you know the difference between Anglicans and Evangelicals? because you soon will, if you are uninformed on the subject."

It was a singular thing that Mrs. Danby and her daughter, being both so perfectly worldly, as people in general would judge, and having led a life abroad the reverse of devout, should now consider it incumbent upon them both to entertain very strong doctrinal opinions, for which they were ready, at all times and all places, to do battle. Each had her own church, her pet parson. Mrs. Danby attended a crowded West-end chapel, where an eloquent young extempore preacher, of sleek face and white-handed appearance set forth to a fashionable congregation the hottest amount of low-church doctrine that could be diluted into a discourse of an hour and a quarter; and, with great self-complacency on the subject of his own election, pronounced judgment each Sunday on the heathenish idolatry and perfect certainty of perdition of the larger majority of Christendom. And Miss Georgy frequented a certain mysterious church, where the dim light scarcely enabled young ladies to read the illuminated letters on their gilt prayer-books, and where intoning, and candles, and flowers, and chorister-boys, gave much scandal to a Protestant churchwarden and the mass of the parishioners. As may be imagined, the ladies' opinions clashed not a little; and as both were very firm, and both invited their spiritual directors very frequently, a good many passages of arms were the result.

"I never heard of either Anglican or Evangelical," said Marguerite, in answer to Danby's question. "My father was Church of England."

"Oh, that is quite old-fashioned now, my dear. However I am old-fashioned myself, and I will take you to Westminster Abbey, for you to hear the English service, next Sunday. Of course you have never heard our Liturgy?"

"Only read by my father; but it scarcely could sound more beautiful than *that*. We used to have our service together every Sunday evening."

"Well, I am glad to hear you were brought up with English ideas, and have not got into the foreign ways of breaking Sunday," Danby observed.

"Oh, Sunday was always such a happy day in my childhood," said Marguerite, her face gladdening as she spoke. "In winter, Manon and I used to dance in the great salle; in summer, when father was well enough, we made excursions into the woods, Manon and all, and dined under the trees; then, afterwards, I would sit making wreaths of the wild flowers we had gathered on the way, while I sang songs and——"

"Danced!—sung songs!—made wreaths, my dear! Are you speaking of *Sunday*?"

"Yes, sir; it was our fête-day—God's day, father told me—the day of happiness."

"Hum!" answered Mr. Danby, shaking his head doubtfully, while the two extremes of church opinion exchanged looks, and met for once in this condemnation of such a flagrant case of immorality, Mrs. Danby deprecating with her hand as though to say that the state of this young woman was, indeed, past recall.

"When you are at Rome, act like the Romans."

At Wiesbaden and Mainz the De Burghs had flaunted, many a score of times, in gay silks and bonnets, to listen to military bands on a Sunday afternoon; but they were now in England, which made a very great difference, and they both regarded Marguerite with the fierce eyes of outraged excellence.

"But," pursued Danby, wishing to smother over everything, "I am sure you will conform to English opinion now, and not dance or sing on Sundays. It might be very well in those wild places, but——"

"Ah, sir," interrupted Marguerite, mournfully, "you need not tell me: I shall never wish to do either here. Those were in the happy times before my father was so ill."

"And can you speak French pretty well?" Georgy inquired.

"Oh," replied Marguerite, in French, "it is much more familiar to me than English. I greatly prefer speaking it;" and she continued talking with that perfectly French intonation and accent to which no foreigner can ever attain.

"It is no gift," Georgy interrupted. "Of course, when you are born and brought up in the country, it would be very strange if you could not speak the language! Can you sing or play?"

"I have not learnt the piano yet, but I can play accompaniments to my songs on the guitar, and I have a very good voice."

"And no bad opinion of yourself," Georgy added, half aloud.

"It is fortunate Miss St. John has such confidence in her own power," Mrs. Danby remarked; "her accomplishments she will probably find needful in her future walk of life. A French accent, above all is desirable for a governess. Oh! how wearied I am!"

And rising with languid dignity, the mistress of the establishment rang the bell, and then commanded a hungry-looking young housemaid, with much asperity, "to summon the servants"—*i. e.*, Wilkins and an unhappy attempt at a page—"to evening readings."

CHAPTER XXXIV.

THE winter and spring passed by, and Marguerite became at least accustomed to her life. Mrs. Danby and her daughter both disliked her in their own way, and strove to make her home as miserable as possible, in the hope of forcing her to go out as a governess; but Danby loved his little cousin, and in the absence of his step-daughter at her gaieties, or of his wife during her fancied illnesses, Marguerite was his only companion.

She liked him, and was grateful; but, as she told Earnscliffe, hers was not a nature readily to take to strangers; and even had any of her new associates been more refined or congenial than they were, she would have been long in becoming attached to them.

As it was, Georgy, whose nearer approach to her own age naturally attracted Marguerite the most, continually jarred upon her. But Mrs. Danby repulsed her even more. The inanition, the selfishness of this woman's life was something so new to Marguerite, after the gentle, uncomplaining sufferings of her own father, that she could scarcely even assume a tone of sincerity in inquiring after her fancied complaints, and in time rarely entered the drawing-room, where Mrs. Danby passed her time between her tawdry morning callers, and homœopathic doctors. When the weather was fine, Danby took her long walks about London, to show her the sights, with most of which she was very disappointed. The Exchange, and the Tower, and the Bank, seen ankle-deep in mud, and through chocolate fogs, were so unlike the London that Philip had described, and she imagined! And Danby was often quite surprised at her very mild enthusiasm.

"Is this the best part of London that we have seen, Cousin? is there nothing more?" asked Marguerite, one February afternoon, when Danby had shown her Regent Street, and Piccadilly, and Trafalgar Square, and they were walking home in the dusk.

"Nothing more?" Why, child, what would you have? I thought, after passing all your life in a ruined old French house in Brittany, anything would appear grand."

"Ah! that was home. But then I imagined London so different to what it is. My own childish fancy misled me I suppose."

"I am afraid you are not happy in yourself, dear, and therefore nothing appears bright."

"Oh! I am happy with you, Cousin. Our evenings are very pleasant together in your own room, when the others are out, and poor Bello may lie before the fire. It was very kind of you to let me keep him, and to tell me nothing of your own antipathy to dogs. I should be *very* miserable without Bello!"

"Um—the dog is old."

"Yes; I sometimes think he will not live very long; the air is so different for him here; and then living down in the area, you see, instead of wandering where he likes—"

"Well, my dear, you know that I have tried to have him more up-stairs; but——"

"Yes, Cousin, you have been very kind in that, as in everything else. You always try to take my part; and, as the others do not like me, I am sure that my presence does not make you any happier in your own house. It would be far better for me to go out as a governess, Miss Georgy says, and perhaps she is right; but, then, I do not like to leave Bello. Do you think I might take him with me if I was a governess, cousin?"

The childish gravity with which she asked the question made Danby smile; but it quickly faded from his face, and he replied—"Marguerite, you would not speak of becoming a governess if you knew how deeply it wounds my feelings to hear you. As I have told you, it was through me that your father became poor; and while I have a home you shall never leave it. Besides this, you are in no dependent position. When Kersaint is sold, and the money it realises invested, you will have a nice little income of your own—enough, on my death, with what I shall leave you, to live very comfortably. If you never marry, little Maggy! you are not quite an old maid yet, you know."

"I shall soon be seventeen, sir. How time goes on; It seems only yesterday that I was a child."

"And, pray, what do you consider yourself now?"

"Well, Miss Georgy says that I look two-and-twenty, and have such an old manner!"

"Does she? It struck me Georgy looked very glum the other evening at their grand *réunion*, as they call it, when you, in your black frock and the flower I gave you, attracted so much attention from all her friends."

"I wished afterwards I had not appeared," replied Marguerite. "I never will again, but Mrs. Danby told me to do so, and said my singing would make the party 'go-off.' "

· "Georgy's quondam admirer, that long-coated young parson, seemed to have a good deal to say to you, Maggy."

· "Mr. Ignatius Shirley? Oh, cousin, he told me I was a true Anglican! I had no idea of it before. And then, when I was describing our cathedral at home, he stared so in my face, and repeated some half-sacred lines, that yet seemed to apply to me. I could not understand him."

· "Nor could Georgy either, I take it. She told me the next morning you were a thorough flirt, Maggy!"

· Marguerite colored. "Georgy does not like me," she said, "and calls me by that odious name, because I dislike it so much. We shall have a nice evening alone to-day, however. They are both going to the thea-tre."

"Not quite alone, dear. I asked Mr. Mortimer this morning."

· "Oh! . r. Mortimer does not disturb us. You and he can talk and play chess after dinner, while I sing my old songs to myself. He never minds my singing, he is so good-natured. I really like Mr. Mortimer."

· They reached home, and found the ladies ready dressed in the drawing-room; for they had dined early, as they usually did when they went to the theatre. Marguerite's face all glowing with health and freshness, as she entered; and, in spite of her dingy mourn-ing, its exceeding beauty made Miss Georgy feel spiteful.

"How fond you are of the London streets after dark, Marguerite! I wonder at your taste for a young lady so pastorally brought up."

"We have seen so much to-day. I never thought of being out late—otherwise I dis-like walking on these dark, foggy after-noons."

· "Oh, of course! Mamma, why has she left off her vail and turned her hair back from her face! A young woman of her age should not be dressed so childishly— it looks quite ridiculous."

"It is very immaterial how Miss St. John dresses," drawled Mrs. Danby.

· "I don't agree with you! People see Marguerite going in and out of our house, and naturally look upon her as belonging to *us.*"

"Perhaps that was the reason your young parson admired her so much," said Danby, "for he used to be very fond of you, Geor-gy."

"Admire her, indeed!" echoed Miss de Burgh. "I do not call *that* admiration. Any girl with a sort of look and manner can get young men to talk to her."

"I think it highly wrong," said Mrs. Danby, languidly, "to put such ludicrous ideas into Miss St. John's head. Her future position will be one in which no respectable

young woman ever allows herself to be ad-dressed by the other sex—unless, indeed, some male dependent of the family should make her an offer of marriage. I remember my dear delightful friend, Lady Louisa Drysdale, used to say it was charming when the governess and butler were engaged. 'It makes them cheerful,' she said, 'and prevents them running after my sons.' "

"Lady Drysdale be——!" interrupted Danby, aroused out of his usual placidity. "What has all this cursed trash of butlers and governesses to do with Marguerite? If any one turns out of my house it won't be her, ma'am—you may be very sure. Come here to me, Maggy darling!"

But Marguerite had become suddenly pale, though she never spoke a word. She walked straight to the door, then up to her own room.

"Can I bear it?" she exclaimed, passion-ately, when she was alone. "Can I live with these people any longer! Oh! I will be a governess—anything sooner than re-main with them. A governess—classed with servants! I was not made for it. Father, if you could see me now!"

She did not weep. She never wept after an insult from these women; but her cheeks burnt, and her heart beat painfully, and she paced up and down her small room impa-tiently, until she heard the house door close after them. Then she bathed her face, smoothed back the dark masses of hair from her temples, and came down slowly and weari-ly to the drawing-room. A figure stood alone in the uncertain light before the fire, and thinking it was Danby Marguerite approach-ed softly, and laid her hand upon his shoul-der.

"Cousin, it *is* hard to bear all they say to me."

"All who say, Miss St. John?"

"Oh, Mr. Mortimer, forgive me! I mis-took you for my cousin."

"What is it so hard to bear?"

"Nothing—nothing that I can tell you, sir." She seated herself by the fire, and strove hard not to cry, while Mortimer stood silently looking down at her averted face. He had looked very hard at Marguerite of late.

"You are left a good deal alone," he went on.

"Yes, I like that. Mr. Danby and I are quite happy together."

"Do you never wish to accompany Miss de Burgh to her gaieties, then?"

"Oh, never!" Marguerite glanced at her black dress. "I would not go to any gay place."

"Not now, of course. But afterwards, I suppose, you will go out with them?"

"Never! In the first place"—Marguerite grew bolder at his kind tone—"I don't think I should ever like the same places or people as Georgy does; in the next, I am going to be a governess. Although my cousin does not much like it, I have quite made up my mind——"

"You—are—going—to be—a governess, Miss St. John?" exclaimed Mortimer, laying an emphasis on each word of the question.

"Yes—they often tell me it would be best, and I feel it so now. I hope that the children will not dislike me, and that I may take Bello," she added in a tearful whisper.

Mr. Mortimer gave a kind of sound between an indignant exclamation and a chuckle. An odd sound it was, that made Marguerite look up, and wonder what he was thinking about.

"Miss Georgy has recommended this plan, I suppose?"

"Yes—and Mrs. Danby too. They find me so useless here, and they say my French accent will make it easy for me to get a good situation. The only thing I doubt about is Bello. Do you think it likely a governess will be allowed to keep a dog?"

Mortimer's reply was prevented by the entrance of Danby, who came up and kissed Marguerite kindly, then joked her upon flirting with Mortimer in the dark.

"I shall tell Georgy," he said. "You must know, Maggy, that Mortimer is an old admirer of hers."

"Am I?" returned Mortimer. "Yes, I admired the whole lot at Boulogne, didn't I? and I admire them more this evening than I ever have before, even——"

"Dinner is announced," broke in Marguerite, quickly, afraid lest he should repeat her half-confidences. "Who will take me?" She laid her little hand on Mortimer's arm, and they went down silently, Danby following. During dinner the two old men talked as usual about their cronies, and the stocks, and a misty kind of politics of their own; while Marguerite, with Bello by her side, for a treat, paid very little attention to either of them. She was still turning over the governess scheme in her head, and thinking that, after all, it might be very much better than her present life. "If I could be with nice people," she thought, "people something more like my father or Philip, who would be kind and not say the bitter things they do here, I might be happy, especially if the children cared for me. I wonder what Manon would say, if she knew I was to be a governess?"

"Lord St. Leger is on the verge of ruin again, I am told," said Mortimer, in the middle of a small radical disquisition upon the aristocracy. The name roused Marguerite's attention in a second, she remembered that he was the father of Philip's wife. "I hear all about it from a friend of mine, who once had the folly to accept some of his bills. He has gambled away nearly the whole of his last inheritance already."

"I remember the man well, years ago in my younger days, when I used to go to the Derby and Goodwood," said Danby. "A cadaverous-looking fellow he was, and a professional gambler."

"Yes; he has been black-balled at half the clubs in London; and can only now prey upon his fellow-sharks or young lads in the dens about St. James's street."

"Has he any sons?" asked Danby.

"No, only one daughter; and she made a miserable marriage three or four years ago. She married Earnscliffe, the writer, who like all other geniuses, was a bad husband, and after two or three years' wretchedness they separated."

"What, legally?"

"Oh, no!—nothing of that kind. Mere incompatability of temper. You know, Danby, the old story."

"By-the-way, Maggie knows Earnscliffe," said Danby, evading the question of domestic happiness.

"Indeed! Ah, talking of authors, do you remember——" and Mortimer began a very long story about somebody they had both known thirty years ago.

He had never looked at Marguerite—never seen the sudden flash, the paleness, the nervous clasp of her hands, at the mention of Earnscliffe's name—had he done so, her future life might have been a very different one. For Mortimer would have married no woman knowing that she had had a former lover.

They went on with their drowsy talk as before; but all Marguerite's thoughts were changed. With Earnscliffe's name came back old hopes, old dreams, old sunny plans for the future. Oh, compared with these, how blank and dreary seemed her prospects now! Her head drooped, and her cheek grew so pale, that at last Danby noticed her; and he exclaimed abruptly—"Maggie child! what ails you? Are you ill?"

"No, cousin," she answered, mournfully.

"You must cheer up, my dear," went on Danby, "and sing to us presently some of your French ballads."

"I could not sing to-night. I have a choking sensation in my throat. Cousin, do you not hear; I can scarcely speak?"

"Have you taken cold, child? Were we out too late for you?"

"No, it is not that; I am—oh, cousin!" (with a sudden outburst of tears) "I am so wretched!"

"Marguerite!"—it was so unlike her to complain before a stranger, that Danby knew her sorrow must be great—"my poor child, you shall tell me all this another time."

"Mr. Mortimer knows; Mr. Mortimer is very kind"—her voice grew thick—"I do not mind saying it before him."

"But what is this sudden sorrow? I know," he spoke hastily—"what Mrs. Danby said to you this evening, and that your feelings were hurt—not more deeply than mine, perhaps—but that is nothing new. You have had to bear similar things before."

"Cousin, you have always been so good, I grieve to leave you; and I think that is one of my greatest troubles to-night."

"Yes," broke in Mortimer, "I hear that you are going to lose Miss St. John, Danby."

"I have heard nothing of it."

"Dear cousin, you know what I said to you to-day. Well, I have quite made up my mind now. It will be far better for me to go out as a governess."

"You never shall, Marguerite—never!"

"Oh, Mr. Mortimer! speak for me. It may be hard to be dependent and a governess; but it is worse—far worse—to live with relations who are unkind to me! I know that I am barely tolerated here, and that all my cousin's kindness makes him more miserable in his own home. Speak for me, sir; tell him that it would be far better!"

Mr. Mortimer rose and walked to the fire, looked into it for a few minutes, then turned round, and grasped his coat tails; and, supported and flanked as it were by this familiar position of fifty years' standing, he spoke deliberately, but with unusual quickness for him, and a certain agitation of manner.

"Danby, I'm a plain spoken man, as you know. Miss St. John, I'm an old man, as you see. I can't make fine speeches to either of you, but this I have to say: If, Miss St. John, you will not forget my age, and my great unfitness to be your husband, but overlook it. and become my wife, you shall have settlements a duke's daughter might be proud of, and all the devotion a plain old fellow like myself can offer."

Danby literally sprang from his chair in astonishment.

"Mortimer, are you in earnest?"

"I don't look as if I was joking, do I?"

"After all you have said about marrying in one's old age, to offer yourself to Maggy! Adopt her, man. You can give her a happier home than mine, adopt her as your daughter. She's only sixteen—she's a child!"

"Thank you, Danby. I have made up my mind with respect to my own determination long before to-night, though I never could bring it out. I only wish to hear what Miss St. John says; how she takes the idea of having such a husband as me!"

He had never glanced at her yet, since he began to speak; and he had kept his eyes fixed upon Danby, even while addressing Marguerite. But now he turned slightly and looked at her. He expected to see her, at least, a little agitated—it is conventional to believe that young women are so, when receiving an offer of marriage, even from a man four times their own age—to see her blush, or tremble, perhaps shrink from him:

but Marguerite did neither. She watched him intently—watching the real emotions. the earnestness of his plain face, and feeling with delighted surprise that again one human being on the earth had conceived an affection for her.

"Sir," she said, at length, "you are very good. I little thought you cared so much for me. How can I thank you enough for your offer?" rising to his side and looking up at him.

"Maggy!"

"Miss St. John! am I indeed so happy?'

Her cool acceptance surprised them both. It was so unlike what either expected, and. for a moment the same thought flashed across them: "Can money so readily win even her fair, young heart?" But one glance at her face—that face where all the sinless trust of childhood yet rested—undid the suspicion; and then a sharp regret smote Danby as he thought Marguerite was promising —she knew not what—in her desire to leave his house.

"Oh, Maggy! I wish I could have made you happier."

"Dear cousin, you have done your best. It was the others who never liked me——"

"Miss St. John—Marguerite, will you indeed accept me?" said Mortimer, very gently. and bending over her.

"Yes, sir, if you will be troubled with me."

Mortimer stooped and kissed her forehead, "May God make you happy, child!" he said, solemnly.

CHAPTER XXXV.

MORTIMER remained late, and they all sat talking round the fire. Mortimer, whose manner had still the quiet agitation of some new-found happiness, although Marguerite did not perceive it, arranged everything as he thought would please her most; where he should take a new house—what carriages— what books—what pictures—she should have.

"And Bello!" added Marguerite, stroking the old hound, as he pressed close up by her side, "Poor Bello! You will not object to him, sir? and all the dear old books from home when they come?"

"Everything of yours, Miss St. John, will be of value to me."

"Poor old Kersaint!" she went on, "I suppose it will be sold soon, or let."

"Well, said Danby, "I heard from the agent in Paris a few days ago, and he tells me there is great difficulty in finding a tenant for such an out-of-the-way place, and that it will be much better to sell. A neighboring farmer has made a tolerable bid for it already—he wants the land."

" And he will destroy the garden, perhaps pull down the manoir itself," added Marguerite, sadly.

" It must pain you to part with your old house, does it not? " asked Mortimer.

" Yes, I cannot bear to think of it belonging to strangers. However it must be——"

" Not now. The old house shall be kept as it is, in case you ever like to pay it a visit. It would be a pleasant summer excursion."

" You will keep Kersaint? Oh! Mr. Mortimer; and may Manon live there, and poor Bruno? Can it be really true that I shall see home again? Cousin, I am so happy!" springing to her feet, and clasping her hands in excitement.

" Poor little Maggy! You look brighter than I have ever seen you. I wonder what they will say!" added Danby, abruptly. *They* always meant his women-kind.

Mortimer chuckled a little. " It will be rather a surprise for Miss Georgy, I imagine, this failure of the governess scheme."

" I am sure Georgy will be glad," said Marguerite. " For she does not like my living here, and——"

" Well, Maggy; why do you hesitate? "

" Oh! Georgy has often said how eccentric it was of Mr. Mortimer not to marry; so she will be glad to see him married at last."

" Delighted, I have no doubt, and her ' mamma ' also!" said Mortimer, drily.

" I am very sure they will be delighted at my departure, if they are not at your marriage," cried Marguerite, laughing. " But they *will* be surprised! Only this evening Mrs. Danby spoke with such certainty of my being a governess."

" A governess!" echoed Mortimer, half aloud. " Such a glorious creature as that— a governess!"

Certainly Marguerite did not look much suited for one at that moment, as she stood before him in an attitude of the most childlike and unconscious grace—her face flushed, her bright curls falling in a perfect cloud about her shoulders.

" Surely you never thought of it in earnest? "

" Indeed I did; although my cousin was so good he never liked to hear of it. Perhaps I should have got on pretty well. I don't know. But, oh! Mr. Mortimer, I like my new prospects so much better; I feel as if I had a home again, now that Kersaint is not to be sold." And she turned her eyes to his with a soft, warm expression that made Mortimer's heart thrill, as it had never done during his sixty years of hard life.

" Cousin Danby must come often; must he not, to see us? " *Us.* How sweet the word sounded from her lips! " Whenever you are alone I shall hold you engaged to me, cousin—remember."

" I shall miss you terribly, Maggy. Nothing but the thought of your own increased happiness could reconcile me to your marrying so young. You seem such a child still —not seventeen, and——"

" Danby, don't begin about adopting again," interrupted Mortimer, quickly. " *You* have preferred marrying a lady of experience; it is my happiness to have won a girl of sixteen."

" And Heaven grant your choice may turn out the best, my friend. I am sure I ought not to offer advice on such subjects, with my own fate as an example of my judgment "

A thundering double knock at the door here made the quiet trio start, and Danby turn quite pale. " Who is to tell them? " he said, nervously. " We must decide at once."

" Not I," said Mortimer, evidently enjoying his friend's discomposure. " Of course, you are the proper person. You are Miss St. John's guardian."

" Well, the fact is—I am rather——"

" Oh, I will, cousin. I knew you would rather not say it. And they cannot be angry with me now that I am so soon to leave." And Marguerite ran to open the door.

Judging from the tone of both ladies as they entered, their dissipation had been rather a failure; at least, Mrs. Danby was complaining peevishly of fatigue, and Georgy, in no pleasant voice, was expressing her disgust for some person or persons unknown.

" I knew them so well at Baden-Baden, and afterwards at Boulogne, and to-night they scarcely looked at me—never returned my bow. What are you doing, Marguerite, up, still? Go and cut me some sandwiches, and move quick, Miss." Pushing her rudely aside. " I want to come in and warm my feet."

" I have something to tell you, Georgy."

" Move away, Miss St. John," cried Mrs. Danby's sharp voice. " This dog again! " as Bello's gaunt face peered through the open door. " For the last time, I say, I will not suffer it."

" Oh, Mr. Mortimer! " exclaimed Georgy, in a suddenly cheerful voice, as she caught sight of him. " I did not know you were here. Marguerite, love, why did you not tell me? "

They both entered and shook hands with Mortimer, who greeted them in his usual quiet way. " An unexpected pleasure! You did not tell me that Mr. Mortimer was coming to dine with you, dear," said Mrs. Danby.

Danby knew what that " dear " portended, and replied, " No, ma'am; Maggy and I were so tired when we came in, that we forgot all about it, didn't we, Maggy? " He looked, and spoke nervously, wondering all the time how his wife would take the news, and what his own life would be for some months after the stock-broker had proposed for " Maggy," not Miss de Burgh.

" Take away my cloak, Marguerite,"

whispered Georgy; she had of late tried to convert Marguerite into a sort of waiting-maid for herself. "And tell me how my hair looks."

"Very uncurled," Marguerite replied, meekly, taking away her cousin's wraps, and laying them on a table. "But it does not much signify. Have you had a pleasant evening?"

"Never mind," was the rejoinder; but in a tone too low of course for the guest to hear. "How dare you sit alone in this way when there was a visitor? Your face so red, and your hair all flung about in that ridiculous manner. You shall have it cut before you go out as governess."

"Georgy, don't be angry with me. I shall not trouble you long now."

Mortimer heard her voice in a second, and came a step nearer.

"Miss de Burgh, it seems you are to lose your young friend soon. You will be lonely without her."

Georgy was sweet and affectionate in a moment, and regretted that circumstances compelled dear Marguerite to go out on the world. and so on.

"Well," returned Mortimer, "most young ladies go out in a similar way, and appear rather anxious to do so than otherwise."

"Ah, yes; and Marguerite is very patient, poor thing."

"I hope her patience will never be so much tried again, Miss de Burgh, as it has been lately."

"Marguerite!" said Georgy, looking round sharply at her, with an expression that plainly said, "Have you dared to complain?"

"Explain, Maggy, explain," Danby interrupted. "Mortimer and Georgy are at cross purposes."

"The truth is, then," said Marguerite, very calmly and quite composed, as she addressed herself to both the women, "all my prospects have changed this evening. After you had left I thought deeply over what you have so often recommended to me, and decided it would really be best to follow your advice—although cousin Danby would not hear of it—and become a governess. I mentioned this before Mr. Mortimer, and—you will scarcely believe in such kindness—he has asked me to marry him, and live in his house for ever."

"Mr. Mortimer—to marry you!" gasped Georgy.

"Impossible!" said Mrs. Danby.

But Mortimer's face soon showed them that it was only too true; and they had to force out something like congratulations.

"You must really excuse our surprise," said Georgy, at length, with a desperate attempt at sprightliness; "but we have always looked upon you as such a confirmed old bachelor, Mr. Mortimer. However, I hope your marriage may prove a happy one."

"Thank you, ma'am; I believe it will. I,

at least, have every prospect of happiness, if Miss St. John can be content;" and he drew Marguerite to him and laid his hand on her shining curls.

———

CHAPTER XXXVI.

THERE were few preliminaries to be gone through before the marriage. Mortimer wished it to take place at once; and Marguerite did not plead for delay. He made the most ample, unconditional settlements upon her; took a new house at Wimbledon, with gardens and conservatories to suit her taste; bought pianos, pictures, books—everything that could externally make the home of a young girl happy.

And Marguerite? She was very calm at first. Simply and childishly happy in the thought of her release from the De Burghs, or the prospect of being a governess, deeply grateful to Mortimer for his kindness in marrying her, and giving her such a home; and for some time she connected all this scarcely at all with Philip and the unaltered love she still bore him. But as the day approached, when the wedding-dresses were actually being made, and the thought was *realised* of her approaching marriage, her spirits sank, her color went and came, her manner was fitful and nervous.

"You are not repenting your decision, Maggy?" said Danby, one evening, when they were alone, and he had been intently watching her face for some time. "It is still not too late."

"My decision—about what, cousin?" with a slight start. "Had I anything in particular to decide upon to day?"

"I was not speaking of silks and pearls, or patterns of damask and ormolu, Marguerite; but of the great decision—your decision of marrying Mortimer. Do you ever wish it revoked?"

"No," answered Marguerite, slowly, and without raising her head; "it was to be, I suppose. I had no other prospect; and Mr. Mortimer seems very well content. I am sure Mr. Mortimer will be kind to me. I heard from Manon, my nurse, to-day, in answer to my announcement, and she is so delighted, and thinks it such a good thing for me. Although she is only a servant, Manon is very sharp-sighted, and I am glad to hear her opinion. How much she will think of me next Thursday."

"Next Thursday!" repeated Danby. "Only three days more! She has never known love," he thought, as he continued to watch her almost infantine face. "She cannot realise the sacrifice of all such feeling that she is making in marrying an old man. Her perfect ignorance will be her safeguard."

The two following days passed by—the evening before the marriage came—and Marguerite was looking at the white silk and orange blossoms she was to wear next morning. A vague, wild hope was there, that yet it would never be; that at the last something would happen, some one die—Philip appear, and tell her that he was free, and she would marry him. She could *not* feel that to-morrow she would be Mortimer's wife; and once, when she woke suddenly from a dream of old days in the night, the desperate thought crossed her, even now, to break it all off—return and live at Kersaint with Manon—do anything, rather than place another barrier against the possibility of ever becoming Philip's. But with the morning came Georgy to help her to dress, and she heard the unusual stir of servants in the house, and the sun shone cheerfully into her room, as with a good omen for her happiness, and the half-formed resolve vanished.

"You do look well, I must confess," said Miss de Burgh, when the bride's dress was completed. "Toilette de Mariee is so exactly suited for peach-colored complexions and downcast blue eyes. I never could look the bride that you do; and then, as you don't intend to cry, the effect will not be spoiled. Most girls cry, you know, and red eyes are the result; but that is not your style."

"When girls are leaving home," said Marguerite, gently—so gently that even Georgy softened—"I can imagine their crying, but there is nothing to make me shed tears."

"Your home has not been too happy here I must confess."

"Oh, my cousin Danby has been very kind; and, if you have not liked me, perhaps it has been my own fault. I hope you will often come and see me now."

Upon which Miss de Burgh kissed her with great unction, and was sure, if she had ever hurt dear Marguerite's feelings, she wished to be forgiven.

Marguerite being of course still in mourning, the wedding was to be a very quiet one; so there was only a small party at breakfast. It went off as such things generally do. Miss Georgy was in an hysterical kind of good spirits, Mortimer radiant, Danby very silent; but Marguerite, who had kept up pretty well hitherto, grew paler as the day proceeded; and when, at last, her lace and orange-flowers were exchanged for a travelling-dress, and the moment arrived for her and Mortimer to leave together, the very hue of death was upon her face. He felt her tremble violently as she entered the carriage, partially saw the stricken expression of her features when she first found herself alone with him, and thought it was all girlish timidity.

"Philip, till this moment I never knew half my love for you!" was her thought.

And so they started for their honeymoon in the Isle of Wight.

CHAPTER XXXVII.

For some time after Philip's arrival in Rome, he was as silent and misanthropic as is the wont of disappointed lovers. His experiment of going into the world again had proved so signal a failure in Paris that he now went into the opposite extreme, shunning all companionship but that of Neville and a few of his artist friends, and wandering like a ghost among churches and picture-galleries, taking lonely rides in the Campagna, and being excessively brief with any unfortunate English people who made advances to him. When, by chance, he was forced into any kind of society, he compared the English-women he met with Marguerite, and they disgusted him. Their faces had no glow, their voices no music, after hers; and he came back to their lodgings—Neville and he lived together—invariably with a fresh accession of ill-humor on these occasions.

"You should go more among foreigners, Phil," said Neville, one evening. "You would get on better with them; and the Italian women would be sure to like you, with your pale face and sentimental conversation."

"Let us speak of a more interesting subject, Neville. I am weary of the whole sex —English, French, or Italian."

"A la bonne heure! I wish from my soul you were. But you are only in a state of rebound. I know you so well. Just the state from which men fall into their worst errors Some pretty face will arise, and undo all your woman-hatred in an hour. The carnival is next week!"

"I shall go into the country while it lasts. It makes me sick to see the buffoonery with which human beings can be amused."

"Well, I am one of the common herd; I shall lock up my studio, and be as happy as any school-boy of fourteen. It does the eye and brain good to be relieved from work a few days: one returns to it with such zest afterwards. And then there are groups of form and color to be seen in the carnival better worth studying than the old masters themselves."

"You have such an object in life, Neville! Everything is sweet to you that can minister in the slightest degree to your one passion—ambition."

"Why do you not call it love of my art? But you would be far happier too, Earnscliffe, with any 'one passion,' as you are pleased to term it. Your longing for distinction was feverish once; but, as soon as won, you are wearied of it, as of everything else!"

"I have not wearied of anything. Exactly *that* of which I could never weary, I have never possessed."

"The reason why you think it beyond the reach of satiety."

"You have never loved, Neville. It is a subject utterly beyond, or beneath you."

"You are wrong, both in fact and inference. I *have* loved, and with an intensity equal to your own—perhaps greater, for I have only loved once, and I have analysed the passion as deeply as you have done."

"Neville, you have actually loved!"

"I am past thirty."

"Oh, of course, every man feels what he dignifies by that name. Not one out of a hundred love."

"I have, and have been deceived, like the rest of us. But to return to yourself. You believe that if you had possessed the object of your last adoration (you have made such half-confidences that I shall probably, unwittingly, hurt your feelings), your heaven would have lasted; that, having lost it, you and she will be eternally miserable. My friend, you will be a very happy man five years hence, when you have passed the age of sentiment, and are beginning to care for position, and have entered the House and shone in your first speech; and as to the young lady, perhaps she is married by this time—at all events, she will not be constant to your memory for a year."

"She may marry: she will not forget me!" replied Philip.

"And so add another to the scores of guileless young creatures who every year swear to love and honor one man with the warm words of another yet thrilling in their heart! I thought your idols were all perfect, Phil."

"This one was! Too perfect for you and me to speak of, Neville."

"Thank you. Well, we will profane her no longer. Come and tell me how you like my last sketch."

Philip rose to look, and their conversation dropped for the present: but the next morning, when they were wandering beneath some ruins a few miles from Rome, he returned to it.

"Neville, tell me more of your own love. I am in a state when it is pleasant to hear of the disappointment of one's friends!"

Neville seated himself on a broken fragment of marble, and leisurely drew from his pocket, first a cigar-case, then his sketch-book.

"I will talk of my love, mon ami, if there is any chance of curing yours by doing so; but I must smoke and sketch at the same time. It is a subject that sends me to sleep by itself: it requires accompaniments."

"Give me a cigarette, Neville."

"Ah, you are mending! You have refused to smoke hitherto."

"The open air—the fact of lying at one's length among the daisies—makes smoking a necessity."

"Don't apologise. I have seen you look enviously at my meerschaum every evening for the last week, and knew what was coming. I cannot conceive why you ever gave it up. In my troubles—when the committee of the R. A. rejected my first picture and hung my second ten feet high in the octagon-room, for example —I smoked more fierce than ever."

"And in your love affair?"

Neville smoked away in silence, and half-closed his eyes, as though intently watching the effect of light and shadow upon the blue Campagna, but there was a dreamy look upon his face.

"It was years ago," he exclaimed, suddenly; "I was quite a boy."

"And which was false?—or was either?"

"Philip, it is not a pleasant remembrance; but as you seem to care about it, you shall hear. I started in life young: you remember what I was when I left Harrow. I came at once to London, with few friends, no connection; and I had to make my way alone unassisted, except by my own energy.

"I lodged in the house of a Scotchwoman, a widow, and a person of a certain position in life. She kept a kind of boarding-house for young men—medical students, young artists like myself, who preferred this kind of life to common lodgings or chambers. The house was respectable; I was recommended to it by decent people: and everything was in appearance quiet and as it should be.

"This Scotchwoman had an only daughter, a girl of seventeen, lovely as an angel, with fair, bright hair and Madonna-like eyes, that seemed too soft to reflect any human passion. All the young men in the house admired her, of course; but I, before I had been there three weeks, was wildly in love with her. I could neither eat nor sleep; I trembled if her dress touched me as she passed; it maddened me if she spoke or smiled with another man. She haunted me till I could not draw a line; and my companions all used to laugh at my white face and my altered manner. In short, I loved her as boys *can* love.

"I got over my timidity and spoke. She trembled, she flushed, faltered, and burst into tears. 'It was madness; we must not think of it, we were so young. But she loved me!' I went half wild with excess of happiness.

"With stolen interviews, a whispered word when we passed each other on the stairs, a pressure of her hand night and morning, I was forced to be content for some months. But at length I grew impatient. I told her that I would wait no longer; either she must fly with me and become my wife by a Scotch marriage, or I would leave her forever; I could not live on in the same house any longer and be as strangers. She hesitated, wavered, consented to become *mine*. Phil, even now I feel the rapture of that moment."

Neville drew his wide, artist-hat more over his eyes, as though to shade them from the slanting sun, and leisurely cut one of his pencils, but his hand trembled very slightly.

"We planned to go to Scotland, and be married; then return at once, and ask her mother's forgiveness; and I should work for both, and we should all live happily together. This was the project. As you may imagine, I had very little money—not enough to take two people half-way to Scotland; and, with much shame, I was obliged to confess this to my beloved, and to tell her that a few days' delay would be necessary for me to try and obtain sufficient for the journey. To my surprise, she answered by taking a little purse full of gold from her pocket, and laying it in my hand. 'It was a present from her god-father. She had had it for years.'

"I don't know whether the circumstance aroused any suspicions in my mind, or whether it was a kind of natural instinct; but, after I had taken the purse and carried it away with me, I felt strangely excited and ill at ease. Though I believed her implicity, the thought would arise, 'Why had she so much money? was it girl-like so quickly to offer it?'

"We had settled to elope that very night, and I had gone out of the house to evade suspicions, but was to return silently when every one was still, and we should then steal out together. I remember I walked on and on through the crowded streets, but saw nothing that was passing around; I felt dull and stupefied, as though under the influence of some narcotic. I at length turned my steps homewards, resolving to remain quietly in my own little attic at the top of the house until the appointed hour.

"I entered with my latch-key, and met one of the women-servants in the passage. 'Where was Mrs. M——?' I asked, as coolly as I could. 'Gone out.' 'And Miss ——?' 'Oh, in her own room; she was not very well.' This was so exactly like the plan we had determined upon, that I felt re-assured, and ran upstairs towards my own room, when, on the second floor, I heard voices that arrested me in-a moment. Hers—I should have known its slightest sound among a thousand—and that of a man.

"Her own room was on the first floor; that from whence the voice came was a small sitting-room of her mother's, to which none of the boarders were usually admitted. I walked up to the door. I stood still there, and listened (for the only time in my life, Phil, it was excusable at such a moment)—listened and heard—thank God! not my shame, for she was not yet my wife.

"I must tell you there was one inmate of the house, towards whom I had always felt an uncontrollable dislike, a young Pole of high birth, and rich, but who was boarding in the family for the sake of learning English. He was there some months before I came, and I had never anything to do with him; but a certain air of impertinent superiority in his manner made me conceive an instant dislike for him the first day we met. I never saw him speak to Miss M——, beyond a passing word of recognition at dinner, if he was placed near her. Indeed, she seemed less friendly with him than with any of the other young men, towards most of whom I had in turn entertained some boyish jealousy.

"She loved him. Had loved him long—guiltily, as I knew the first moment I heard the tones of their voices together. And the money that was to have assisted in making her my wife came from him!

"'Difference of position,' I heard him say, 'would not allow him to make her the reparation of marriage. But Neville will do it,' he added, laughing, 'and we can hoodwink him hereafter, as we have done already.'

"I entered the room at once; not bursting with fury, as you might imagine, but quite cool and collected; only I felt that my face was bloodless, and my teeth clenched.

"'Good God!' she exclaimed, starting up, and advancing towards me for a second, then shrinking back to him as though for protection. I only looked at her once—never spoke to her; but I walked up to him.

"'Monsieur Neville, your return is unexpected, and, permit me to say, undesirable. You have mistaken your room, I think.'

"Phil, I wonder I did not kill him, for I had the strength of a young Hercules at all times, and now the whole fire of my nature was up! I dragged him to the top of the landing—lost though she was, I respected her presence sufficiently for this—and then, I repeat, I wonder I did not kill him! When his cowardly white face was undistinguishable from the mass of blows I had rained upon it, I hurled him with all my force down stairs; and have a dim recollection of women shrieking, and doctors being sent for, and Mrs. M—— wringing her hands as she came in and found her best lodger lying a bleeding mass in the passage; but I left the house without even collecting my things, and saw none of them again.

"Of course, I expected to hear from the count, for he was'nt dead; but no message came, and one of the other boarders, a fellow-student of mine, told me they seemed anxious to hush the matter up, and prevent it from being known out of the house.

"Two or three days afterwards I discovered the purse still in my pocket, and sent it back to Miss M—— by my friend, who was just going to leave for Italy; and from that day I never have known what became of her, or whether the mother had connived at the whole thing or not. In short, I have never heard their name, nor have breathed it until now. But, Phil, I have never loved again. *Loved*, mind; for that was pure, perfect love. I have felt as others do a dozen times.

. "Pah! my cigar is out. Give me a light, old fellow, and let us go on before the noon-day heat. I can finish my sketch at home."

They walked on silently for some time, then Philip exclaimed, "But you must admit, Neville, that yours was an entirely exceptional case, one from which no sweeping deduction can be drawn."

"Yes, in the utter depravity of so young a girl, it *was* exceptional. Without precisely resembling my own case, however, are there not thousands of others where one or both have been as miserably infatuated, then deceived? Look at yourself, you have been so a dozen times already."

"Ah! but none of this dozen was the true one. You confuse the Eros with the Anteros. I have not been deceived now."

"Well!" replied Neville, impatiently, "but something—circumstance—Fate—what you will, has stepped in and thwarted your devotion and your happiness. Give up such love, as I have done. Be content with the common hopes, the coarser pleasures of humanity."

"I wish I could," returned Philip.

* * * * * *

Late in the evening of this day, when Neville was at work, and Earnscliffe, lazily outstretched, was reading the English papers, an exclamation broke from him which made the artist start round.

"Good God! Neville, she is married!"

The *Times* fell from his hands, and Neville, picking it up, read at the head of the list of marriages, "William Charles Mortimer, of Portland Place, London, and Chestnut Grove, Wimbledon, Esquire, to Marguerite Lilla, only child of the late Percy St. John, of Kersaint Manoir, Brittany, Esquire."

"It *is* soon, Phil; sooner than I expected. But it was sure to be so; and these things are much better ' got over ' at once. If your wife had died you might have married Miss St. John, and both have been wretched for life—it is much better as it is."

"She will not forget me!" said Philip, abstractedly.

"The devil she wont!" exclaimed Neville. "A pleasant prospect for William Charles Mortimer, of Portland Place and Chestnut Grove! However, I suppose you will return to life, now that the dream is over."

"It is *not* over. My love was just as hopeless before as it is now that we are both tied, yet I indulged it."

"Well, for everybody's sake, it is to be desired that you will keep away from England—for the present at least. When Mrs. Mortimer is an elderly matron, with grown-up children, you might see her again with safety."

"I have no wish to do so, I can assure you. Except an occasional visit to my uncle, while he lives, I shall spend my life abroad."

"A few years of it only. The objectless, nugatory life of continental Englishmen would not suit you after thirty, as it may now."

"I shall begin a new book to-morrow," said Philip, after a long silence.

"Bravo! You would not have written for six months to come but for Miss St. John's marriage. And, Philip, I predict that this will be your best work—better even than that famous one wherein you felled and trampled upon all your great friends. I suppose womenkind will come in for their share of sarcasm in this?"

"On the contrary, there will be very little about them. I am weary of the subject."

CHAPTER XXXVIII.

Two years had now elapsed since Marguerite's marriage—two unchequered and serene years, wherein no one month had greatly differed from the preceding or following ones. But surrounded by all that wealth can give, and Mortimer unchanged in his kindness and devotion, her life palled heavily upon her. The worn out simile of a bird imprisoned in a golden cage could never have been more aptly employed. She rose each day, and her French lady's maid attired her in her elegant morning dress; she breakfasted with Mortimer from Sèvres and Dresden, after which he started for the City, and then she had only herself to please for the remainder of the day. She might look at her costly rooms, or walk into her conservatories and gaze at their rare contents, or order her carriage or her horse, or play on her magnificent piano, until dinner-time; then Sèvres and Dresden and her husband again. After dinner he fell asleep, and there was the evening to be passed in somewhat the same manner as the morning.

Oh, how she wearied of it all! With a feverish longing she would think of her old free life, that sweet, untrammelled liberty of her childhood, and feel how gladly she would give all that she now possessed to return to it. No flower in her conservatory gave her the pleasure of those wild-flowers on the Breton heaths. She felt that her life was void; and although her great sweetness of temper, and the real regard and gratitude she felt towards Mortimer, prevented her manner from ever expressing discontent, there were often times when her youth would rise irresistibly strong within her, and the *want* of her existence become an actual pain. The indistinct yearning she had experienced at Kersaint, before she ever knew Philip, returned now with tenfold strength; for this vague desire was no longer without an object. Marguerite, in the interval, had loved with all the strength of a deep and fervent nature: and her heart actually sank, as she looked forward to years and years—her whole life, in fact—still spent in the same way as now. No other love than what she felt for her husband, no higher object than her own amusement.

Her husband's acquaintance were, for the most part, men of about his own standing; he had never cared much for women's society, and knew little of their wives and daughters; and the few families they did visit were none of them congenial to Marguerite. Once or twice a month he dined out: occasionally they had a dinner party of old men at home. The conversation, on these occasions, as may be conceived, was not of a nature likely to afford her much interest. The presence of Georgy de Burgh was quite a relief to her at these festivals, especially when Mrs. Danby was not able, from her delicate health, to attend; and Marguerite was only too happy to lend her her carriage or riding-horse, or to send her bouquets of hot-house flowers; she was quite glad when these things could give any one else more pleasure than they did herself, and had long forgiven the petty slights which Georgy had shown her in her cousin's house.

"Are you very happy, dear?" inquired Miss de Burgh, as they sat on the sofa, after one of Mortimer's dinner-parties, and while the men were still in the dining-room; "you look so pale to-day."

"Happy!" Marguerite started and colored. "Oh, yes! He is very kind to me; I have everything I wish."

"I see—under similar circumstances, I *should* be happy. You think too much of Philip Earnscliffe, dear."

"Georgy!—indeed!——"

"No, Marguerite; don't deny, nor wince, as if I had done you some dreadful injury. I do not blame you in the least; still it is a pity that you should do so. You are quite losing your fine color, and look years older already."

"I am glad of it. It makes the difference seem less between Mr. Mortimer and myself."

"Oh, oh, Marguerite! *I* cannot believe that you wish to pass for a 'Goody Two-shoes;' but every one else will, if you talk in that way. Fancy a woman of your age liking to look old! The fact is, you are too much moped—no going out, no society (for these fusty old dinners are worse than nothing). Why in the world don't you go to the opera, like other people?"

"Well, I have thought of it; but Mr. Mortimer comes home tired, and we dine so late—and, besides, I do not think he cares much for music—I mean, not as I do."

"But these are no reasons why *you* should not go. So fond of music as you are, it is absolute cruelty that you never have any opportunity of hearing it."

"I should like it very much indeed" said Marguerite, her eyes glistening. "How kind of you to think of it for me!"

"Nothing about my own place in your box," thought Georgy. Then aloud—"Well, dear, I really do not like to see you leading such a lonely life. I shall speak to Mr. Mortimer about it this very evening."

"Oh, I will ask him, thank you. He would prefer it from me. I need only go on those evenings when he dines out, so he will not miss me. And would you come with me the first time please? I have never been to a theatre in my life?"

"To be sure I will," Georgy cried, delighted at the success of her manœuvre. "There is to be 'Lucia' to-morrow, and it will be a benefit night in addition. Make your husband take us places for it, even if he cannot decide about a box."

"Oh, I know that he will get a box the very day I ask for it," returned Marguerite, simply. "It gives him such pleasure if I express a wish for anything." Her face was still lit up with the child-like pleasure the thoughts of the opera had awakened, when some of the men entered. Mortimer was one of the first. He came to his wife in a second, looking, with his red face and portly figure, as unlike her husband as possible.

"How merry you seem, Marguerite. Miss de Burgh, you must come and see us oftener. You brighten up my poor lonely wife."

"Ah, we are conspiring," said Marguerite, with her sweet smile. "Perhaps you will not be so well pleased when you hear what we are speaking about."

"Try me. I am not often offended with you."

"Well, I am so very fond of music, and—Georgy has been saying that the opera would be such a treat to me sometimes, if you thought you would not mind taking a box for me."

Mortimer looked delighted. Although he was always trying to please her, Marguerite would seldom ask him for anything.

"Come here, Danby!" he cried to his friend, who had just entered, "and see how we are all changing. Your demure little ward has just asked me to get her a box at the opera!"

"Ah! Georgy must have had a hand in that, I suspect," said Danby. "Madge never heard of operas at Kersaint. Did you, Mrs. Mortimer?"

"Never—that is—" her perfect truthfulness compelling her to speak. "Cousin, I did *hear* of them once," and Marguerite blushed deeply.

"Well, there was no great harm if you did, child," said her husband. "What are you looking so red for?"

"Who used to talk of operas at Kersaint?" went on Danby; "Philip Earnscliffe, I suppose."

Oh, what would Marguerite have given to master herself better! When Earnscliffe's name was mentioned, or even any other subject that remotely bore upon him, the blood *would* always rise crimson to her very temples, and her hands turn cold in a second. Was she never to overcome her old girlish feelings, now that she was another man's wife?

"Come here, Marguerite," cried Georgy, who was watching her narrowly, "I want you to tell me about your new songs, and to know if you can lend me some waltzes?"

Marguerite felt only too thankful for the interruption, and going quickly to Miss de Burgh's side, leant down over a heap of new music until her long hair almost covered her burning face.

"Take any you like, Georgy," she said, in a low voice. "I have not even tried them over yet. Mr. Mortimer brings me something new every day."

"Marguerite," interrupted the other, in a whisper, "you are very demure, and very excellent; but if I were your husband, I would not wish Philip Earnscliffe to appear in London."

CHAPTER XXXIX.

WHEN her toilette was complete the following evening, Marguerite surveyed herself with more pleasure than she had felt in her own appearance since her marriage; and, devoid of vanity though she was, she could not be insensible of her own extraordinary beauty. Her luxuriant hair was partly gathered round her head, partly fell upon her neck, in a style peculiar to herself, and a magnificent set of pearl ornaments—a present from her husband that day—well became her youth, and fair, satin-like skin. In her bosom was a bouquet of rare hot-house flowers, all white.

"Am I, indeed, as beautiful as Philip said?" she thought, when her maid had left, and she was waiting for the announcement of the carriage. "What would he think of me now?"

She started, and turned from the glass, as her husband's step was heard entering her dressing-room.

"Well, Madgey, child, how do you look in your finery! Not so bad upon my word!" He drew her to him, and kissed her forehead. "You seem very happy, little woman, at going out alone for the first time."

"Oh, Mr. Mortimer! I should be more glad if you were coming too."

"Quite sure, Marguerite?"

"Quite; I mean"—with her usual sincerity—"if it were anything but to the opera. But, perhaps I *shall* enjoy that more alone, than if you were there, and I knew you were wearied to death with the music."

Mortimer looked the least in the world disappointed, then he replied, kindly, "Marguerite, you are a good child to speak the exact truth. It is not likely that what pleases you should me. See the difference between us!" He pointed to a cheval-glass, where the two figures stood reflected. "What do we look like, Madgey?"

"Father and daughter, sir: I have always said so. And no father," she added, gently, "could ever have been kinder to a child than you are to me, or have more merited her gratitude."

"Ah, Marguerite! if I was a younger man you would feel very differently. Gratitude never enters into love, I am told. However, you know nothing about *that*"—she turned her face quite away—"and, perhaps, you are as happy as many who make love marriages. At all events, what has never been felt cannot be missed!"

"I have every reason to be happy," said Marguerite in a low voice; "I have no wish ungratified since I have been your wife."

"Well, enjoy yourself as much as you can to-night. I hope the opera will be a new source of pleasure to you; perhaps you have been too much alone hitherto."

Georgy was ready dressed when the carriage stopped in Tavistock Street, and appeared in high spirits when she jumped in.

"Marguerite, how exquisite! I never saw those pearls before."

"Mr. Mortimer gave them to me to-day."

"And that darling little cloak?"

"Another present."

"And your lorgnette, and your bouquet; oh, and mine!" as Marguerite gave her one containing all the rarest flowers of the season, and Miss Georgy held it up to the light. People say riches cannot make happiness! I am sure they could make mine! I hope we shall be in a good place! You will create quite a *furore* with your style—and—your newness! Perhaps you will condescend to say what you think of *me*."

Georgy was really looking very handsome in a pink satin dress, unusually *decolete*, and a profusion of diamonds in her hair. Her high color, jetty curls, and cool, undaunted air, formed an admirable foil to the delicate hues of Marguerite's complexion, and her youthful, girlish manner; and when they entered the box, which was one of the best and most conspicuous in the house, they did, to

Georgy's intense delight, create quite a sensation.

"Who is she?"—"What is she?" passed from mouth to mouth, the moment Marguerite appeared, and always with the same reply. No one knew. The overture was nearly over, but Marguerite's attention was instantly riveted to the music; and, listening to Grisi and Mario, such a new world of delight, such undreamed-of enjoyment opened upon her, as would have paralysed all power of expression, had she attempted to give utterance to her feelings. Her eyes glistened and the color went and came in her cheek, as she leant forward, her hands clasped together over the front of the box, in an attitude of the most unconscious attention, while the eyes of half the men in London were fixed upon her.

"At length!" exclaimed Georgy, as the first act ended. "I have spoken to you in vain about eight times. Now, will you kindly be a little more like other people? Perfect though hands may be, it is not usual to clasp them together at a theatre, as though you were praying. And so very unconscious of all the men who are staring at you!"

"Hands—praying!" echoed Marguerite, dreamily. "Oh! Georgy, have I done anything improper?"

"Not at all, dear! You have succeeded, however, in being singular; and, as every lorgnette in the pit appears to be upturned to your face, you are probably satisfied."

Unwilling though she might have been to offend a connection who would take her to the opera, and ask her to dinner, this young creature's jealousy could never repress itself at Mrs. Mortimer's superior beauty; and Marguerite, feeling by the tone that she meant to be spiteful, colored deeply as she leant back in her chair. The flush remained on her cheeks, making her tenfold lovelier, and people looked at her more that ever.

"How every one looks at me, Georgy!" she whispered. "It is not very polite of them to do so, even if they see how unused I am to these places! Have I done anything very strange?"

"For pity's sake, remember there is no one to hear, and do not be so simple with me," replied her companion, harshly. "Accept your rôle of new beauty, and play it through. The men will not look at you half so much when you are known, or some new face has arisen to eclipse yours."

"I hope not," answered Marguerite, quietly; and then (seeing that Georgy was not in the sweetest of tempers at the small attention her own satin and diamonds excited) she remained silently gazing about the house, whose lights, and tiers of brilliant women, seemed like the realisation of one of her childhood's fairy tales.

In the next box to their own was one individual whose eyes scarcely for a second had quitted Marguerite's face; but it was not until the middle of the performance that her own glance carelessly rested upon him. For an instant her heart leaped wildly—she thought it was Earnscliffe! The delusion was momentary: it was one of those accidental likenesses more of contour and general style, than of feature, or even expression; still, it was sufficiently strong to arouse a thousand old feelings in Marguerite; and, even while Mario was singing, to make her glance timidly at the stranger's face.

"Do you know him—do you know him?" whispered Miss de Burgh. "You seem to be looking at him a great deal."

"I—oh! I know no one; but I should like to know his name."

Georgy knew: she knew everything. "The Marquis de St. Leon—a young man of very high birth, and rich. I wonder whether he remembers me! I danced in the same quadrille with him one evening, three or four years ago, at Homberg! I shall bow when he looks next!"

"Please do not bow, Georgy," returned Marguerite, quickly.

"Why not, Mrs. Mortimer? May not one person, out of all your admirers, be permitted to look at me?"

Marguerite felt that their neighbor was not looking at Georgy; but she was silent, knowing that in her present temper, any opposition would make her more resolute, and also that it was not in the De Burgh nature to let a living marquis be unmolested, if there were the slightest clue to acquaintanceship.

Not until the conclusion of the act, could Georgy attract the attention of the young Frenchman, who was still intently watching Marguerite's averted profile, while he apparently listened to the music; but when at length the curtain fell, and Marguerite leant back, so that her face was hidden from him, his eye casually rested on that of Miss de Burgh. She bowed, and smiled in a moment. The marquis half rose, and made a profound salutation, but with the most unequivocal look of surprise, for of course Georgy's face was utterly foreign to him; and this circumstance, united to her general appearance and dress, gave him at once an impression the exact reverse of favorable of the lady.

"Grisi est ravissant ce soir monsieur," leaning over towards him.

"Mais oui madame!" with a stare of astonishment at her coolness.

"I see, Monsieur le Marquis, that you do not recognise me."

He was about to reply in a strain more complimentary than respectful, when he glanced towards Marguerite—who felt what was going on, and her blush of shame—her innocent young face—made him retract his unfavorable opinion of her companion.

"Mad, probably," he thought—"utterly mad, like all other Englishwomen." Then aloud, "Madame, I must infinitely regret that I do not recall to myself the exact circumstances under which I formerly had the honor——"

"It was at Homberg!" cried Georgy, delighted with her progress. "We used to meet nearly every evening at the Kur Saal, and once, Monsieur le Marquis, I had the pleasure of dancing with you at a grand ball given to the Duchess Stephanie!"

The pain on Marguerite's face was now becoming so evident that the marquis told Georgy he remembered her perfectly, and that his near sight must plead his excuse for not having done so sooner; and he was soon so polite, and so evidently anxious to improve the acquaintance, that Georgy grew radiant—not considering how small a share she had in the cause of his *empressement*.

They continued talking for some minutes, and then Georgy touched Marguerite's arm thinking it must appear strange to the Frenchman that her companion looked so steadily away from him.

"Monsieur, allow me to introduce you to my cousin, Mrs. Mortimer, nee De Josselin St. John."

The marquis slightly started, then bowed very gravely. "De Josselin!" he repeated.

"Her mother's name," Georgy hastened to explain. "The De Josselins of Beau Manoir in Brittany—a very ancient family."

"I may then claim relationship as an introduction," he remarked, in an extremely different tone to the light, easy one in which he had been chatting with Miss de Burgh. "My father and the mother of madame, were, if I mistake not, cousins german."

"And we are all related!" cried Georgy, "how delightful!"

But Marguerite looked at him very earnestly, and with the most perfect simplicity, said:—

"Monsieur, it gives me real pleasure to have met you. You are the first of my mother's family I have ever seen."

"I must demand a thousand pardons," said the marquis, now speaking in his own language, and bending towards Marguerite, "for having looked so often at your face this evening; but I have been vainly endeavoring to recollect where and when I have met you before. Now the mystery explains itself. I am in possession of a miniature, in which there exists the most extraordinary likeness to yourself, and that miniature, madame, is the portrait of your mother, Lilla de Josselin, taken in her early youth!"

"My mother's portrait!" repeated Marguerite, eagerly. "Ah, I possess no likeness of her!"

"And is she no longer living? Pardon me, but it is years since I heard the news of any one bearing the name of De Josselin."

"My mother died when I was born, monsieur. The tears started to her eyes.

"Need I say the pleasure it would afford me to be allowed to restore the picture to one who has so strong a claim upon it?"

"Would you really give it me? I scarcely like to rob you of such a treasure!"

"I prize it," replied the young man, gravely, "as having belonged to my own father, who valued it above everything on earth; but it would give me infinite pleasure to see it in your possession."

"Then come and see us to-morrow, and bring it with you, if you will, indeed, be so generous. Oh! this *is* unexpected pleasure. How much I shall have to tell Mr. Mortimer!"

"Can it be possible that she is married!" thought St. Leon. "She has the face and simplicity of a child. And *what* a face!"

His manner soon displayed such intense admiration, that Miss Georgy, although well content that she could claim any connection with a marquis, felt by no means pleased at the turn things were taking, and the earnest conversation in which she bore no part.

"You are forgetting the beloved music, it appears," she whispered maliciously.

Marguerite felt her meaning, and turned away towards the stage; but her heart was full at the unexpected meeting with one of her own race and nation, and for a moment she could hardly repress tears at Georgy's unkindness—for she always could discern by the tone one of Miss de Burgh's little implied sarcasms. Soon, however, in the absorbing interest of the last scene in that touching opera, into which Grisi's genius throws so deep a pathos, she forgot even her new cousin; and when the last notes of "Lucia" died away, Marguerite was trembling and breathless with excitement.

"Is it over?" she said, turning nervously round. She was looking so strange that Georgy was startled, and exclaimed, "Heavens! Marguerite, what ails you?—are you going to faint?" And the marquis, who had already risen to depart, bent towards them and inquired anxiously "if madame was ill?"

"Oh, no," returned Marguerite, trying to smile; "I am only rather nervous. It is very foolish, I know; but this is the first opera I ever saw."

"You silly child!" said Georgy. "Did you think Grisi was really dead?"

"If I might presume to offer my escort?" St Leon hesitated.

"We shall be really grateful," returned Georgy, promptly; "for, strange to say, we are alone this evening."

He joined them at the door of their box; and they were soon endeavoring to make their way through the crowded lobby.

"Lean on me, madame, I entreat," he said to Marguerite. "You look terribly overcome."

"It is nothing," she whispered; "only a

passing faintness. I am unused to these great crowds, and shall be better the moment I breathe the air."

Just then one of Georgy's former friends happened to pass them on his way out; a young lordling it was that she had once picked up in Switzerland, when he was still in jackets, and with whom she had contrived at intervals to keep up a bowing acquaintance ever since. Seeing her with the new beauty, and accompanied by so well known a man as St. Leon, he condescended to be civil, and they shook hands—the lady very warmly.

"What an age since I have seen you, Miss de Burgh! Will you take my arm? it's too crowded for three. Good evening, marquis. Deuced hot, aint it?"

St. Leon answered with a stately bow. He was, however, overjoyed to get rid of Miss de Burgh, and be able to devote all his attention to his lovely companion.

When they reached the vestibule, Georgy and her young friend were nowhere to be seen.

"They are probably in advance," said St. Leon. "Let me conduct you outside for a few moments; the air will refresh you. Indeed, unless you wait very long, you will probably be obliged to walk some distance to your carriage, owing to the crush to-night."

The cold night air revived Marguerite instantly. "I am better now," she said, glancing up at her cousin. His figure looked so like Earnscliffe's, seen in that uncertain light, that involuntarily her hand pressed upon his arm—then trembled a little.

"That is right," he answered. "Let us walk on, madame, somewhat apart from the crowd. The air is the best thing for you now, and it will give your friend time to join you; they are probably detained by the crowd."

Miss de Burgh was not likely to hurry when resting on the arm of a lord; and it was fully twenty minutes before they all met. During this time the marquis had learnt the name of Marguerite's husband, and their address, and had promised to bring the miniature the following day, "if madame would do him the real favor of accepting it." And her glistening eyes, as she turned to thank him, were sufficient reply. After Miss de Burgh had joined them, they had still to walk to the carriage at some little distance. And all this time the young Frenchman was thinking that he had never, in all his experience of beauty, met with any woman to compare to his English cousin, and complacently exulting at her very amiable reception of himself; while Marguerite's quiet reflection was, "He is like Philip—certainly like him, but not a hundredth part so handsome or so noble-looking; all the fine intellect is wanting, and the resemblance half pains me from its incompleteness."

When they were on their way home, Miss Georgy displayed a great accession of spirits.

"What a delightful evening—a lord and a foreign marquis! I saw those odious Miss Malcolms looking at me as we came to the carriage. They were stalking by with their mother, like three great spectres in the moonlight, and no vestige of a man with them! Lord—— was so attentive, and he is coming to call. I heard you asking the marquis. Do you admire him, Mrs. Mortimer?"

"Yes—or rather there is something about him which attracts me."

"Indeed! Well, you are candid."

"A nameless something. I cannot explain what it is, Georgy."

"Do not trouble yourself; I perfectly understand. Heigh ho! here we are at my hideous old home. Thank you for my pleasant evening, Marguerite, and take me again as soon as you like."

And Miss Georgy, yawning extensively, ran up the paternal door-steps, leaving Marguerite to drive home in the moonlight with the sweet notes of the "Lucia" still vibrating through her brain; and the voice, not of St. Leon, but of Philip, in her heart.

CHAPTER XL.

FROM that evening a new life seemed to have opened for Marguerite. Delighted that, at length, something could be found affording her real pleasure, Mortimer insisted upon her frequently going to the opera; and it was a source to Marguerite of such genuine, unmixed enjoyment, that soon these two, and often three evenings in the week, were looked upon as a matter of course, and anticipated each time with all the zest of a child.

She loved music passionately; she went for the music, and listened to it as few English people can listen—came home to dream of it, and sing what she heard to her own piano, and for herself. Her voice had greatly improved; and after the constant instruction, for two years, of the best masters in London, Marguerite now sang as not many in private life are ever heard to sing. She often thought of Philip's prediction about her voice, and wondered, with a half-sigh, what he would think of her now that she had so much improved.

Of Philip himself she never heard. One long letter he had written her from the Tyrol, two or three months after they parted—a letter that had been read and re-read until known by heart, and then stored away with her other most precious relics—but after this she heard no more. Still, however, she thought of him—still was his name never forgotten in her prayers—still his books were treasured—and all this with the most entire unconsciousness of wrong. But, perhaps, that which kept Philip's image most strongly alive was the likeness that she traced to him in her cousin.

The young marquis called on the following day after their first meeting,' with the portrait of Mrs. St. John, and Marguerite had received him with all the unreserved cordiality of a relation, and made him stop to be introduced to Mortimer, and dine with them. From that day he became intimate at the house. Although his society possessed no *charm* for Marguerite, she liked him. He was refined, well-educated, superior to every one else around her, and had all those minute graces of conversation and manner in which a well-bred Frenchman excels. But he was artificial, and to Marguerite this deprived him of all the interest he might otherwise have inspired. Everything that in Earnscliffe was natural, St. Leon seemed to have learnt. Although he was never vapid —seldom actually common-place—he rarely said anything forcible or striking.

"I shall be jealous of your handsome French cousin, little wife," said Mortimer, one evening. Marguerite accompanied by Georgy and St. Leon, had been spending a long morning at the Exhibition.

"Jealous, sir!—surely you cannot mean it. Do you wish to be like Gaston?"

"Not that kind of jealousy, my dear. Jealous!—jealous of his being your companion so often."

Marguerite laughed. "Don't you think Georgy de Burgh would like to marry him?" she asked.

"I think Georgy would marry any one."

"Oh, yes; but I sometimes think she really likes Gaston."

"And do not you, Maggy?" looking rather earnestly in her face.

"Yes—I like him—very much, at times; and then, he is my only relation, except my cousin Danby. But he seldom really interests me. This morning, among the pictures, even, I forgot so often what he was talking about. When we were looking at that exquisite thing, 'The Awakened Conscience,' I had just read all the story of the girl's life in her suddenly anguished face, and, turning to Gaston, I began telling him it; when he interrupted me, and said, 'the finish on the carpet was painted *à ravir!*' It was so like him. He cannot appreciate the wild-flowers in my wilderness half as much as the rare exotics in your hot-houses, sir."

"Well, I don't blame him there," said Mortimer, complacently. "Our flowers at Wimbledon are the finest of any near London (without doubt the young man never saw anything like them in his own country, for all he's a marquis); and your wilderness, as you call it, Maggy, is a horrid damp hole. However, if he does not like your weeds, I am sure you seem to like the same books;

or I find you reading together, or talking of what you have just read, when I come in."

"Yes," said Marguerite, smiling, "but we never agree in our criticism. Gaston always admires the very parts that I pass over, and detests anything like sentiment, which, you know, I *do* like."

"Poor Maggy! you like what you don't understand. But I am glad to hear I need not be jealous."

"Oh, Mr. Mortimer! what is cousin Gaston to me?" And the perfect truth in her face must have dispelled it, if a slight shade of jealousy had really crossed his mind.

"It was very kind of him, though," Marguerite went on, "to persuade this grand countess to call and invite me to her house; but I don't care much about going. I am not shy; still I tremble a little at appearing among hundreds of strangers, and knowing no one but Gaston. I wish you would go, Mr. Mortimer; it is not too late for you to change your mind."

"My dear, I am not suited for the Countess of E——'s parties. With your beauty and manners, you are fit company for the Queen; but it would spoil the effect for *me* to be shown as your husband. Besides this, I'm not fond of music, and ten to one but I should fall asleep when some of the grand singers are in the middle of their bravuras, or else clap my hands when I ought to be silent. No, child; go and enjoy yourself. I shall be quite content with your description to-morrow morning. It is time for you to dress, Marguerite. Go and see how grand you can make yourself."

"I do not care about it," she replied, slowly preparing to leave the room. "I would much rather be going to the opera."

"But *I* care for it," said the husband. "With your own appearance, and my money. you *ought* to be in the best society in England!"

From the first moment he knew her, St. Leon had longed to see his lovely young cousin in the same world as that in which he himself moved. With Mortimer's great wealth, the fact of his being on 'Change was a misdemeanor it was just possible for the English aristocracy to forgive; and, for some months past, he had been thinking over every possible plan for obtaining an introduction for Marguerite to the house of some of the leaders of fashion, whose mystic stamp would afterwards enable her to pass current among the *confrèrie* of London exclusivism. At length he had been partially successful. The Countess of E——, at whose house he had long been intimate, was about to give the largest musical entertainment that had been attempted during the season; and at this entertainment St. Leon determined Marguerite should be.

"Your party will be charming," he said to the countess, as he sat next her at a dinner party, the day after the cards were issued.

"All parties at H—— House must be so. But as yet your invitations have not included the best amateur voice in London."

"Is it possible? I thought I had asked every one."

"But this is 'no one.'"

"Ah! The fact is, marquis, I have often attempted those sort of people at my large musical parties; but they are invariably failures"

"But the lady I alluded to is 'no one' in the language of London life; but I have the honor of being her very near relative," remarked St. Leon, a little stiffly.

"Oh, a foreigner! But, do you know, my dear friend, that *that* makes all the difference? A foreigner may be of the highest rank, yet not have chanced to bring introductions to England. I shall be delighted to make the acquaintance of your charming relation."

The countess had three exceedingly plain daughters, and lost no opportunity of being gracious to young men of good property.

"My cousin is, however, married to an Englishman," St. Leon pursued, demurely; "Mr. Mortimer, a very rich stockbroker."

"Heavens, what have I got into!" thought the lady. "It will be such a crush," she mentally added, "that perhaps these dreadful people will not be seen, or pass for professionals." Then aloud, "You must tell me Mrs. Mortimer's address, or write it down for me. My poor head is so overladen with names of people I care nothing about, I may forget those whom I should like to know."

But St. Leon did not allow her memory to fail in this instance; and a day or two afterwards, to Marguerite's surprise, the card of the Countess of E—— was left in Portland Place, accompanied by an invitation to H—— House, for the 15th of the following month.

"What does all this mean, Gaston?" she cried, when he paid his next visit. "I am sure you know something about it."

"It means this:—The Countess of E—— is one of the leaders of your London society, and has so constantly heard me speak of my accomplished cousin, Mrs. Mortimer, that at length she has ventured to call and ask you to her house: when she sees you, she will find how great a gainer she is by the introduction."

"Fi donc! You have so often promised to pay me no compliments. Am I really to go, Gaston?—do you think Mr. Mortimer would like it?"

"Mr. Mortimer!—toujours Mr. Mortimer! can you never pronounce for yourself what you would like, ma cousine?"

"Well, I think I wish to go; but he will decide best—he is so sensible!"

And Mortimer, who soon afterwards came in to luncheon, gave his opinion, with very little hesitation, in the affirmative. Marguerite thought St. Leon's account quite simple about Lady E——'s wish to know her; but her husband was more flattered and pleased at the unexpected grandeur than he cared to acknowledge. To do him justice, the feeling of gratification was for her, not himself; and he hastened that very afternoon to order her new diamonds and a new dress, in his desire that her first appearance should be a brilliant one.

From the beginning Mortimer very sensibly declined the invitation for himself, and said his pleasure would be in Marguerite's enjoyment. But, when in her sheen of white brocaded silk and diamonds—and, more than this, in her glorious bloom of youth—she entered the dining-room for his approval on the evening of the concert, the natural thought crossed him of the admiration and flattery to which she would be exposed, and the charm this new life must soon possess for one so young as his wife; and something painful was in the thought.

"Marguerite, you are indeed magnificent! Dress and diamonds can add even to the perfection of your face. We grow more like Beauty and the Beast every day!"

"Mr. Mortimer, I will not hear you say those things; tell me you do not mean it, sir!" coming close to him, and looking steadily in his face. "Does it give you the slightest pain my going without you to this grand party?" she added.

"No, Maggy. Have you ever known me so selfish?"

She did not reply, but still looked at him very earnestly, as though striving to read the expression of his face; then she repeated, "I wish I had not decided upon going."

"What! when it gives me such pleasure?"

"Yes; I feel that it would be better for me not to go."

Was it some unbidden presentiment of the future, some dim foreknowledge that in the great world of London life she would again meet Earnscliffe, that influenced Marguerite as she spoke?

The carriage was announced, and her husband led her to it; then kindly kissing her, bade her be happy, and sing her very best. Afterwards, with dignified pride, he told the coachman to drive to H—— House. But, when he returned to the empty dining-room—still thinking of his wife, and this new sphere of admiration and excitement into which she was thrown—there was a mixed feeling in Mr. Mortimer's appreciation of their freshly-arisen grandeur.

CHAPTER XL.

THERE was actually a hush of admiration when Marguerite made her appearance in the Countess of E——'s stately reception-rooms, unattended, unknown; but with the quiet self-possession that was innate in her, and covered with diamonds that might have formed the dowry of a young duchess.

Lady E—— was exceedingly civil in her reception of Marguerite, and her regrets that Mr. Mortimer was unable to come; for St. Leon was already at her side, and hearing every word she uttered.

"I am really indebted to you," she whispered to him (but so loud that Marguerite heard it). "At the close of a season, such a face, such matchless grace as your cousin's, is indeed refreshing among all the well-known pale faces of London! Mrs. Mortimer, allow me to introduce my sister to you—Lady Millicent Gore."

A pale, interesting-looking woman, seated near the countess, bowed to Marguerite, and made room for her by her side. "My sister is so engaged in receiving her guests, that you must allow me to take her place in introducing you to our friends, Mrs. Mortimer. As a foreigner, most of the people about you must be strangers."

"I know no one, madame, except Gaston," glancing at her cousin, who remained hovering about her, as though to afford her encouragement. "I have never been out before!"

The lady, of course, thought she meant in England, and returned, "I fear our English society will not please you as much as your own. All my early life was spent abroad, and when I first returned to England. I was incessantly struck with the great difference in the tone of our manners—the want, above all, of that perfect ease and absence of restraint which characterises good foreign society, that of Paris especially."

"I was never in Paris. Until I came to England, all my life was spent in Bretagne."

Gaston advanced to her side.

"More of the old *noblesse* of France, and of their old courtly manners, yet linger in Bretagne than in any other of our provinces, madame," he said, addressing Lady Millicent.

"So I have heard; and that strangers are very rarely admitted among them. From what part of Brittany do you come, Mrs. Mortimer?"

"From the very wildest part of the extreme west—a part that few English people, I find, have ever heard of."

"You speak English so well—with scarcely any foreign accent."

"My father was English—so either language is familiar to me."

"You speak it better than your cousin," said Lady Millicent. "The marquis has an excellent accent, but he has not our idiom."

"No," replied Marguerite; "and he will alway render French idioms into English, word for word. Gaston, do you hear that

mine is pronounced the best English? We often argue that point."

Some acquaintances of Lady Millicent's stopping to speak to her, her attention was taken from Marguerite, who turned towards St. Leon. "Gaston" (in French) "how kind of you to be here already for my sake! I know that you dislike going to early parties."

"But you do not want my protection, Marguerite. You look as composed as though you had been to every party this season."

"I do not feel so, I can assure you. My heart beat violently when I came in. Do you know, at the very last, I tried to persuade Mr. Mortimer to accompany me?"

"Thank all the gods he stayed away," thought Gaston. "Ah! you will not mind going out alone the next time," he said, aloud. "Ce n'est que le premier pas qui coute!"

"Yes, that is all very well; but I do not suppose I shall have any more invitations."

"Ah, some one is going to sing—who is it? I surely remember that handsome face."

"That handsome face belongs to Mario, madame. He and Grisi are going to sing a duet."

"And I shall be expected to sing in the same room with them. Oh! I do feel shy now."

"More than you did at the prospect of singing before dukes and countesses? You told me yesterday you had no dread at all."

"Before them, certainly not. They may know no more of music than I do; but before great artistes,—yes Gaston," in a low voice, "I should like to be introduced to *them*."

"N'en parlez pas, ma cousine! One is not introduced to professional singers! If you ever require them in your own house, you will engage them, and pay them so much a-night. You do not suppose that they are acquaintances of the Countess of E—— ?"

"Hush! they are beginning. Ah, now for real enjoyment!"

After the duet, which was delicious, a great amateur harpist performed a long piece, with the assistance of an amateur pianist, of immense execution and no taste (all of which Marguerite thought remarkably unpleasing). Then the Duchess of Somebody sang—very mildly; then Herr Some One Else played on an extraordinary instrument, that he had been fifteen years in constructing, and fifteen more in learning to play; then Lady E—— came to Marguerite. She had been introduced to several people in the meantime by Lady Millicent and Gaston, and was now surrounded by a little circle—a Russian prince, an English earl, one or two younger sons, St. Leon, of course, and a celebrated author. To the latter she was speaking with much more animation than to any of the others. She wondered whether he had ever known Earnscliffe!

"Mrs. Mortimer, I have come to claim your kind promise. Marquis, will you take Mrs. Mortimer to the piano?"

Lady Millicent good-naturedly followed, thinking Marguerite must feel timid amidst such crowds of strangers. "Shall I stand beside you?" she whispered.

"Oh, if you will be so kind, I should greatly prefer it! But I am not very nervous now."

"Have you notes?" asked Gaston, much more flurried than she was, about her success.

"No; I never use notes. What would be best for me to sing?" (to Lady Millicent) Italian or English?"

"Italian, perhaps, as the last song was an English one; but let your own taste guide you."

After a few bold chords—she seldom played the regular written accompaniments to her songs—Marguerite began an Italian bravura, and in a second every one seemed electrified. Marguerite never sang better in her life. Constant attendance at the opera, and first-rate instruction, joined to singular natural ability, had given her an artistic style of expression almost unknown among young ladies—a style which made even Grisi rush hastily to the concert room, to see if some new singer had arrived beside herself. During amateur performances, the artistes usually waited in patient resignation, and without hearing a note.

"Ecco una voce! Gran' Dio! Ecco una voce!" Could Marguerite have seen the face of the great artiste, her triumph would have been far greater to herself than it was at all the praises that were showered upon her at the conclusion of her performance. Lady E—— was almost in tears of delight that such a début should have been made in her house, and seized both of Marguerite's hands as she was going to rise from the piano.

"One more, Mrs. Mortimer—only a little ballad—anything you like; but really we cannot so soon lose your exquisite voice!"

Marguerite smiled, and re-seated herself.

"One of your Breton romances," whispered St. Leon, close beside her. He knew too well the secrets of effect not to be aware how a plaintive ballad would tell after the Italian bravura.

She chose, this time, the wild dirge she had sung to Earnscliffe on the first evening he had ever heard her; and, perhaps, that recollection gave more than usual pathos to her voice. The lights, the strange faces around her vanished. She was by the open window again at Kersaint, with the summer sun-set streaming into the old room, and gilding the graceful outline of Philip's figure, as he stood in the deep embrasure watching her. When she concluded, amid a universal and genuine murmur of applause, the only words she heard were those of St. Leon.

"Thank you, Marguerite." His voice sounded so exactly like Philip's that she turned round with a start; and something in her cousin's attitude at the moment completed the resemblance.

"Phil—Gaston—oh! cousin—I mean." Her color went and came, and a sudden emotion shot through St. Leon's heart. He was no coxcomb, but, while handing Marguerite to her seat, he ventured, very slightly, to press the little hand upon his arm.

"How you blushed, Marguerite, as you finished your last song; were you conscious of it?"

"No—yes. Oh, Gaston, my thoughts were far away."

"You are complimentary, madame. Am I completely beyond consideration?"

"Why I see you every day, dear Gaston. You know I could not be thinking of you."

"What a dreadful coquette!" remarked some well-trained English girls, who were watching Marguerite and her cousin. "Look at the way she smiles and beams up in that man's face! But then all Frenchwomen are the same. And a married woman too, which makes it worse!"

"Let me take you to supper," whispered Gaston. "I see our hostess bringing up some one to introduce to you, but remember that you are engaged to me."

*   *   *   *   *   *

From that evening Marguerite became the fashion. Much as we talk of exclusiveness, our aristocracy is probably less exclusive than any other in the world; and great wealth or great talent can at any time gain admittance more easily into London society than into that of half the capitals in Europe. Marguerite, too, had riches, talent, beauty; and, at least, on her mother's side, high birth. And besides all this she was half a foreigner—a circumstance which in itself casts down many barriers in England—so her husband's business and himself were tacitly ignored by the great people who wished to secure Mrs. Mortimer for their parties. He was asked as a matter of course, but had the good taste invariably to decline; and Marguerite gradually became accustomed to go everywhere alone. The slight feeling of uneasiness he had experienced on her *début* wore off. as he perceived how little her new kind of life altered his wife. She told him so exactly the admiration she received, the compliments that were paid her—poor Gaston included—that it would have required a more suspicious nature than even Mortimer's to harbor any feelings of jealousy; and he was soon prouder than he chose to confess of his wife's success, and of her entrance into "grand society."

"But Marguerite," he said, one morning at breakfast, as she described some brilliant ball on the previous evening; "does not the thought often cross your mind, among all these handsome young men, of your old plain husband at home, making you wish that you had not chosen so young, and before you had seen anything of the world?"

Confess, Marguerite; such is sometimes the case!"

"Never, Mr. Mortimer. I have never yet met any one among them who really interested me. I still like Gaston far the best among all the young men I am acquainted with—and you know precisely how I feel towards him."

"Then, Maggy, must I believe that your heart is pre-occupied?"

"I believe it is so, sir," she replied, in a very low voice.

Mortimer knew not the unacknowledged memory which made all others seem so poor and weak compared to it—knew not that his own strong safeguard was in the shade of his wife's old lover!

That season passed away—another came —and Marguerite's popularity rather increased than waned. Her extraordinary voice made her a welcome acquisition everywhere; and the whole musical world were now as anxious to engage her for their concerts as they were to get Grisi or Alboni.

When Georgy said that the world and amusement would soon efface Marguerite's recollection of Philip, she was, to a limited extent, correct. To forget him was not in Marguerite's nature—to love again was impossible; but she had not now the time to think of him as formerly. The desire of distinction that lies dormant in every human heart—desires which, had she married Earnscliffe, would never have germinated in hers —now took the place of a softer interest in life. Young, gifted and admired beyond the usual lot, Marguerite was happy—if such a life can ever make a woman's happiness — at all events, her existence flowed smoothly on, and no longer stagnated as in the first dull years of her marriage.

As may be conceived, Georgy de Burgh and her mother made indefatigable efforts to get acquainted with "great people" on the strength of their dear Marguerite's success. But this she knew from the first was impossible; and Mortimer at length made one or two such unmistakably plain speeches on the subject (when they had been wearying his wife with supplications to get them invited to Lady Someone's ball), that they had taken serious offence; and although Danby still continued to call as usual, Marguerite now saw little of either of the ladies.

But St. Leon was a most constant visitor at the Mortimers'. His relationship gave him, of course, a claim to more than ordinary intimacy, and, whatever his inmost feelings might be towards Marguerite, he had as yet so scrupulously concealed them, that she had not the slightest conception of anything more than friendship on his part. Her own manner to him continued the same as it had always been—quite open and unconstrained. As she had told Mortimer, she preferred her cousin to any other man with whom she was acquainted, and, perhaps, had her heart been

wholly unoccupied, there might have been danger in this constant intimacy. Remembering Philip, however, she saw precisely where Gaston was shallow and unreal; if his voice softened she knew he was acting: if he read to her, or sang to her, or walked with her, she remembered how she had done all this once before with Philip beside her, and the present seemed in a moment as a faint, cold shadow compared to that warm and golden past.

And yet, while Philip's recollection always stood between Marguerite and St. Leon, the resemblance, real or fancied, which she traced to Earnscliffe in his features, was the greatest interest her cousin possessed to her; and a sudden look or expression of his would often so bring back Philip and old days, that —utterly unable to master her emotion—she would blush and tremble, just as she had done years before at Kersaint. These blushes, these tremors, fatally misled St Leon.

CHAPTER XLII.

FOUR years passed away after Earnscliffe had parted with Neville in Rome before he returned to England. The first eighteen months he had spent in Italy and Greece; the latter part of the time in the East among the wildest, least frequented districts of Arabia and Syria. During this period, but only at intervals, he had continued to write, and each successive work bore evidence of deeper thought, and was imbued with a healthier tone than had characterised even the best of his earlier writings. In this long intercourse with nature, freed from the enervating influences of social life, Philip had regained much that the world, with its pleasures and disappointments, had taken from the fresh genius of his youth. In the absence of all human companionship, he had created for himself a wild and lonely peril, that was eminently calculated to strengthen into self-dependence his formerly yielding, somewhat indolent character; and he was now returning home, unconscious of the change, with renewed ardor and ambition, and his whole moral being braced in a manlier, more vigorous tone.

An event had occurred too, during this interval, which, Philip was obliged to confess, removed his strongest reasons for living abroad, and his morbid distaste for England. He was once more free! After three years of ill health, spent, first in the spendthrift grandeur of her father's house, then in poverty, uncheered by either affection or respect, Lady Clara died. Earnscliffe did not hear of her death without a certain emotion, although it was impossible it could cause him anything like real grief. He had written to his wife after Lord St. Leger's break-down, offering all the assistance in his pow-er, and entreating her to receive some allow-ance from him. "For my sake I ask you to accept it," he had written, "for the sake of our childish days. Show sufficient generosi-ty to give me this pleasure!" But, whatever softer feelings Clara's better nature may have prompted, the letter remained unanswered: and Philip heard of her no more, until he accidentally read the announcement of her death in an English paper at Smyrna. She had then been dead some months; and, by the following spring, Earnscliffe finally quit-ted the East, and resolved to return for good to his own country.

Although, in his exile, he had often tried to persuade himself that deserts were far more suited to him than cities, he could scarcely repress the pleasure with which he once more found himself in Paris.

He met several old faces among the idle crowds on the boulevards; but not one that lit up with an expression of recognition at seeing him—(Philip was greatly changed, sunburnt, and stouter, and a beard of two years' growth completely metamorphosed the once soft, dreamy character of his features); and, at last, he turned in to a solitary dinner at Les Trois Freres, where he was soon obliged to allow that *coquilles de volaille à la financière*, *egigrammes d'agneau*, and *meri-gues glacés*, tasted excellent, after the wild meals improvised by himself in Arabia Pe-træa; and that chablis and hock were prefer-able to black coffee and arrack of the desert.

"Neville was right," he thought. "I re-member, he told me that at five-and-thirty, I should have done with sentiment, and be glad to return to the substantial things of this world. I am not quite so old, but I have certainly no sentiment left; and, as for the world—garcon, bring me the bills for the theatre to-night." He glanced over the names of the performers, and it gave him an old feeling to perceive that they were nearly all strange ones. "I am like an unrolled mummy, or Robinson Crusoe," he thought. "On the earth, but not belonging to it. I wonder what has become of Celeste and Fridoline, and poor little Rose!" And Phil-ip sat long over his dessert, thinking of his old loves, as he sipped his wine, but looking by no means miserable.

"Eh, mon Dieu, est il possible?" burst at last from the lips of a Frenchman who was taking coffee at another table, and had been intently watching him for about half-an-hour. "Can I really see Monsieur Earnscliffe?" coming up to him with both hands extended. After a second's hesitation, Philip recog-nised a rather silly looking young man, Monsieur Deschamps, by name, with whom he had formerly been slightly acquainted in Paris; and, glad to meet with anything that connected him with the land of the living, he cordially returned the friendly greeting of the Frenchman.

"I am surprised that you know me," he remarked; "several of my countrymen pass-ed me to-day, with no signs of recognition."

"Until I heard you speak to one of the garcons, I was uncertain; but I could not be mistaken in the tones of your voice. My wife—I am married, now—has often said to me, 'Monsieur Earnscliffe's was the only pleasant voice she ever heard in England.'"

"I congratulate you on your happiness. But, have I indeed the honor of being an ac-quaintance of Madame Deschamp?"

"My wife's former name was Madem-oiselle Celeste——"

"Celeste!" exclaimed Philip. "Do you mean——"

"Yes, monsieur, the celebrated Celeste. But she has long since abandoned the stage," he added, with dignity. "Half the year we live on our estates in Normandy, the other half in Paris; and we shall be charmed to see you *chez nous* Hotel Rohan, Rue St. Maur, Faubourg St. Germain. Indeed, to-night is one of Celeste's receptions, and I am sure she will be delighted to see again so distinguished a personage as Monsieur Earns-cliffe."

Philip bowed to the compliment, and promised to call at the Hotel Rohan in the course of the evening.

"You will meet several of your compatri-ots; for Celeste admits many strangers to her societies, in consideration of the happy years she spent abroad, especially in your country. Lady Kentish and Mrs. Dodd Tracy are of her friends the most intimate."

It was late when he arrived, and the guests were long assembled. The house of Celeste's husband was exactly such a hotel as used to be considered aristocratic in "the Faubourg"—*entre cour et jardin*—and dull, huge, and damp. It had been purchased from some ruined family by the father of Monsieur Anatole, and he considered that it gave a kind of halo of good birth to reside there himself; although poor Celeste's own taste much more warmly inclined to a cheerful, noisy apartment in the Faubourg St. Honoré.

Celeste knew Earnscliffe instantly; and advanced with a blush and exclamation that were not acted, to meet him. "Oh, Philip!" in a very low voice, "this *is* unexpected!"

He told her in two words of his meeting with Monsieur Deschamps, and how gladly he had availed himself of his invitation.

"You must stop till all these people are gone," she replied, still in the same tone. "It is already late, and then we can talk over old times. But the world, and your compa-triots especially, are so censorious, that I must not even appear glad to see you now. Let me introduce you to some of your own country-people!"

"Who in the world can all these people

te?" thought Philip, after he had looked about him. "They certainly look respectable."

He did not know anything of a certain class of English in Paris, or he would have felt no surprise at seeing them at Celeste's house, or anywhere else. A class made up of odds-and-ends of society—Mrs. Dodd Traceys and Lady Kentishes—who, for some little reasons, are just not received in London, but manage to pass current better abroad—these—and others brought by them and of a still more mystic origin—constituted Celeste's British guests.

Her husband—who had married her in a silly freak, or perhaps with the wish to do something remarkable—was really a man of tolerable property, though of low birth ; and some of his connections—decent shopkeepers mostly—made up the French part of the company, and were looked upon by the English as models of foreign breeding and high birth. Better bred they certainly showed themselves than his own country-people ; for, when Earnscliffe's name was known, the latter all crowded round him, and solicited introductions, until he was literally bored to death. And it was with the feeling of the most intense relief that he watched the last of them—Mrs. Dodd Tracey—depart about midnight, and found himself alone among the chandeliers with Celeste.

"You have grown so handsome, Philip—I can call you so when no one hears : but you look much older."

"You are still handsome, Celeste ; and look younger than ever."

She shook her head and smiled ; but then said her quiet life now was, of course, less wearing than it used to be when on the stage.

"And happier?"

"Oh, yes!—I was getting tired of acting, and ovations, and suppers, and all the rest of it. And now I have everything I like, a very nice house, as you see—only rather dull—a dear little carriage of my own, and—better than all—a son two years old, with black eyes and long hair, beau comme un ange. I should like you to see him. But sit down—not there—here, where I can see you, and talk. I do like to hear your voice ; it reminds me so of old days!"

Philip seated himself as she requested. "You must have a good deal to tell me, Celeste."

"Yes, but your story first. All that has happened to you from the very last day I saw you."

Omitting all mention of Kersaint, Philip gave her a resume of his wanderings, describing just the scenes and people she was likely to care about ; and Celeste listened with great interest, and her plump hands clasped in a charming attitude of attention.

"Voilà tout!" she cried, as he finished.

"Ah! and you have become quite a philosopher among these dreadful deserts without doubt. Mon pauvre ami, how sentimental you used to be!"

"Very long ago ; I do not look sentimental now ; do I?"

"Oh, no ; you have quite lost that indescribable expression ; that softness—not of voice, that is the same as ever—but of face. All your youth is gone."

"It should be, I am getting old."

"Do not speak of it, what must I be?"

"For some people time remains stationary."

"Ah! you never used to make pretty speeches, poor little Fridoline often said that was your great charm."

"Fridoline!" echoed Philip. "I had almost forgotten her. Where is Fridoline? a great actress she must be by this time."

"She is gone," said Celeste, gravely. "No, not dead ; but returned—vanished as she came. Some news respecting the death of a relation reached her, and she never could be induced to go on the stage again. Imagine the rage of the manager! She had to pay an immense sum to get off her engagement so suddenly."

"But when did all this happen? Is she really gone—for ever?"

"Oh! it happened two or three years ago. One night, just as she was going to the theatre, she got the letter ; and a week afterwards had quitted England, accompanied by an old servant, whom you may remember. She came to see me in Paris—it was just after my marriage—looking years older, and in deep mourning. I was surprised at her coming here ; for, of course, it took her out of her way in returning to Norway ; but she said she had a visit to pay near Paris, before leaving France forever. That visit was to Pere la Chaise—and I accompanied her.

"Then you know more about her now than you used to do?"

"I know all ; and should like you to do so too. Tenez! I had entirely forgotten it ; but I have a letter for you from Fridoline herself. She gave it me, blushing and confused, the day she left ; and made me promise to keep it for you, saying, 'You will see him again, or hear of him, at least—I never shall.' Do you know, Monsieur Earnscliffe, I believe poor Fridoline loved you?"

"Me, Celeste? Never. We were friends, as two young men of the same age might be—nothing more."

Celeste shook her head. "I don't believe in these kind of friendships ; if on the one side, the feeling lasts as it began, it is sure to become warmer on the other. However, you shall have the letter when you have read it, you can judge for yourself. It is close at hand among my old letters. Here it is."

"I will read it to-morrow ; let us speak of nothing but old times now." And they spoke antil the timepiece just beside them, chimed two; and Madame Deschamp started at its sound, and appeared suddenly to recollect that she was no longer Celeste.

"I hope you are not leaving Paris yet?"

"A polite way of bidding me good-night, madame! You have not told me of all our mutual friends yet, or, more interesting still, half enough about yourself."

"Mais voilà Anatole qui rentre!" exclaimed Celeste, as a man's step was heard on the staircase; "and two hours in the morning!"—speaking English.—"It is frightful, these Paris husbands."

Monsieur Anatole entered, and smiled affably to Philip. "Ah, Monsieur Earnscliffe! I am charmed that you have honored us. She is looking well, is she not?" taking his wife's hand affectionately.

"Remarkably well!" answered Philip. "I was just telling her so," he thought, "when you interrupted me." However, he was silent. There seemed such perfect harmony and good understanding in the *ménage*, he could not for worlds have disturbed it.

"I have already trespassed too much on your kindness, madame. In talking over so many old friends and scenes, I have forgotten time," he said bowing to Celeste: "and now I must have the pain of again wishing you good-bye; only this time I trust it will be for months, not years."

"Ah, you are hastening back to London so soon!"

"Yes; I am obliged to leave to-morrow morning: but next winter I hope to return to Paris for some months, and——"

"You will come to see us—you will count us of your friends?" said Celeste's husband, warmly seizing both his hands, and with actual tears in his eyes.

"The French are a singular people!" thought Philip, as he walked home in the moonlight to his hotel.

CHAPTER XLIII.

When he was half-way between Paris and Boulogne, the following morning, Philip took Fridoline's letter from his pocket, and broke the seal. The contents were as follows:—

"I shall never see you more, Monsieur Earnscliffe. When you receive this letter, my name will come back to you like a dream long forgotten. You will say, 'Ah, poor little Fridoline! I remember, now, there was something about her I never understood.' And just for this reason I write you. In the eyes of the world I care nothing how I am remembered. I may be merely called eccentric, or classed with all other actresses; but to you—I know not why—I would appear as

I really am. The time is past when it could injure any one to disclose the secret of my life—the reason for secresy, alas! exists no longer. Philip, let me tell you briefly why I left my own country—why I followed a profession, and associated with a class, that was abhorrent to me!

"My earliest recollections are of a Norwegian village, buried in the depth of pine forests and wild mountains—where, for more than half the year, the snow never melted; and of a large, old farm house, of which only a few rooms on the first-floor were furnished, and where I lived with my Aunt Christina, and one servant—Hulda, who has never left me.

"My aunt was tall, and thin, and severe; and appeared to be of immense age—although I suppose, in my childhood, she could not have more than reached middle life. She loved me; but with an austere kind of love that chilled me instinctively. If I danced and sang, she shook her head, and looked away from me—when I played childish tricks upon Hulda or the cat, she told me the devil was in my heart. Once, when I was about six years old, I collected a quantity of spring flowers in the forest, and made them into a wreath for my own hair, then climbing up to the glass in her bedroom, I was surveying myself with great satisfaction, when my aunt suddenly entered. 'Vain already, child,' she cried passionately. 'You shall be dressed in your old winter things all the summer.' And she flung my flowers far away through the window. Afterwards, when she joined us by the kitchen stove in the evening—for I had taken refuge as usual with Hulda in my disgrace—I saw that Aunt Christina's eyes were red with weeping, and I wondered where was the sin of making flower wreaths! But Hulda told me I was too young to understand such things.

"As I grew older, I was never allowed to associate with any of the other girls in the village. People seemed to look upon us as something doubtful—my aunt held aloof from everybody; so we had no visitors. I think she only received about two letters a year, on each of which occasions her eyes always grew red, and her manner to me redoubled in severity. If I asked, why I had no father or mother, or sisters, my questions were checked so sternly, that I felt it was very wrong indeed for me to wish to be related to any one. Still, I was not unhappy. It takes more than loneliness or occasional punishment to subdue the natural spirits and loving heart of a child.

"So the time went by till I was fifteen. On that day I fancied myself a woman, and I told my aunt so. 'Do you, Fridoline?' she answered. 'Then as you have decided it yourself, so it shall be. To-day your childhood ends.' She was right. From that day I never felt young again.

"I remember well with what interest I

seated myself by the open window on that bright June morning—eager to devour every word as it fell from the lips of Aunt Christina, as she sat opposite me in her favorite stiff horse-hair chair. She told me who I was—what was my mother. Oh, Mr. Earnscliffe! I shrink from repeating it to you even now—nothing could make me do so but the feeling that my own character must always remain misunderstood unless you hear my history. Knowing also that you will not be harsh in your judgment upon her who is gone; and that, when you have read, you will burn this letter, and never allow its contents to be known to any but yourself.

"They were early left orphans—these two sisters;—but my mother was years the younger, and gifted with extraordinary beauty and talent. From the difference in age, Christina loved her almost with the love of a mother; and when, at sixteen, in spite of their religious education—in spite of all she could say against it—her young sister embraced the life of an actress—it almost broke her heart.

"The success of the lovely Pauline was instant, and in a few weeks all the young nobles of Christiania were at her feet. Christina continued—great as was her repugnance to theatres and actors—to watch over her, even when she had to bear with harsh words for her untiring surveillance. But it was all in vain. Natural vanity—levity—I must call it by no harsher name—was too strong in the heart of the young actress. She became the mistress of Count Z——f—one of the richest nobles in Norway—and, by the time she was seventeen, was my mother.

"Christina had not seen her for months; but a fortnight after my birth, she called at the costly house which Count Z——f had fitted up for Pauline, and had a long interview, in which she made use of every appeal, both to affection and religion, in her endeavors to win her back. But to no avail. In the height of her youth and beauty, the voice of poor Christina had little charm to lure her from her guilty splendor and the apparent devotion of a man like Count Z——f; and she declined every proposal to leave him, and return with her sister to the country. 'Then give me the child, at least!' said Christina. 'Let me save her innocent life from contamination, and bring her up' with a horror of all that has lost you!—far away from the world and its temptations.' It was some time before my mother would consent. The strongest love of humanity was not so dead within her that she could give up her helpless infant without a pang! At length, however, she yielded; Christina receiving me on the sole conditions that I should be as entirely hers as though my parents were actually dead, and that she never should be asked to receive any presents or money from my mother on my behalf. 'From that time,'

my aunt concluded, 'I have never seen her. She left soon after for Paris, and I believe acted there for some time. Count Z——f deserted her at the end of six months. And then—but I wish to enter into no more details to you, child—enough that your mother still lives—is still guilty. You will not blame me now that I have been severe with you; and have checked all approach to that levity which was her ruin—although in any other child it might have been innocent."

"I shrank away from her—I hid myself in my room—I prayed to God that I might die. The whole earth seemed suddenly dark and hideous to me; and for many weeks afterwards I was dangerously ill with brain fever.

"Just as I was slowly recovering my strength, my Aunt Christina died suddenly, leaving me all the small property she possessed, and perfect mistress of my own actions. I do not think I felt her death much at the time—indeed, I was glad of my newly-acquired freedom, for I thought it would enable me to carry out a scheme, first framed in the delirium of fever, but which I had pondered over calmly and ripened since: to go to Paris, find out my mother, and endeavor to win her from her present life.

"It was a wild idea, but yet we carried it out—I and Hulda. We travelled, and in winter, the long, long journey to Paris; and then, child as I was, I had to search for my mother, with no other clue than the address of the hotel where she had lived some years before. I cannot enter into the hateful details of that search—you may imagine them; but, strictly as I had been reared in a simple cottage, ignorant of all vice, save in name, nothing daunted me, and I found her.

"She was living in splendor at the hotel of some great Russian prince, and it was with difficulty I could gain admittance to her presence. 'Madame was out'—' Madame was ill '—' I was not commanded '—' I was an impostor,' and so on. However, I was not to be deterred; and, after waiting about for more than two hours, I contrived to steal up the back staircase among some of the women-servants, and then asked one of them to show me to madame's room, offering her five francs for her trouble. She led me along one or two passages, and then pointed to a door, saying that was the bedroom of madame, and I must knock for myself—she would incur no further responsibility. In my eagerness, however, I forgot to knock; and, entering the room, I saw a lady richly dressed, sitting in an immense fur-covered fauteuil by the fire embroidering. She turned with some surprise at being interrupted; but, on seeing my pale face and worn black dress, doubtless thought I was one of her workmen come to solicit charity.

"' Sit down,' she said, kindly, to me, ' poor girl, and tell me what I can do for you.'

"The sound of her voice made me turn

quite sick with emotion. 'Madame,' I faltered out, 'I am Fridoline!—I am your child!'

"She turned deadly pale, and, for a moment, I thought that she had fainted; then she started up and came to me, caught me in her arms and kissed me wildly, passionately. 'Fridoline, my own—my very own. Child, how have I yearned to see your face! my child—my own!' She clasped me to her breast; and, with no more words than such as I have just written, we passed two hours.

"Ah, Philip! I knew that she was a lost, stained creature, but yet the deepest joy I have ever known was in those moments when I rested for the first time upon my mother's bosom, and felt her kisses upon my face.

"I thought from her intense delight at seeing me, that she would at once leave Paris, and return to our quiet home with me; but, with each secret visit that I paid her, this hope died away. When at length I had courage to approach the subject, and, as delicately as a child could do, besought her to turn her thoughts to another world than this, and let me devote all my future life to hers, she evaded the question: and at length I saw—not that she was entirely without remorse or any better aspiration—but that wealth and luxury had become part of her very existence, and were ties too strong for her to give up; and that it was these that bound her to life.

"Then, for the first time in my life I wished for money, and for her sake, and an inward conviction told me that, if I chose, I could win it by becoming an actress. As a child, I had always possessed great powers of mimicry—although my aunt punished me severely in her hope of checking it. And often in the long winter evenings, when I was not more than six years old, I used to convulse poor Hulda with laughter at my representations of everybody in the village, including the pastor and Aunt Christina herself. But I turned with loathing, at first, from the idea of following the same calling that had been my mother's, and only stifled my prejudice against it as the conviction gradually strengthened upon my mind, that it was the sole thing open to me in which my abilities could be brought to bear. Finally, I resolved upon making the attempt; crossed over to England—where I heard I had a better chance than in Paris—and accepted a small engagement at the French Plays, you are aware with what success.

"I begin now to think that my scheme was a false one, and that even money could not have effected what maternal love had failed in. But for years no doubt ever crossed me; and this one object kept me ever on, untiring in my profession, undismayed by difficulty or, worse still, by all the horrors of vice that beset me. I corresponded at intervals, and by stealth, with my mother. She always wrote with the most touching affec-

tion: said how she gloried in my success, in the name I was creating; but, above all, in my fair, unspotted fame; and then there would be regrets and faint resolves of her own, soon to leave Paris for my sake. Very faint they were, but still enough to keep me on unwearied at my work.

"I was beginning to think that I should soon have amassed sufficient money to enable us both to live well upon in Norway, when news arrived that rendered my efforts objectless for evermore: my mother had died suddenly one night on her return from the theatre. The letter was from her own waiting-woman, the sole person who had been admitted to the secret of our relationship, and she added that my name was the last sound upon my mother's lips before she died.

"I never acted again. My life has lost its aim now, and I shall return to my own country, unknown, unnoticed—as I left it.

"Philip, do not quite forget me.

> "FRIDOLINE."

CHAPTER XLIV.

A VERY grand ball was to take place at the French Ambassador's, to which Marguerite was invited. Without knowing why, she was much more anxious than usual about her dress for this occasion. Her dressmaker was astonished at the number of times she changed her mind, and the numerous visits she paid her before the day came—Mrs. Mortimer, who generally decided upon a toilette at once, and never looked at it again until she wore it!

"Can you tell me the time, Mr. Mortimer? I am sure all the clocks must be slow!"

Mortimer was dozing in his arm-chair by the fire, and Marguerite, seated at one of the drawing-room windows, was watching the last fading hues of the April twilight, and the cold-looking moon that rose among the leafless elms in the distance. They were now living in Mortimer's house at Wimbledon, where he fancied the air agreed with him better than in London, and which Marguerite also preferred for its gardens and conservatories.

"Time, child—how you startled me! Is not the time-piece striking something?"

"It must be slow; surely it is long past eight!"

"How anxious you are to put on your finery, Maggy. Well, I will ring for lights and coffee at once, and you can go."

"You shall not have your coffee earlier on my account, sir; there is plenty of time," replied Marguerite, a little ashamed of her own anxiety on the subject: and she came and seated herself by Mortimer's side. Her face was very flushed, and she gazed long and steadily in the fire.

"I feel to-night," she went on, "some unaccountable weight upon me: something almost warning me not to go to this party [much as I wish it. Shall I go, Mr. Mortimer?"

"Silly child! of course you will go. What can happen to you?—the horses are as quiet as any in England. You are getting fanciful, Maggy; you do not take exercise enough."

But Marguerite could not shake off her fancy, not even when she was dressed and far on her way to town. It was, as she had said, a vague presentiment—not precisely amounting to a foreboding of evil, but a feeling that something was to occur that evening of no common importance. As she approached A—— House, however, the crush of carriages, the noise and excitement, took her thoughts from herself; and when she entered the brilliantly-decorated rooms, amidst the blaze of countless lights and the open admiration of every eye she met, no wonder that all gloomy thoughts vanished!

"La belle Mortimer never looked so lovely," said one knot of young men, who were watching her entrance.

"I thought you were acquainted with her," remarked a friend.

"Of course I am."

"Oh! she never bowed to you in passing, that was all."

"She is as capricious as other beauties," said the first speaker—a silly-looking youth: one of the crowds whose attempts at idle compliments Marguerite's quiet dignity had set down. "Even the marquis is thrown over sometimes. At Lady Dacre's party, her fancy was to talk to some hideous little author the whole evening. However, he was beneath St. Leon's jealousy, I suppose."

"St. Leon is Mrs. Mortimer's cousin," said a young man who had not yet spoken, gravely. "Of course they are intimate! But little Grot"—turning towards the youth—"is always so sharp-sighted when there is nothing to see."

A tall figure was standing close beside the group, his face turned away, but intently listening to all they said. When the last speaker finished, they changed their position slightly, so as to be out of hearing; and the stranger—for something about his appearance and bearing made him look unlike the London *habitués* of the room—moved on also, his eyes still following Marguerite as she advanced to the graceful hostess.

"Are you engaged for the first contre-danse, madame?"

"Gaston, you quite startle me, speaking in such a solemn tone! Monsieur, I *am* engaged for the first, but not for the second."

"You will promise it me, then?"

"Certainly; but, cousin, on our usual terms—not to dance it! Even if one cared for dancing, which I do not, who would

struggle and faint through such a crowd as this, for a mortal quadrille, when they might pass it coolly in some dim-lit conservatory? Look out for one, dear Gaston—you know what we both like; and, above all, one with few intruders."

"She is too open," thought St. Leon, as he watched Marguerite led away by the partner who came to claim her; "no woman on earth ever made such a remark as that to a man she loved! And it is better so— far better!" he added, with a half-sigh. "She is happy as she is; and yet, sometimes, her blushes, her faltering answers—. Would it were decided; I cannot pass my life in these doubts and hopes for ever."

Like most Frenchmen, Gaston had small religious belief. No compunction as to morality, or even the ruined happiness of another, ever crossed his mind when his wishes were concerned—his own passions to be gratified. Sensitively alive to honor (on all points which men of the world have decided to constitute it), he could visit daily at Mortimer's house, and receive his hospitality, with the systematic intention of one day winning Marguerite's love, and feel none of the conflicting irresolution—the agony of remorse—which a man like Earnscliffe would have done, even although he had not sufficient strength to fly from temptation.

"Violá notre contredanse, mon cousin!" He started as Marguerite's gay voice aroused him from a long reverie into which he had fallen—a reverie in which his secretly-cherished hopes of coming into power under the new Imperial règime of France, and his hopes with regard to her were strangely blended. "Have you forgotten all about my request? You look extremely absent."

Gaston offered her his arm without reply; but when they had left the ball-room, and were passing through the crowded vestibule, he whispered, "I *am* absent, madam—distrait—miserable; but of all others, you must pardon me."

"Gaston, do not be sentimental!" she answered, with a laugh. "I always tell you that your greatest charm is in being unaffected. It would not suit you to be poetic and wretched."

St. Leon led her on, through one after another of the magnificent suite of rooms that were thrown open. "Will this crowd never lessen?" she exclaimed. "I am sick of so many human faces."

"You should have employed your time, then, while I was dancing, in finding out some cool, undisturbed spot, Gaston, instead of indulging your poetic fancies."

"I was thinking of you, madame; do not blame me."

The abrupt manner, the subdued tone, if it was acting, was excellent, and would have told with the majority of listeners. But Marguerite drew away.

"We have gone far enough, cousin. It is not too warm here, let us rest and admire these lovely statues."

"You wished to be among flowers and moonlight just now! You are changeable to-night, madame."

"Let us go on, then!" she returned, gently, guessing from his face that he was offended, and too yielding ever to contest a point; "if you really wish to be away from the crowd. No one seems to be entering that door on the left—shall we try it?"

The door was closed; but yielded to Gaston's hand, and they went in. It was a small morning-room or boudoir, that, although not formally closed, had not been included among those rooms which were to be thrown open: and an alabaster hand-lamp, left, probably, by accident on a centre table, was the only light. Gaston quickly closed the door before any other wanderers in search of quiet and cool air had discovered their retreat or attempted to follow them; and Marguerite, who otherwise would have hesitated at entering a room not intended for guests, found herself thus obliged to remain, or show too plainly her unwillingness at being alone with St. Leon.

"Gaston, this quiet and repose seem almost fairy-like, after the lights and murmur of voices we have left. Had we better remain here? the room looks scarcely intended for strangers."

"You told me, madame, in the ball-room to select a spot free from intruders—surely this must answer the description?"

"What a bright moon!" remarked Marguerite, turning towards the window, which opened upon a balcony leading to the trellised roofs of some conservatories. "And the air does not feel cold, although it is long past midnight."

She stepped out; but hastily retreated, "Gaston, some one is here before us. I am sure I saw a figure at the further end of the balcony—a tall, slight figure. Cousin—let us retire, we may be intruders."

"Let me see!" St. Leon answered, springing down the steps which led from the window, and taking a hasty survey around, then quickly returning to her side. "You were deceived, Marguerite," he said, "I have looked around, and no one is to be seen."

"But I am positive I saw the figure of a man."

"It may have been a servant, then," he replied, carelessly. "But, whoever it was, is gone now. Come in, Marguerite! the air is too cold for you to remain without."

"The calm night is so refreshing!" she answered, lingering—her eyes fixed dreamily upon the dark gardens beneath, as though she longed to pierce their shadows.

St. Leon wheeled a chair close to the window. "Sit here, then," he said, "where you can feel the air without being exposed to it."

"Thank you; that is delightful. And you, cousin?"

He seated himself on a low ottoman, almost at her feet, and looked up in her face.

"Here is my place, Marguerite!"

"Nonsense, Gaston! Only imagine any one entering, and seeing you! Although we are cousins, people would think I was a coquette—a character that I am not anxious to acquire."

St. Leon rose in a minute. "I wish I could believe you no coquette, Marguerite."

"Gaston!"

"I repeat it—I should indeed be happy—wildly—tumultuously happy, if I believed you were not a coquette."

"Cousin Gaston! do you know what you are talking about?"

"I know too well, madame—and it is impossible that you do not understand it also. No—you shall hear me!" He caught her hand as she half-rose. I have been silent too long, and I can conceal the truth no more. That truth which you must have guessed a thousand times, Marguerite—I love you!."

"Love me!" she stammered, turning very pale. "Yes, dear Gaston—cousinly love—as a brother——"

"No, madame, not as a brother. Je vous aime" (the conversation was in French, of course)—"je vous aime d'amour."

The hand which he held turned quite cold, and he felt her tremble. "Gaston," she said quickly, "I cannot remain here, now—let me go."

"Not until you answer me, Marguerite, ma cousine." Very gentle was his voice; he misunderstood her reply, and drew her nearer to him, but she shrank away.

"Cousin, you must not speak to me thus, never recur to it again—let us be friends, as we have been. I—I——"

"Marguerite," he interrupted, "tell me honestly and plainly, with all the truth of your nature, do you love me?"

"As a friend?"

"No, madame; as a lover?"

"No—a thousand times no." She took her hand away, and looked him very full in the face.

"Then you have trifled with me cruelly—trifled with me as I could not have believed you capable of doing, with your youth, and your seeming innocence."

"I do not understand you, monsieur!" Even her soft temper was aroused by his bitter manner, and the sneer which accompanied his last word. "How have I ever trifled with you?"

"Marguerite, can you recall no time when your voice has suddenly lowered as you spoke to me—when your cheek has flushed, your eyes have sank beneath mine? Have you never started at my voice? Oh, Marguerite!" he went on, his tones growing low and agitated with these recollections, "it could not all be acting. Speak; tell me that although I may hope for nothing more, there *have*, at least been moments when you loved me. Tell me only this one word. Even now you are pale, you tremble."

Marguerite's head had sunk as she listened to him, until he could only see the averted line of her profile, and her hands were clasped together nervously. A sudden self-reproach shot through her at Gaston's words; and, in her lowliness of self-estimation, she at once transferred the guilt of his love to herself.

"I have deceived him," she thought. "When the likeness to Philip has made me blush and tremble against my own conviction, he has thought it love for him! Yet, how can I undeceive him?"

With cheeks now burning with shame, she looked up timidly in her cousin's face. "Gaston, I *have* unconsciously deceived you," she whispered; "Nay, do not misunderstand me—not as you think I have—— Cousin, there is some one without, I know I heard a step——"

"No—no, it is nothing. Go on, Marguerite, all my hopes in life hang upon your next words!"

"I have, Gaston, never loved you; but, early in life," she lowered her voice, and glanced hurriedly towards the open window, "long before I was married, I parted with one dear to me; one whom I have never met since, shall never see again; and, oh, Gaston! how must I tell you? there is a likeness in your features. At times you have so reminded me—and——"

"Madame!" interrupted the marquis, with the most frigid politeness, "I beg of you not to be so discountenanced. It is no unusual occurrence. Most English young ladies have loved before they marry; and with me your secret—such as it is—is perfectly safe. Only, another time, when you may trace any fancied resemblance in one of your friends to this—early lover, it might be well to explain the circumstance at once; before so many blushes, and starts, and tremors have led him into being the fool that I am. You have honored me with your regard from my likeness to another! I thank you, madame!"

"Gaston—you are unjust!"

"I have been deceived. You cannot enter into my feelings."

"And I have been wrong—so wrong," her voice faltering, "but let my ignorance of the world be my excuse. If I could have guessed in the slightest degree your feeling towards me, cousin, I would have died sooner than mislead you on such a subject. I have few real friends—no relation but you, and now I have offended you for ever. Oh, be generous enough to forgive me!"

He turned away with an assumption of indifference that ill accorded with his agitated face, for he was touched by her artless, pleading manner. "I can never think of you, Marguerite, but as an image of everything most sweet and lovely; but we cannot continue friends; I have hopes and ambitions in France, in which I shall, doubtless, be able to forget the dream of the past year. After to-night, we shall meet no more."

The tears rose in her eyes; but she was silent. She could not *now* ask him to be her friend still, or oppose his intention of leaving England.

"Shall I conduct you to the ball-room, madame?" offering her his arm with just his usual manner, and seeking to banish from his voice all traces of recent emotion. "Your absence may be noticed; and, I believe, I am engaged for the next dance."

"Then go—pray go—and leave me here until it is all over. I am so flushed—so agitated yet—it will be well for me to remain quite alone for half an hour."

He left her, without another word; and Marguerite remained alone—alone in her beauty, her youth, and brilliancy, but with tearful eyes, and a feverish weight about her heart, more even than her rejection of Gaston was sufficient to occasion. In hearing words of love once more—although her heart no longer beat to them—the past seemed to have arisen again. These long, cold years of separation rolled away; her youthful passion, her glowing Kersaint life returned. She thought of the first hour when her heart acknowledged its love for Earnscliffe; of the day when they had parted—the promises she gave him then——

"Philip," she murmured, half aloud, "I *have* been true to you—I have loved no other."

"Marguerite," answered a low voice, very softly, but whose tone made her whole blood rush wildly to her heart. She looked up, and close before her stood Earnscliffe.

CHAPTER XLV.

ON his arrival in London, Philip met with a much warmer reception among his old friends than he had anticipated. Small jealousies, petty rivalries, are forgotten in five years; and, with our natural proneness towards the past, men remember only the brighter side of youthful friendships, and imagine they were infinitely warmer than was in reality the case.

He went straight to his uncle's house when he arrived; and the intense delight of the old man in once more seeing his boy, rewarded Philip sufficiently for his intention of making England henceforth his home. He was soon overwhelmed with invitations, and the soft eyes of many a young *debutante* looked kindly at him wherever he appeared. For he was now again eligible—the heir to Miles's not inconsiderable property (which the old man's good management and economical habits had greatly increased since the time of his failure); and, last of all, handsomer than ever, and with just such an amount of scandal connected with his name as serves to give additional interest to a man in the eyes of young ladies.

He never thought of meeting Marguerite. The name of her husband had escaped from his memory, or whether they ever lived in London; and when he heard the perfections of the lovely Mrs. Mortimer described, he little knew they spoke of Marguerite.

"She is as lovely as an angel, and as faultless," said one of his friends; "far too excellent for my taste! However, you will see her at A—— House this evening, and you can judge for yourself; perhaps she may be in your style."

"As I do not know what that is, I cannot answer. I generally look devoutly at every fair face I meet, and forget it in five minutes. At my age, men are past enthusiasm about beauty."

When Marguerite entered the salons of the Comtesse de P—— that evening, amidst the murmurs that her appearance always excited, Earnscliffe saw and recognised her in a moment. His astonishment may be conceived on meeting Marguerite St. John in the celebrated Mrs. Mortimer, and beholding into what glorious beauty her girlish promise had ripened; and an emotion, of which an hour before he would not have believed himself capable, smote his heart as he thought of all he had *once* been to her; and how completely the world and her success must now have effaced him from her memory. He observed her meeting with St. Leon; and, in her free, unconstrained manner, saw that there, at least, he had no rival, although, with the jealous quickness of a lover, he read, at once, on the face of the marquis, that his were more than ordinary attentions which every one pays to a lovely woman.

"She may not care for *him*," thought Philip; "but to how much devotion like his must she have been exposed! Fair though her fame is, among all the men in London who are at her feet, is it possible that no new fancy may have sullied the old love?"

He had next to watch Marguerite as she danced with some young Austrian officer, to whom she had just been introduced, and to mark her smiling, animated manner during the whole quadrille. Then to see St. Leon approach her again, and Marguerite take his arm, with an air of the most complete intimacy, laughing merrily as she told him of his solemn manner.

"She has become a coquette—she is like all other women, now!" thought Earnscliffe

fiercely. "How I detest this hot throng of people;" and he walked away from the ball room, and from Marguerite. Chance led him to the boudoir already mentioned: and the fresh, bright night tempted him into the garden without, where he paced hurriedly up and down, thinking over this sudden meeting with his old love, and the emotions that the sight of her awakened. "I laughed at it all this morning," he thought, "and said that men of my age could not feel the passion of boys; yet, my heart has beat more wildly at meeting Marguerite, than it did years ago when she first said she loved me; more than hers would now, I imagine, on seeing me. Our characters are changed from what they were in the Kersaint days! Marguerite is a woman of the world; and I shrink and tremble—but this is folly." He stopped short in his walk, and turned again towards the house. "I will return, and ask to be introduced to Mrs. Mortimer. If she treats me as an ordinary acquaintance, or feigns altogether to forget old times—let it be so! I will not wound her pride or disturb her composure by recalling them."

So he retraced his steps, and was about to enter the window, when he heard the sound of voices in low, eager conversation; and paused, as one instinctively does on interrupting an interview of this nature. His first thought was to withdraw as he came, and find another entrance to the house; but as he noiselessly turned with this intention, he caught the agitated words of Marguerite, —"Gaston, I have unwillingly deceived you;" and he knew in a second that it was her voice.

Fastidious almost to a fault, on smaller points of honor, Earnscliffe would not have stooped to listen even had his own dearest interest been concerned; but he was literally so spell-bound by Marguerite's voice, that it was some minutes before he could reflect upon his position, and that he was overhearing a conversation not intended for other ears. And in that time he had learnt all—her rejection of Gaston—the meek acknowledgment of her old girlish love—the half confession that that love still lingered.

"Unchanged!" he thought. "And still so gentle—so utterly distrustful of herself. Oh, Marguerite, that I could claim you for my own at last!"

He waited until St. Leon had gone, then silently advanced and gazed on her subdued mournful attitude — her drooping head; scarcely breathing, lest the sound should disturb her. But when he heard his name on her lips, he could remain silent no longer.

"Marguerite!"

She looked up—she knew him. To his last hour that expression of her face will never fade from Earnscliffe's memory. Delight —pure, passionate delight—like that of a mother's welcoming back the child she had believed dead to her, shone in every feature.

She clasped his hands—looked up into his face with the eager gaze of one recalling every line of the well-known features. "Philip! Philip!"

He was the first to recall anything of the present to her mind; and Marguerite unclasped his hands and drew slightly back.

"It is so sudden," she said, faintly. "Forgive me. I forgot everything—but seeing you again—imagine my surprise—"

"Imagine mine—on discovering that the celebrated beauty of all London was Marguerite St. John."

Both spoke somewhat abruptly, and with the hurried intonation of deep excitement; then, after a few seconds, they began to speak on indifferent subjects—as those always speak who meet like this, yet dare not give expression to their real thoughts. Marguerite asked how long he had been in England?—Earnscliffe inquired politely after her husband. But, even as they spoke, the eyes of each sought the other; each felt that, under that assumed calm, lay words of passionate joy at meeting—thoughts of that tender past which every look and word recalled.

"You are so changed, Phil—Mr. Earnscliffe."

"Yet you knew me instantly."

"I knew your voice; but, of course, I should have recognised you anywhere—at any time. You look older, Philip" (his name would come); "scarcely so grave, though, as you used to be. Ah! you were so pale when—when I last parted from you."

"I am only outwardly changed, Mrs. Mortimer."

"Only outwardly changed!" She looked up into his face as he bent towards her, and thought till this moment she had never seen the perfection of human expression before. How could she ever have called Gaston like him?—Gaston — Mr. Mortimer. With a sudden flash of thought, Marguerite remembered her husband, her home, and her gloomy forebodings of that evening before she started, and all the brightness of her dream faded.

"It is getting late," she hesitated. "I think I shall soon leave."

"So soon? After five years of separation, can you not spare me one half hour? Mrs. Mortimer, I have much to hear."

"Perhaps," hesitating still more, "you would call upon us. I am sure Mr. Mortimer would be glad to see you, and——"

"And you? Do you really wish me to come?"

"Oh, Philip! can you ask?"

The caressing tone and quick, upward look were so exactly Marguerite in her old girlish days, that Earnscliffe almost started. Her manner, had of course, acquired something of the conventional tone of the world; but at this moment she looked as childlike as on the first morning when she ran beside him on the sea-shore.

"How shall I ever remember to call you by your new name?" he whispered, as they returned towards the ball-room; and Marguerite's cheeks were yet glowing with the blush this remark called forth when they entered.

St. Leon saw them instantly. He was not dancing—indeed his engagement had been only a pretext for leaving her—but was standing alone, moodily thinking over the blow his vanity, and such love as he was capable of, had received. A fierce pang of jealousy shot through him when he saw Philip.

"Who is that stranger with Mrs. Mortimer?" he asked of an acquaintance near him.

"The little man with red hair, that she is speaking to?"

"Bah! the man on whose arm she leans."

"That? oh, mon cher! is it possible you do not recognise Earnscliffe the writer—just returned from the East? Mrs. Mortimer looks more animated than usual. It is not often celebrities take to each other so well!"

Gaston moved impatiently away; he guessed, by one of those intuitions peculiar to persons of his subtle nature, that he was looking at Marguerite's old lover; guessed it by Philip's quiet manner—by her face; and he saw, with fresh bitterness, the error into which he had fallen in believing that Marguerite loved him.

"She loves him still," he thought. "Poor little fool! and will call it friendship. Celui là me venger de son indifference!"

CHAPTER XLVI.

It was very late when Marguerite reached home, and the few hours intervening between her arrival and Mortimer's early breakfast were spent, not in sleep, but in agitated reveries over meeting with Philip, and anxious endeavors to form some right plan for the future. She would tell her husband, at all events; her truthful nature forbade concealment for a second. "Mr. Mortimer understands the world better than I do," she thought. "He will decide upon what terms I ought to meet Philip now—how great should be our intimacy." Marguerite knew not that, after all that was past, she had but one safeguard—to see him no more.

"Did you enjoy your ball as much as you expected, Marguerite?" said Mortimer at the breakfast-table, glancing up from the newspaper. "Lord, child, how pale you look! I shall be glad when all these dissipations are over, and I can take you off quietly to the sea-side."

"I am more tired than usual to-day; there was so much excitement last night, I mean." She grew nervous, and began to stir her untasted coffee. "I met——"

Mortimer, however, was not listening. He was particularly engaged in reading the City article, and, much as he loved Marguerite's voice, would just as soon it had been silent at that moment.

"I have something to tell you, sir!" with sudden energy.

"Indeed, my dear!" very unwillingly looking up from his paper, and keeping his forefinger on the spot where he left off. "What do you want now, little wife? wasn't your dress fine enough?"

Something in his manner so utterly forbade the delicate confidence she was about to make, that all Marguerite's courage forsook her, and scarcely knowing what she said, she turned abruptly to another subject.

"Cousin Gaston is going to France, Mr. Mortimer."

"The best place for him, too. He has been discontented and out of humor for months past. He will get into place under the Emperor, no doubt, staunch loyalist though he used to be: a Frenchman's politics can always turn round at a day's notice. When is he coming to say good-bye?"

"I don't know sir—perhaps not at all; I said something to him last night which he did not like, I am afraid." Marguerite quite regained her composure in speaking of Gaston.

"Um! I can imagine what it was. He has been hovering about you too long, even for a cousin. These young Frenchmen have not our feelings upon honor and good faith. Is this the news, then? Cousin Gaston's departure?"

With a burning blush, Marguerite forced herself at length to bring out Philip's name. "She had met an old friend—a friend of her father's—Mr. Earnscliffe, the author."

"Indeed, child! I never knew your father had any English friends since you were born. However, I am glad you have met some one to talk over old times with. Just let me finish my City news, and you shall tell me all about him."

The utter unsuspicion of her husband made Marguerite's task more difficult to perform. She sat watching his face as he read, and wondering how, with his strict, almost stern ideas upon such points, he would receive the intelligence that, years ago, as a mere child, *his* wife had had a lover—a married man, too, even then—and that she had now met him again in the world!

"Sadbrook Brothers, by Jove!" exclaimed Mortimer, with a vigorous descent of his large hand upon the table, which made the Sevres breakfast-service start from its aristocratic composure. "I said it—I knew it—for days past, and no one believed me! Gone—aye! to everlasting smash! They will not pay a shilling in the pound, and I

was fool enough to keep one of their bills, against my own conviction. I beg your pardon, Marguerite, but I must start for town at once. Thank God! it's only for a thousand pounds; but poor M——s will be let in for half he is worth. Ring the bell, my dear; don't you see I am in a hurry?"

Marguerite shrank aside as Mortimer, his red face all flurried with the news of Messrs. Shadbrook Brothers' failure, bustled from the room. He forgot to say good-bye to her even, in his excitement; and five minutes afterwards she heard the carriage roll off that took him to the City.

And so ended her attempted confidence respecting her old lover. She had not the courage to attempt the subject again. And Mortimer never knew how far more important to him were the trembling words that hung impending on Marguerite's lips that morning than any City failure could have been, even though it involved the loss of a thousand-pound bill!

Earnscliffe's last words, the night before, were—"Then, to-morrow, I may call, if you will allow it;" and Marguerite passed all the forenoon in a feverish, unsettled state of excitement, expecting him; half regretting, at one moment, that she had not spoken to Mortimer; then glad, poor child! that she had been silent—that once, at least, she was to have the exquisite happiness of being again with Philip.

Philip was shown into Marguerite's morning-room, where she usually received visitors, and, after a few minutes' pause, to recover her composure, she joined him.

She shook hands with him in silence; then seated herself at some distance, her face turned aside, her hands clasped together in just her old timid gesture. Once more with him she felt that all her acquired manner of society vanished; she was exactly as she had been at sixteen. "I have watched for you all the morning—I mean—I——" stopping suddenly short as she recollected how she was betraying herself.

"This room looks so like you!" said Earnscliffe, pitying her evident embarrassment: "the books, the flowers, the absence of all those artificial nothings with which most women think it necessary to be surrounded. I could fancy myself at Kersaint."

"Ah! but this is not my room. There I have indeed all the dear old books from home; this is called my morning-room, but I receive visitors here. I could see no stranger in *my* room."

"Then I shall not be admitted?"

"Yes, I should like you to see my father's books. You are not a stranger, Mr. Earnscliffe."

"Nearly so; after five years, old recollections are as nothing with most people. Those only who possess a peculiarly happy organization can forget."

" Happy ! " she turned her full gaze on his face. " Happy ! my life would be utterly barren if there were no past."

" In the world—in society—who thinks of it ? "

" In the world—in society ? But *that* out of one's existence ? In the early morning— of a summer's evening—of a winter's night— oh, Philip ! in all the times that make up our real life, the past is everything. It is the poetry of the present."

" To old people it may be so; but with the young, all golden dreams lie in the future."

" Ah ! I spoke only for myself." returned Marguerite, sadly. " I never look onward."

There was a moment's silence; then Marguerite resumed. " Will you let me show you my garden? There is one part of it I should like you to see, although it is too early in the season for it to look perfection."

She rose, and opened the door of a glass alcove, leading into an immense conservatory, where tier rose above tier of the rarest hot-house plants—all grouped and arranged by one of the first gardeners in England. She then led him through a winding path for some yards; and, turning round, said—" This is my miniature of the forest lake at home, where the water-lilies grew. Do you remember it, or see any resemblance ? "

It was a clear pool of water, artificial, of course, but natural enough in appearance— ferns and water-plants were planted round it, all of the same kinds as really grew in Brittany; and a profusion of water-lilies, not yet in flower, floated on the surface.

" I remember well," said Philip; " it was our first walk together."

Oh ! dangerous conversations, when every sentence commences with, " I remember ! " They stayed long by the little lake, talking of old days, old scenes—but both tacitly avoiding all allusions to their last parting, or anything that had happened since then.

" Poor Bello was with us that day by the lake ! " said Marguerite. " I fancy now that I can see him darting off into the forest for game. Do you recollect him ? "

" Perfectly well ; is he still living ? "

" No; he died about a year ago. I grieved for his death more than I should have thought it possible to grieve for an animal. But then he was all that remained to me of my home ; and he was so faithfully attached to me, up to the very last."

" And your home—Kersaint—who has it now ? "

" Mr. Mortimer would not let it be sold, when he saw how much I cared for it. Manon lives there with poor, half-witted Bruno. She writes me a strange letter twice a year, quite her own style and orthography, but full of affection and all the simple news that she knows I care for—about the peasants and the garden. Yes ; Kersaint is still mine. We have often talked of making an excursion there ; and I do think this summer Mr. Mortimer will take me. Poor Manon ! can you not imagine her wild delight ? but you look so very thoughtful, Mr. Earnscliffe ; what are you dreaming about ? "

" I was thinking what a happy man your husband must be ; able to forestall every wish of yours, and read the pleasure in your face for his reward ! "

" I believe Mr. Mortimer is happy," she answered ; " most kind and generous, I know that he is. But tell me "—seeing the clouded expression still upon his face—" does this mimic lake really remind you of our forests —of Brittany ? "

" Yes ; I am only too much reminded," said Philip, " of things it would be far better to forget."

" Yet you have seen so much since, I wonder that you can have such a good recollection of poor Kersaint. You have been everywhere — Vienna, Rome, Jerusalem, Thebes—while I have seen nothing but London, and a few watering-places all these years. Which place—I mean which city—that you have visited, would you like to live in best ? "

" Rome. At least it suited my mood best at that time ; and my friend Neville was with me there. But," added Philip, looking steadily at her, " my recollections of Rome are bitter ones ; for it was at Rome I first heard of your marriage ! "

Marguerite turned away, and plucked tiny pieces from the grass beside her very quickly. " You must have been surprised," she said, in a low voice.

" It was very soon, that was all. I expected it would be so, after a lapse of time ; but it *was* soon, Marguerite."

" I—I—should have written ; but I did not know where to send my letter. I did not want you to hear of it first through the papers, without any explanation. I should have liked you to know all the circumstances, and how very unhappy the life was that I left, when I married ! "

" You acted perfectly wisely, of course. My feelings, I confess, were intensely selfish ones. I ought to have been glad to hear that you had again a home and protector, but I could not feel so. As I said, my recollections of Rome are bitter ones ! In ten days after hearing of your marriage, I left it for ever."

" For ever ! shall you not, at some future time, return to Italy ? I cannot imagine your living long in England."

" Well, I cannot imagine myself living long anywhere. I am so accustomed to change and unquiet that—— However, I shall now have different objects in England to those that I have had before. Perhaps, they may fill the void of life better than any of the former ones ! "

" Do you care much for going to the opera now ? Oh ! how you used to tell me about it, and how vainly I tried to picture it all. It is my greatest amusement, my *real* pleasure."

"Then I am sure I shall care for it," answered Philip. "But I have forgotten all about operas, of late years. Do you remember how I told you once that your voice only wanted cultivation, to be the first in England? I was right, you see; I have heard of your renown."

"Yes—I sing well, I know; but my singing does not give me greater pleasure than when I could not tell a note, and sang only wild ballads to my father——"

"And to me. I remember well the first evening I ever heard you sing to the guitar—with the sunset falling on your face through the open window, and I thought it was the face of the Madonna, out of some old painting. Have you quite forgotten?"

"And how you stole away afterwards, and I watched you pacing up and down the terrace, in the twilight. Generally, I ran after you myself, I remember, in those long summer evenings. Oh! Mr. Earnscliffe, what must you have thought? I was so very free in manner; so very different to what I now know is correct for young ladies to be."

"Shall I tell you what I thought?"

"No, no; it would only be a compliment."

"Of which you hear so many, that you are tired?"

"Of them, and the people that pay them too. It is so delightful to speak again to some one who is a real friend, and with whom one can talk of subjects of greater interest than people and parties, and all the repeated nothings which form common conversation."

"But, surely, you have some friends who do not come under such general denunciation?"

"None; with perhaps one exception, that I can call a friend."

"And that exception?"

"Well, I think Lady Millicent Gore cares for me more than any one else."

"And the marquis de St Leon?"

"Cousin Gaston? Oh, yes; he and I were great friends. But he is not like you; he is conventional, and never can see things quite as I do. Still, I have liked Gaston; the tie of relationship is something in itself, and it was so unexpected to meet with a relation of my mother's, that my heart warmed towards him from the first. But he is leaving England for good, now; and——"

"You will miss him extremely, I suppose, Mrs. Mortimer?"

"No—I mean it is better Gaston should go—that is——Mr. Earnscliffe! an idea is flashing upon me." Marguerite's cheek became crimson, and a whole forest of tiny leaves were soon lying upon her white dress. "Last night, when you found me alone—had you heard?—did you hear Gaston's voice?"

"Most unwillingly," replied Philip, "I confess that I heard some of a conversation not intended for other ears. Something I heard before I had time to withdraw; then, I caught the tone of your voice, and forgot everything else in listening to that again!"

"And you heard——, tell me! I would rather know!" cried Marguerite, in her generosity only thinking of Gaston's secret; "tell me what you heard him say."

"I scarcely heard the voice of your companion, and have not the faintest recollection of his words. I thought but of your voice."

"That is right. Gaston would not have liked a stranger to hear what he was saying. His political career in France is just opening, and we were talking of things important to him, and——"

"Not to you?"

She looked up quickly, and saw from the expression of his face that he had heard enough to guess the nature of their interview; and her eyes sank with shame as she recollected that her own last words contained the confession of her former love.

"I have forgotten all about it," she stammered. "Let us speak of something else."

How lovely she looked at this moment; resting in an attitude of the most excessive grace upon the turf-bank where they were sitting together—her face turned half-aside, her eyes downcast, unconsciously pulling to pieces the petals of some daisies that she had plucked.

"Your own flower, wild-Marguerite. Will you not give me one now, as you used to do in bygone times?"

"No, I was a child then. Children may give or say anything. I will give you this piece of jessamine," taking it from her waist-belt; "and it is a very early and rare kind, and much better worth having than my poor namesake. But I must confess I prefer all wild flowers, however common."

"Do you remember our lesson in bouquet-making?" said Philip, approaching nearer to receive the flower, "that bright May morning? and how you told me——"

And so on, with those endless recollections and replies—so tiring for other people—so interesting to those concerned—until the sun warned Marguerite that the afternoon was quickly passing.

"I must show you the library and the old books," she cried, as she rose; I had no idea the time had passed so quickly."

"And I have kept you out in this cold east wind," replied Philip, as they walked slowly towards the house. "You are much too thinly clad for our wretched English spring."

"I never wear a bonnet. It was part of my education, you must remember, to brave all weathers; and England has a better climate than Brittany——"

By comparison, perhaps. I hate all these northern climates, after the warm south, where every breath one draws is an actual enjoyment, and life flows on so sweetly one does not know that it is indeed passing."

"Yet you have left this delicious climate?" observed Marguerite, smiling.

"I was alone in Italy, Mrs. Mortimer; I rather spoke of what life might be there, than of what mine actually was. Alone, existence is much the same everywhere."

Marguerite did not answer; and entering the house together she led Earnscliffe upstairs into her little library. The oak panneling—the plain book-shelves—all were in exact imitation of her father's library at Kersaint; and his own books, with a few of Marguerite's favorites were on the shelves.

"In this room my in-door life is passed," she said. "I read here for hours every day. Take this seat—no—not where you can look out and see the difference between Wimbledon Common and the green sea at home—but here turned towards the fireplace—and now, fancy yourself at Kersaint!"

"May I, indeed, do so?" was Philip's reply, and the blood rose crimson in Marguerite's cheek at the tone. It was in the library she had told him that, whatever happened, she would never love any other but him; and she felt that the whole scene must return upon his recollection.

"I did not mean——Oh, Philip! I can keep up this appearance no longer," she exclaimed, passionately. "Let us speak once of old days, and then, be silent for ever! Remember how young I was—how ignorant of the world——!"

"Marguerite," interrupted Philip, rising and taking her hand, his own trembling as it met hers; "do not speak as though the past contained anything you could wish forgotten. If there was wrong, is was my own: if there should be a remorse, it is for me. You have always been as you are now—most blameless."

"But Philip, hear me; for this once I must speak. You know how—then—I loved you," the words came reluctantly from her lips, "and when we talk so much of old times, it recalls old feelings to my heart, that *should* have died long ago; and it is wrong, for I am married now—married to one whom I respect more than all on earth, and I must not have a thought apart from him. Will you help me in not recurring to the past? I am weak still, you see, and I look to you for assistance."

She spoke quickly, nervously, and changed color every moment. Ignorant that she was betraying to Earnscliffe that which a woman of the world would have hid from her own heart, namely, that his influence over her was as powerful as ever, she said simply what she believed it was her duty to say; hoping that, having done so in this first interview, their future intercourse would be placed upon a right footing.

"Help me, Philip, in not recurring vainly to the past, or wishing any part of life undone. We have both so much to make us happy still—you in your genius and ambition, and I——"

"You hesitate, Marguerite."

"I, in the kindness and affection of Mr. Mortimer," she added, but with an effort. "In the home that he has given me—in striving to make him happy in his old age. Tell me that you think it right that we should agree to forget the past?"

"Agree not to speak of it rather! it can never be forgotten. The one bright spot out of my whole existence—those few short months, when however guilty, I loved—was near you; no Marguerite! it is impossible me to say, 'I can forget it.' If any recollection of that time makes it bitter for you to see me now, I will never intrude upon you again. Tell me to leave you, Marguerite—tell me that as a married woman there is wrong in your being with me again; but do not ask me to forget the past, or to feign an indifference that I can never feel!"

She looked up in his face; her heart thrilled at his words (cold and dull when written, but oh, how eloquent spoken by Earnscliffe!) and, wrong or right, let those judge who have been likewise tempted—Marguerite could not bid him see her no more. What weight had thoughts of duty or prudence as she listened? The five lethargic years she had passed without Philip were gone; and they were again together as in the earliest, fondest days of their love. She fancied the beatings of the waves came in through the open windows—her father smiling at her from his old place by the fire!

"Philip, I can never ask you to leave me again—never believe that there is wrong in seeing you."

"Oh, Marguerite! you do not know the happiness those words hold out to me. After the loneliness of years, to be once more near you—occasionally to be allowed to visit you, hear your voice, gaze silently upon your face, will be delight I can scarcely realise. But you look flushed and tired, my——Mrs. Mortimer, I mean. Tell me that you are not wearied with my long visit?"

"How could I be wearied with you? I am flushed—but not with fatigue. Are you really going so soon?" as Earnscliffe rose with signs of departure. "You have not looked at the books yet, or at my drawings—I have learnt to draw since I saw you last —or at a portrait of my mother that I wished you to see. Do stay a little while longer!"

And Earnscliffe stayed until the golden sunset flooded the room, and the timepiece struck seven, and the hour of his dinner-party in town was over. And all this time every word of Marguerite's, every gesture, every wave of her dress, as she flitted lightly before him with her books and drawings, was recalling his old passion, and making his pulse once more tremble like a boy's—he—who yesterday declared he had outlived love! And poor Marguerite! safe as she believed them both, after their candid avowal and her own resolutions, looked up with her frank, confiding gaze, and spoke unreservedly as ever, and once even touched his hand with her old familiar gesture, and believed that it was all friendship.

———

CHAPTER XLVIII.

" How pale you look, Marguerite! and so dreadfully nervous! You scarcely hear a word I am saying. All your gaieties are not improving your beauty! "

It was Miss Georgy who spoke. After remaining for some months indignant with Marguerite, she at last bethought herself that Mrs. Mortimer's own parties, and an occasional place in her opera-box, were infinitely better than nothing. So (about a month later than Philip's first visit to Wimbledon), Miss Georgy came down unexpectedly one fine day, to see " dear Marguerite; " prepared, as she said, to forgive everything, and have a long, friendly morning together.

The standing commencement of these " mornings " of female affection being for one friend to say something mortifying to the other, Miss de Burgh had opened proceedings by commenting very plainly upon her young relative's ill looks. But Marguerite, fitful in spirits, after the now daily excitement of meeting Philip, and weary from the effects of a feverish, sleepless night, cared nothing for any comments on her beauty.

" I must be pale I know," was the reply, " for I feel far from well, and so weary "—leaning her head down on the silken pillows of the sofa. " I believe I go out too much."

" Ah, yes! " returned Georgy, with one or two nods; " but I always foresaw it all, as you know. I am not surprised. I always told you," she added, " what it would be, if you and Earnscliffe ever met again."

" Georgy "—her pale cheek coloring up in a second—" I don't understand you. I ——"

" My dear Marguerite, the time is past for any excessive innocence now. After a flirtation with your cousin, and now with all London talking of you and Earnscliffe, simplicity is almost out of character."

" All London talking of me! Georgy, you must jest."

" Not in the least, dear; I hear your name a great deal oftener than is creditable for a married woman, especially when in connection with a man of the notoriety of Earnscliffe."

" What can they say of me? Who can be sufficiently interested to mark my actions? "

" About that I do not know; what they say, however, is very soon told—that you are carrying on a most desperate flirtation! However, it does not signify much, as long as your husband hears nothing of it," she added with a laugh.

" As long as your husband hears nothing! " These careless words awakened a vague chill of terror in Marguerite's heart. Could the world be really speaking evil of her? Could there be a chance of Mortimer's hearing it? She felt that any anger her own explanation might have awakened would be nothing compared to that.

Georgy read her face directly; and, for reasons of her own, repented she had said so much. She did not wish Marguerite and her husband to have scenes and explanations, or leave London just then.

" Oh, I was only half in earnest," she cried quickly; " but you take everything so extremely au serieux. English people always invent scandal about each other, you know; it's one of our national peculiarities. But Mr. Mortimer is not likely to hear the on dits of your world. He never goes out with you, does he? "

" Never! " repeated Marguerite, sadly. " I go out entirely alone."

" Well, it's trying for you; but then, from the way you used to talk, we all thought you were quite removed from the temptation of ordinary mortals. 'Gaieties had no charm for you.' 'You liked to look old for Mortimer's sake,' and so on. I always knew, though, that it could not last. Are you going to Mrs. Lorrimer's fête? "

" I don't believe I shall go. I dislike those long, day-light entertainments, especially now that I am not well."

" But you can go late," said Georgy. " There is to be a ball, al fresco, and the grounds illuminated, and I know not what besides."

" I wish you were going in my place, Georgy."

" Dear Marguerite, how kind of you! But that is impossible, you know; one person cannot accept the invitation of another. If you were going, it would be different."

" Oh, if I were going, I could take you easily. I know Mrs. Lorrimer so well, that I should not scruple to bring you with me."

" Ah! dear Marguerite, do go, for my sake," pleaded Georgy, in her softest manner. I have had such a dull season; and mamma cares less for anything but her own fancied complaints every day."

Marguerite would infinitely have preferred remaining away; but Georgy looked so eager, she did not like to refuse, especially, after the cold feeling that had lately existed between them.

" Well, as you like," she answered. " What day is it for? I have forgotten all about it."

" June the first, dear; that will be next Friday—in three days. Marguerite, how good-natured of you to take me! What must I wear?" Georgy's manner was so child-like, it was difficult to believe that she was ten years older than her intended *chaperon*.

"Wear? Oh, Georgy, I have so many dresses that I have never worn. I wish you would take one of them. It would be really a kindness; for this will probably be my last gaiety this season, and by next year they will be old fashioned. Eulalie could make any alteration you liked."

Miss de Burgh was not too proud to accept the offer, and accompanied her to her dressing-room; where, after a long inspection of numbers of costly toilettes, she chose the most expensive she could see, and Marguerite's last bonnet from Paris, with the small addition of French gloves and sleeves.

"Are you quite sure you can spare them?" said Georgy, after Mademoiselle Eulalie had carefully packed up her spoil.

"Oh, yes. Indeed, I care nothing for gay dresses myself. It is Mr. Mortimer who insists upon my having all these rich things."

"And yet, with all your extravagances, you seem to have plenty left for charity. I see your name at the head of every list and subscription."

"Yes, out of our superfluity. We feel nothing that we give. I have never spoken to a poor person since I married."

"Of course not. In your position, and living in London, or near it, you can't do those things as though you were a curate's wife, on a hundred a-year, in the country."

"So Mr. Mortimer says; and of course he is right——"

"Talking of country curates, Marguerite," interrupted Georgy, "do you remember your admirer—Mr. Ignatius Shirley?"

"Who said I was an Anglican? Yes, I remember him."

"Will you believe that, after all his profession, and shaving his hair close to his head, and intoning the service, and saying (when mamma demanded an explanation of his attentions to me) that the Catholic priesthood should not marry, he has gone completely round. His new rector was Low Church, and very rich, with one daughter; and the mean little wretch was in Broad Church in a week, then as Low as possible, in the hopes of getting her. However, I am happy to say, the girl married some one else; and Shirley has just been well pulled up by his new bishop—who is an Anglican again—for saying in one of his sermons that 'baptism was a pleasing form.'"

"And what has become of your own opinions, Georgy? You went even further than Mr. Shirley, I remember."

"I am developing," said Miss de Burgh, solemnly.

"Into what?" asked Marguerite, to whom the phrase was new.

"Is it possible that you are ignorant of the beautiful theory of development? Oh, Marguerite! my future life will show it you."

"And who is your preceptor in this new —system?" Marguerite inquired, aware that without a priest no faith would do for Georgy.

"My present counsellor is the Comte de Montravers—a man to whom England will yet owe her regeneration. We shall meet him I trust, on Friday."

"I am surprised that those to whom such serious questions are all-important can care for the frivolties of society," Marguerite remarked.

"Yes," returned Georgy, with a pitying shake of the head, "that is how the world speaks, knowing nothing of the beautiful elasticity which is our chief characteristic. We go into society for society's sake—not our own."

Marguerite wondered, as this was the case, that Georgy should care for Brussels lace, and Paris bonnets; but concluded it was part of the elasticity she spoke of.

"But I never dance now," said Miss de Burgh. "What I can, without singularity renounce of these follies, I do. Is that your lunch bell, Marguerite? I must make an early dinner with you. To-day is a fast, and I attend complin."

They went down to the dining-room; and, from Miss de Burgh's vigorous onslaught upon chicken pie and jelly, Marguerite concluded that fasting was an exercise to which she had not yet yet "developed."

"What time shall you call for me?" she inquired, when her little meal was finished. "Let us go late; the effect is much better on entering fresh, and when other people are beginning to be tired."

"Certainly—we shall have fewer hours of it—five, do you think?"

"Oh! at the latest, Marguerite. Remember it is an *al fresco* affair, and the dancing will commence early. Suppose you say that you leave your house at four; by the time you have picked me up, and we drive to Richmond, it will be late enough, in all conscience. Good bye."

"But you do not walk, surely?"

"No. I came—I was obliged to come— in the omnibus."

"Then wait, at least, till I order the carriage round for you. I am going to ride on horseback this afternoon."

"Oh, you dear, kind creature!"

And after more kisses, and much amiability, Georgy took her leave, to be in time for complin; but not forgetting to have Marguerite's presents carefully stowed away in the carriage.

————

CHAPTER XLVIII.

MARGUERITE said rightly that Earnscliffe had much to make life desirable in his genius and ambition. He had returned, no longer a dreaming boy, with morbid feelings towards one class because they had slighted him, towards another because they had misappreciated his books. Great and settled principles had dawned upon him in this interval; and, as at thirty every man must strengthen his onward or retrograde path, the turning point had arrived from whence Philip's was to be recognised as one of the leading intellects of the day.

The downfall of a ministry—only held together because any change at that crisis was dangerous—was imminent; and, under a new administration, Earnscliffe's intention was to enter Parliament, and take an active part in the social reform of which he was now a supporter.

Meantime, he went as much as ever into society, and soon had an only too engrossing object there—an object before which, for the time, even his own political advancement was secondary. In three weeks from the day of their first meeting, Philip knew that he loved Marguerite with a passion compared to which even his former love for her seemed tame and poor. He strove with it—he felt that it was madness—putting aside any higher consideration of religion—that, even if Marguerite were to become his, the misery of both would be sealed; yet he could not resist temptation by leaving London, or seeing her no more. He loved her beyond the bounds of prudence and reason. He had not learnt in his youth that where reason stops, paralysed and forceless, a higher principle can conquer; and that only religion—warm, heartfelt religion—can combat the frailty of our erring nature, and still the wild dictates of earthly desire. He had to learn it by a bitterer lesson than any which his life had yet taught him.

Earnscliffe went rarely to Wimbledon, and when he did so his visits were short. Unlike St. Leon, he shrank from receiving the hearty grasp of Mortimer's hand, his ever ready hospitality, his cordial and frequent invitations. The absence of all distrust or suspicion in the old man, his utter confidence in Marguerite, were irresistible appeals to one of Philip's generous nature. Although he had not the courage to withdraw from the wrong itself, he shunned communication with the man whom his conscience told him he was injuring, and at last only met Marguerite in the parks, or at parties and the opera, but then these meetings occurred, at the least, every five days out of the seven!

"I hear grave things of you," said his friend Neville, one morning when Philip was alone with him in his studio. Neville lived in a good house now; and was, according to his own ideas, a very rich man. "Every one is coupling your name with that of Mrs. Mortimer. Surely you would not let the fair fame of the woman you were once ready to die for, be sacrificed to gratify your vanity? Whatever are your faults, Phil, that is unlike you."

"Who mentioned my name with hers?" exclaimed Philip, angrily, "Who dared to breathe one word in detraction of Mrs. Mortimer? Neville, you are bound to tell me."

"My good friend, be cool! When you are devoted to Mrs. Mortimer at every party where you meet her, are always seen in her box at the opera, or riding beside her in the park, I suppose—ignorant as I am of such things—that it is just to call you her very warm admirer, and not unmerited to speak lightly of herself. Married Englishwomen don't encourage these innocent friendships, you know, as they do in France or Italy."

Philip made no reply. Something in Neville's plain way of speaking brought the real truth before him; and he shuddered to think that Marguerite's name was being sullied by all the idle men and loungers in clubs, and that he should be the cause.

"These things are incomprehensible to me," pursued Neville, throwing himself back in his chair, and sending forth a perfect volcano of smoke from his short meerschaum. "The kind of entanglement into which you are now entering is a madness I can neither understand nor pity. *Yours*, mind—I pity her, by Jove! The world is wide, there are hundreds of women of all ages and conditions whom you might easily win, yet you still pursue and hunt down this poor little creature, who very nearly lost herself for you before, when she was a child. Leave her, Phil! How is it all to end? that is what I ask. By her deserting her home and husband for you? Oh, you turn away! but such is the conclusion of this kind of attachment. Then—what is the result? At thirty—just when your life is really beginning—you are saddled with a woman for ever, whom it would be infamy to desert, yet whose presence, after six months, will be a literal burden to you. A woman,' uncorrupt in heart, yet classed by the world with the vilest of her sex—always in tears, always devoured by self-reproach that she would vainly seek to hide—such would be your household companion. Suppose a step further—there is a divorce, or the husband dies, and you marry her—as a man of honor you must do so—worse and worse still! You are now married to a woman society will never receive; you can never forget what she was (what you made her—mind!) before she was your wife; you can never feel respect for her, or she for you. If she is still young and beautiful you will be jealous of your most intimate friend; remember the fair face with which she deceived her first husband, when she was encouraging you; and never be alone with her writing desk without the secret wish to break it open, and discover if the same sort of notes are lying there which you remember to have existed in the time of Mr. Mortimer, defunct."

" Good heavens, Neville! have you done?" interrupted Philip, impatiently. "I never heard any human being talk so fast or so incessantly as yourself. You go on with your imaginings until you make me out a thorough villain, betrayer, seducer—almost murderer. I wish you would reflect upon what you are saying."

"It would be well for you to do so, my friend!" replied Neville. "However, some day you will remember my counsels, and wish you had attended to them."

" Neville!" exclaimed Philip, springing up, and speaking very earnestly, " you misunderstand me altogether. I would give my right hand sooner than Marguerite should be ill thought of. But you know not all the history of her past life and mine; you can, however, guess my feelings, for you have seen her. Tell me what I ought to do—how act as a man of honor."

" How act with honor, Earnscliffe? Leave her at once—how can there be a question? Break it off directly."

" And her feelings?"

" Oh! her feelings are already engaged then, too? It is even worse than I thought. I will tell you what, Phil, no half-measures will avail now. Leave town immediately— go abroad again—to Scotland—anywhere you will, and stay there till the whole affair is past. When you return, it will be comparatively easy to avoid the snare once escaped— feign another love, for example. Are you listening to a single word I am saying, mon cher, or only meditating, after the common manner of human nature, how you will not act upon the advice you asked for?"

" I have heard you," replied Philip, slowly, "and know that you are thus far right. It must be broken off at once, or never."

" And between these two you hesitate? Between common sense and common honor, and eternal——"

" Neville!" he interrupted, abruptly, "there are some points upon which no third person can give an opinion. Thank you for your good intentions, and—good morning;" and before his friend could speak again he had quitted the room.

" And I have lost half my morning," soliloquised the artist when he was gone. Oh! the folly of arguing with a man in love."

That evening Marguerite was at the opera, more fresh and youthful-looking than ever, in a white dress and natural flowers (Earnscliffe had said how much he preferred seeing her without her rubies and diamonds, and of late she had never worn them when Mortimer would allow her to appear in public dressed according to her own simple taste). During the second act, she saw Philip enter a box on the other side of the house, and seat himself beside one of the youngest beauties of the season, to whom he began paying—or appearing to pay—the most marked attention. Perhaps he was already trying to follow Neville's advice—perhaps he wished to test how Marguerite would brook divided homage. She was, however, devoid of all small jealousy; and thinking it quite natural Philip should sometimes like to talk to others beside herself, she smiled and chatted with just her usual manner to the bevy of box-loungers, who approached her between the acts.

" That Eastern man," lisped Mr. Grottiesley, or " little Grot," as his friends called him—a young guardsman, with straw-colored moustache and moonlike face, who had long wished to be one of Marguerite's admirers. " What is his name? Earnton, Earnley——"

" Mr. Earnscliffe, perhaps."

" Oh!—ah!—he really has something to say, I suppose; Miss Carlton Vere appears actually listening as he talks to her?"

" Yes," replied Marguerite, smiling, " one always remembers, at least, what Mr. Earnscliffe is talking about, which is not the case with every one, I must confess."

" Oh!—Ah!—yes!—tombs, I suppose, and all that—ah!—dreadful bore, men who have been to Thebes and Petræa, and such places, and talk about what they have seen. Now I have been all over the world—Egypt —Jerusalem—Crimea—St. Petersburgh — but you would not guess it, would you?"

Oh no!" Marguerite answered, in her most simple manner. " I should have thought you had only just left school. Is it possible that you have really travelled?"

" Miss Carlton Vere is not half as pretty as she is usually called," remarked a friend, who was listening with pleasure to little Grot's failure. " Do you think anything of her, Mrs. Mortimer?"

" Indeed I do!" replied Marguerite; " hers is just the style I admire—finely chiselled features, and pale, alabaster complexion."

" A poet's beauty, in short. Earnscliffe seems to consider it so."

But Marguerite's calm expression did not vary for a second; and the young guardsman who disliked tombs remarked to his friend, when they had left her box—

" That woman is the deepest hand I ever knew; she never even changed color at my sarcasm about that puppy, Earnscliffe."

Philip, meanwhile, was absent and distrait. He was intently watching Marguerite all the time that he seemed to be so attentive to the lady at his side, and wondering how she could be so happy and smiling without him—

nay, more, while he was apparently devoted to a fresh object. Had he, after all, given her credit for deeper feeling than she possessed?—would the idea of parting from him again affect her as deeply as he had told Neville? His impatience soon overcame all previous resolution; and, feigning some excuse, he actually started up in the midst of one of Miss Carlton Vere's prettiest young-lady remarks, and came quickly round to Marguerite's box.

She heard the door softly open, and knew, without turning round, that it was Earnscliffe (at all times she could feel his presence without seeing him.) They had met already that afternoon in the park, and Philip seated himself without any salutation, in the farthest corner of the box, where the deep shadow screened him from observation, while Marguerite still kept her eyes upon the stage. Without exactly knowing why, she felt embarrassed, and waited for him to speak first.

"Is it possible," he thought, as he scanned her features, "that she is only trifling with me?—coquetting, like any other woman, and as for ought I know to the contrary—she may actually have done with that French cousin already?" From the beginning of time, whoever has loved has been unjust, at the slightest breath of jealousy. "She did not look—when talking to that young fool just now—as though it would break her heart to part with me. However, it shall be put to the test."

After a few minutes' silence, Philip said, shortly, and with no preparation—"Mrs. Mortimer, if your attention is not too much engrossed with the music, I have come to wish you good bye!"

She started round and faltered—"Good-bye! Oh, Mr. Earnscliffe! only for a short - —"

"For months—a year, perhaps—my absence will be quite indefinite.

She looked at him in utter astonishment as he spoke in this cold, strange tone—looked at him with compressed lips, tearful, dilated eyes, as no coquette in this world ever looked.

"Another parting!" she murmured; "oh! how shall I bear it?"

Then she turned away, and Philip saw her hand clasp tightly over her side, with the old gesture that any sudden pain called forth; and at once he was re-assured of poor Marguerite's sincerity. "Could he leave her after this?—was he justified in breaking off their friendship, now that he was certain of having awakened all the long-buried love of that gentle nature?"

"Marguerite, can my actions indeed affect you so much? Will you bid me remain?"

She looked round, very slowly this time, and, without saying a word, held out her hand to him. Earnscliffe took it; its pressure thrilled to his very heart, and from that

moment all further irresolution on his part was over, all fainter warnings of his better nature unheeded—he felt that Marguerite must be his.

"How could you so trifle with me?" she asked, after a time. "You could not indeed mean to leave again, when you have only just returned to England, and are so occupied with your political prospects? How foolish I was to believe you! But these are cruel jests! I have too few real friends to bear the thought of losing one of them."

"You could really feel pain at parting with me?"

"Really! Oh, Mr. Earnscliffe, I know how badly I dissemble—you must have read it on my face!"

"I am afraid to read your face now—afraid lest my own wishes should read differently to the truth—afraid even to read the truth."

"You speak strangely to-night; I scarcely understand you."

"Shall I be plainer, Marguerite?"

"Oh, hush! we are not listening to the sweetest notes of the Piccolomini"—and she turned from him, blushing.

"I only hear one voice," replied Earnscliffe; and during the remainder of the opera neither spoke again—but, for them, silence was now only too eloquent.

When the last act was over, Marguerite rose to leave (she never stayed for the ballet), and Philip, as usual, escorted her to her carriage. They had to wait some time before it came up, and both seemed constrained and disinclined to speak. Earnscliffe dared not trust himself to do so, and Marguerite, without knowing why, felt herself trembling nervously as she held his arm. She tried a dozen times to make some common-place remark to break the silence, but each time the words died on her lips; and at length, with an effort, she exclaimed suddenly, with a forced laugh, just what she least intended to say—

"I wonder what makes us both so dull to-night?"

Earnscliffe bent down and whispered—something that made his companion shrink and turn cold.

"No, no—impossible. I cannot listen to such words, even from you."

"Then why ask me not to leave you? We can continue no longer as we are now; either our intimacy must cease at once or—" his voice became so low that only Marguerite's ear could catch its sound.

They were standing apart from the crowd, and where a deep shadow fell across them both, but Earnscliffe could see the whiteness of her face, as she looked up to his, and how her lips quivered.

"Never," she replied, slowly, and as though each word was wrung from her with pain. "I will never leave him, nor forget all that I owe to him. No, not for your sake."

"Then I have been mistaken," said Philip. "I believed that you loved me; that, loving me, you would make any sacrifice, even that of name or position, for me. I believed you incapable of trifling with me—as you had already done with your cousin Gaston," he added, sarcastically. He had not anticipated so instant a rejection, and his pride was wounded by her tone.

"Gaston!" echoed Marguerite. "You accuse me of trifling with him, and compare my feelings towards you with what I bore him! Then you shall hear me—I will tell you the exact truth, Mr. Earnscliffe. I never cared for Gaston more than as a cousin; I misled him unintentionally—and—I *have* loved you—loved you as a child, when I was ignorant of my sin in doing so—shall never cease to love you, now even that I know my guilt. But," she went on, passionately, "I will not bring dishonor on my husband—I will never cause a moment's sorrow to the only one on earth who has been my friend. Though my heart may break in the effort, I—I will part from you, Philip."

She took her hand from his arm, and strove to move away, but Earnscliffe could see that she trembled too violently to be able to walk; and, fearing observation from the crowds of people who were near, he whispered, hurriedly, "Mrs. Mortimer, I entreat of you to take my arm. I have been most wrong to speak to you thus, and at such a time—pardon me. I will offend no more."

She accepted his arm, for she felt that her limbs were powerless to support her; and neither uttered a word until Marguerite had entered the carriage. Then she bent forward, unable to part with him in anger, and already reproaching herself for the pain she had caused him.

"Philip, if I spoke harshly, forgive me. It is better that you should leave—that we should not meet again; but, forget this evening, think of me with kindness, for I shall be very miserable."

The carriage drove away, and Philip stood gazing after it in the dim light, his arms folded, his lips compressed. "She is mine," he thought, "mine already! Her last frail defence is pity for the old man. An hour—a moment—will overthrow it. The desire of my whole life is attained; the only woman I have really loved, won." And he turned and walked homewards, yet with no feeling of elation at his heart.

———

CHAPTER XLIX.

AFTER a few hours of feverish, troubled sleep, Marguerite awoke to the misery of another day. She had to listen to Mortimer's usual stories and extracts from the newspaper at breakfast, strive to make replies—parry his questions about her pale face and confused manner—tell him what she had done, and whom she had seen the night before.

"Mr. Earnscliffe!—ah, he liked Mr. Earnscliffe. Why did he not come oftener to see them? why would he not accept their invitations to dinner now? It was very strange, as he was an old friend of her father's." And so on, while Marguerite's hands grew colder and colder, and her breath came so thick she could scarcely articulate a word.

She felt intensely relieved when Mortimer departed, with the announcement that he should not return till dinner-time, and she had at least the solace of being alone and unquestioned. During all the forenoon she remained in her own dressing-room, unoccupied and tearless, but with somewhat the same dull, leaden sense of oppression upon her that she had experienced before leaving Kersaint. After luncheon she shut herself in the library, with orders that no visitors should be admitted, and then strove to exert herself to read; but though the words floated before her eyes, her mind did not receive their meaning, and would recur to the all-engrossing object of her previous thoughts. So, after mechanically turning over the pages for an hour or two, she laid the book aside; and then, opening a private drawer in one of the cases, took out a manuscript book of her own writing, and, seating herself by the table, made a short entry on its last leaf.

This book had been given her by her father on her twelfth birthday, when he told her she should try and note down in it the progress of her own mind and feelings from that day onward until she was a woman; and, faithful to every wish of his, Marguerite had continued to do so even to the present time; so that it formed a complete history of her whole inner life from her childhood till now.

The story of her love for Earnscliffe was written with the most entire truthfulness: her confession of it to him on the day of the storm, her anguish at parting with him—all was there without a gloss of concealment. Then came her dreary life with the Danby's; then her marriage. After this there were, for two or three years, few entries; occasionally, a subdued expression, not of complaint, but of her want of interest in existence—a fear that, for Mortimer's happiness, she had committed an error in marrying him. Later on came the description of her entrance into the world, and of all the admiration she received there; but still with allusions to the one great object that her life lacked, and whose place no triumphs of her beauty and talents could supply. At last came her meeting with Earnscliffe, and Marguerite trembled as she read over all that she had written since then, and compared it with the early description of her love for him at Kersaint. There was so slight a difference—only the childish simplicity of style was altered; the feeling was the same—or deeper!

"It would be better destroyed," she thought. "This journal records no very happy life; and if I were to die suddenly—not an unlikely event I know—it would fall into Mr. Mortimer's keeping, and render him miserable in the thought that I was less contented than he believed me. I had better destroy it. It is strange that my entry of to-day should fill the last leaf! Is it that after this my real history will be over—my life have nothing more to record? or——" and a vague but solemn presentiment whispered that perhaps her life, *indeed*, was almost past.

"I had better destroy it at once," she repeated, slowly, and approaching towards the fire. But those pages recalled so much: the early entries, before she had ever known Earnscliffe, so brought back her childhood and Kersaint that, after hesitating some time, Marguerite decided she would not burn it yet. "And, besides, it was her father's gift." And so the book was again laid in its former place, and then, falteringly she drew forth some notes and papers that were always kept in the same drawer with her journal. On some of them the ink was faded now, the paper discolored. These were scraps of poetry, half-playful, half-serious, that Philip used to write at Kersaint—all carefully treasured, even then—and with them was the long letter which he had written to her from Tyrol. But Marguerite knew all these by heart; and, after holding them in her hand for a few seconds, she replaced them; and then, but very hesitatingly, and as though other eyes than her own were in the silent room, took out another packet of letters. These were, however, freshly written, and still in Philip's hand.

As Marguerite read and re-read some of the ambiguously-worded notes he had lately written to her—but to every syllable of which her heart could now attach a different meaning to what it had done when she first read them—a knock came at the door of the library. It was only her own maid, but Marguerite's heart fluttered and her cheeks glowed with all the confusion of guilt as she entered.

"Un billet pour madame," presenting on a salver one of those notes which Marguerite knew was from Philip at a glance.

"I see: there is no answer," she said, with forced calmness: and Mademoiselle Eulalie withdrew, not in the least deceived, for, though all the world may be blinded in such matters, a French lady's maid never can; and the first downward step in a woman's career is when her own servants suspect her.

Marguerite tore open the letter. There were only these words:

"Marguerite, The time has now come for you to decide. If I see you at Mrs. Lorrimer's on Friday, I shall consider your sentence of last night is recalled. If you are not there, I leave England *alone*, the following day."

The paper fell from her hand, and a sharp pain struck at Marguerite's heart. "Cruel," she murmured, faintly—"cruel to make me decide upon our separation, and force it upon me so soon. Yet it must be so, sooner or later. I might have known it could only end thus; it is better finished at once." Then she laid her head upon the table and wept with one of the wild paroxysms of her childhood—as she had not wept for years; and thus a full hour passed away. She was careless if the servants entered and saw her so—careless even of Mortimer's return: only the one consciousness of losing Philip was present to her, and she would scarcely have heeded if the whole world had been present to witness her desolation.

At last, slowly, she raised her pale face, and again read the note through, but with eyes so hot and painful she could scarcely trace even Earnscliffe's bold, clear writing. "If I am not at Mrs. Lorrimer's he will leave England. If I go—but—no—no," she cried, vehemently, as a wild thought of happiness would cross her brain; "I must not meet Philip again. If I am even there, he will consider my sentence recalled. I shall see him no more then; he will leave me for ever, and my whole life is bound up in his. Oh, my God! pity me, and guide me in my weakness and my anguish!"

She rose, placed Philip's last note with all the others, locked the drawers, and went into her own room, where she bathed her face and strove to become more composed before her husband saw her, for it was already nearly the time for his return.

As it happened, he came home rather earlier than usual and very hungry: and, for almost the first time since her marriage, Marguerite was late for dinner. Punctual himself to a fault, nothing disturbed Mortimer's temper more than the want of punctuality in others. He actually spoke harshly to her when Marguerite appeared, at five minutes past seven, and faltered some gentle excuses for keeping dinner waiting.

"Yes, ma'am; when I, with all my business, can always be in time for everything, I do think that you, with nothing but your own pleasures to think of, may manage to remember my hours. What kept you out so late to-day, pray?"

"I have not been out at all, sir. I felt very unwell, and have been by myself ever since you left."

"Of course there is some reason always. What made the carriage late, then, in calling for me yesterday in the City? You were so hurried going off to the opera last night that I was not able to ask you; but I *will* have more order in my house."

" I am very sorry you were kept waiting, Mr. Mortimer; but Georgy came to see me in the morning, and I sent her home in the carriage, which I suppose caused the delay."

" Of course, if one of those women could get into a private carriage she would drive all over the town to show off!—your own sense might have told you that. So Georgy has been here again, eh? and you were all affection together, I suppose, after the manner of women."

" I received her in the spirit with which she came. It is much better there should be no further coldness between us."

" Will you take my arm, Mrs. Mortimer?" he interrupted, with grim politeness. " My fish is cooling, which of far more importance to me, you know, than the cooling of young ladies' love." With which sorry attempt at wit, he led Marguerite to the dining-room.

The stately meal passed off in absolute silence. Mortimer was not a man who quickly recovered himself when he was ruffled, and Marguerite was too nervous and weakspirited to trust herself to speak.

When the servant had withdrawn and the wine was on the table, Marguerite began timidly. " Georgy asked me to take her to Mrs. Lorrimer's *fête*, yesterday."

" I thought she came to ask for something besides forgiveness," returned Mortimer. " What did you say?"

" Oh, she seemed so earnest about it — I did not like to refuse."

" Well, poor thing!"—Mortimer's temper was a little improved after his first glass of port—" I suppose she is making one last desperate effort to be married. She is looking very old and thin; so you don't mind taking her. A good foil, ma'am, eh?"

" Well, the truth is, I wanted to ask you how I must get out of my promise. I told Georgy I would go—and now—and now—"

" You won't take her, I suppose?"

" Not exactly that. I have changed my mind, and don't intend to go myself."

" Why?"

" Because—the fact is—I mean I have changed my mind."

" A mighty sensible reason, upon my word! 'I mean—I thought—I have changed my mind.' I never expected fashionable life would make you silly and capricious like other women, Marguerite; but I see it is having the common effect."

" It is not caprice, indeed it is not; I have reasons."

" Let me hear them."

Never did a tone so completely repel confidence; and Marguerite could only stammer out something about " not feeling well."

" It is not that at all. You change merely **because** you **have promised** that wretched

woman to take her among your grand people, and now you think you'll be ashamed of her when she gets there. You will blush, next, if I am seen driving about with you." Mortimer was working himself up with his own words, until he grew fixedly obstinate in determining to oppose Marguerite. " It looks monstrous unkind of you, ma'am," he pursued, " and I must say is very unlike your former character. Besides, how can you make the excuse to Mrs. Lorrimer of illness, when she sees you riding about every day, perfectly well? Her husband has been a client of mine for twenty years, and I desire you, Marguerite, not to be capricious with her, whatever you are with all your other acquaintances."

" Very well, sir. I was quite wrong; but it was not caprice, I assure you. I will go," answered Marguerite, her own heart, alas! not combating the point too resolutely.

" And—if this important question of going or not going is settled—I shall have my sleep," said Mortimer, stretching out his large feet, and shutting his eyes. " I am tired, ma'am, and my cold fish has disagreed with me."

And Marguerite stole up in the twilight to the library, and with a tremulous hand wrote—

" I shall be at Mrs. Lorrimer's on Friday; but I recall nothing."

Folded, sealed, directed the note to Earnscliffe, and committed it to the velvet paw of Mademoiselle Eulalie.

————

CHAPTER L.

EARNSCLIFFE only saw Marguerite once from their parting at the door of the opera until the day of Mrs. Lorrimer's *fête*, and then but for a moment, as he was walking with Neville in Hyde Park. She was on horseback, and bowed to Philip as she passed by; but with a visible embarrassment most unlike her accustomed calm demeanor.

" By Jove! she is lovely," was Neville's exclamation, " and so young and innocent looking. Spare her, Phil, she is too good to fall."

" Neville—even on the strength of our old friendship—there are some things I will not hear you say. What on earth do you mean by the expression? How am I to 'spare' Mrs. Mortimer?"

" I am unhappily quick at insight," returned the artist, quietly; " and know as well how things stand between you and her as you do yourself. Why have you not followed the advice you asked me for, and left town?"

" I have acted as I considered right," replied Philip, coldly. "Let us change the subject."

"Oh, as you please. It is of more importance to you than to myself—of more importance to her than to either. *Apropos de rien*—do you remember, Phil, how we walked together near these 'bowery glades of Kensington,' as somebody calls them, six years ago, and saw Rose Elmslie driving along in Count B——'s pony phaeton? You were indignant with me 'about some love matter, I remember.'"

"Poor little Rose! what became of her I wonder?"

"Poor little devil! you should say. After you left England she went to perdition with a rapidity greater even than what I predicted for her. Left Count B—— for some one else, and then sank lower and lower—took to drinking, I believe, and was hissed off the stage."

"Is she dead?" asked Philip, quickly. "I never heard this before."

"You never remembered to ask, probably. She is not dead, my friend—or, I should rather say, was not so last winter. A few months ago I was returning home quickly in the dusk—after a long walk into the country to mark the effect of the red sunset over the frozen woods—and, as I was taking a short cut through some of the back streets near the Haymarket, a woman—pale, haggard, desperate—touched me on the sleeve. I turned round, and, pulling my arm from her with a gesture of disgust, told her, in no gentle tone, to leave me. 'I ask you for money,' she said, 'because I am starving. Do you refuse? As she spoke I caught sight of her face, and saw that it was——"

"No—not Rose?"

"Yes, it was Miss Elmslie. I remembered her directly. I scan every face I see too deeply for it to fade from my memory: and hers was not one to forget. She had a peculiarly moulded chin—do you recollect?—small, and with the slightest dimple in the centre."

"Yes, yes!—go on."

"Well, I knew her by that in a moment. 'You are Rose Elmslie,' I said; not concealing my horror, as you may suppose. She started aside at the sound of my voice, and tried to push her way through the coarse crowd along the pavement; but I followed, and entreated her to stop—at least, accept such assistance as I could offer. 'Leave me,' she said; 'I shall die soon. I want to see none of you again.' Her voice was very weak, but unnaturally low and hollow. 'And you refuse any assistance?' I repeated. 'Yes, from you,' she answered. 'You were one of Earnscliffe's friends, let me pass on!' and again I lost sight of her."

"And you saw her no more?"

"Yes, as I passed the door of a gin palace, a few minutes later, I caught a glimpse of the same drooping figure, waiting silently by the counter for one of the glasses of 'forgetfulness,' that a smart-looking woman was serving out. Poor wretch!"

Philip felt sick. "Great God, what a world is this!" he exclaimed.

"Yes," returned Neville, "it is much as we make it. The world God sends us into is fair in itself; men create sin, and call the world dark. But," he went on, "Rose Elmslie was worthless, in heart, the first day you ever saw her—tainted from her childhood; her misery afterwards is the natural conclusion to such a career, and is nothing, in its blackest horror, compared to the remorse of one who *has* been pure and without reproach. No hell, you know, burns so fiercely as that of the fallen angels!"

"Good morning to you," said Philip, abruptly. "I see an old friend whom I have not met for years." And crossing the ring, he left his friend alone.

For a moment Neville watched him. Then, raising his slouched Italian hat upon his forehead, and folding his arms behind him, he marched on. Philip's friend was an old club acquaintance whom he had afterwards met abroad, and who had now just returned to England; and, glad to escape from Neville and his own thoughts, Earnscliffe took his arm and they walked townwards together. But again the same subject was, singularly enough, forced upon him.

After some minutes' conversation upon their mutual wanderings since they parted, his friend remarked, "I have wished to see you for several days, but have been too engaged to find you out, and never could see you at the club. Oh, I forgot, you don't belong to mine now. *Nous avons changé tout cela!* and, like every one else, your politics are altering."

"Conforming to our present exigences."

"Oh, that is the term, is it? However, I was going to say, I have often heard of your name and of more than your political prospects. It appears that you are *au mieux* with this last wonder, *la belle* Mortimer. Your old luck."

"You should rather say the old scandal of English clubs," replied Earnscliffe, with assumed indifference. "Mrs. Mortimer's father was a friend of mine, and I am intimate with them."

"*Them!* Is the husband ever seen by mortal eyes? I thought the venerable old stock-broker was a kind of myth—only heard of as supplying Madame with diamonds and his name."

"You have been misinformed throughout, then," said Philip, shortly.

"Eh, *mon cher!* I see the case is serious. When a man denies these things his friends had best be silent. But to turn to another theme. What has become of all our old friends of the coulisses, then? I suppose we may speak of them?"

"I know nothing of them now—I have

other interests and other things to think of," returned Earnscliffe. Neville's story of Rose was too fresh for him to risk the mention of her name.

"The devil you have! Well, after being abroad so long as I have, one does not know what to speak of on one's return. One man has become a dissenter,—another a papist, a third a .Gladstonite—and a fourth turns up his eyes when actresses are spoken of, and denies his *bonnes fortunes*. For Heaven's sake, Earnscliffe, come and dine with me, and let us talk over old days."

But Philip pleaded an engagement — as glad to escape from his friend as he was, five minutes before, from Neville—and, tired of the sunshine and crowds of people, returned to the solitary room at his hotel, and flung himself on his sofa, not to sleep, although he had not slept for two nights, but think. Think—commune with his own heart for the last time before the overwhelming temptation which he knew the morrow—only a few hours more—would bring. From the moment that he received Marguerite's note saying that she would once more see him, he knew that she was his (even if any doubt before existed.) The contest was too unequal to last much longer; her exceeding trust in him, her ignorance of her own danger, made the result but too certain. And again, as it had done so often years before, the accusing thought would present itself, "You are betraying God's holiest work, the innocence of a child."

It was no pleasant thought! He rose and paced uneasily about his room, striving—not to combat with the wild dictates of passion; they had remained too long uncontrolled to be under his power now—but to seek out some extenuation with which to satisfy his own conscience. "She was mine, in reality, years ago," he said, half aloud. "Mine, heart and soul, from her childhood. What is any mere conventional tie compared to that? If I left her now, her existence would be one long-continued misery—constantly endeavoring to fulfill her duty as another man's wife—seeking vainly to crush what is part of her very life—her love for me! But, if this remorse Neville speaks of is, indeed, inevitable, will not *that* be a bitterer anguish? for one so pure to feel that she has become—— Pshaw! my devotion will make her forget all that—and everything beside— I wish the dragging hours would wear away! I shall be calmer when all is decided. Will to-morrow never come?"

He waited impatiently until evening; then, when it was dusk, unable any longer to bear the oppression of solitude and of his own meditations, he ordered his horse and rode down to Wimbledon, where he dismounted at the inn, and walked on towards Mortimer's place, but without entering the gates. He saw nothing of Marguerite, of course; she was alone all the time in the library,

writing in her journal—the last entry she ever made there—but it was enough that he breathed the same air, could catch a glimpse of the walls that enclosed his idol, and he lingered, unnoticed by any one, until near midnight, and then, under the solemn starlight, rode back to town.

Not quite unnoticed, Mr. Grimes, the butler, had been out on honorable business of his own, and calling on his friend the innkeeper, heard that Earnscliffe had left his horse there.

"And not come to us!" pondered Grimes. "What's up now?" And that worthy man dodged and peeped, and found Philip, and stole after him, and saw how he looked towards the house, and paused, and half spoke, and walked quickly on, only to return and gaze again. And then Grimes returned home, well pleased with what he had seen, and burning to relate it in the servant's hall.

The next morning shone out bright, but not sultry; and by the afternoon it was one of those sweet, still summer days, of which there are about six in the English year—the very weather for an out-of-door *fête*. At four o'clock the Mortimers' carriage called in Tavistock Street and found Georgy ready-dressed, and in great excitement at the expected dissipation, and the pleasure of breathing the same atmosphere and looking at the same trees and flowers as three or four hundred "great people," during a whole long evening.

She returned to Wimbledon for Marguerite, and had to wait for some time in the drawing-room, before she appeared. "Marguerite had had a headache," her husband said, "and had begun to dress late."

"Quite unusual to see you at home, Mr. Mortimer; I thought you were always in the City at this hour."

"I am not very well; I have not felt myself for the last week, and Maggy persuaded me that I ought to stay at home and be quiet. However, I must go to town for an hour or two when you are gone."

"Dear Marguerite has not been looking very well either lately."

"Dear Marguerite has been to too many parties, Miss de Burgh. She will be as blooming as a rose after I take her to the sea."

"Oh! I am delighted to hear that it is nothing but fatigue that made her so pale, but she seemed so very low and nervous."

The door opened and Marguerite entered, her complexion brighter than usual, and her whole appearance giving the most direct denial to Georgy's kind misgivings.

"Very like an invalid," said Mortimer, proudly. "But, Maggy, dear, how oddly you are dressed! That white muslin gown —plain little white bonnet, and no ornaments. What is this new fancy for dressing like a school-girl, eh?"

"My dress is very handsome," returned Marguerite; "it is the new-worked muslin you gave such a price for last week; and my bonnet has only just arrived from Paris. You know it is my French fancy, sir, to dress simply, and with only real flowers for ornaments, at a summer *fête*."

"Well, you always look well, child, however you dress. At least, here are fine flowers for you," and he presented her with a bouquet, composed entirely of early moss rose-buds and Cape jessamine.

"How lovely!" said Marguerite; "how exactly my taste. It looks more like a French bouquet than one of Campbell's making."

"I don't know that it is his," replied Mortimer; "I found it just now on the table, where some of the servants placed it, I suppose."

"I ordered two—one for each of us," said Marguerite. "What is Campbell thinking about!" She rang the bell, and her page answered it, with two gorgeous bouquets of hot-house flowers on a salver.

"Then, who brought this one?" she inquired, coloring, without knowing why.

"That was left by a servant on horseback, madam, an hour ago. There was no message."

"From some of your numerous admirers, I suppose?" said Mortimer, when the page left the room.

"One who knows Marguerite's taste well, at all events," added Georgy. "Cape jessamine and moss-roses are your favorite flowers, dear, are they not?"

"It looks mighty well with your white dress, Maggy, whoever sent it. I suppose you'll neglect *my* rare flowers now?"

"Which shall I take, sir? I don't care," hesitated Marguerite.

"Little hypocrite!" thought Georgy.

"Which shall you take?—whichever you like the best, to be sure! Perhaps, the simple flowers suit your style best."

"Old idiot!" thought Georgy. "Earnscliffe sent it, and it means something if she wears it."

So Marguerite took the roses and Cape jessamine for herself, and placed the bouquet Georgy did not choose in a vase on the table. Then she turned to her husband. "Do you feel really better now?" she whispered. "I scarcely like leaving you, if you are unwell."

"I am much better, thank you," returned Mr. Mortimer, who hated to be thought ill. "It was nothing; I shall go into town for an hour, and return home as well as ever for my dinner. That reminds me, Maggy—what did you do with those papers I gave you yesterday morning, when I left in such a hurry. I hope you have them safe?"

"I locked them up with my letters," replied Marguerite. "Do you want them? I will run and bring them for you in a moment."

She went up to the library, unlocked the secret drawer, where, for safety, she had placed Mortimer's papers, took them out, and then—flurried by the incident of the bouquet, and thinking nothing of what she was about—came down again leaving the drawer open. That drawer contained her diary and Philip's letters.

"Here they are," she said to her husband, "quite safe, although I had the charge of them."

"Thank you, my dear. And if you will give me permission, I shall go and sit in your own sanctum myself for an hour. It is the coolest room in the house of an afternoon."

Little knowing what the seemingly trivial request involved, Marguerite smilingly assented; and in a few minutes she and Georgy were on the road. As they approached Richmond they passed, and were passed, in return by numbers of gay carriages and young men on horseback, all on their way to the *fête*.

"We are not late," said Georgy, "at all events. Judging from the numbers of people we see, there can be scarcely any one there yet."

"Oh!" returned Marguerite, "I knew we should be in good time."

"What hosts of people you know, Marguerite! Every one we have seen yet has bowed."

"I know 'everybody,' as the English phrase is. I am literally tired of bowing already."

"Who is that girl who passed us last? she is pretty."

"Miss Carlton Vere. She is considered the beauty of the season. That was Digby Grant, the dandy, *par excellence*, who was riding by their carriage."

"Yes, I know him by sight: he has four thousand a-year; and his uncle is Dean of Coventry, and his cousin is member for B——. I should like to be introduced to him, dear."

"I can introduce you to any one you wish, Georgy; so mind, if you do not meet many friends of your own, you must tell me whom you wish to know."

"Oh, thank you! the Count de Montravers will be there, however, and in *his* society I naturally care for no other."

"Georgy, I begin to think you are engaged to the Comte."

"One need not be engaged to everybody in whose society one finds pleasure," said Miss de Burgh, tartly, "as you must be well aware."

Marguerite colored, but made no reply—she seldom did to Miss Georgy's speeches—indeed, she forgot what they were talking about a moment afterwards. She was looking nervously at every group of young men they passed, wondering, hoping, fearing whether Philip were among them. But she saw nothing of him; and they soon arrived at Mrs. Lorrimer's pretty villa, where the crowd of carriages and people, sounds of music, and distant marquees in the grounds, announced the gay scene that was going on.

The entrance-hall was completely wreathed with flowers; and through this they were ushered to a room on the ground floor, opening upon the lawn, where Mrs. Lorrimer received her guests, before they dispersed into the grounds.

Marguerite presented Georgy with her usual quiet grace; and Miss de Burgh was quite flattered at the well-bred smile of Mrs. Lorrimer, which she mistook for the commencement of an acquaintance, although in truth the lady never thought of her again from that moment to this.

"I advise you to take refuge in the gardens, Mrs. Mortimer; you will find the lower lawn by the river delightfully cool, while the sun remains so high."

And a crowd of young men surrounded Marguerite, all anxious to dance attendance on the celebrated beauty, who, in addition to her lovely face and irresistible charm of manner, possessed the strongest attraction of all—that of being the fashion—and the fashion too, with so notorious and fastidious a man as Earnscliffe!

"Mr. Hollingsworth, let me introduce you to my cousin, Miss de Burgh," said Marguerite, addressing a boyish-looking youth with an incipient moustache, who colored to the eyes, and at once became the victim of Georgy's charms, without hope of release for an hour or two.

"Isn't it delightful?" she cried, as they followed Marguerite and her train upon the lawn. "I love these free, wild things in the open air so much better than balls; don't you?"

"I haven't been to many—Cambridge is so slow."

"Cambridge! dear me! Have you not left college?" (Mr. Hollingsworth looked about fifteen.)

"No; this is only my first term."

"And do you care for dancing?"

"I have only danced at school," would have been the truthful reply; but Mr. Hollingsworth merely said—"Not very much;" and Georgy returned—"Nor she either. Really pleasant conversation was far better than waltzing. Did Mr. Hollingsworth know where that darling little shady walk led to? Could it be to the river?"

And Georgy and her new friend soon disappeared, rather, it must be confessed, to Marguerite's relief, who, though perfectly above the vulgar feeling of being ashamed of any one, was not anxious to have Georgy's close attendance the whole day.

She walked about, and felt that every eye was bent upon her as she moved. Among all the brilliant women there, hers was the most recherchée toilette—hers the loveliest face. Never, in her first season, had she

created a greater sensation than to-day; and, of course, she was aware of it. But to herself the whole scene was without interest, all the admiration she awakened was worthless. Earnscliffe was not there, and in his sense everything beside was blank.

CHAPTER LI.

"DEAR Mrs. Mortimer," said a kind voice close behind her, "it is so long since I have seen you!"

Marguerite turned and recognised Lady Millicent Gore, one of her earliest friends. They shook hands, and Lady Millicent made room for her on the seat beside herself.

"You young people will have so much dancing this evening, you must reserve your strength, and not stand or walk while the day continues so hot."

"I never dance now," replied Marguerite, "but I am delighted to have found a place by you."

"Never dance?" repeated her friend. "Is it possible that you have renounced dancing at your age? You used to be so famous for your waltzing."

"I don't think I really cared for it; but I found it dull at balls to sit out and watch others dancing, without doing so myself. I have given it up now, I am not very strong."

"You look well; but perhaps you are flushed at this moment. You must make your husband take you abroad this summer, to get over all the fatigues of your London season."

"Oh, that is already settled. We are going to Brittany in a few weeks, to visit my old home there."

"I remember you told me all about your place in Brittany, the first evening I ever saw you, at my sister's house. Speaking of that evening reminds me of your cousin, the Marquis de St. Leon; what has become of him lately?"

"Gaston has returned to France: he forms one of the new government already."

"The new government? I thought he was an ultra-Legitimist."

"So he used to be," said Marguerite, smiling, "but——" she turned white, then flushed crimson. In the distance her eyes had caught one glimpse of Philip. "What did I say?" she added, vaguely.

"Poor thing!" thought Lady Millicent. "Is it possible her cousin interested her so much? with such a husband, however, it is not wonderful." And delicately changing the subject, she began speaking of some of the people who were walking up and down on the lawn before them. "Miss Carlton Vere is very pretty," she remarked, after a few dear friends had been discussed. "But it is not a style I at all admire—do you?"

"Oh! every one must think her lovely," replied Marguerite, in rather an absent tone.

"Yes, but her consciousness of her own beauty greatly diminishes its charm. She wants your unaffectedness, Mrs. Mortimer. Look at her now, as she walks with Mr. Earnscliffe, and shakes back her long fair curls while she looks up at him. Do you suppose it is a case of serious attention?"

Lady Millicent went so seldom into the world, that she was unaware even if Marguerite and Earnscliffe were acquainted; and continued making the most unconscious remarks upon his apparent devotion to Miss Carlton Vere. "He is really distinguished-looking," she said. "Not only his face handsome, but his manner, and whole air are so unlike most young men that one sees. Do you not agree with me?"

"Mr. Earnscliffe is good-looking," answered Marguerite.

"Good-looking! my dear, what very qualified praise. Of course you have read his writings. Are you not warmer in your admiration of them, than their author? Oh! you are acquainted with him then," as Earnscliffe passed, and took off his hat to Marguerite; "now tell me what his conversation is like?"

And Marguerite had to talk of Philip for a good half-hour to Lady Millicent Gore (who felt an especial interest in authors), and all this time to watch Philip in earnest, and apparent devoted conversation with Miss Carlton Vere; while that young creature smiled and blushed, and shook back her curls more playfully each time as she passed the spot where Marguerite was seated.

"The sun is pouring full upon us," she cried at last—too weary and impatient to listen even to the gentle Lady Millicent. "Will you not change your position?"

"Thank you, my dear. I like this place; and I don't feel the sun in the least. But I will keep you no longer; you have already devoted nearly an hour to an old woman—which, for the *belle* of a *fête* like this, is indeed sufficient."

So Marguerite rose, and taking the arm of Digby Grant—who had been hovering patiently near her for some time—walked with him towards the river. He was an agreeable man, in spite of his affectation, and only too anxious that Mrs. Mortimer should consider him so; but she was strangely absent to-day, and replied à *travers* to his prettiest speeches while he led her, unconscious how far she was going, to a remote part of the lawn, where, as yet, none of the others had penetrated.

"Would you like to escape this terrific sun, Mrs. Mortimer?—that rustic boat-house looks inviting."

"As you please; yes, certainly." And Marguerite entered, really glad to be away from the crowd, and only wishing her companion would leave her.

"Pray don't let me take you away from everybody, Mr. Grant. I am so tired, I shall remain here for half-an-hour; but do return to the lawn without me. You may come back for me as late as you please."

"I am only too thankful to be away," he replied; "these odious mixed things are my horror—people of all kinds—you don't know who is who! The last time I was at Mrs. Lorrimer's she had some dreadful Syrian wretches, whom I remembered as shoe-blacks in their own country. To-day there are still worse atrocities. Actually I saw that man, calling himself the Count de Montravers—a man who would be received in no decent society in France; but whom English people will invite, and listen to, while he descants on the regeneration of England. I had only one object in coming here, Mrs. Mortimer."

"Could you not shelter me from the sun? Thank you. It fell full upon my face."

"Let me hold your parasol? No. Your bouquet, then—your hands are full;" and he took Marguerite's—Philip's—bouquet, and inhaled its fragrance with great gusto.

"Pray do not shake them to pieces," she said at last. "See, one rose-bud has fallen out already."

"Which I may keep for my guerdon," he replied, picking it up, and preparing to place it in his coat.

"No, no," interrupted Marguerite, eagerly; "give me the flower, if you please, and I can replace it. I never give away my flowers."

"Are they so valued for their own sakes, or for that of the donor?" in rather a piqued tone at her refusal.

"For their own sakes," replied Marguerite, coloring; "flowers are my passion—I——"

Just then she caught the sound of a well-known step, advancing on the gravel path beside them; and, in another moment, Earnscliffe's tall figure was visible. He was alone, and after glancing at her and her companion, walked slowly on with a very slight salutation, and his face calm and grave as usual.

"He must believe that I am happy without him," thought Marguerite. "That I am encouraging the idle attentions of another already." And this idea, that to many women would have been one of entire satisfaction, gave her such intolerable pain, that she rose hastily, and proposed returning towards the house at once.

Meantime, Georgy had lost Mr. Hollingsworth, who, after a series of manœuvers, contrived to slip away from her among the crowd; and, for about half-an-hour, failing to spy out Marguerite, she had wandered along, as is the habitude of obscure persons at large assemblies, unnoticed by anybody, except those few who languidly raised their eye-glasses, and classed her among Mrs. Lorrimer's "oddities." At length, she met her friend, the Comte de Montravers, and seized upon him with an avidity that should have been most flattering to the foreigner. Like Miss de Burgh, however, he was on the look-out for great people himself, and he was not particularly anxious to be the attendant of an unknown person of two-and-thirty, nor nearly so *empressé* in his manner as when they took morning walks together in the mystic regions of Brunswick Square; and he passed on, after a short conversation. So Georgy was again discomfited; and, when, at length, she joined Marguerite, was not in the best of tempers.

"Where in the world have you been?" she exclaimed. "Since I saw you disappear in the distance, two hours ago, with Digby Grant, I have never met you. It appears *he* is your adorer, after all, not Philip Earnscliffe, who, I can assure you, has been devoted to that lovely ' iss Carlton Vere the whole afternoon. I have met them a dozen times together. But how pale you look. Can't you introduce me to some one as you promised you would? Mr. Grant for instance."

"He is talking to Mrs. Lorimer at this moment. Tell me the names of any other people you wish to know."

And Marguerite—weary and spiritless though she was—tried to exert herself for Miss de Burgh; and, ever ready to please another walked about with her, and introduced her to everybody she wished, even to Digby Grant, who raised one eyebrow and bent his head just sufficiently to move his topmost curl at the introduction. But Georgy was radiant with smiles, and soon appended herself to some of her new acquaintance with such determined pertinacity, that Marguerite felt she was fairly disposed of the remainder of the evening, and also that she would have to wait many a long hour before Miss de Burgh would choose to leave.

The dancing was now at its height; and the two large marquees on the lawn, brilliantly lighted, were thronged with dancers and lookers-on; while many there were better pleased to wander about the grounds, where hundreds of colored lamps glimmered in the dark summer night. Marguerite was standing somewhat apart from the entrance to the principal tent, and through her moment unattended; her head turned away from the light and music, towards the silent river beneath, when, close beside her, she heard Philip's voice.

"Mrs. Mortimer—Marguerite, may I dare to offer you my arm?"

She started, and her heart beat so violently she could not answer. Then she placed her hand, almost without knowing that she did so, upon his arm.

"Can you spare five minutes from all this gay scene; from all your admirers, while you say good-bye to an old friend?"

"Philip!" (The altered tone of her voice shocked him.) "I am very weary; I hate all this crowd and glare; and I should have left already, but——"

He led her down a narrow sidewalk—the same Georgy and Mr. Hollingsworth had previously discovered—and, in a few minutes, they were as completely alone as though they were at Kersaint. Only the sounds of the distant music were there to remind them of the scene they had left. The warm, soft air—the odor from the garden flowers—the uncertain light of the stars—the presence of each other—was all they were awake to. In those few minutes, the world, and all belonging to it, were forgotten. Marguerite's hand was upon his arm; she heard his voice again—more dear even from those few days of separation—and her life, that had just before seemed so void, was again a glowing, delicious heaven.

"You are pale now, Marguerite! and yet so flushed a few hours ago; are you not well?"

"Did you really notice me before this? I thought you were too much occupied to think of my appearance."

"You could not really believe it. I might as well affect jealousy of the butterflies that have been hovering about you—of Digby Grant, because I saw you with him alone, when he was holding my flowers for you. Marguerite, our feelings are too deep for these small fears."

"Your flowers? they were indeed from you, then?" and the hand that held them unconsciously pressed them closer.

"Did you not feel that they were from me? Believing they were from a stranger would you have worn them? Oh! do not let us attempt any longer to dissemble. Marguerite, the hour has come when *that* has passed for ever. I received your note telling me to be here, and I am here. My conduct to-day has only been assumed to mislead the idle world, who already may have spoken of the attachment which I have vainly tried to hide——"

"But I told you to hope nothing—that I retracted nothing. I came here that this might be our last meeting. Oh, Philip! you do not know the agony that I have passed through since I saw you, how I have striven and prayed—as much for your sake as my own—to overcome this love that can only end in misery."

"And in vain, Marguerite! tell me so; whatever happens, let me once more hear from those dear lips that you love me—once more."

They had now reached the river, whose liquid masses floated by in their black stillness beneath them, and Marguerite shuddered as the chilly air from the water struck upon her heated cheek. She shrank to Philip's side, and his blood became fire as he felt her slight form clinging as it were to him for protection. He thought of the world's cold breath, already raised to wither Marguerite's good fame, and—strange sophistry!—felt that his honor constituted him her protector.

"Philip, you could not urge me thus, if it were wrong. You are so much better and wiser than I—Philip! will it really make you happier if I once more tell you the secret of my existence—the secret that will make my whole life a blank evermore? Then hear me —I love you still as I did at Kersaint!"

Her voice sank to the lowest whisper, but Earnscliffe heard it still. He seized both her cold hands suddenly within his own—

"Marguerite!"—(his voice, too, was low, and altered in its sound from what she had ever known it before)—"let this moment, then, decide our destiny. You say that you love me still—that that love will make your whole life a blank without me—be mine, then! I know the sacrifice I ask of you— the sacrifice of good name, of position, of all that women hold dear, and that against this, my passionate love, my utter devotion, are all that I have to offer. Come with me to another country, where in our love all the disappointments of the past shall be forgotten, and we will live for each other alone;" and his arm was thrown round her trembling form.

But Marguerite even yet shrank back. "Let me go!" she whispered, very faintly. "Let me return to my home—to my husband; I will not bring dishonor upon him!"

"As you will, madam!" He released his hold instantly. "I was wrong in supposing that for my love you could so readily give up your fair fame. You speak of his honor, and forget that I, too, should forfeit every ambition, every prospect in life, and deem their loss as nothing if I possessed you. Oh, Marguerite!"—his voice sinking again into its deepest, most passionate tenderness —"forgive me! I know not what I say. I cannot lose you! Oh, Marguerite, Marguerite! remember all the years that we have loved each other—that you were mine, in heart at least, before your husband ever knew you—that years ago you promised me never to love another."

"Philip, I have kept my word."

"Then redeem it now—now, when all my happiness in this life depends upon your decision."

"Philip—ah, may God help me!—I can have no will but yours."

He folded her to his breast; he knew that she was his. But, even at that moment, he could hear the unnatural throbbing of her heart, and mark that the face upturned to his was one of agony. The hell of a fallen angel had already begun. With the first breath of guilt a dark shadow had fallen across Marguerite's love.

"Mine, mine!" whispered Earnscliffe, tenderly. Death only shall part us now."

"Death!" she repeated, with a shudder; "yes, you are right to speak of death——"

"When years of radiant life are spread before us? In Italy, in the sweet south, my Marguerite, we shall at length be happy together—happy as we should have been long ago, if fate had not divided us."

"Aye, fate!" she answered, dreamily; "there was an evil fate in my mother's destiny and in mine. Both married where they could not love; she died young, as I shall."

"My own love, do not speak of dying. In my new born joy, do not cause me the torture of thinking that I could ever lose you."

"Philip, I am yours—wrong, lost though I may be—I am yours. I shall never part from you now. My love is interwoven with my very life, and can only end with it. But it will not be for very long. Something tells me, even at this moment, that I shall die. When the summer comes again, and you are breathing another warm night such as this, you will be alone: but you will still think fondly of me, still hold my remembrance dearer than all other, and in that thought is almost happiness sufficient."

She looked up at him with one of those ineffably sweet smiles that I never saw on any countenance but hers, and laid her head upon his arm. The gesture was so natural, so innocent, so like Marguerite, so unlike guilt, that Earnscliffe's conscience recoiled even yet from her betrayal. "My life's devotion must atone to her for all she loses," was his inward resolution while he bent over the pale, upturned face.

As though any human devotion could make atonement for sin to a nature like hers!

* * * * * *

"How frightfully ill Mrs. Mortimer looks!" said one of a group of friends, when, leaning on Philip's arm, she re-entered the ball-room; "and so wild and haggard! See how her eyes wander round, as though she saw nothing, and how she clings to him! Things are approaching a crisis."

"Oh, I have foreseen it long; indeed, I have not taken my Sophia Jane at all latterly, when I called at the Mortimers'. From the first moment I saw her and Earnscliffe together, I knew how it would end: there was something so bold-looking about her to me."

"Mrs. Mortimer bold-looking!" chimed in Digby Grant, who, though a rival, was more generous than female friends. "She looks more like dying than anything else at this moment; but who could ever call such a face as hers bold?"

"Oh, of course, Mr. Grant! men always admire that style of person. I cannot appreciate the excessive innocence of a married woman who carries on these kinds of desperate flirtations. If I were Mrs. Lorrimer, I should dislike having the dénouement at my house—for a dénouement there is I am certain."

"She is fainting, by George!" exclaimed Digby.

"Look at Mr. Earnscliffe's face! What a disgusting exhibition!" broke in two or three plain young women; and soon a score of different stories were in circulation—"Earnscliffe had said something to Mrs. Mortimer, which made her faint dead away on the spot!"—"Jealous of his attention to Miss Carlton Vere!"—"Fainted as Earnscliffe was running away with her in her own carriage!"—and so on.

But Marguerite knew and heard nothing. She was in a deep swoon; and when at length she partially recovered, she found herself in the open air, with only her kind friend, Lady Millicent, beside her.

"Where am I?—Is he here?" were her first incoherent words.

"You have fainted, my dear Mrs. Mortimer—you are ill," said a gentle voice, which Marguerite at once recognised. "As soon as you have recovered, you had better return home at once."

"Home!" said Marguerite wildly. "No, no—not home! anywhere but there. I cannot return home!"

Lady Millicent's face became very grave. "Can all this possibly arise from any recollection of her cousin?" she thought. "Every one is mentioning Mr. Earnscliffe's name; but this morning they seemed barely acquainted."

"Dear me! what is all this scene, Marguerite?" cried a loud, woman's voice. "Have you really fainted?"

"Georgy, let us go. I am very ill."

"Go? at nine o'clock? Thank you, my dear! I have made a great many agreeable acquaintances, and I have not the least idea of going."

Lady Millicent looked round with perfect horror at Miss de Burgh.

"Are your movements controlled by that —lady?" she whispered to Marguerite.

"I brought her with me. I believe I must wait until she is ready. But I am, indeed, weary and ill, Georgy," she added, looking imploringly towards her.

"Can I take care of your friend?" interposed Lady Millicent, overcoming her repugnance to the friend's appearance, in her kind feeling to Marguerite.

"Oh, Lady Millicent! you are too kind."

"Lady Millicent" sounded sweet to Georgy's ears, and she became affectionate immediately that she discovered the little, plainly-dressed old lady was an earl's daughter.

"Dear Marguerite, if you are indeed ill, of course, we will go at once. I thought it was merely a passing weakness.

"My chaperonage and escort are entirely at your friend's service, again remarked Lady Millicent. "Only let me see you safely

into your carriage at once. You are not in a state to remain one moment in yonder crowded rooms." And a servant was sent to order Mrs. Mortimer's carriage; while Georgy, with many smiles, tried to ingratiate herself with her new acquaintance.

"Dear Marguerite was not very strong, did faint sometimes; the cool drive home would refresh her; it was so kind of Lady Millicent to offer to chaperone herself!" and so on; during all of which Marguerite still clung weakly to her friend's arm, whose disgust at Miss Georgy's selfishness increased with every word she uttered.

Earnscliffe was hovering near, though afraid to attract attention by approaching closer; but when the carriage was announced he advanced and offered Marguerite his arm.

"Good-night, my dear Mrs. Mortimer. I shall come and see you to-morrow morning."

"Good-night, Lady Millicent!" lingering wistfully, as they shook hands. "You have been very kind to me. Good-night." Marguerite felt they were parting for the last time, and her voice was thick and husky. "Good-night, Georgy."

And then, threading their way through the crowds who pressed round them, to stare upon her altered face, Earnscliffe led Marguerite to the carriage.

"Farewell, my own love!" he whispered, as she took her place. "We shall meet to-morrow, and part no more—only a few short hours."

"Oh, Philip! a strange fear is upon me. I tremble at being alone," she replied.

He bent forward, as though to present her bouquet, which he still held, and pressed his lips upon her hand. It was icy cold, too cold, even for his kiss to warm it, and he felt that she was trembling violently.

"Drive home as fast as possible," he said to the coachman. "Mrs. Mortimer has been taken ill." And in another moment he watched the carriage disappear which bore her from him.

Then Philip returned to the ball-room, where he paid so much attention to Miss Carlton Vere, that people began to think, after all, they had been mistaken in their suspicions; and Miss Georgy reflected with pleasure how she would tell Marguerite that Mr. Earnscliffe seemed to enjoy himself a vast deal better after her departure.

CHAPTER LI.

ALONE, through the silent night, Marguerite drove home. The lights, the confused sounds of music, were still flashing through her heated brain; but, clear above them all, rang Philip's last words—"To-morrow, and we shall part no more;" while ever, like a death-knell to that tumultuously happy thought, her own heart echoed—"To-morrow, and no more peace; to-morrow, and I shall no longer dare to speak of my childhood or my father. My father!" and the remembrance of his poor, passionless face, of his perfect integrity, his unwavering principle, awed her into a sense of her own guilt, deeper than what any thought of Mortimer could have awakened.

As she proceeded, every object by the way-side took the form of something connected with Kersaint. The waving branches of the Park trees, overhanging the road, seemed to her excited imagination the ancient Breton forests; the groups of laborers, returning late from hay-making, bore semblance to the peasants she had not seen for years. She passed a cottage garden, and some white lilies, shining calmly in the moonlight, brought back the altar in the old cathedral, decked for early mass. And all rose up in judgment against her.

"But it is for *him!*" she exclaimed, in her terror at the invisible presence she felt around—as though the mention of his name could overpower that—"to be with Philip, who is dearer than life itself! Whatever the sin, whatever the misery, he wishes it; and I have no other will."

Then she leant back in the carriage, and closed her eyes: she could not bear the light of the stars to-night—even they seemed watching her reproachfully. And, in addition to this tension of mental pain, there was a fiery sensation in her brain, a quick, uneven throbbing at her heart, different to what she had ever experienced before, and which heightened into actual agony as she approached home.

To meet Mortimer again—once more to lay her head beside the old man's trusting heart, and know that on the morrow she would leave him, in loneliness and dishonor—was something so utterly abhorrent, so foreign to Marguerite's nature, that, even under the strong sway of irresistible passion—with Philip's kiss still warm upon her hand—she shrank loathingly from herself and the task before her.

"Better," she thought, "never to see him again—never more enter the home he has given me—than thus betray him to the last!"

And once the desperate purpose half arose of bidding the coachman drive on to town—anywhere except home. But where could she go?—to Philip?—she revolted instantly from the thought. To Lady Millicent Gore? What pretext could she form for such an extraordinary action? And thus, while she deliberated and wavered, an abrupt turn of the carriage told Marguerite that she had already entered her own lodge-gates—she was already home.

When she reached the front door, her limbs trembled so that she could scarcely totter from the carriage to the house; and, but for the servant, who caught her arm, she would have sank upon the threshold.

"Where—where is Mr. Mortimer?" she gasped, hardly conscious what she said.

"My master is in the library; he has been there all the afternoon," answered the man, terrified at the ghastly paleness of his young mistress. "Lord, madam! has anything happened?"

"Give me a light," said Marguerite, in a calm, composed tone. "In the library!" she murmured to herself, and the fact of having left the drawer open which contained her letters and journal, flashed upon her mind with sudden clearness. "Then he knows all!" she thought. "Thank God that, at least, I am spared the guilt of further concealment!"

She took the light with a steady hand, and walked so firmly up-stairs, that the servant stared after her in astonishment, and thought her pallor and wild looks on entering must, after all, have arisen from some accidental faintness. She went straight along to the library, never stopping for a moment on her way, then opened the door, still without faltering, and in perfect silence.

Mortimer was seated at the table by a lighted lamp; and before him, as Marguerite's forebodings told her, lay her open diary, her papers, Philip's letters, dried flowers, that he had given her years before at Kersaint—all the hoarded records of her love.

For a moment neither spoke: then Marguerite walked close up before him, her large, dark eyes unnaturally dilated, her hands clasped tightly together upon her bosom.

"Madame! *you* here?" She did not attempt to speak. "You have returned then to my house—to your *home*," with bitter emphasis on the word. "Has your lover failed in his appointment, though you were true? or is it convenient that I should be honored with your presence for one night more?"

Still she never answered, only her lips parted a little; but there was no sound.

"Speak!" he thundered, rising from his seat. "I command you to speak—the time is over for any more of your cursed innocence."

"I do not pretend to be innocent," she replied, very low.

"No. With such evidence as this," pointing to the table, "even your hypocrisy is confounded, although it is the blackest that ever a woman's blasted beauty covered since the world began. Some women go to perdition after years of marriage—that is bad enough! but you have never been pure—you were corrupt in your childhood."

"Sir!" raising her clasped hands towards him, "do not speak to me so. Kill me, but do not say that I was guilty when you married me."

" Oh, kill you, madam! You may spare me those theatrical expressions. Keep them against the time your poet lover deserts you, they may tell upon him! Not guilty, you say when I married you? then what do all these letters mean—these entries in your own hand-writing? "

" A girlish love, sir—not guilt."

" Girlish love for a married man?—girlish love still, I suppose? only that he is free, you married. But you forget by——! aye, and your paramour, too, that there is another in the case now—that you have a husband implicated in your dishonor, and one that is no fool to look on, and smile at his own shame, as some in your fashionable world do! Oh! the fool that I have been already," he went on passionately, " to think that at your age, and with your face, you were going into the world innocently. Fool to believe all your own accounts that you amused me with, as a cover to your intrigues. By Heaven! I believe that this is not the only one ; and that your cousin Gaston came in for a share of your girlish love."

" No, no, sir," she cried vehemently ; " guilty though I am, do not accuse me of such infamy as that! You do not—you cannot believe that I am so utterly lost?" looking steadily at him.

He moved his position uneasily, and turned away his head, as though afraid to look down into that truthful face that had already deceived him.

" Well, I believe you!" he answered, after a minute. " One is sufficient. And such love as you have borne your first lover was not likely to be shared, I own. How proud I have been of you, Marguerite!" he went on more softly—" how I have boasted that *my* wife was above even the shadow of reproach!—how I have studied every wish, every thought of yours——"

A sudden sob choked his words ; and even more touched at this gentleness than at his angry words of reproach, Marguerite sank upon her knees.

" Oh, forgive me!" she cried. " I acknowledge my sin—my utter unworthiness—my ingratitude ; but say that you forgive me! Do not let your last words to me be curses! "

" My last words!" he echoed, scornfully, all the momentary weakness over. " My last before you join Philip Earnscliffe, I conclude. No, madam, they shall not be curses. I have forbearance enough for that, and you will be sufficiently cursed in your own after-life. Rise up, pray, and leave me. I am in no humor for scenes now. I will not disgrace you before the servants by telling you to quit the roof you have dishonored at once —but never let me see your face again "

She rose—she turned, and without a word, she tried to move towards the door ; but strange lurid lights flashed before her eyes,

an intolerable pain was about her heart, and her limbs refused to help her.

" I—am—ill," she said faintly, leaning heavily against the wall.

But Mortimer's heart was steeled. He believed her far guiltier than she was, and thought it all acting.

" Leave me, madame!" he repeated, fiercely. " Do you hear me? Leave my presence!" Still she never moved ; only her head sank down, her hands clasped more convulsively for support. " Then as you refuse to do so, I will go myself. I will remain no longer in the same room with the woman I have called my wife, until I knew that she was——"

The cruel word had no sooner escaped him, in his passion, than he wished it recalled. To his last hour Mortimer will never forget the wild scream that burst from Marguerite's lips—the expression of her face as she turned it full round to his. Both will haunt him, as I am told the mute anguish of a stricken deer has, years afterwards, haunted the memory of him who smote her.

" Not to me!" she cried, staggering forward a few weak steps. " Say it was not to me!—not to your little Marguerite——"

She threw her arms forward, as though once again to clasp him, then sank, like a thing of stone, at his feet. Mortimer believed that she had fainted, and raised her instantly ; but as he did so, a crimson torrent broke from her mouth, dabbling her neck, her dress, her flowers, with the dark tide of death. In that moment of fearful excitement the vague dread of her whole life was realised. She had ruptured a blood-vessel.

Still she strove to look up at her husband, and her lips moved inarticulately, as though asking him to recall his last words.

" Forgive me!" she said, at length, with an almost superhuman effort, while the blood literally poured from her mouth as she spoke.

" I was not *so* guilty; and tell Philip—Philip——"

But a film gathered over the upturned eyes —a sudden spasm contracted the features— and so, while she yet uttered his name, she expired.

CHAPTER LIII.

When Philip returned home to his hotel from Mrs. Lorrimer's *fête*, he did not attempt to rest ; but remained up the whole night, writing letters to his uncle, to Neville, and a few other friends, telling them of his sudden departure from England. He made all his business arrangements—wrote to his banker for letters of credit—to some of his political supporters, saying for the present he had abandoned his intention of standing for L——; and all this with a strange calmness at which he himself was astonished. Although he knew that Marguerite's promise once given, she would never fail him, he could not realise the truth that she was to be actually his—actually leave England with him. From the first it had been so completely a part of their love to look upon it as hopeless, and for him to consider Marguerite as the type of all purity and innocence, that, even amidst the very preparation for their flight, his mind refused to see the evidence of their union and her guilt. When morning came he could only swallow a cup of coffee, and afterwards pace up and down the room, waiting impatiently for eleven o'clock. At that hour he proposed going down to Wimbledon, finally to arrange with Marguerite for meeting her in town, towards evening, in time to reach Dover for the night mail. But an unusual tremor was upon him. His strong nerves started at the slightest sound. Every footstep in the passage he fancied was approaching him with some message, some ill tidings from Marguerite; and, at length, unable to support this kind of uneasy suspense any longer, he hastily changed his dress, and ordered his horse, resolving to linger on the road, and so get rid of the lagging hour-and-a-half which yet remained.

When he reached Wimbledon it was only half-past ten. "No matter," he thought; "she will be alone by this time, and the interview is better over, for both of us. My poor Marguerite! I know well the feverish uncertainty she must suffer. It will be soon finished now."

He left his horse at the hotel, and walked on towards Mortimer's house: the gates stood open, and he entered without speaking to any one. The gardener's children were not playing, as usual, in the lodge garden: no servants were about; there seemed an unusual gloom about the whole place, or it appeared so to Philip's excited fancy; and he walked on hurriedly to the house, and knocked. Marguerite's little page came to the door, with pale, horror-struck face, and eyes swollen with crying.

"Is Mrs. Mortimer at home?"

"Oh, sir!—my mistress—have you not heard?"

"Heard what?" exclaimed Philip, seizing the child's arm so suddenly that it deprived him of all his remaining fortitude, and, instead of replying, he burst into tears. Just then a stealthy step approached from the other side of the hall, and the butler's solemn face appeared.

"Mr. Earnscliffe — sir," not speaking above his breath, "my master has given orders that you should be admitted."

"And Mrs. Mortimer?" asked Philip, eagerly.

The man shook his head. "If you will follow me, sir," he replied, "my master will tell you himself."

Philip felt that something of importance had taken place; either an explanation had occurred between the husband and wife, or Marguerite had already quitted her home; no glimmering of the truth, however, crossed his mind. He was ushered into the dining-room, and waited alone for about ten minutes in all the misery of suspense, and while each moment seemed to him an hour. At length Mortimer entered. For a second Earnscliffe did not recognise him. In one night his appearance had altered from strong middle life into decrepid old age; his face haggard and pale; his step uncertain, his gait drooping.

Earnscliffe advanced to salute him.

"Sir—do you offer me your hand?"

The hollow tone made Philip actually start back; he felt that Mortimer knew everything.

"I should not have come——"

"Had you known all! No—probably not. There is no attraction for you now, Mr. Earnscliffe! You have finished your work well."

"Great God! sir, tell me—how is Marguerite? Is she here?"

"Aye she is in my house still. You will be content to leave her with me now, I suspect."

"I can bear this no longer!" cried Philip, vehemently. "If you will not tell me how Marguerite is, I will find her—see her myself." And he approached the door.

"Will you so?" Mortimer answered. "Then let me take you to her chamber. I am not a jealous husband, you perceive, Mr. Earnscliffe! although I am aware of your attachment, I conduct you to your love myself." And he motioned to Philip to follow him.

"The old man is mad," thought Earnscliffe. "He has discovered all, and is doting in his jealous rage."

But he shuddered with a vague foreboding of ill, as he followed Mortimer's tottering steps up the staircase. When they came to the library Mortimer trembled visibly, and attempted to pass on quicker; and Marguerite's little spaniel, who was silently following them, shrank fearfully away. Philip saw all this with that quick perception to external things which the mind frequently experiences under the most violent emotion; and when at last they reached Marguerite's sleeping room, and Mortimer noiselessly turned the handle of the door, the cold dews stood thick upon his forehead.

"Tell me, in pity tell me," he whispered, "is Marguerite there?"

"Oh, go in!" returned Mortimer. "So gay a gallant surely never fears nothing. Go in, sir! I have brought you to your love!"

And, with a powerful effort, Earnscliffe

forced himself to enter the room that already his tortured sense told him was one of death.

Upon the bed dressed in white, lay Marguerite, her face uncovered. A sweet, loving expression was yet upon her features: her hands lay in an attitude of natural repose upon her breast, and all that told of death were one or two gouts of blood upon her night-dress, and a faint streak across the parted lips.

With a burst of agony, before which Mortimer's own sorrow quailed, Earnscliffe flung himself by her side, covered her cold hands with kisses, called upon her to awake to him by all the names that the fervor of his nature could pour forth.

"Oh, it is well for you to recall her, who have been the cause of her death!" said Mortimer, in a low, concentrated voice.

But Philip never heard him: unconscious, even in his presence, he continued sobbing with such passionate excess as is rarely witnessed in a young, strong man. "Marguerite, return to me; remember *how* I have loved you! Marguerite, my child, my own!"

At length, jealous of the kisses Philip pressed upon her cold, insensible hands, Mortimer came round and touched his shoulder.

"Leave sir!" he whispered. "You have seen all that I intended you should. Your place is not here now."

Philip sprang to his feet, and turned upon him a face of anguish before which Mortimer shrank back.

"This is not my place!" he repeated between his teeth. "Not mine!—who have loved her with my very life—before you ever knew her—not mine!—who have been the cause of all her sorrows. Leave me with her, sir!" he went on fiercely; "my place *is* here—I can injure you no more now. No——" as Mortimer was beginning to reply—"in her presence let there be no unseemly words—afterwards I will hear all you have to say; but now I must be with her—and alone."

After a moment's irresolution, Mortimer left the room in silence. He went down to the dining-room; and, seating himself in his arm-chair, wept feebly like a child; and, for an hour longer, Philip kept his watch with the dead. During that hour, what tongue can tell the dread remorse—the resolves—the meditated atonements of Earnscliffe's heart? They rest between him and Heaven, and his future life alone can test their sincerity. At length, pale, but tearless now, he rose, and bent down over her scanning, for the last time, her waxen features, as though to imprint each line upon his memory for ever!, then he stooped, and kissed her lips. That long, lingering kiss which poor humanity gives to the clay which once held its idol before yielding it up for evermore!

* * * *

The dining-room door stood open, and Mortimer met him as he passed.

"Not now!" said Philip, waving him back! "I will speak to you any other time —not now."

"One word, Mr. Earnscliffe—I think I have a right to demand it—I have one question to ask!" And struck by the softened tone, the wistful expression of the old man's face, Philip mastered his own emotion, and entered the room. Mortimer closed the door, and turned round to Earnscliffe, a strange look of dawning remorse and doubt contracting his features, as though with some sharp bodily pain.

"You are right," he began, huskily, "that is no time for you—and me—to speak together. By the dead body of her you have quitted—by your own honor—was she pure still?"

"She was as spotless as the very light of heaven!" returned Earnscliffe, solemnly. "Whatever were my own guilty hopes for the future, I swear to you that Marguerite was pure——"

"Then, I was her murderer!" Mortimer interrupted, hoarsely. "Leave me, sir. You are the less guilty of the two."

CHAPTER LIV.

MARGUERITE'S sudden death and the circumstances attending it furnished conversation until the close of the season. Actually for four consecutive weeks one subject continued to be spoken of in the great world with unflagging interest!

The exact circumstances of the last night of Marguerite's life were never actually known. All Mortimer could be brought to say was, that his wife returned home flushed and over-excited from Mrs. Lorrimer's *fete;* that she complained of illness; and, while they were speaking together, was seized with the attack from which she never rallied.

Meanwhile, the confidential talk of servants gained far more ground than the asseverations of the husband. Mr. Grimes had heard his master's voice speaking in loud, angry tones before the bell rang which summoned him to the fearful scene of death in the library. Mademoiselle Eulalie had been bold enough to take a glance at a few of the papers upon the table, which, in those first moments of terror, Mortimer had taken no heed of. Mademoiselle Eulalie saw that they were in the same handwriting as the ones her mistress had so constantly received—saw that they were signed "Philip Earnscliffe."

And all this, and much more of a like nature, was related to the countless servants who came "to inquire" for Mortimer. And soon in every club and *coterie* it was told, "that Earnscliffe had long been Mrs. Mortimer's lover—years ago, even before she was married; but that the husband, as usual, was blinded longer than any one else; that, at the Richmond *fete* Mrs. Mortimer had besought Earnscliffe to take her with him from England; that he had returned home half distracted: Mortimer, in the meantime, had broken open her desk, and found all Earnscliffe's letters. Fearful explanations had ensued, ending" (in this, at least, they could weave no falsehood) "with Mrs. Mortimer's rupturing a blood-vessel of the heart, and her death."

Even Georgy found herself quite of importance, from knowing so many details of the story, flaunted from house to house in the French bonnet and dress Marguerite had given her—the relationship was too distant to require mourning—eager to tell all she knew, and say: "How very melancholy it was! but she must confess she always thought Mrs. Mortimer was completely French in her notions of morality, and much too fond of admiration for a married woman!"

And thus, while those who had so long courted and fluttered round Marguerite were casting each an additional stone at her blackened memory, she—the best and purest among them all—was carried to her grave—a new grave in some new cemetery; and laid there, with only two old men for mourners—Danby and her husband.

Only two mourners at her funeral! But when the summer twilight was deepening, a stranger bribed the keeper of the gates that evening to open them for him to enter. And throughout the first dark night that Marguerite was in her grave, this stranger kept watch, kneeling upon the new-laid turf in such tearless, rigid anguish as can smite the heart but once in a lifetime, then leaves it blank and dead for ever.

*   *   *

When Neville called upon Earnscliffe the following day, he started at seeing his face. Every remaining look of youth was gone; around his eyes was a deep hollow shade; and already many a silver line streaked his dark hair.

"You have suffered, Earnscliffe! You are fearfully changed!"

"I have," replied Philip, without looking up or extending his hand to him. "I have gone through all the bitterness of remorse that any man *could* do, and yet live."

———

Time has passed on, and Earnscliffe has again interests in life; deeper, graver interests than any of those which engrossed him in his youth. All desire for personal distinction is gone; and if in his fresh political career he has won success, it was unsought for. He has firm convictions now upon the points where he once so wavered—a stronger sense than formerly of his own responsibility; and in strenuously supporting the cause of social reform, in devoting himself wholly to the welfare of others, his high powers of mind have found at length a genuine and lasting scope for action.

Neville is, as of old, his greatest, his only friend (for political partisanship, however warm, can never constitute friendship to a nature like Philip's) and he always looks forward with relief to the close of each session, and the lonely autumn which he and the painter shall spend together in Scotland; for Neville is still the same untiring student as ever; and, celebrated though he has become, works from Nature with all the fresh zest that he had at eighteen.

But Philip has never written since Marguerite's death. Either he feels no more inspiration, or the constant excitement and turmoil of political life leave him no spare time for literature. He rarely goes into the world—never into the society where he once so shone, and whose leaders would still receive him with open arms, did he choose to return to their small distinctions and applause.

Is Earnscliffe happy?

Oh, reader! is there not some shadow across your own memory—some grave over which no flower can ever grow, to answer that question?

THE END.

www.ingramcontent.com/pod-product-compliance
Lightning Source LLC
Chambersburg PA
CBHW020231030726
47497CB00009B/3046